The

Reconciliation
of Gentry

The
Reconciliation
of Gentry

Karen G. Berry

For Brother Steve, my friend and champion;
I wish you'd been able to read them all.

We easily forgive a child who is afraid of the dark.
But we find tragic a man who is afraid of the light.
—*Plato*

SUMMER, 2000

Gentry

She catches my eye in the rearview mirror as we head over the bridge. "You missed the exit!"

I don't hear that.

I feel Mel's hand on my arm. "She needs to go home." I don't hear that, either. "You have to take me to the airport tomorrow morning." I don't hear, I don't plan to hear anything until I pull up to the beach with Gretchen and Mel. "I know you can hear me, my boy."

I don't hear a thing.

"GENTRY, I REFUSE TO SIT HERE AND YELL AT YOU! SO GET OFF THE GODFORSAKEN FREEWAY!!"

I take the next exit and pull into a parking spot.

This is a tough neighborhood. Homeless people walk past us. One man has on a pair of purple jeans, and I think, what could be worse, adding insult to injury, being homeless and having to wear purple jeans. "Just go up Burnside." This is Gretchen. "Gentry, did you hear me?" If I were that bum, I would panhandle for jeans. "Just go up Burnside and turn right on 25th."

That's not how you get to the beach.

⸻

The Jeep ran like a dream. I left the top off and the sun beat down on me, and I no longer look like a ghost. Or feel like one. During the day, Gretchen told me about her school, living in Portland, going to Europe. We had three years to cover.

While she slept, I talked to Mel. I confessed everything from the time I left Detroit until he walked in the door to take me out of Oklahoma. I asked God's forgiveness. And Mel's. We took our time. We had more than three years to cover.

Mel kept saying, "No hurry, my boy."

The nights were cool and beautiful. Sometimes I was too tired to talk. Mel drove, then, and Gretchen curled up in the back of the Jeep like something waiting to be born. I'd lean back, my eyes on the stars, sending up a prayer.

God, thank You for the painful weight of happiness on my heart. Amen.

We went from one overwhelming landscape to another. Mel said, "Going west, you feel God's presence. You sense His recent passage." We saw the desolation of the Great Salt Lake, the coastline of Big Sur and the redwoods. At the Eastern Rim of the Grand Canyon, we gazed out on two hundred miles of a vista none of us could comprehend or describe. I had to turn my back to recover. Gretchen took my hand. "What are you doing?"

Mel spoke for me. "He is marveling."

She rolled her blue eyes. "You can't marvel forever."

The hand of God was in the landscape, but so was the work of man. The Hoover Dam made me want to throw up, the idea of what it held back, what it could drown and bury. Who thought of this? Who could trust his puny human math?

"Come on." Gretchen pulled my hand and we ran across.

She is fearless.

Gretchen thought the fact that I could order for myself in restaurants was the greatest wonder of the American West. "This is more amazing than the Mystery Spot, Gentry. But I was looking forward to picking out your food. Can't you just let me?"

I said not yet. I was afraid to backslide in this area and get stuck again, umming and vacillating. Mel and I prayed over our food, and Gretchen watched us, and it was not an issue.

But she was correct. You can't marvel forever.

My time in Oklahoma has stripped me back to the studs, as Brother Victor would have said. I have no idea who I am anymore. I have this Jeep and the promise of a job and the use of Kathryn's house. I never even thought about being there alone. In my mind, Gretchen was there with me. And now what? She's not eleven anymore. She lives in Portland. A fifteen-year-old girl is not going to walk out of her mother's house and set up housekeeping with me as if I were her dad. Gretchen is not mine.

I still don't have my own, God. If there is a plan, please reveal it.

Amen.

I feel her touch on the back of my neck. "It's just until Friday. If you dig some clams, I'll cook chowder."

Mel smiles. "Fish on Fridays. That takes me back."

Gretchen directs me, calling right here, up this street, left now, okay then right here and then follow the road, here it is, park at the curb.

And she told me correctly, they live near their old house. The new place is twice as large as that house, and sits against a hill near the old hospital. It is a work of Craftsman art. I compare it with the only house I've ever owned, and I don't feel stupid or inadequate or poor.

I feel hopeless.

"Come on, Mom's *dying* to see you!" Gretchen hops out over the side. Mel extracts himself, groaning. I sort of scramble out. We trudge up a few massive steps to a tiny, manicured yard, the evidence of Kathryn around me, her roses and other flowers spilling down the hill in a controlled cataract of beauty that is nothing in comparison to her as she steps out onto the porch and smiles. Her eyes shine.

Oh Kathryn, come here.

I slip my hands around her head and pull her close and kiss her. She tastes of tears and lipstick.

Mel clears his throat.

We pull apart, but she leaves her arm around my waist and I leave my hand in the wisps of her fine, cropped hair.

She smiles and puts her hand on my belly. "What's *this*?"

Hm. Ignore that, Kathryn, all right? Yes, ignore the stomach, and south of there. Maybe if you stopped touching my stomach?

A wiry old man steps forward, extending his wizened hand. "Jack Fankhauser."

Hey, Jack. This is awkward for me, Jack. Is it awkward for you? Do you know who I am? Can you tell what I've done with your wife? Can you tell what I'd like to do with her right now?

I shake his hand. "Hey. I'm Gentry. It's nice to meet you."

Kathryn's eyebrows fly up. "You sound like someone from Oklahoma."

Mel smiles. "You should have heard him after five years in Georgia."

Gretchen rolls her eyes. "I'm sure it'll go away."

My throat is closing. I have to talk fast. "Hey Kathryn? Can you take Mel to the airport in the morning?"

"What? You're not staying? Gentry." Her eyes are puzzled. "I have so much to talk to you about. Please, come in." Gretchen pulls my arm, Kathryn takes the other, don't pull on me, please, PLEASE.

They let me go.

Mel nods. "Let's walk, Gentry. Stretch the legs." He turns to the confused knot of people I've driven from Oklahoma to see. "We will return shortly." I stride down the sidewalk as if I have somewhere to go, Mel behind me. I walk up the block with him following. My heart is trying to beat its way out of my throat.

Mel watches me pace out my anguish. "Is it under control?"

I nod.

"I'll explain for you, my boy. Just make your good-byes in a mannerly fashion."

They wait by my Jeep. They are not phantoms born of longing, human mirages. Look at them, standing on their feet like real people. Corporeal. Present.

I focus on the feet.

Kathryn has on little clogs, the kind with staples to hold the leather to the wood. The lace of Gretchen's sneaker trails on the concrete. I kneel down before her and carefully tie it like she's a child, but when I stand up, her blue eyes are nearly level with mine.

Hugging Gretchen good-bye is just one more thing not to cry about. Her voice is small. "Please stay here." I shake my head.

Jack staggers under the dismissible weight of Gretchen's bag, and Mel carries his. Gretchen retrieves my Becca pillow from the back seat. "Can I have this? It smells like you." I nod. Kathryn hands me house keys and talks about the paper, the post office box, like I don't know about those things. I hug her again, carefully, kind of sideways. I keep nodding, I let Mel hug me, I get in my Jeep, I nod, I wave, I pull away from the curb with a jerk as Mel gathers them up and urges them inside with officious waves of his little hands.

I make it about two blocks before it shakes me so hard that I jerk my Jeep over into the curb.

God, this is pain.

I know it was ridiculous what I tried to pretend, what lie I fed myself. What did I think, truly, after four years, what fantasy did I live in? It would be impossible. Did I really think he would come out of that door to jump up and sniff me and kiss me hello?

Bosco is dead.

I put my head down on the steering wheel. I submit. He's with You, he deserves that, and I believe it, it's stupid and sacrilege but I have to believe it so forgive me, all right? God, let him be with You.

Forgive me. Amen.

When I finally raise my head, a woman stands next to the Jeep holding out a box of Kleenex. "Are you all right?"

I can't answer, that's how far from all right I am.

She's tall and wears glasses, and even though it's a beautiful day, she has a blanket around her shoulders. "I'm sorry for asking. If you were all right you wouldn't be crying." She should leave me alone because I'm a man and there isn't a man alive who wants someone to watch him do this.

I get hold of myself. A shuddering breath. But I stop.

"I'm fine."

She almost laughs. "Would you like to come in for a minute before you go on to wherever it is you're going?"

This kindness almost undoes me all over again. Please, God, make me stop.

I drag my sleeve across my face. "Could I, um, wash up?"

"Oh sure. Come on in." She leads me up wide stone stairs into a baronial entrance hall and shows me to a crooked little half bath hiding under a huge staircase.

I barely get the door closed and my pants open.

Ah. Relief. I go for a good three minutes. I open the tap, drink this sweet Oregon water until my stomach hurts. I wash my hands, my face, find a toothbrush in one of my pockets and brush my teeth with cold water, which makes them ache. I wish I could shave. I use my wet hands to push my hair out of my face. I think, when I see myself in the mirror, that I would never let me in a house. But a man who weeps in the street is probably not perceived as much of a threat.

I step out and close the door. She's not waiting for me.

I can't leave without thanking her, so I stand there in the dark glow of all that wood, wondering what to do. This place could use a suit of armor. Maybe two.

"I'm back here!"

I walk through three enormous, mostly empty rooms to find her. This is the second-nicest house I've ever been in, somewhere between Daniel Shaw's ancestral mansion and Mike's house.

She's making a tiny cup of coffee in a kitchen of mammoth proportions. The blanket is gone, and her hair is twisted up behind her head and secured with two crossed pencils. The sweep of her bare neck, that old-fashioned dress, her flawless white feet make me feel I've stepped back in time.

"I'm making you an espresso. Sit, please." I know exactly where to sit, because on the table is a box of Kleenex and a brown paper bag with the top folded down. "My name is Fiona."

"I'm Gentry."

"Gentry. It means courtesy, but you know that."

"What does Fiona mean?"

"White." She sets the coffee before me.

"Thank you." The cup is so small that I'm reminded of tea parties with Lucy Rose. "This coffee is great."

She shrugs. "I'll take your word for it. I prefer tea." She sits down on the blanket, which was draped over a chair, and pulls it around her so she's completely wrapped. Her eyes are the color of wet sand. "Are you feeling any better?"

I'm not much for explaining myself, but she's been extraordinarily kind. "My dog died. I left him with some friends, they live up here, and I just stopped by their house and found out. I didn't want them to see me cry."

"They live around here?"

"A block away."

She angles her head. "What did your dog look like?"

"I'm, um, not good at describing things."

"Try. Try describing him to me."

I have such a clear image of him. "He was huge. He had thick brown fur, very soft but not that long, with some funny whorls in it where his head fit on his neck, like his head and his body were from two different dogs. His ears weren't that big but they didn't stand up or anything. His tail was long and whacked everything. And big feet that started turning out when he got old."

She smiles. "There was a dog exactly like that in this neighborhood. A tall girl with blonde hair used to walk him. I saw him almost every day. He had a silver face. Like a mask."

"How long has it been since you saw him?"

"A year, maybe? I think it was last spring."

"That would have made him seventeen."

"Seventeen? Are you serious?" We shake our heads and sit, paying a silent tribute to the big dog that lived seventeen years. "Wasn't his name Rosco?"

"Bosco."

"That's it. He was out with the girl, or this little lady in her fifties. He didn't walk very well. Sometimes he'd lie down on the sidewalk right in front of our gate. I think he liked the dog next door, she keeps up a racket. And whoever was walking him would wait, and talk to him until he was ready to get up."

"He could still run when I left."

She shakes her head. "I don't think he could even see anymore, to tell you the truth. But I patted him. He was the softest dog I ever touched."

I'm undone.

Oh, Bosco. How could I have left you? My dog, so old and stiff, but still waiting. Waiting for me to come back because I always came back. His eyes gone blind, his face gone silver, that sounds so beautiful, Bosco in a metal mask, like Agamemnon.

Fiona doesn't say anything, or do anything. She just sits, wrapped in her blanket, keeping me company in this cold kitchen, this dark place.

"Uh, hi?" The man of the house has arrived. In his suit, with his briefcase.

I drag my sleeve across my face and stand.

"Oh, Hugh, this is . . . Gentry, and he . . ." Her eyes plead. "Hugh, do you remember that dog the blonde girl was always walking?" She smiles at him so hopefully. "That really old dog."

"An old dog." He thinks. He is a guy in a suit with a briefcase who can afford to buy a house like this for his wife, and he frowns and thinks. "The big one they never had on a leash?" Fiona nods. I sniff.

"Yes. He belonged to Gentry, and he died while he was out of town."

Hugh nods. "I'm sorry. He seemed like a nice old dog." We stand in an awkward agony. "So, you're . . . our neighbor?"

"I, um, have to go. Bye." Hugh follows us out, shaking his head, giving me a look that says, wow, wives do some strange things, don't they, like invite in crying strangers for coffee, and as a fellow man I must commiserate.

I commiserate with no one.

I climb in the Jeep and she puts a long white hand on my arm. I wonder how she can hold me in place with something so slender. "You should go back up to your friends."

She's probably right. But I leave, because the beach is where I promised to spend this night, and I keep my promises.

∽

I'm flying, now. Hey, Highway.

I tried to describe this highway to my wife. She wanted me to share and I never shared, but I tried to talk about what was important to me. I would say something general. She said that I wasn't telling her anything specific.

I tried to be specific.

I tried to describe Mel. When I talked about his hands, she shuddered. She was certain those hands had been all over me. I tried to explain my school, which was terrifying in an exhilarating way. She saw it as a Catholic sex shop. She wasn't interested in the growth of my faith, the growth of my mind. She wanted to know if the boys got into each other's beds.

I never even tried to explain what it felt like to teach in Detroit, where every student took his life in his hands by walking in the door. Every teacher, too. Nothing could have been of less interest to her than my years in Detroit. I was celibate.

She wanted to know about Oregon. I talked about this highway, the trees, the pass, towns full of buildings that looked like three or four shacks joined together. How damp, green and foggy it was, how every little market had a hand-painted plywood sign announcing the sale of espresso and Keno tickets, as if a person would have to stop every half mile or so for caffeine and gambling just to stay awake.

She said, "Who cares?"

It's all still here. I didn't make it up, and it didn't disappear. The little stores still sell Keno tickets and espresso. The pass still makes my ears pop. The ocean still takes my breath away.

This is to give thanks. Amen.

The smell of salt and the cold air hit me at the same time, and I remember where to turn, what to watch for, a glimpse of the ocean, and it's different. They changed it. It used to be white. There are cedar shingles, now, and green trim. Why did they change it? They even shingled the little house, sitting out there like a room that wandered away from the main house.

I start shivering. It must be down in the 60s. Maybe the 50s, and the wind blows in over the cold Pacific. My teeth are clacking and it hurts. I have to use a key to go in the big house, and when I step inside I can't understand where I am, because this is a completely different kitchen.

Am I in the right house?

The flooring is wide planks of honey brown, like Gretchen's skin when she's been in the sun. This range looks like Eve's. Has Kathryn taken up feeding combining crews? A dishwasher? Kathryn had a dishwasher back then, and it was me. I could take a bath in the sink, and what's this island doing in the middle of the room? Bar stools? Bar stools belong in bars. Cookbooks? She never needed any cookbooks. Even the phone is different.

Where's the little table?

I need a drink. Of water, a drink of clean Oregon water, that's all, God.

I run a hand along a cabinet, open a noiseless door to inspect joins as careful as those in the cabinetry of the old sacristy. At least the glasses are familiar. She bought them after that night she smashed every single glass in the house. We had to drink out of jars for a couple of weeks before she bought these. We all had our own jar. The first night I drank out of mine, my milk tasted faintly of green olives.

Well, the red couch is still here, and like a Pavlovian response, I'm rock hard. Great. That's all I need, God, to see that couch and remember Kathryn with the new knowledge mixed in there that Gretchen saw us. Will I ever get this untangled?

I go upstairs. I think I only went up there three times, so if it's different, I won't be too weird about it.

Gretchen's room is much the same. Fairytales left behind on the wall, because she isn't a child. She must have her computer in Portland. I miss my computer. The door to Marci's room is closed. I never went in that room then and I won't go in now.

But I will inspect the room I spent a night in.

Kathryn has "redone" her bedroom. "Redoing" involves money I never had, so my home stayed undone. This room is beautiful. A larger window on the west side for this perfect view. Kathryn now sleeps in a huge, high bed. I hope that means that she and Jack sleep without touching.

I need to leave it alone.

They installed a skylight. The rain on that would drive me crazy, but these are Oregonians, they're used to the rain. Kathryn lies under that old man and stares out that skylight, I guess.

I can shut myself up anytime.

Ah, a fancy bathroom. I took a shower in here once. This room wasn't that big, but it's big now. How do you do that? Grow a bathroom? A huge new bathtub. What I could do to her in that bathtub, because I'm not old.

Quit, now.

It's infantile what I do. But I go right into the tub. And then I wash my hands, of course. And rinse the tub.

Well, I wonder where I'm supposed to sleep. In the new oversized bed? In Gretchen's room? In Marci's? The couch looks just right. I need a drink as badly as I ever have, but there will be no poison here. I'm safe. God, keep me safe.

I drag a blanket to the couch and pray for dreamless sleep.

Amen.

〜

God, You hate me.

"Fankhauser here." I can hardly make a noise. "What? Speak up. Who is this?" His voice is old, tired, angry.

I hear her. "Is it Gentry?"

"How the heck would I know? Whoever it is mumbles."

Her concerned voice in my ear. "Gentry?"

"Get Mel."

"Of course. Just hold on."

I hold on.

"Gentry? I'm here." Something chokes out of me, not words. "I am here, boy, I will always be here. Would you like the Psalms?" He speaks the words until he hears my voice join his. We say psalms together until he hears me cry. I can sleep if I cry.

I hear Kathryn speaking to him in the background.

"I leave for the airport soon, Gentry. I suppose you just called at this hour to say goodbye to me, that is the type of wonderful boy you are. I am never farther away than your phone. Remember that. Will you sleep, now?"

"Yes," I whisper, and he hears me, and I hang up.

God, this is to thank You for sleep without dreams.

〜

I'm up at dawn to dig clams. I wonder, as my hand closes around the shell of this rudimentary animal that shoots water back at me, spitting in protest, who first had the idea to eat these. I drop it in the bucket.

Digging makes me wonder where he's buried. Is he buried? Did they take him to the vet because his hips were so bad, and the vet kept him? Was he thrown away? Did he disappear one day? Did a wave take him once he was too weak to swim? I don't know where he is, God.

I'm shivering again, even though I wore three shirts.

I go back to my digging. My neck and back and arms ache, my right hand goes numb from reaching down where it's cold. When the bucket is full, I carry it up to the house and leave it in deep shade. I'd put oatmeal and herbs in the water if we were steaming these, because Gretchen likes the clams' bellies stuffed. But I'll be cutting these up for her later. When she gets here.

I get some coffee and drag a bar stool over to the kitchen window. Just me, my coffee, some marveling.

God, I would like to stay here forever.

Amen.

∾

There's a place I visit on the cove. Gretchen and I walked past this place, we rode past on bikes. This is the grave of someone lost, someone who washed up, unknown and alone, who was buried with love. There are always flowers here. Other people visit this spot, but I'm alone today. I brought a bunch of roses from a florist who smiled as if she knew that Bosco used to lift his leg on Kathryn's bushes. I place them with the carnations and wildflowers brought by other people.

Known Only To God.

God, watch over him, because he watched over me. Amen.

∾

Gretchen arrives late Friday morning. I wondered if over the course of three days, everything would change and I would be denied her again. But Kathryn pulls up in her new expensive car, and out hops Gretchen. "Hi!"

"Hey. Hey Gretchen? What do you want to do today?"

She smiles, shy. "Everything."

Everything sounds good. Kathryn waves and pulls away without getting out.

"We got Mel to the airport. He said to give you his love. And this." She wraps her arms around me, and I put my face in her hair. She smells like the sun on grass.

My chest warms from the inside out.

We visit the tide pools, and we sit on the sand and talk about science camp and riding lessons and school. We talk about my terrible job in Oklahoma. I tell her the funny parts to make her laugh, only the funny, never the terrible. She asks me if I want to talk about my wife and I tell her I don't. "When you want to, you can."

"I won't ever want to talk about it."

"You might." I might. But not with her. Nothing like that with her. I lie back on the sand, one arm behind my head to keep the sand out of my hair. She lies back, too. "Is Mel Irish?"

"Australian. But he does sound Irish."

"I like to watch you two. He's like a father, the way he bosses you around."

"He's nothing like a father."

"Of course he is, dummy. He's Father Mel."

I close my eyes and doze.

Gretchen is surprised that I've grocery shopped. I changed, too, little girl who grew up. She cooks, and we eat the fine chowder she learned to make from Kathryn. She's surprised again when I turn on the television after dinner. "I thought you hated TV." She snuggles into my side and lets out a happy sigh. I think it's safe to put my arm around her. We watch television. I let her have the remote. I breathe in her sweet hair. Like prairie grass.

God, thank You for this.

She falls asleep on my shoulder. I lay her down on the couch and cover her. I get my sleeping bag and lie on the floor below her.

I fall asleep listening to the sound of her sweet breathing.

Gretchen

"Gentry, wake up, wake up, WAKE UP!" He jumps up, hitting out. And then he sees it's me. "It's okay. It's just me. Come sit here." He's on the couch fast, face white and eyes round. It isn't the cold that makes him shake like this. I put my blanket over him, wrap my arms around him. I don't think you're supposed to wake people when they're having nightmares. Or maybe that's sleep-walking.

When he's asleep again, I go upstairs so he won't hear me cry.

⌒

When Mel called my mom and asked if I could meet him in Oklahoma, Mom wanted to say no but I wouldn't let her. I had to be the one who went to get him. Mel knew it, I knew it, and she knew it, too. Unless I went to get him, he wouldn't come back.

I flew down to Oklahoma alone. A flight attendant walked me off. I was way taller than her.

I'd only seen Mel once, but I recognized him. He had on his black suit and collar, but he still had to show ID. That was kind of funny, the flight attendant asking a priest for his driver's license.

All he asked was how was my flight. All I said was fine.

We rode through that city in a taxi and it was so flat and ugly and hot. It didn't seem like an environment Gentry would thrive in. A tiny old lady with shining amber eyes answered the bell. Mel said, *Hello, I am Gentry's uncle Mel and this is his friend Gretchen, and we've come to pay our respects to Miriam, his wife.* She said she was Miriam's mother and to come in and meet everyone. And Mel said, *Yes. But where is Gentry?* She said he was in the other room.

Gentry walked out. He was pale and his belly stuck out, not like he was fat, but sort of like he was malnourished. And his hair. It went down just past his shoulders. He was a ghost of the Gentry I knew. But the worst part was the flinching. He always did that when he woke up, mostly with his eyes. When we went to hug him, he flinched with his whole body.

Mel put his hand on my arm and whispered, *Give him a chance to get used to us.* He steered me around, showing me how to pay our respects. It was interesting, like there was a script. Mel said things like, *I never had the pleasure of meeting your niece, but I understand she was a woman of tremendous spirit.* People nodded and smiled and cried and said things like, *Oh my gosh yes.* Gentry followed us, staring at me like I was not real.

This scared me.

Mel said, *It's time for us to be going, my boy.* Gentry said goodbye to everyone and then we got him out of there. We went to some post office place and he mailed everything off to make room for me in the back of the Jeep. Gentry kept pulling away when anyone got too close. So, I decided to habituate him to the stimulus. I held his hand or put my arm around his waist when we walked places. Eventually, he stopped flinching.

He talked a little during the day, asking questions about Europe and school. Mostly he wanted to listen. But at night, when Mel was driving and they thought I was asleep, Gentry talked a lot. Well, I thought it was talking, but I figured out he was confessing.

Confession is private. I was never very good at letting Gentry be private.

He told it in order. I wrapped his pillow around my head while Gentry said whatever he was going to say about my mother, but I wanted to hear what he said about my sister. I always wanted to know if there was more than what I saw that day in his house. But Gentry didn't remember. "I remember I was in the kitchen, I was standing there with a box. I woke up in the hospital. I have no memory in between."

"Tell me who you *think* did it."

"A student named Garret."

I always thought it was Garret, too.

"Why didn't you tell the police that?"

"I'm afraid . . ." he choked up. "I'm afraid of why it happened. What I might have done. To deserve it."

"To *deserve* it? What would you do that would entitle someone to beat you almost to death, Gentry?" The Jeep flew along the highway, the tires on the road vibrating up through the duffel bag and into my head, which was full of ideas of how he could have answered that question. But he didn't answer. I guess he really didn't have to. "She is still in Oregon?"

"She's up in Washington."

Mel sighed. "Oh, my boy. I suggest you think about how you plan to handle this. And pray. Let's pray about this." There was lots of praying about Oregon and my sister and guidance and memory and compassion and understanding and self-forgiveness and other things that bored me so much that I dozed.

I woke up when he started talking about someone named Becca in Georgia. He was "with" Becca back when they were both in college. Neither of them were married, so that was "fornication." After he left Oregon he was "with" her again, which was not fornication for her because now she's married and has a baby with a Disney character name. She "committed adultery." Gentry didn't "commit adultery," though. He just "fornicated." Gentry "committed adultery" on his honeymoon. He was even more upset about that than he was over what he did with Becca. There was this entire fertility clinic experience that he went on about. Strange, to think of science as a sin.

I learned a whole new vocabulary. The vocabulary of sin. The whole thing sounded ridiculous to me. "I lusted after my friend Paige." I mean, seriously, how can lust be a sin when it's a basic part of human biology? None of it makes sense to me, but I've never had sex, I've just studied sex.

Mel seemed to agree with me. "Gentry, lust is human. God forgives you, He's the author of your humanity. Forgive yourself." Mel was firm about Gentry having what Mel called a "physical life." "You are thirty years old. And you can find a way to have physical life that doesn't violate your principles or threaten a marriage or ruin your career."

"What if I can't?"

"I believe you can. You could try marrying a woman you love, for one thing."

They didn't say anything for a while. "Look at my life, Mel."

"Nothing you have ever done is inconceivable, Gentry, or unforgivable. You can figure it out, my boy. You have to stop denying what you are."

"And what am I?"

"You are a man, Gentry, a normal man, and you need a physical life."

"But isn't that my worst sin?"

Mel sighed. "Please, Gentry, stop thinking like a sixteen-year-old boy. It sets you up for such terrible falls. Instead, please think like a man who wants to live in accordance with God's plan for you."

"I don't know what that is."

"Of course you don't. Faith is trusting without knowing. God has a plan for you, but you show no faith in it. You live in a state of fear and sin because you fight God's plan for you. You must pray for it. Constantly, sincerely, with your whole heart and soul. You must submit."

This made no sense to me in any way, but it made sense to them. Gentry dropped his head and closed his eyes, and Mel drove, and they prayed for a long, long time. Sometimes Mel said things out loud and sometimes Gentry did, and then they said things together, Hail Mary and Our Father and I guess it made them feel better. It put me to sleep. Finally Mel said, "Your sins are forgiven."

Gentry asked, "So get up and walk?"

"Get up and walk."

Gentry started to laugh. A big, strong bark of a laugh, like he used to have. And then in the middle of the laughing, it turned into crying. We rode along, me pretending to sleep, Mel driving, and Gentry bawling like a baby because he was so relieved.

Forgiveness could make it all better like that?

There's still something wrong with Gentry. I don't know what it is. Mel can't fix it all with his magical God spells.

Gentry is broken.

Gentry

I pick up the phone and there must be twenty of the brothers singing to me. Yes, there are speakerphones at the monastery. Mel and I talk a little, and then I go back to the couch and roll up in my sleeping bag, wishing I hadn't driven Gretchen upstairs with the spectacle of how messed up I am.

Happy Birthday to me.

I go back to sleep.

❦

My head is pounding. She's quietly sweeping. Kathryn put a wood floor in a beach house kitchen, which means sweeping several times a day to guard the finish. If I keep my eyes closed and still my mind, I can pretend that she's still a little girl in there, singing and sweeping like a child in a fairytale.

I open my eyes to hers. And she is not a child.

"Happy birthday, dummy. Who called you that early?"

"Mel."

"Did he wish you a GODFORSAKEN birthday?"

I laugh through the pain. "He sang. They all sang. Hey Gretchen? Will you shut the shade? My head hurts."

"I bet it's caffeine withdrawal. It happens to Marci when she sleeps in. I'll make you an espresso."

"Okay. But the shade."

"Addiction is never pretty." She closes the shade and goes away with her broom.

Before I moved south, I was there with the brothers on my birthdays. I spent summers at the monastery even after I started teaching. I cultivated corn, hayed, did early combining. I needed the money and I liked the work. So I was with him for all my birthdays and the brothers always woke me, singing.

Mel never asked me what I wanted at first. He figured it out. When I was eleven, he gave me more things than I'd ever had in my life. At twelve, he taught me to drive. At thirteen, he gave me the right kind of soccer boots. When I was fourteen, he made me ask for what I wanted. He said it was time to learn to ask.

He swallowed hard when I asked for a dog.

I wasn't sure what day my birthday was until Mel told me. I could have asked a teacher, but I was too embarrassed. I just got older every summer. It was strange to get older, not knowing when or how. I do remember asking. I'd been to a birthday party. I got invited to those. I showed up by myself and left by myself and I never brought presents. After a particularly nice one, I came home and asked what day my birthday was.

Your birthday was the worst fucking day of my life. That was your birthday.

I sit up and breathe. Where did all that come from? Take that away right now, God. Amen.

Gretchen enters with a cup of coffee. "Are you okay? You're shaking."

"It's forty degrees cooler here."

"Do you want another blanket?"

"I'm fine."

"Are you sure? You look weird."

"Thank you."

She laughs. "Okay, birthday boy. What do you want to do to celebrate?"

"I want to fly a kite."

She whoops like a child.

Thank You, God.

Gretchen

I wanted things to be easy and fun. I wanted him to smile. And he kept smiling. The weather was perfect. As soon as his headache let up, we went out to breakfast and then to the kite store. He made me pick out a kite.

At first we couldn't even begin to get it up in the air. "It's like the kite's doing it on *purpose*, Gretchen," he said when the kite slammed into the sand.

"I think you were born for this." He laughed so hard he had to sit down.

We discussed thermals and updrafts and currents, but none of that actually made the kite go up there to ride on them. Finally a little boy came by and coached us through it, and we finally got that kite up in the air. We anchored it on the sand and lay on our backs and watched it dip and fly. It was beautiful. Gentry fell asleep. He smiled in his sleep. When he woke up, he got the kite reeled in and gave it to the next kid he saw. He was so happy. So was the kid.

We walked up to Broadway and played games at the arcade. We found one where he was still the top scorer after four years. We rode those old bumper cars and the tilt-a-whirl, and went to Leonard's for caramel corn. "Hey, Gentry." "Hey, Joe." Joe gave us the right size. I paid, because it was Gentry's birthday. This is a funny old place, and he still loves it and so do I.

Some things don't change.

We walked down Broadway to the turnaround, with that bronze statue of Lewis and Clark at the end of the Oregon Trail. I can't say that I never noticed it before, because I notice everything, so I'd seen the dog. He lay there under the feet of his master, so huge and patient and loyal. Seaman was the base of the statue, the foundation that held up the other figures. He was a Newfoundland.

Gentry stopped smiling.

"You look weird again." I put my arms around him. I felt him pull away, then hug me back, his hand reaching up to stroke my hair. He started to shake. "Are you okay?"

"Cold," he said, his teeth chattering. It was 78 degrees.

When we got home, he lay down on the couch with the TV on. I let him sleep until dinner.

Gentry

She surprises me this evening with chicken and dumplings. Perfect.
"Time for your presents." I am not used to wrapped presents, the ripping, but I get it open. "Do you like the color?"

"Perfect." I put it on. "I'll never take it off. I've been cold since I got here."

She strokes the sleeve. "Every Oregonian has to have a fleece. It's a rule."

Mel sent a package that she picked up at the post office on her way here and hid from me because she knew I'd open it early. The package contains a John Deere cap. "I'm jealous. Tell Mel I want one, too." I take her seriously, of course, because who could not want a John Deere cap? "Are you going to wear it in the house? You can, you know, on your birthday. It can be your party hat. Your John Deere party hat."

I wear my cap in the house.

This kid. God, You sent her to me, and this is to give You thanks. Amen.

When did she learn to make chicken and dumplings? She ladles me a huge bowl, the dumplings are fluffy, she even has some little peas for me to mix in there. Mel has to have told her about that, because how would she have known about the little peas? I give even more in the way of thanks than usual, and take a big bite. The heat hits the molars on the left, and I drop the spoon and hold my face. This gives Gretchen a clue that I'm in pain, that face-clutching gesture, and of course, my howl, the loud agonized howl I make.

I wish I swore.

I wonder how I did it as a kid. Because I don't remember much, but I remember my teeth aching all the time. I think tooth pain was the undercurrent of my whole, sad childhood.

"Gentry, if you need a dentist, you should go into Portland."

I nod and stir my chicken to cool it down, because it tasted good even as it hurt me, like sugar did.

Like pop. And ice cream.

I remember.

I turned eleven just after I went to live with Mel. So Mel, being Mel, bought me a bike and a fishing rod and new boots and a new set of Narnia books. He gave me the bedroom in that little apartment, and all those things sat in that room, even the bike because it would be stolen if we left it outside. I sat on the bed and stared at it. It was all mine. It was too much.

He took me over to the rectory, where the brothers sang and someone had baked me a cake. I sat at the big rectory dining table with a piece of chocolate cake in front of me. My right arm was in a sling, so I held my fork in the wrong hand. My teeth hurt too much to take a bite.

What is it, Gentry? I'd kept the pain in my mouth a secret for so long, I wouldn't have known how to tell it even if I had been able to speak out loud. *Gentry, it's just fine if you don't care for any cake. You don't have to eat anything you don't wish to. Would you like some ice cream?* I couldn't even think about ice cream. *Is there anything, anything at all that you'd like?* I wanted a lock for the door of my room.

He sat down next to me and took the fork away and held both my hands. I hated it when men put their hands on me, but I could always take it from Mel because his hands were so small. *I need to go over to your house. Would you like, perhaps, to come with me?* I must have cried, because he pulled me over on his lap. *Hush, my boy. Hush. Here is the plan. I will go over there, and I will pack up whatever you might want someday, all right? Just whatever seems like it might matter to you. But is there anything you want to have in the apartment? Anything?*

I wanted my grandparents.

The next day, I waited in the church while he went over there. I prayed and waited and lit a candle. I wished for my grandparents. It was a Thursday night, and they came.

I saw them every Thursday and Saturday night, every Sunday morning. I still couldn't say a word in English, but every week we stopped outside the church and talked in their language. They patted me with small brown hands, showing the teeth they were losing to age and decay in broad smiles. After I left for school, I still saw them on breaks. They asked me over but I wouldn't go back there. But they were so proud of me. I know because they told me. All the time.

The first thing I said out loud in English was, "My teeth hurt."

The first time the dentist put his hand in my mouth I bit him so hard that he swore. I wanted to hide, I promised not to bite, but every time he tried to put a finger in my mouth I bit at it like an animal. Finally, the dentist gave me a shot of something and Mel held my hand and we prayed. I spent hours in that chair, but a shot in the arm and Mel beside me with kind hands and a prayer, and I was all right, I could let him put a hand in my mouth.

I loved my teeth, then. Everything fixed, clean, and no pain. I smiled all the time. I began my relentless brushing campaign that continues to this day. For the first time in memory, I could eat candy, I could even eat cake, but I was careful, not trusting that it wouldn't hurt me. But it no longer did.

I have to tell Gretchen. "I did drink pop for a while. I did. When I was eleven. I liked root beer." I tell her about sitting there with that cake, and then the trips to the dentist, how ashamed I was of biting the poor man, the shots, Mel, my neighbors. I talk and talk, I tell her everything because I promised I'd tell her whatever I remembered.

She listens, her eyes round, holding my hand. "And your neighbors, that's why you speak Vietnamese?" I nod. "Why was your arm in a sling? You bit the dentist?"

I shake my head.

The chicken is cold now. She puts it back in the pot, warms it up, and we eat but it doesn't feel real to me. It feels like what I remembered was real, and sitting in the kitchen with Gretchen, eating, that's the dream.

Is that the plan, then? Do You want me to remember?

I pray for the strength to submit to Your plan.

Amen.

⁓

Gretchen asks to come to church with me on Sunday morning.

"I'm sorry but your mom said I'm not supposed to take you to church."

"That was years ago." She rolls her eyes like her sister used to. "I'm always in church now. I have to go to chapel at my school, and I have to take Religious Studies. I call it my Wizardry class."

"You can come with. But I have to take a shower."

Hot water helps a headache.

When I come downstairs, clean and dressed, she stands in the kitchen shifting from one sandaled foot to another, serenely stroking a Chapstick over the mouth she inherited from her mother. She wears a short skirt and a close-fitting shirt. The bracelet I gave her on her eleventh birthday encircles one slim wrist. She turns to me with a smile.

She is so beautiful, God. It is almost blinding.

∽

Father Steve is no longer here. There's a new priest, younger than me. I know I should respect all your priests, Lord, but I like the older ones more.

"It's a lot like at school," she whispers. I hear her stumble a little at the slight variations between Catholic and Episcopal hymns. Her voice is as pure as ever, but stronger. Certain notes trill out like birdsong.

She doesn't take communion, of course. I can, I confessed to Mel, I can, Oh Thank You, God, melt on the tongue of a penitent man, Lord.

The wafer tastes like forgiveness.

I light the candle, because I always light a candle. Today, I remember the prayer I used to say, every single time until I forgot it. That forgotten prayer.

Please God. Bring her back. Amen.

Dizziness. Gretchen takes my arm, steadies me. "Are you okay?"

I'm not okay. Something is wrong with me.

∽

In the parking lot, we say hey to Vu's mom. I wrestle my tongue through my side of a conversation, and receive an exuberant description of his latest misadventures. He's fine, just fine. But I feel strange. Is it the difficulty of speaking that language? Is it remembering? We get in the Jeep. "I need to sit here for a minute."

She puts her hand on my arm, she always touches me, she held my hand all through the Mass. "You sing nice, Gentry."

"Thank you for lying."

"I mean it. Were you ever in choir?"

"In school, but not in church. I was an acolyte."

"I can imagine you up there in the red robe, so serious."

I took it seriously. Usually.

I remember when I'd just turned thirteen, helping Mel serve Mass. He glanced at my feet, blue eyes dancing behind his glasses. He almost laughed out loud because I had on my new soccer boots. Wrecking the floor with the cleats.

I ran in those. "I ran."

"What?"

I can't explain. The sun is too bright to me, and I don't want to go home. My stomach hurts. I'm probably hungry, though I don't feel hungry. "Do you want to go to breakfast?"

She smiles. "Sure." We collude, here. Her mom will arrive soon to carry her off to Portland. If I take her to a restaurant, Kathryn will have to wait. But I feel too strange to drive and I can't stand the thought of eating.

"Gentry, when you take communion, you don't have the wine."

"No, I don't."

"Why?" She deserves the truth. I've never said the truth out loud, except to Mel. Please, Gretchen. Please know, please know without my saying. "Are you an alcoholic?"

I stopped taking the wine long before I knew that, Gretchen, long before. Because the wine was sweet. And I have to put my head between my knees because I remember.

Oh, Dear God, let me forget.

I remember standing in an alley one summer night while a priest shook my shoulders and screamed in my face. I was home for the summer, thirteen years old. I was drunk, so drunk on that sweet wine. Another altar boy and I were partners in crime.

I'd loved the wine since my first communion, the only sweet thing in my mouth that didn't hurt it, almost numbed it. My neighbor sometimes packed my teeth with chewing tobacco. It made me sick, but I never told her that. She was only trying to help.

But that's not what I remember, God, is it. It was me, the wine, the other acolyte. We were supposed to be folding some cloths, and we got into the wine. All the altar boys got into the wine. What a delight, a fire in the belly, a fire in the mind, and the forgetting. The forgetting was the best part.

Father Peter found us. The other boy ran. I tried, but I was too drunk and once again I'd worn my soccer boots. Father Peter had no trouble overtaking me behind the church, catching me by the arm, pulling me up short while those cleats skated across the pavement.

He held my shoulders tight, and one still ached and he pulled it, I was drunk and scared, he pinned me and his face twisted and his voice rose, what did I have to *say* for myself, what was *wrong* with me, his face was too close, he told me to take myself back into the church right now, to get *in* there but I kept trying to twist away and get to the rectory and I wasn't going *anywhere* and did I know what I had *done*, his teeth in my face and the spray of his spit in my eyes, that was sacramental wine, it was supposed to be blessed, blessed, what kind of a low and sinful boy would do such a thing, shameful, *pulchritudo eorum confessio eorum*, is that it? you look so pretty but you're full of sin, of course you are, I remember your parents, I know where you come from, I see you with Mel, I know how you *are*, what you *want*, you pretty, sinful, beautiful boy and he pushed me against the wall and pushed himself up against me, hard, put his mouth on mine, his tongue shoving against my teeth to get in

Oh Dear Jesus I will be sick

I brought up a fountain of sweet wine turned sour, filled his filthy mouth and fouled his robes as he pushed me away, the wine spattered on his feet like blood. I heaved, grateful to be sick because the wine burned the taste of his mouth out of mine while he gagged and spat, spat and shouted, *That might have been the blood of the* Savior, *the sweet blood of our* Savior, *and you vomit it onto the* ground, *Gentry!*

The blood of Christ saved me.

And I'm sick over the side of the Jeep, I sick it up, please don't let me be sick from Your blessed body, Please, Forgive me, please, I knew it was wrong to drink that wine and why do You make me remember? After all this time, I'd forgotten, please, I beg You, please give me the strength for this.

Because I'm sick, and not from the remembering. I'm sick, terrible sick, the first time I can ever remember being sick when it wasn't from drinking. I can't move, I'm shaking too hard, and I make Gretchen get the priest. She doesn't understand, she watches with horror while the Host is recovered and taken away. "What will they *do* with it?"

"Burn it."

"They'll burn your *vomit*?"

"It's His body."

She shakes her head and cranks the starter. "Wizardry."

I have to shift for her.

I would stay on the couch forever, but Gretchen pushes me upstairs. "You need to go to bed." Dear God. Marci's room. This is Kathryn's old bed, I'm sure, made up for me in my sickness. She unties my boots and pulls them off. I'm too weak. She pulls off my socks, and even my feet look sick.

"I can do the rest."

"Are you sure?"

"I can, I'm sure." But first, I have to die.

Finally, I get under the blankets, and I never knew, God, that there could be a sick worse than a hangover.

I'm crazy.

Miriam, you're dead.

Bosco, chase her off.

Good dog.

⌒

Kathryn comes in to see me. Are you really here? She takes my temperature, feels my forehead. She is here. Her hand, so cool . . . I'm too hot, Kathryn. Cool me.

They stand outside the door and talk.

"Mom, he's too sick. I can't leave him."

"What if you get sick, too?"

"I already had the flu."

"What if it's a different flu?"

"Then I'll call you and you can come take care of both of us, okay?" Gretchen is pleading, please, I don't want to be sick and alone, Kathryn, please have mercy on me, please . . .

"Is he drinking? Have you seen him drink anything at all?"

"No, Mom, he didn't even take wine with communion."

Wine, oh, I lurch up, I fall down, I crawl to the bathroom, barely, hug the bowl, the floor tips, help me . . . she's here, she holds my head, there's nothing to heave up but still I retch, this is violent, my eyes ache, Kathryn, thank you, this is disgusting but I'm grateful to you. "Sh, sh. It's all right. It's okay . . ."

She helps me back to the bed, unbuttons my shirt, yes, do that, take off my jeans, okay? That feels so good. Now take off the rest. Kathryn. No? Why not? She pushes me back, puts a cloth on my head. Too cold. Kathryn you make me cold. I will freeze. Get in here, Kathryn, make me warm. Come here.

Her gentle smile. "Oh Gentry."

The bed rides like a boat on the waves, and she leaves me, don't leave.

I hear her voice in the hall. "You're right. You have to stay. If you feel at all sick, you call me. And one of us will come immediately. This is a bad one."

I sleep.

⁓

Fever dreams, senseless, fast, hurtling through my head. I need the phone, if I dial it the right way, if I just hit the right combination of numbers, I will reach Miriam and I can tell her don't do this, don't do it, you don't need to do it, it doesn't have to happen for me to leave, but I can't find the phone, oh God, someone bring me the PHONE.

Nothing can stick, nothing stays. I sleep.

⁓

Ice. I am ice. Gretchen is here, her eyes are ringed with slivers of ice, the ice around your eyes, Gretchen, you are pure frost just like your mother, and she covers me, and I'm ice, she covers me, she brings more and more and more, she will suffocate me before I'm ever warm, I will shake to death, I will never be warm, I am ice, Kathryn did it. She froze me with her blue words. She froze me.

"Sh, Gentry. Sleep. Sleep now."

⁓

I wake up, heat pours out of my hands and feet, pours out like waves, waves like blood, pouring out like the hot blood, out of me, and I fight it off, I am sacred tinder, immolated, my thighs burn, there has to be a flame, my skin splits with this fire, I am splitting open so the heat can leave me, where is Kathryn, would you please get Kathryn, let me pour this heat into her, she's always so cold and I can pour my fire into her make her a crucible and she will tremble and shake and shatter, her ice will finally melt from the fire that consumes my body, God, rage through me, purify me, make me fuel, I surrender my fire . . .

I sleep.

⁓

I have a silver mask. I touch my face. My palms are gilded. She strokes my gilded face and sings to me, a song from my church.

Mel had a postcard of a Christ on a cross with hinged arms. A collapsible Christ. "People are made of parts, and so are machines. We're all parts."

"Have some water. Come on."

"That might rust me."

"Sh. Just a sip."

My hands and face are made of metal.

⌒

I'm sweating cold oil.

"Hey Gretchen? What is this? What's coming out of me?"

Gretchen is beside me, wearing my clothes. Is she me?

"It's sweat. Your fever broke."

"No, it's chrism."

"Chrism is just oil. And this is just sweat." She mops my face with her hand and sniffs her palm. It's blessed. She's blessed. I sleep.

⌒

I wake.

It's dawn. I have about fifty blankets on me. Gretchen's rolled up in my sleeping bag on top of all of them, the princess and the pea.

My voice is a croak. "Gretchen. Are you awake? Hey Gretchen?"

She opens her eyes. "Hi."

"I need to get up. Right now." She rolls off. She still wears my sweats and T-shirt.

"I can't stand up."

"We'll do it together." She helps me up.

"If you let go I'll fall down."

"I'll hold on, then." She steers me into the bathroom, the floor keeps tipping, and she braces her feet and holds me around the waist and lays her cheek against my shoulder.

The room spins but she won't let go. "Don't look."

"I'm not going to look at your stupid penis." She keeps hold around my waist while the room spins like the carousel down on the strip and once she rode that and she took a white horse and I watched because I didn't want to ride because I wanted to see her float up and down on that white horse and the room spins like that.

She helps me back to the bed.

"I don't want to sleep anymore."

"I don't blame you. Your dreams have been really interesting. Do you want the TV on?"

"Yes."

She brought a television in here. I'm so weak that I can't move. We watch the spectacle. A panel composed of people with bad teeth and ugly clothes yell at each other, and then, the audience with their bad teeth and their ugly clothes yell at a man on the panel, and then the host, with her nice teeth and her nice clothes, says, "Really? And you let him do that? I can't believe that," in her low, intelligent voice.

"I liked her better fat. She was more interesting."

"I like her however. I like her, fat or thin. I just like her. I hate every single person she ever has on her show. But I like her." Babble. Gretchen turns to me and smiles.

I sleep beneath her smile.

Gretchen

"Hi, sicko. How do you feel?"

"Worse. I feel worse." He's been having a tearing, wet cough while he sleeps. He starts to cough and gags on it. "I feel like I'm trying to cough up a dishcloth."

I point to a stack of paper cups on the nightstand. "Jack says swallowing it is a bad idea. So spit." The fever had him for over two days. He would sweat it out and then heat up again, and the whole time, he babbled this crazy religious dream talk. I'm glad it's done, but now he coughs.

"I can't smell anything." He sounds scared.

"It's just part of being sick."

He coughs and coughs and coughs.

I call Mom and we talk about the cough. She says, "Why don't you rub some Vick's on his chest?" I say okay, and then she says, "No. Don't. I mean, have him do it himself."

When Gentry wakes up, I bring him the Vick's, and he smells it and almost passes out. "Okay, I can smell that. Please take it out of here."

Not a great idea, Mom.

Jack says he needs an expectorant to keep things loose so he doesn't get exhausted from the effort of coughing. But I know Gentry won't take it. I ask him, though, when he wakes up, if he could try to take a little. I hold out a spoonful, and he stares at it and starts to gag. "I can't, Gretchen. I'm sorry."

"Don't apologize. I'm just worried about you."

"I wish I could take a bath."

"So do I," I say, and he laughs and then he coughs until he chokes. Well, he does stink, not like body odor, but like sweat. I'm bored, helping him to the bathroom, carrying out his spit, watching him hack. "You can at least change your boxers." They're stuck to him and as stiff as paper. I empty out his duffel to get him a clean pair. "What's the deal with this ridiculous underwear? It's all so . . ." I wave around a pair. "Can I buy you some new, and then can I have these?"

"Why would you want my ridiculous underwear?"

"I just want to show it to Mom and Marci."

He laughs, and that makes him cough and I feel bad, because it hurts his chest. "You can have it all if you buy me what I used to wear."

"Deal. My dad has a shirt just like this. It's his favorite shirt." He seems embarrassed. "Gentry? What happened to all your clothes?" He coughs. I hand him a cup. He spits. He's so weak and skinny. "You should drink juice for the calories."

"I can't drink juice, Gretchen. I can't drink anything sweet, okay?" He sounds anxious.

"You don't have to."

I bring him hot tea. He drinks, then has the worst coughing fit yet. I hand him a spit cup. He gags and hacks and practically fills it up, which is terrific. I hold out my hand to take it.

"Hey Gretchen? I would gag if I had to carry around other people's body products like that."

"I really don't mind."

"I don't see how you can stand it."

"I'm a scientist, remember? Just hand it over."

"I don't. I remember . . ." and he won't finish, and he's confused, pale, handing me the cup, like he forgot where he is, and he stares at the cup, and he looks like he's going to cry. He always looks like he's going to cry.

I carry off the paper cup but don't check it until I'm out of the room. It isn't green. I have the feeling that if I checked Gentry's phlegm in front of him, he'd be ashamed for having any.

He falls asleep. "Miriam, I'm sorry." He says it out loud. He'll start to beg, soon, and pray in his sleep. And then he'll be fighting something, kicking the footboard, wearing himself out with nightmares.

I rub his forehead and whisper to him. "Sh, Gentry. Sleep is for resting." He mumbles something about handmaidens. I start to sing, very softly.

He sleeps.

Gentry

I cough and cough and cough. She brings me hot tea, hot broth. I drink it and hack up the contents of my lungs. We watch television. I taste nothing, I smell nothing. I cough. We sleep.

The week is gone. Kathryn will be back for her today.

Jack calls. I hear her because she is sitting on the kitchen stairs, answering questions, explaining. She calls him Jack, not Dad. Why does this relieve me? Of course she calls him Jack, Mike is Dad. "He's holding down liquids. I keep pushing them, like you said. No, he gags at anything solid. No. He just sits there and gags. Okay, I'll try crackers in the broth. I think he needs to rest more. Okay, see you in a few days."

God, this is to give thanks.

She wants the cable up here. "I could tell you how to do it, what to buy and how to hook it up, if only you could drive."

"I can drive, dummy. Remember?"

"I have to shift for you."

"I've been paying attention. I can do it."

I send her to the hardware store for a splitter and some cable, and I tell her how to do it, she runs the cable through a heat return, and we have cable.

She still watches the Learning Channel, but her real obsession these days is a show about this petri dish approach to young adulthood. Gretchen is fascinated with it. I think this is cruel, this whole idea. Thanks to a marathon, we watch four years of the show in one weekend.

We reassemble the casts. We arrange a nice cast, where the show would be boring, and a creative cast, where everyone would be busy actually doing things. We put all the snakes, psychos and losers in one cast, and try to imagine what they would do to each other. Gretchen, of course, would like that show the best. It would be the most "interesting."

∽

One night the phone rings, and I hear her yelling.

"You're SICK, you know that? Just SICK. I don't CARE what you found out. He would NEVER to do that to me, he would NEVER do that, never, never, NEVER!"

She comes in and wraps herself in my sleeping bag, and curls up at the end of the bed instead of next to me. I can hear her cry.

We sleep.

∽

I wake up, and she's beside me. "Gentry? I don't remember you ever being sick when you lived here. Except that Thanksgiving. Remember?"

"That was a hangover. I've never been sick except for hangovers."

"Never? How about in school?"

"Especially not in school. There was an infirmary. Nuns took care of you."

I shiver and she puts on more covers. I sleep without dreams.

∽

I feel a little better. "Gretchen, where are you? I feel better." I put my feet on the floor and try to stand. Not happening.

Her voice from across the hall, calling like a flute. "Do you like your baths hot?"

"I don't know. I never take baths."

"Let's find out." She steers me into a room that smells overwhelmingly of steam and Kathryn. I haven't been able to smell anything for days, and this combination is overpowering.

"Do you need help?"

Steady. The counter is right there, the counter is steady. "I think I can do it myself."

"Are you sure?"

"Yes." No.

She starts to go out, turns back. "Gentry, I was thinking, maybe in a few minutes I could come in here and wash your hair? Here's an extra towel, you know? To cover up. I really don't care if I see your stupid penis, I'm just thinking about all the other people who would be freaked out if I did."

My stupid penis. I want to laugh and I want to cry, but most of all I want to get clean. I decide while peeling off my shorts that I'll ask Gretchen to burn them.

I fall into Kathryn-scented bliss, sliding all the way below the water, letting the air out of my lungs so I can curl on my side and lie on the bottom like a flounder. Maybe I can lie here until both eyes migrate to one side of my head. That would be nice. So nice, even though my heart hammers and my chest burns. I never take baths, I always take showers. Why? I come back up gasping, my hands pressing my eyes.

Everything is too close to the surface.

She put a razor in here, so I shave. That takes about sixty seconds from lather through rinse.

Gretchen knocks. "All clear?"

"Wait!" I arrange the towel to cover the offending area. "Yes."

She enters, takes a look and snorts. "Nice diaper. You look like Jesus in a hot tub. Have you seen that old website?"

"Of course."

"Did you laugh?"

"Of course."

"Good. Lean back." She massages in the shampoo. Dear God, I always loved having hands in my hair. "Dad warned me that your hair was short."

"A year ago it was an inch long. It stuck up like a brush."

"That sounds ridiculous."

"It was."

"Then why did you *cut* it?"

I could tell her the truth, that my wife took a scissors to my hair while I was passed out drunk. If I reveal this to Gretchen, maybe she can help me understand what happened to me down there. Because Gretchen is the smartest person I know.

We're silent as she rinses, puts in conditioner. I spend a fortune on this stuff now, thanks to my nice stylist in Oklahoma City. Her name was Bernadette. "Knock, knock."

She smiles. "Who's there?"

"Bernadette."

"Bernadette who?"

"Bernadette the stake." Gretchen laughs politely. I could explain about Saint Bernadette, and the Bernadette who loved my hair. The thought of this exhausts me.

Gretchen inhales. "Sandalwood. This smells nice. But you always kind of smelled like this, you know. Even your sweat smells like this." She rinses out the conditioner. "You sent your ponytail to me."

My hair. I did that, I sent it to her. I wanted it to be safe.

"I still have it. I thought about burying it with Bosco, but I couldn't do it. I did put some of it in there with him. I'll show you where his grave is once you can walk again."

He has a grave, I can visit him, he didn't disappear or get burned up or thrown away.

I press my hands to my eyes and slide back under the water.

⁓

I'm well enough to eat toast. This means she is going to leave.

I called Kathryn this morning to ask if I should drive her home. And she said in her calm, cold voice, "No, Gentry, I'll come." Oh will you, Kathryn? For me?

Why is this all I think about? Ever? I'm an idiot, what will I do? That phone call at my office, what was I doing? What if Fanny had walked in there, or Ben?

Gretchen says, "What? You're blushing." I shake my head. I'll stay away from your mother, Gretchen, because she's married, and because of what you saw.

I turn my attention to the egg in front of me. It seems like a lot, this fried egg. I think I can eat it. Maybe. "I fry eggs, now."

"Really?" She smiles.

"I'm good at flipping."

"Eggs are hard to flip."

"I have a system. I can show you."

"You can fry the eggs when I come down next time."

"When?"

"Well, I have riding lessons, you know. And there are some things coming up I want to go to. You can always come to Portland."

"I have to tear down the old lab and take it all over to the middle school and set it up, and then I have to set up the new lab at the high school. You could help me."

She shakes her head. "I'll be back soon."

When? Why won't she say when?

I eat my egg. She does the dishes. We don't talk.

Gretchen

"Come on." I walk out the back door and wait. He steps out and I take his hand and try to lead him across the driveway, but he panics, pulls back. "We won't go in the little house. I want to show you something else." And I pull, and he follows, and we go around to that narrow strip of land between the little house and the bluff. The edge of the world. It's right under the window. I marked it with white stones in the shape of a cross for Bosco, the Catholic dog.

And he's on his knees.

I cry, then, because I have to tell him. He left and Mom got sick, and I just knew she was going to die. But she didn't. She had the surgery and she got better, and then she was seeing Jack. And there was no way I could write him and tell him that my mom liked this old guy. I cried about it to Dad and he said, "Let your mother tell him. This is not your job, sweetheart." So I didn't write and she got married and no one told Gentry.

How could I tell him that Mom got married?

We brought Bosco back here almost every weekend. The first thing he did when he got out of the car was check the little house to see if Gentry was back where he belonged. Then he would walk to the top of the steps, smell the air, wave his tail and carefully walk down, two front feet, two back feet. He'd patrol the sand and say hello to the other dogs. But going up the stairs was hard for him. We had to help him.

He kept slowing down. He'd lie on the floor of the sun porch in Portland, basking and smiling. Sometimes when I got home from school, Mom would be out there asleep beside him, her arm round his neck. That's how big the dog bed was, she fit on it, too. Both of them on there in the sun. He'd watch me through his milky old eyes like he was warning me not to wake her up. I would notice his face going silver and his hips getting bad, and the way he still smiled and wagged his tail, and I would think, Gentry has to hurry up and come back.

But I told him not to come back. Because he married someone besides my mother.

Bosco started to fail. We had to put his bed on a tarp, and clean him up. Jack said, "This is not humane, Kathy." And my mother said, "Don't even say it out loud, Jack."

That last summer, we took him to the coast. Mom said we were just going to stay there. She didn't say until what. She didn't have to.

Bosco could still get around a little. He would walk out the kitchen door and follow his nose to the edge of the world and smell the ocean. He was deaf and blind. He didn't even try to use the steps anymore. And then he stopped eating and drinking.

I built a windbreak in front of little house, right under the bathroom window. It was in the sun and out of the wind. He spent his last days here, sleeping in the sun. I'd tempt him back to the house at night, when it got cold.

And one morning, he came out and lay down, and he never got up.

I tell him all of this. I can't stop crying. Gentry leans again the house and pulls me back into his arms. I can feel his heart beating against my back. He holds me, puts his face in my hair. I tell him how Jack cried when he was digging the hole. Mom cried. Even Marci cried, she sat out here and cried a whole entire night over Bosco.

I can feel Gentry's tears falling in my hair. We just sit there. And I remember how that felt when I was eleven, his heart, his arms, and I cry because he's back, Gentry is back, four years I waited and he finally came back to where he belongs.

And now it's time for me to go.

Gentry

My hands are shaking as I wash my face in the sink.

I refuse to follow her around while she gathers up her stuff. I make coffee. I sit down to drink it at the stupid island thing, what was wrong with a table?

She comes down the kitchen steps, bag in hand, and puts it by the back door. She pours herself a cup and goes to the fridge and adds a little cream. Always, these moments when I see that she's grown up while I was busy down south trying to convince myself that I could come back to her.

She sits down beside me. "You know, there are kids in Dad's neighborhood who go to the same prep you did." She watches my face when she says this, watching my reactions. "I think it would be hard to be in high school and not have parents."

"It was easier at that school. Everyone was away from his parents. Not just me."

"That makes sense, actually. Did Mel take you there every fall?"

"Just the first year. After that I went by myself. But he always came for parent weekend. He stayed in the rectory."

She smiles. "I'm glad."

"I was glad, too."

"Did you ever play any sports?"

"Yes I did."

"Right. I mean, like, organized sports."

"Right. Team sports. I played those."

"Like soccer or baseball. You never played any of those, did you?"

"I think we just covered that." Why does this surprise her? I can follow rules, I'm not slow, I have long arms.

"What were you good at?"

"Everything but wrestling. It's supposed to be a good sport for kids who are small and strong. So I tried. The first time someone put me in a hold, I broke his nose. So. No more wrestling for me."

"What did you end up playing?"

"Soccer and basketball. Soccer because it has the highest standards of sportsmanship of any game, so I had to keep myself in check to play. I loved basketball, so they me play that, too. I really wanted to play lacrosse, but it was decided it was best if I didn't play anything that involved a stick. So no lacrosse, no baseball or softball. I ran track."

"Distance or sprints?"

"Sprints and javelin."

"A javelin is a stick."

"You don't hit anything but targets with it."

She stares with those blue eyes. "What happened to that picture of you and Mel?"

"At my commencement? I put it in that box."

"What box?"

The box I was holding the night it happened.

I sit there for a minute, feeling the world shift. I stood in the kitchen and the box was heavy. And she walked down the stairs, wearing my robe.

"Are you okay?"

I nod. I can see it, the old kitchen overlaid on this new kitchen. Marci in my robe. "I had a box full of your mother's stuff out in my house, and I put the picture in there."

Her eyes narrow. "I never saw *anything* like that in your house."

My head is starting to hurt. "It was from your old house, and it ended up out with my stuff. I'll find it for you." I press my hands to my eyes to push it all back in. "Why are you asking me all these questions about high school?"

"Oh, I don't know." She studies the countertop. "I guess because I'm in it, now. I've been wondering what you were like, that's all."

"I was twelve when I started, so I was a scared little kid who sucked his thumb and had bad dreams, but at least I didn't wet the bed." She laughs. Does she think I exaggerate? I don't. Those poor kids who wet the bed.

"Did you make friends?"

"No. I was always fighting. People left me alone."

"It's so weird that you got into fights."

"I wasn't joking about the sticks, Gretchen. I was a rough kid." I remember that counselor chiding me, *You can learn a new vocabulary for your anger besides violence.*

"Boys can always fight. It's male breeding behavior. I have no idea how to fight."

"When you're smaller, you have to fight dirty. That's the trick. Scare them, kick them in the privates. Even if they're a foot taller and forty pounds heavier. Never be afraid, because that scares them, the idea that you aren't."

"Were you really that small?"

"I was short until I turned fifteen. And then in one year I grew ten inches."

She stares down at her coffee. "I know someone who grew like that. He said it hurts."

"It was like being on the rack. I was still growing in college."

"That must have been strange to be in college that young. Wasn't Mel worried about your social development?" That sounded like Kathryn, her tone, her expression, her general air of judgmental concern.

"Mel is a priest. He was worried about my spiritual development. He was worried that I wouldn't be ready for my Latin form. That was the kind of thing Mel worried about. He did teach me to ride a bike when I was eleven, and he taught me to drive when I was twelve."

"Twelve?"

"Yes. Twelve. He taught me to drive the rectory's old Rambler wagon. I had a picture of me driving it. I was so little, it looked like a nine-year-old was driving. We were lucky that most of the local cops went to our church."

"So you have pictures? Besides the lost one?"

"Yes. I have school photos and yearbooks and all that stuff."

"Seriously? Can I see?"

"Mel keeps it for me. Do you want me to have him send it out?"

"Please."

"Okay."

"Don't forget, please? Don't forget to ask him."

"I won't forget." Why is she so curious what I was like all those years ago? God, do You realize that I started high school twenty years ago? "Hey Gretchen? How old do I look?"

She studies me, thinking. "You used to look about seventeen. Now you definitely look old enough to drink." She shakes her head. "When my dad went down to Oklahoma, he said he didn't recognize you when he got off the plane." I remember that moment. He looked right through me. "He said you looked like a scared little kid dressed up in his dad's suit." Gretchen glances out the window and rises to her feet with a womanly grace that stops my heart. Kathryn is here. She doesn't stay long, just long enough to ask after my health and steal her daughter.

⌒

This is the emptiest room in the house.

The closet in here is like a small room. Shelves, bars, even a window. I see something familiar balled up on the floor at the back. My big brown robe. Dusty. I put a hand on the doorframe to steady myself, because when she came down the stairs, she was wearing my robe. I don't know why she had on my robe.

God, what did I do before I left?

She left things behind, a few dolls and toys. A box with photos, the yearbook, two framed pictures of her with Garret. Some pictures of me from the day I taught Gretchen to ride her bike. I did look seventeen. Boxes of old clothes that still have her sharp smell, like the air after a lightning strike. A stack of CDs. I used to have this one. And this one. And this one.

Ah, here it is. The box. I pick it up, it's heavy and dusty and full. I remember the feel of it in my arms, the smell of that old paper, like carrying a dead body into their house. I'm too weak, I have to set it down on her bed.

I kneel and press my hands to my eyes.

I'm ready to face it, God. What happened.

You can let me remember.

⌒

I knew where the new key was hidden, but the door opened without it. They'd been locking up since Alex Fournier came prowling around, but they must have forgotten. Probably Mike Mumford came in to get Gretchen's bag for the weekend and he stupidly forgot to lock the door because he never knew how they did things, he lived his pompous, ignorant existence oblivious to his original family's daily life, when they woke, what they ate, what made them laugh. He didn't even know where they sat at the table.

My knees kept trying to go out from under me, but I couldn't drop that box.

I stepped into the kitchen where I hadn't set foot in weeks. It was dark, very dark, but a blue light shone from the living room.

The television.

I couldn't blame the television on Mike. I would turn it off on my way out. I'd lock the door. But I just wanted to stand there for a moment, only a moment, and think about my time in that kitchen. Sitting at that table. Marci pouring me a cup of coffee. Gretchen combing my hair. Kathryn doing the crossword with me. That was all. God, it was so much more than I'd ever had.

It should have been enough.

I was standing there, having my little moment. I'd earned it by loving all three of them in my own incomplete and messed-up way. I wished I'd known how to do it better, how to love them right. Maybe things would have been different.

That box was heavy.

A dark shape rose up over the back of the couch, a torso, a face lit with blue, small eyes and a carnivorous grin. The hair on my arms rose, but I knew that was not a ghost, not a demon. That was just a short kid with a bad attitude and worse teeth who smelled like engine oil and chewing tobacco.

If he was here, so was she.

She came down the kitchen stairs slowly, one careful step at a time, taking her time. I could smell shampoo in her wet hair. She reached the kitchen and stood there tying my robe closed around her, her fox-like chin lifted in challenge. I felt the words rise up, the babble, about why was she not at the all-night party and her mother would see she was gone and where was his truck parked and what was she thinking, letting him in the house?

Too much to say, so I said the only thing I could. "I found this box." She held out her arms and I gave it to her. That was it. I didn't do anything to her, with her before I walked out of that kitchen forever.

But I didn't go get my dog. I didn't get into my Jeep.

I didn't leave.

I stood by the garage, where he'd parked his stupid Chevy short box with the eight-inch lift kit. There were tree limbs and branches on the ground. I'd never finished cleaning up after the February storm. Too many other storms to worry about.

Apple is a hard, hard wood.

I said a new prayer, something like, Oh God, Oh God, Oh God, and this prayer made my blood surge, my ears roared with this prayer, and my heart sang with a mean and evil joy because when I was finished with this prayer, there was no glass left in his truck.

Amen.

Time to start on the fenders.

He stepped out of the front door that no one ever used, but he waited on the step. *Why, God? Why, when I'd watched him hate me all this time, holding himself back, why was he waiting?* I saw the branch in my hands, the impediment to his approach. He flinched when I threw it against the house. It slid down the siding into the grass, a wooden snake, rigid and dead.

I held out my empty hands. *Come here.*

But still, he wouldn't. So I went to him.

I slammed him into the side of the house, felt the satisfying impact of a young body on a hard surface as his breath left him with a gasp. I had not yet caused him pain but I had caused him fear and I held him there, saw it in his eyes, Lord, I tasted his fear, drank it in. It would sustain me.

He spoke in a high, weak voice. *You wrecked my truck.*

I did. I slammed him against the house, heard the crack of his head on wood. Now he'd feel some pain. *Don't touch her again. Or I'll wreck you.*

Something cleared in the murk of his brain. The fear left his eyes and he grinned that horrible grin I saw over the couch, it *wasn't* the light, he *was* a ghoul, laughing at me. *You mean Marci? I don't have to touch her. She can't keep her hands off of me. You should've fucked her, you really should've. She's great.*

His gut was tensed to take the blow. The impact of it traveled up my arm to my shoulder, wrenched it with the impact as it traveled up and into me. My arm and my shoulder were on fire, my hand numb. He was panting, gagging, but he wouldn't fight.

It was a brutal instruction. I told him not to touch her. Not to call her or talk to her. Not to look at her face if he saw her in public. I told him he wasn't allowed to talk *about* her. *Did you hear me, Garret? Don't even say her* name *again.* He took his medicine like any child who knows he's at the mercy of someone older and stronger.

I let him fall.

He shook his head, trying to stand. He got as far as his knees. *You can't stop me. You won't even be here, asshole. You can't stop me.*

Then I'll tell her what you did to Tiffany.

You fucker. He spat. *You tell her and I'll kill you.*

What about Tiffany? Her voice rang out from the open door, her voice that sounded like her mother's but without the music. I turned away from my handiwork to face her. To tell her. She stood on the step, arms crossed, her eyes shining. *Tell me, Gentry. What did Garret do to Tiffany?* I could tell by what radiated from her eyes, the hatred and betrayal, that she already knew. She turned away and closed the door forever.

Her pain was my fault.

The blow to the back of my head held a certain mercy, in that before it hurt, it stunned. But pain followed like a deep ringing tone, it rang me like a bell. Pain sang up from the back of my head like a choir of agonized angels. I started to fall, I knew I had to fall. I had come there to fall.

But God, it was the slowest fall.

I felt a clean snap as my jaw slammed the concrete step. I couldn't move as he silently went to work on me with his boots. I prayed to black out because I thought I'd known pain in my life, a thousand blows for the first ten years, but I'd never felt pain like this.

Oblivion, finally.

I don't know how long I was out. I woke on my back, arms out, unable to see, unable to move. God, I was so ready to die. I waited for Your voice, the voice that would call me to my rebirth, when I would finally be made right, free of this body that chained me to sin.

Gentry, open your eyes.

It wasn't You. It was her. I wanted You, but her face shone closer by, and put out Your grace.

She pulled open that robe. *Look at me. Just once. Please* see *me.* The desperation in her voice. I did. I looked upon her nakedness and felt myself rise, I felt lust and pain and grief come pouring out of me like the words that burned my mouth as I smashed that truck, like my hatred for that ruined boy, shame and blood and rage and come, pumping out of me as I died.

You can't die of shame, even if you want to. I didn't die.

I submit to this memory.

Amen.

Eventually, I get up off my knees and go to the bathroom to throw up. I wash my hands and face with ice cold water. I drink from the tap until my stomach complains. I take off my sweaty shirt, dry my face with it, take it downstairs to the laundry room with my dirty robe. I take off everything else and put it in the washer. Everything can be made clean, yes? I want to get in there too.

I open the back door and stand there in nothing. This is what I have, today. A hot cup of coffee. The steady noise of the washer. The roar of the ocean, the salt smell of the air. A memory I have to live with.

All of it is water.

Everything can be made clean. Even me.

I'm supposed to make things right. Whatever that takes. I have no doubt that this is Your plan, God. And I submit. But I'm tired of doing this alone. I want to talk to Mel. I want to pet Bosco. I want Gretchen to take my hand, to turn it palm up and study the lines as if they mean something to her. I am so tired of being alone.

I dry my eyes and go inside to shower.

⁓

Time to work.

This equipment was impressive four years ago. Now it's slow and pathetic. The LAN at Ben's office was better than this.

The middle school has a volunteer team of students who show up at the high school to help me tear down the lab, excited about reassembling it in their school. Kids this age are hard for me. They are raw and hopeful with their unwashed hair, awkward shoving, the cracking voices of the boys and chipped fingernail polish of the girls. But they're eager to work. We spend hours rolling, marking the right cables. The kids are better at tracking down the miles of connections than I am. Volunteers show up with vans. We go to the middle school and build a network. Connections and current and configuration.

I come back to the house each night and cook myself some rudimentary dinner. I start to plan in my head how I'll set up the high school when the equipment arrives. I sleep at night, soundly. I wake to the sun, the sound of the ocean, the peace. This is to give thanks, for work and waves, for sun and sleep. For all the water.

Amen.

Hoan-Vu

I heard old Gentry was going to come back. Why anyone would want to come back to this place is beyond me, but I heard he was on his way.

I was up at my mom's hearing in exhaustive detail about all the things that were currently wrong with me. I decided to take a break from that fascinating and self-esteem-building topic to see how old Gentry was doing.

I heard he was married two years ago. Marci told me during a rare lull in her recurrent bitch attack. Actually, she was a little broken up over the whole thing, that Gentry married someone. It surprised the hell out of me because I figured if he ever gave up the undercover high school priest act, he'd never be stupid enough to get married.

I knew his wife wouldn't be up at the school, but I was hoping to wangle a dinner invitation to check out Mrs. No Name Gentry, because I was frankly as curious as hell.

I went in there, and he didn't hear me because he was concentrating on some-thing and he had the radio on. He looked just a tiny bit more pathetic than he used to. His hair was shorter and it kept falling out of this funky looking little ponytail he had. He kept pushing it back. He looked tired, and he looked as young as ever, as young as me, even though the guy is really old, thirty or something now.

"I thought I would come carry stuff for you, watch you drop things for a while, Jesus, Gentry, don't hug me, Jesus!" He picked me up and carried me around. I would like to point out that I don't especially like being carried around, but oh well, whatever makes him happy. That's what it was all about, right, keeping Gentry happy, I guess. After I suffered the indignity of unwanted physical contact with some creepy old white guy, he set me down. "You look good, Vu."

"You look the same, Gentry."

"Thank you." Of course I did not mean that as a compliment, but it was a com-pliment as far as he was concerned.

I said, "So, I heard you got married."

"Where did you hear that?" He was surprised. Didn't he remember how small this town is, how everyone knows everything?

"Marci was the bearer of those glad tidings. Is your wife here? How does she like the Beaver State?"

He stared at his feet. "My wife died."

"Oh, hey, Gentry, I'm sorry. I didn't know. I never heard that she died." No wonder he looked a little more pathetic. People should have to wear signs when something like this happens so I don't make such an asshole of myself all the time. "Marci probably would have told me, but I'm not tight with her these days."

"She didn't know."

"Oh." Yes, well, this is indeed awkward, what with the reason they aren't in touch being one of the hot local topics of speculation of the most sordid kind. In general, people thought it might have had something to do with Marci, which, if Gentry indeed did mess with the young woman who occupied most of my waking dreams throughout my high school years, he did deserve an ass-kicking. But whatever Gentry did, I doubted it was bad enough that he deserved to be kicked to death by Garret. "She's too much for me, I'm afraid. She's just basically a first class bitch, if you want to know the truth. I mean, she used to kind of keep it under control, but now, she's like a wild, out of control permanent PMS bitch. Scary."

"Hm. Whatever happened to Tiffany?"

"Oh, this is great. You know how Marci is taking journalism, right?"

"I heard that, yes."

"Well, Tiffany got a job last year at this magazine, this *American Cheerleader* magazine. And Marci is furious over it."

"Wait. Vu, are you telling me that there's a magazine for cheerleading?"

"Yup."

"And Tiffany is a cheerleader journalist?"

"Yup. She's a cheerleader journalist." And Gentry laughed out loud, and I don't remember hearing that all that often. I stepped away because I was afraid he might pick me up and hug me again. Boundaries, Gentry, boundaries.

"Hey Vu? I could sure use some help, here."

"Ah, I was afraid you would say that." Actually, I was hoping he might say that. Because I did always like helping out old Gentry. "Do I get paid?"

"You do."

I told him in Vietnamese that I'd only do it if we only spoke my language, and he agreed in perhaps the worst Vietnamese I have ever heard in my life. So for a few days, I helped him, and listened to him mangle my mother tongue, and I told him my tales of big city life, and I told him about the four different jobs I've had in the three months since I graduated college, because I still have ambivalent feelings about rampant capitalism.

I caught him up on all the kids. But one, I didn't mention. We would get to the point where the reminiscence would logically move to his name, and we would stop, and we would step over or around that place like it was a steaming fresh dog turd. But finally, I just said it. "Garret joined the Navy that summer."

And we left it alone. I always hated that asshole, anyway.

We worked. I talked and he laughed. He seemed to like it that I did most of the talking, and I certainly liked it that way, seeing as how listening to him speak the language was excruciating. But he got a little better with practice. "Say, Gentry, have you and Coach Gilroy resumed your love affair, yet? I think that wife of his is just a jailhouse substitute for you, and you better get ready, because I think he'll dump her now that you're back in town."

"Shut up."

"Boy, your verbal brilliance, there. That's the only thing you say perfectly." And he smiled, and I knew I could kid him all I wanted to. He would put up with me, because I helped, and as usual, Gentry required some help.

Actually, we took an entire week instead of the three days it should have taken, and we spent that week doing things right in the perfectionist, anal-retentive obsessive-compulsive manner of Mr. No Name Gentry. My mom or my grandma brought us lunch every day, and then sat there and watched him eat, making sure he ate enough, I guess, laughing so hard at his attempts to speak. In spite of all these meal breaks, we finished the job and I actually got paid for it.

Gentry was pretty excited. He sat down at the server and did his magic, and when everything started up with no glitches or bugs, he looked like he always looked in church, that same sanctified glow, that priestly face. I was afraid again of that physical contact, but he just said, "Thank you."

"No problem. Anytime. Seriously, anytime."

"Hey Vu?" Oh, God, no, not this one. "I could sure use some help with one other thing." He gave me that lost look.

Ah, fuck it. "I noticed a certain repetitive element in your wardrobe, there. You look like you were just let out of prison with a change of clothes and a one-way bus ticket. This convict look, very nice, but . . ."

"Can I just give you some money?"

"Sure." He gave me a pathetically low budgetary figure, apologized, tried to explain. The last thing I wanted to hear is how some person older than myself managed to be broke. I was hoping that being broke was a temporary state, one that I would have remedied by the time I hit his age. He said he was waiting for his house to close and his paychecks to start. He mumbled something about funeral costs, and he did look sad, then. That was the closest the man got to the subject of his dead wife. "Gentry, don't worry about it. I can fix you up. Vinh will get me his discount."

"And you'll get things, um, baggy?"

"Yes. I'll make sure that both you and Coach Gilroy will fit in your pants." He laughed again.

"Thanks, Vu."

"No problem." It truly wasn't a problem. I didn't mind doing it. I always liked helping out old Gentry. Just as long as I never had to set foot in a store with him again, I didn't mind at all.

Gentry

God, even if he never holds a job, Thanks to You for Vu. He helps.

Three weeks, God. Three weeks until school begins, and the thought fills me with joy and dread. Do I remember how to do this? I haven't even made a lesson plan. I used to do them in my head in the combine cabs. All I've done is get the lab ready. That's just the hardware. I'm as bad as Lorrie Gilroy.

I'm anxious, God.

It took seven calls and an edge of homicidal desperation in my voice before they finally traced my computer and got it delivered. I set it up in Gretchen's room.

I still have some old lesson plans. I can do this. I can teach. I'm a failure in some basic ways, but I'm a good teacher. It's all I ever wanted to do. You brought me back to it, so You must be there, and this must please You. This is part of Your plan.

I submit.

The phone rings, and I answer it because it won't be a bill collector. "Hey."

"Good morning. I'm just letting you know that we'll be there for the week before Labor Day." Kathryn sounds happy. "I'm looking forward to catching up."

"Hey Kathryn? I'm going to see Mel that week." What am I saying? I have no plans to see Mel. She hangs up, hurt and confused.

It isn't a lie if I do it, so I call Mel and tell him to expect me. His voice shakes with happiness at the prospect. God, could You explain to me why he loves me so much? My behavior in this life doesn't merit the love he gives me. Not at all.

This is to give thanks. Amen.

Mel

As a lad, I'd heard of changelings, the wild children who swapped themselves for human boys and girls. They were a camp tale, something trotted out to make us shrink and shiver. We had no faeries, no forest, no woods in our part of the world, just dust and rocks and scrubby grass that barely fed the sheep. But elsewhere on our continent there were dripping forests of hollow trees with high branches where the changelings lived. They stole away the human children, and these strange, knowing creatures took their places.

When I first saw this boy, I thought he was one of them.

I'd stopped him on the steps of the church to enquire after his father. I'd never met the man, but had heard of his rampage through the rectory, turning over the table, tearing sconces from the walls, demanding information we simply did not have. When a 6'4" iron worker decides to tear apart a room, he does a thorough job. He left before the police arrived, and it was decided not to press any charges. The boy, you see. Everyone was concerned about what would happen to the boy if he lost his father, too.

And so, we lived in a state of uneasy truce with Payton Gentry. Some of the brothers felt the current state of affairs, in which his son attended Mass without him, was sufficient. Others felt it was best if even his son were not there, as the father might come along behind him. A few felt we should reach out. I had never met the father and only knew Gentry from his presence in the pews with the Nguyens, but I thought some action should be taken.

So that Sunday on the front steps of the church, I called Gentry back to me.

He halted. I watched his back stiffening. He shoved his hands deeply into his pockets as if hiding an act of thievery, and turned to meet my eyes with the dark and liquid gaze of a wild animal. But he did not speak in the ancient tongue of changelings, or the Vietnamese his neighbors taught him. He spoke English in a regular boy's voice, low and pleasing, a slight hesitation before his consonants.

He was an intelligent child. And he was angry.

⁓

And so, he is returned to me. This boy who learned *De Profundis*, and prayed it on his knees every morning of his first year with me. This man who is a gift beyond measure.

Thirty-two years old.

I have done what I can. And with God's help, we have muddled through. I saw him through the first year. That shattered, silent boy crying each night on the other side of the wall, alone in his room, the only sound he made for weeks.

I wanted to keep him with me forever. I was prepared to leave the priesthood behind if I needed to, to forsake my call. But he was curious about a school that would challenge him, and I was too old to adopt him, and I thought his life might change if he went to a school where it was not a punishable offense to be intelligent. I wondered, what did he think of a pre-sem? Because the boy seminaries still existed in those days. He turned to me with his dark, worried eyes, so afraid to say no, so afraid not to. This was not a young priest I had on my hands.

I kept him home for one year so he could regain his voice and get ready for a real education. And then I let him go. I saw him through adolescence, his years of hunger. Those famished eyes, ever hopeful for more. How could such a small boy eat so relentlessly? The summer he turned sixteen, I saw him through a season of growth so painful that I thought I could hear his bones creaking. He got out of bed in the morning, stiff, eating pain reliever and gulping milk, and went to pump fuel. He had such tremendous industry, a ceaseless desire to be at work and of use.

Yes, he went off to college. And he learned everything there. That next summer I found myself trying to ease the suffering of a tormented seventeen-year-old boy who had known and lost a young woman. He could not bring himself to tell me of what had happened. What I have heard over the years, the acts that men commit, the acts that God forgives. And he was afraid that his common mortal failings would lose him my love.

I tried. Always, I have tried to help him find his way. I stand uselessly at the edge of his life, praying to God for oil to calm the troubled waters of his soul. I have watched over him as best as I can. He has watched me with the eyes of a hunted doe.

He has his mother's eyes.

∽

When my nephew visits the monastery, his first order of business is to check out the equipment. It is a point of pride with him that it runs well. It does.

He seems better. I no longer have to watch the man flinch in the manner of the child when he first came to me. But his face is full of pain when he is not guarding it from any expression whatsoever. Oh, my boy, it is a fine and beautiful thing to have a face like yours, one that broadcasts your emotions. But I know it was a burden. And I wonder, my boy, why you are here, so soon, and so quiet.

I show Gentry the changes I've made to the site, and he compliments the graphics. "It looks very nice." He scans the forms. "Have you thought about a no-frames option? When you're on a laptop and using a touchpad, they're annoying."

"I see. This means I have to build two pages?"

"There are shortcuts. I'll help." He turns his hurt and beautiful face to me and blurts, "Do you know why I hate peanut butter?"

"No, my boy, I do not."

"When I was five, I ate some rancid peanut butter and threw it up. He put my face in it, like a dog. He made me eat it off the floor."

I am possessed with a degree of loathing that makes me shudder.

"Pray, Gentry. Pray for compassion."

"Compassion." His face is stone. "I won't pray for that."

And we go to Mass, and I pray.

∽

He tunes up the ancient van, that malfunctioning case for automotive euthanasia. He works on a riding mower someone donated, what a Godforsaken piece of crap it is, but he gets it going. There are two functional riding mowers, then, and Victor rides one, and he rides the other, and Gentry wins whatever mowing competition they set up because Gentry loves to win.

I tell him that we are having trouble with the stove in the canning kitchen. He goes over it carefully and decides the elements needs recharging. We go see the man who does that. Gentry explains the situation, the sauce tomatoes piling up, the canning requirements of the brothers. He smiles that smile of his. "This time of year every burner is important." The repairman does it quickly while we wait and he will not accept payment.

On the ride back home, I wait.

"Hey Mel?"

"Yes?"

"I keep trying to remember what you said to me about masturbation. I can't remember."

I pinch the bridge of my nose and search my memories. "It was when you were eleven. I taught you how to ride a bike that day. Can you remember? It had only been a month since you came to me. I ran behind you, but I became winded and had to let go. I let you fall, and you hurt your knee." And set up a wild keening at the blood.

He nods. Pale in the face.

"Do you remember, Gentry? That night? I thought you were asleep or I would have knocked. I wanted to make sure you were all right but I interrupted you." That tiny boy, alone in that room, sleeping in his clothes, he always wanted to sleep in his clothes.

"You told me it was normal. You said every boy in the world did it. And you told me to be careful what I put in my head."

"Do you remember anything else?"

"No. But something's wrong, I can't . . ." He stops. "I feel like if I do it, the world will come to an end."

"Pray for memory."

He watches me from behind his beautiful mask. "I won't pray for that."

And we go to Mass, and I pray.

⁓

It rains for a few days, disastrous for the crops, but rain falls without intention. He stays within the walls, oiling hinges and fixing doors that stick. He mends floor tiles, replaces what can't be mended. The brothers step around him. The brothers have always left some room around Gentry, who brought us a way to keep ourselves afloat financially, who comes back every year to make sure we have what we need. I feel pride in him, and pride is a sin. But I have always been guilty of that sin where Gentry is concerned.

He spends time in the library with me. When I ask him, he reads aloud. That was how he found the courage to speak again as a boy. He read to me from the newspaper. As a man, he reads to me from Latin texts.

But today he cannot concentrate. He stares at his hands as he speaks. "I remembered about Father Peter."

"Ah. I didn't realize you had forgotten that."

"He said it was my fault. What he wanted to do."

"The swine." I came out of the rectory and found Gentry, shaking and gagging and smelling of wine, Peter with that same guilty, stolen wine vomited down his robes. I sent the boy in and demanded to know what happened. Peter spoke of the temptation of Gentry, his beauty, as if it were an excuse to assault a thirteen-year-old boy in an alley. "Your staying at the rectory on your breaks wasn't provocation. You were innocent."

"He didn't think I was innocent."

"You were. And he was sent away for treatment."

"Does that work?"

"I defer to the wisdom of others in this area, Gentry. But every priest who does this hammers in another nail and hands the hammer to the next generation. It will be the death of our church, I fear."

He shakes his head with the hopelessness of an ancient. Lifts his palms in a gesture of helplessness and appeal. "Every time I open the paper, there's something else. It makes me sick."

"I have no answer. Maybe, I don't know, women? Yes. I think that will be the answer. I just pray it happens in time. Pray with me, Gentry." And we pray for the impossible. We pray for the ordination of women.

"Amen."

"Amen."

And we go to Mass. I pray.

In the kitchen, Gentry has only ever washed dishes. This visit, he helps Loren to cook. I walk past and hear Loren explaining the mysteries. When we sit at the long tables, we say grace over the meals Gentry helped to prepare.

After we eat, we walk. The evening wind is hot. The rain ruined everything and left.

"I remember something about court. Some joke, when the judge said you were my father." The judge smiled, kindly, and he said, I guess the Father is your father. Making a joke. Gentry shook his head. He didn't want a father, so we worked it out that I could be his uncle. "She's still alive, isn't she?"

My heart leaps. "I can . . ."

"No." There is no mask that can cover his face for this pain.

"Pray for understanding."

He shakes his head. "I won't pray for that."

And we go to Mass, and I pray.

∽

The next day, we hear his heavy boots over our heads. There are some loose roof tiles, and of course the gutters. The chimneys are often clogged with nests. It is work and it has to be done, and when we see him at noon, he is covered from head to toe in various filth. He seems happy.

He chills easily, but never complains about our cold showers. We sit at a wooden table in the kitchen. He cradles a cup of hot tea in both hands, and shivers, blue-lipped, in the brown robe I bought for him all those years ago.

"What did you tell me about my name?"

"I said you could change it, Gentry. I said you could pick out any name you wanted, but you wouldn't." His child's face set in stubbornness. "Do you remember why?"

"No."

"Try to remember." The man's face is set in the same stubborn way. Refusing to remember. And then it gives.

"She couldn't find me if I changed my name."

What I see in his eyes cracks my heart. I take his hands in mine and he lets me.

Oh, my boy. Pray to have compassion for those who deserve none. Pray to remember that which is best forgotten. Pray to forgive that which is unforgivable. Pray to understand that which can never be understood.

Pray for peace. Pray for the strength to submit.

I hear the bells calling, the slap of sandal on stone as my brothers in Christ move to the chapel.

We sit at the table and pray.

Lorrie

Well, hell, you never know.

Right before I leave for Canada, and I mean right before, I'm on the way out the door with the kids yelling and Vicki telling me to hurry up and the sonofabitching phone rings and it's Kathy Mumford. Oh, great, my favorite bitch in the whole wide world.

But I'm polite to the woman, I see her in the store and I'm so nice it makes me want to puke, because of him. Sometimes she had news about him. And she says that she's going to call him because the school board is finally replacing the worthless, lazy, piece-of-shit jerk who took his place. Somebody else in town told her about it, and she calls me to yell at me for not calling her about it. Like that's my job.

And I say, well, the guy is married, he can't just pick up like he used to do, I was going to write him about it but I figured why the hell, he's probably making a hell of a lot more money now than he ever did as a teacher, especially here, so why bother?

She says, well, she's heard that things are not good with the guy. "Michael saw him, and he's not doing very well, Lorrie." And I know what I hear in her voice, she's sniffing around for information, and I'll be damned if I tell her highness anything. Not like I know anything to tell, but if I did, she's the last one who'd hear it.

I tell her I'm outta there, I gotta go, call me and leave me a message if the tape isn't full which it probably will be, but try anyway and tell me what the hell he says.

And the whole time we're gone, I keep wondering. Will he finally come back here? And what the hell's wrong with him?

So I get back, and there's a letter from him, mailed from Oklahoma a couple weeks ago.

Dear Lorrie,
    I am coming back. See you at the school.
              Gentry

That was it. That was the sonofabitching letter waiting for me when I got home from Canada.

I can't wait, I jump in the Ford and I hightail it up there, and I push in that back door and all those Mumfords are up there. A whole house full of them.

I'm polite, I'm always polite to her royal highness. Now. So she says do you want a cup of coffee, Lorrie? And I say well that would be nice, like I don't even hate her. And we sit down all cozy-like and she tells me he went to North Dakota for the week to see Mel. And so I ask, did the wife go with him to the monastery? Because I didn't think that they let the wife into those places, I thought monasteries were where a person might go to get away from the wife, see. And then Kathy tells me that Gentry's wife died last summer. A year ago. And that she does not know one goddamn detail beyond that, her ex went down there to help him out, and he's the one Gentry told.

He needed help and he called her ex?

I got four sonofabitching letters from him last year, and they all said the same sonofabitching thing, that he was fine and the fishing was good and not to worry about Y2K. What the hell kind of bullshit was that? Because I never knew him to lie, Gentry is not the kind of man who tells lies. He's too damn honest, to tell the truth.

Kathy says, do you know anything, Lorrie? Anything at all? I say, nope. I know less than anything.

And that little girl, Gretchen, she's not so little anymore. She stares at me, cool as a cucumber, and it hits me that she might know everything.

What the hell happened to my little buddy?

Gentry

I drove back without speeding tickets, and without Bosco, and got there way too late on the night before school started, which was fine because I was probably too nervous to sleep anyway.

Two notes waited on the table.

Dear Gentry,

    We had to go back to Portland because (duh) tomorrow is school. Coach Gilroy came by. I hope you had a nice visit with Mel. Did he yell? Jack is coming to play golf next weekend, and he will bring me back here if that's all right with you.

    Gretchen

That's all right with me.

Gentry,

    Well, this is one fine how do you do. I finally get back and I get up to see you and it is nothing but a house full of Mumfords. And you are off in the monastery, praying, or some such shit.

    See you tomorrow, little buddy.

                               Lawrence Gilroy

I brought in the box I promised Gretchen and put it up in the closet next to the other.

I slept a little on the couch, without dreams.

This is to give thanks. Amen.

FALL

Gentry

I have to get there at 6 AM to beat him in, because Lorrie always comes in early. I guess he wants to get a head start on doing a terrible job of teaching.

His classroom looks much the same.

I turn on his machine. Can I hack his password? I could use my admin password, but I like a challenge. NFLFOOTBALL. No? How about FISHING. No? Let's try FISHING69.

I'm in.

I scroll through his bookmarks. The NFL Home page, www.GLoomis.com. He still likes Betty, or Bettie, or Bette, I see. He needs a bigger hard drive to handle all this Betty. Lorrie has learned the magic of the right click, and no one ever added her names to the filters after I left. But he has the lesson plans for this year worked out on that funny little program I wrote.

I open his daily planner and stick a note on there for him.

Dear Lorrie,

I decided to get in here and snoop around in your private files. I see you actually use this thing. What's the world coming to? What can it mean when the great hunting, fishing, coaching, Martial Artist lays down his club and begins to type like a sissy?

I see you even get up on that Internet! What's next? Will you sit in the basement typing all night, arguing about the technology of science fiction television shows on message boards? Or will you become some kind of an online sex addict? Where will this all end? Keep it up, and I will have no choice but to relieve you of your fine woman, your sturdy children, to spare them contamination.

I'll see you at lunch.

Gentry

I put his cursor in the no sleep corner so he will see this first thing. Lorrie's classroom is next door to mine. I come back to the lab, and write my four rules on the board.

GENTRY'S RULES
1. No food or drink or chewable substances in the lab, under any circumstances. Ever.
2. Respect the equipment.
3. When I tell you to talk, talk.
4. When I tell you to shut up, shut up.

Several kids come in early. One has a Coke. I point to rule number one, and he shoots me a look. Well, if the last guy let them have stuff like that in here, that explains the filthy state of the machines I took over to the middle school. Unbelievable.

The kid takes his can full of pop and drops it into my metal wastebasket. It makes a nice clang, a sound to really set the teeth right on edge, and it splashes all over the place.

He smiles. I smile back. "Name?"

"Drew Dosier."

"Drew, get some paper towels and clean that up." He does it. Good. Then he sits down and gets on the net.

Things have changed here on the Oregon coast. Well, it was 1996 when I arrived here. And now it's almost 2001. Everything has changed. These kids talk to each other about the new machines, and they talk about what they have at home. Well, good. We might be able to have some fun, after all.

I check my class list. Most of the names are unremarkable. Two Hillarys. A Hoan and a Trang and a Vin. We have an Old Testament theme, with Naomi, Leah, Isaac and Moses in here. Hm. And I have a kid named Zebediah. Is there a new religious commune here on the coast?

And then I hear it. Low, loud, booming. Oh Dear God, every peal of his laughter rings my heart like a clapper in a bell.

And he is here, he pulls me out of my chair, he has me in a bear hug, he shakes me, mauls me, slams me against the wall, Oh Lorrie, go ahead and rattle my jaw, crush my spine, break every bone in my body, just to see you, finally . . .

And my students get to see this shaking, this joy as he picks me up and throws me around like a dog with a toy and I laugh and laugh and laugh.

Hey kids? Get used to it. I'm your teacher and these are my rules.

⌢

I go through the lunch line and Darlene is there. I can smile at her. She doesn't smile back. But she gives me a double portion.

"Hey Darlene, you'd better load me up, too, or I'll tell on you."

"No way, Lorrie. You're too fat already."

"Screw you, Darlene, not that I would unless you paid me."

Some things never change. We sit down. "Lorrie, she looks terrible."

"Aw, she married Royal, that jerk that almost took your head off that night?" I pretend to remember, but it was vague five years ago. "He's a merchant marine, see, and he comes home and knocks her around and knocks her up, and then he leaves again. She has two kids and one on the way. Hey, little buddy? You all right?" I nod, waiting for the shudders to stop. He tries to pat me, which doesn't help.

"I'm all right."

"Well, you don't look all right. Are you cold? I know it's a whole hell of a lot hotter down there."

"Just in the summer." He watches me until I stop shaking.

"I wanted to ask you something and I keep forgetting." Oh no. Questions. "Look, Gentry, it's something I wanted to ask you the whole time you lived there." His gaze is steady. His eyes are concerned. I steel myself.

"Okay, just ask me."

"Did you ever get to that Cowboy Hall of Fame?"

"Yes, as a matter of fact, I did."

"Larry Mahan's from Oregon, you know." His eyes glow. "Hell, did you see the saddle?" And I start to tell him about it, but Vicki approaches the table and lifts me from my seat in her iron grasp. "Oh, Jesus Christ, Vicki, would you put him down already? Put him down, everybody's staring at you, for Christ's sake."

"Will you come for dinner tonight?" she asks in her low voice. I nod. Her physical magnificence and rib-crushing strength have temporarily deprived me of my powers of speech. She releases me and I sink back to the bench. "I have lunch duty," she explains. I watch her walk away, in awe of her backside. I fight an urge to slap her glossy flanks. She looks better pregnant than any woman I have ever seen in my life.

"Put your goddamn tongue back in your mouth, Gentry."

"What?"

"Just forget it." He loves her so much it hurts him.

This is to give thanks. Amen.

That evening, I pull up to the Gilroy family home. Lorrie does his yard work. Or maybe Vicki. I need to be careful of my assumptions. I knock. A three-year-old boy who looks about five opens the door. "Hello. Who are you?"

"Hey. I'm Gentry."

He smiles and takes me by the hand to lead me into the Gilroy domain, still the home of the largest television ever manufactured. But the car posters are gone, the zodiac wheel is gone. A display case full of trophies and family photos dominates the room. I have copies of these, Lorrie stiff and sweaty, Renata squirming in some feminine swirl, Walter and Vicki calm and dark-eyed.

A little girl sits on the black couch I laid on for a week back in 1997. She's pulling stuffing through holes in the cracked vinyl. "She could eat that." I can't help myself, she's only two, and she could choke on that stuff.

Walter looks. "No. She tried it and she doesn't like it, so she doesn't eat it anymore."

"I see." This must be a different approach to the idea of choke hazards and accidental poisoning. Let them sample it. If it doesn't kill them, they'll avoid it. "Hey, Renata." Renata smiles and swings her legs off the couch, this is a huge child, and she runs over and clips me.

I fall.

"She's a poophead." Walter sounds apologetic.

Renata, once she gets me down, sits on my chest and smiles broadly, and a drop of drool escapes her mouth and heads for my face. I really have a problem with this, I don't like spit in my face, but I catch it, and I laugh. She laughs, too, and then she looks me in the eye and speaks.

"Pussy."

I lift her off me, then. She weighs a good ton. I pick her up and carry her, and I go to find the parents that produced these kids, Lorrie's daughter and Vicki's son.

When I enter the kitchen that smells of the things I never seem to be able to cook for myself, Vicki enfolds me again. She leaves her arm around my shoulder when she turns to stir something. "Do you like boulettes?"

"I'm sure I do, whatever it is."

"Meatballs." She turns back and hugs me again. I hope he loves you, Vicki. I hope he worships you. "He does," she whispers in my ear.

"Oh what the hell, do you two have to cuddle all the sonofabitching time?" Lorrie yanks me away from his wife and into the bear hug, the man hug. "Come on. Do you want a beer? How about a Coke? Well hell, I'm just being a host. Come on, I'll give you the whole tour, let you see the whole enchilada." We head for the case of trophies. "These are mostly Vicki's." He sniffs. "I have a few over here. She can't compete right now, see, with the bun in the oven, but she'll be back in shape and kicking butt before you know it."

"Well." What am I supposed to say? I'm glad my wife never took up martial arts. "Vicki's amazing."

"That she is." He beams.

"Nice kids, too. Walter is smart. Renata clipped me."

He shines. "I taught her that."

"And those are some big kids, Lorrie."

Now he will burst with pride. "Really? Aw, you're just saying that."

"No. Seriously. Those are some huge kids. I mean it, those have to be the largest children I've ever seen."

He's so proud that he has to look away. "Yeah, well."

God, thank You.

❧

The rest of the tour consists of the contents of the hangar-sized pole barn that they use for a garage. Some of it is familiar, the old Alumaweld, the truck, Vicki's Bronco, parked and tightly tarped. There are mats and a kickbag in one corner. Lorrie shows me the Ford Excessive they drive. "What do you think, little buddy?"

"Incredible."

He sniffs with pride. "Gets about five miles a gallon. Vicki looks good driving it."

"Well, I like that package. How's the Bronco?" I covet Lorrie's wife's rig nearly as much as I covet Lorrie's wife. "Is it running?"

He gives me a look of outrage. "Of course!" He puts a tender hand on the fender. "We have to keep the damn thing hid. If the garage door's open, somebody knocks on the door asking to buy it. It happens at least once a week." He strokes the shrouded flank of that Bronco, reverent.

I like his tools. They appear to be completely unused. He has a new Vise-Grips that I'd love to try out. I sold almost all my tools to Derek Cook before I left

Oklahoma, and there is nothing in Kathryn's garage like this new Vise-Grips. "Can I borrow your tools?" He laughs, hits my shoulder.

"What I have is yours. Except for the wife, of course."

One wall is covered with gear, a sapling grove of rods, and their waders hang side by side, Lorrie's wider, Vicki's longer. He sees me looking. "Hey, little buddy, we need to go fishing."

"I don't have a rod anymore."

"Shit. No shit? Well, we can loan you one." They could loan me ten, I think. "We take turns, you know, until the kids are a little older. So you can go with one of us anytime. Anytime at all, Gentry."

"Thanks." I've missed this man, and I've missed fishing, but I think what I miss most of all is my yellow Berkeley ugly stick with the Zebco reel.

"Are you there? Wake up there, buddy."

"I'm here."

"You're not going to cry, are you?"

"No." I'm too happy to cry.

"Oh, you can fucking cry. I'm glad to have you back, you little pussy. I missed you so goddamn much, you little asshole, I even missed your crying. I'm so son-ofabitching glad to have you back." Me too.

Oh God, I never thought it would happen.

This is to give thanks. Amen.

⌒

Once I've stuffed my stomach to the point of rupture, I watch the children eat. Renata brings appetite to a meal, and what she lacks in fine motor, she makes up with gusto. Walter eats calmly. He stares at me for most of the meal, and finally speaks. "Dad?"

"What?"

"I want a pigtail and a peersteers."

"A what?"

Vicki understood him. "Let's discuss that after dinner, Walter."

"What the hell did he say? Is he talking about livestock?"

"We'll talk about it later."

"Fine, screw me, later is fine."

After dinner, Lorrie, who has hardly stopped talking, stands up and goes to a cabinet and gets out two small glasses and a bottle of something brown. He pours out a shot and holds it towards me. "You gotta taste this, little buddy, I got it for my birthday." Bourbon, I can smell it.

Nice bourbon.

I shake my head. And Lorrie doesn't call me a name. He looks at the drink in his hand. "I guess this one is mine, then." He puts the bottle away. "Would you like to watch a tournament? One of Vicki's?"

"No." I couldn't watch a tape of people hitting each other, even if there were rules.

"That's fine, Gentry. Let's talk."

So Lorrie talks and we listen. I want to ask Vicki how her French classes are going, but I don't have a chance because Lorrie has so much to say about his teams for the four years I was gone. They were fine seasons. Lorrie's boys made the playoffs every year, and even the finals year before last. Lorrie sniffs. "Vicki's girls are undefeated two years running. Basketball, of course."

"I wish I'd been here. To see it."

"Aw, hell, you're here now, and that's what fucking matters."

"Yes, Lorrie. That's what fucking matters."

And he laughs so hard that he starts to cough, and Vicki has to pound him on the back.

⁓

And when the evening is over, after the kids' baths and a few bedtime stories which I got to read to them, and some of Vicki's peerless pie and perfect coffee, and more in-depth conversation about mutual acquaintances (Tom Seidenberg is principal at Cannon Beach Elementary, Bill Bongers married a woman he met on the Internet), and more talk about sports and fishing, he walks me out to the Jeep. "Well. Are you okay, little buddy?"

"Yes. Now."

"Then I want to ask you something, seeing as how you're okay and all."

"I already told you about the Cowboy Hall of Fame."

He frowns. "Aw, cut the crap. Hell, Gentry. I know I'm a stupid son of a bitch, but I'm not so sonofabitching simple that you couldn't have told me that your wife died." He sniffs. "So, I thought about it, see, and I thought, that's not right, that you didn't tell me. So I thought about what would make it so you wouldn't tell me. I thought a lot about it. And you know what I think? I think your wife killed herself. And that's why you didn't tell me. Is that what happened?"

I nod.

"I was *right*?" His face. "She *offed* herself? Jesus at the Rodeo Christ, I knew you picked out a crazy one. I think you LIKE them that way. Why can't you ever pick out a *good* woman?"

If he touches me, I'll hit him.

"I'm sorry, Gentry, I'm sorry I said that."

I can't look at him.

"Look, I know you and I know you blame yourself. But you can't. That's a crazy thing to do, see, to kill yourself, and you can't blame yourself for what a crazy person does. Crazy people do crazy shit and it drives everybody else crazy. But it's not your fault."

I shake my head.

"Ah, shit." He's trying to find the words. "Well, hell. I thought about how I'd feel if something happened to Vicki. But I'd have my kids, see. You know why we named Walter what we did?"

"I wondered."

"Well, you know we got married on Valentine's Day, right? And then we went up to Timberline, because we went skiing for our honeymoon. And we got up there and Vicki got out that poem you sent her when she wrote you and told you we were going to get married."

I've always wondered if he liked that poem.

"Well, I thought, if the damn kid is so goddamned broke that he can't send a sonofabitching present, he could just send a goddamned card, you know, not some piece of shit poem from some pussy fag poet. Jesus."

I guess I don't have to wonder anymore.

"But Vicki brought it along, and she read it to me. I wouldn't listen to her before, but when she read that poem to me on our wedding night, I could not believe it. That was one fine poem, little buddy. I still remember what it was called. A Woman Waits For Me. And we made him that night. And his name is Walter for Walt Whitman, and Gentry, for you." He gives me his hanky and looks away. My tears embarrass him, and my loneliness embarrasses him, and his good fortune embarrasses him the most of all.

"I'm going to tell you something about Vicki, little buddy. I'm going to tell you this because I know you won't think less of me as a man if I tell you this about my wife." He looks away toward the bay. "Vicki can dry fly fish. It's kinda like a religion with her. You should see her cast. A thing of beauty." His voice chokes. "A woman like that. Jesus. How I ever got so lucky." I return his hanky, soggy and crumpled, and he uses it anyway. "One waits for you, too. Somewhere, I know it, she waits for you."

He goes in to his good woman. I leave.

Where does she wait for me, God? Where? At the Wet Dog, or Uptown Annie's?

Pent up, aching rivers. Keep me away, God. Keep me safe.

⁓

Kathryn calls. "How are classes?"

"Busy. Busy, Kathryn. I have twice as many kids." And the idiot at the middle school keeps calling me over there because he knows nothing.

"Gretchen says your teeth are bothering you. Have you made an appointment with a dentist?"

"No. I haven't had time." Between getting the classes set up and seeing the Gilroys and fishing every free second I have and being terrified that if I ever sit down in a dentist's chair again I might never get out of it because that's how bad things are in my mouth. "I have a number. Lorrie's family goes to . . ."

"You need to see a Portland dentist." Kathryn has made an appointment for me on Saturday, and it's a personal favor kind of a thing because the dentist is her dentist and also her friend, and she expects me to drive up on Friday and spend the night because she really hasn't had a chance to see me, and it's been almost two months, now, by the way. "So, you'll be here for dinner Friday night?"

"Um, sure." Do I have a choice? I seem to have no options. I have some mandatory dental work and some mandatory visiting to do. Kathryn insists.

⁓

She deserves this life.

I like her kitchen. The table. "Here it is."

"I couldn't imagine a morning without it, so I brought it here. I had the wobble fixed." She pulls me through an open set of French doors. "And I brought this one, too." Her small hand strokes that smooth wood.

God, help?

We move on. I make all the appropriate noises, the appreciative "hms" and "ahs." I nod quite a bit, raise my eyebrows. I notice, I admire. I think, for a spurned man on a forced march through the domain of the chosen one, I do a passable job of being polite.

Dear God, how much house can there be? Will this never end?

She studies my face and smiles artificially. "Michael said you had a nice little house down there in Oklahoma."

"Hm. He was right about the little."

That makes her laugh. But I know how to make her cry.

Okay, stop that.

She brings me into their bedroom, of course, which is the size of the entire upper floor of the house at the beach. "The view from this room is beautiful at night." I nod, smile. It takes all the strength I have not to lift her up and lay her down on that enormous bed.

Enough.

She clears her throat. "Well!" She takes me back to the hallway, opens a door. "I put you in here for tonight." Great, it's next to theirs, maybe I'll hear them while I'm trying to sleep. She seems nervous. "It's somewhat feminine, but you won't mind, will you?" I shake my head, smile. This room is one of those colors I don't know the name of, like a pink but with a hint of something darker to it. It makes me think of women's mouths. And other parts.

It might be better if I laid her down on this bed. Less disrespectful to Jack.

"May I see Gretchen's computer?" She's surprised by this request but she takes me down the hall. Gretchen has another yellow and white room. That yellow doll sits on her bed. I sit down at the desk. "This isn't the printer I gave her." I sound accusatory.

"She wanted an 11X17. For charts." Charts. Of course. I should have thought of that. I should have sent her a better printer. But this company didn't make an affordable model with a tabloid output back then. What does she have on here? "You let her get online, finally?" Kathryn nods. I check her system. What's this? I can't believe it. "Kathryn? Did she put more memory in here?"

"A friend of hers did it, I believe."

Who? The memory is perfectly configured. Who did this? I push away from her computer table, I handle my ridiculous feelings of printer rejection and RAM displacement.

Kathryn is trying very hard not to laugh at me as we leave Gretchen's room. She gestures toward a closed door. "Marci stays in that room when she deigns to visit us." She opens a different door. "And you can use this bathroom." Great, just keep me away from the bathtub.

She takes me back downstairs. The way she patters down the stairs, her feet small and light. I sound so loud coming down after her. Giving chase.

All right, I need to stop this.

She stops me in the living room. "Why don't you sit down? Would you like something to drink?" Is this a test? Because a shot of poison might help.

"I'd like some water. If that's okay."

"I think water would be fine." She's laughing at me. Well, fine, just so long as I've amused a Mumford woman. That's why I'm here.

I follow her into the kitchen. Following her is its own special agony. I want to do something inappropriate. Something that involves the parts of her that I see so sweetly outlined in jeans that follow every new curve. Kathryn, I would sell my soul at this moment if you would come over here and take hold of what I have for you. And then we could put the wobble back in the little table.

"Excuse me, but I need some air."

I push out her kitchen door and breathe.

∽

I'll take a walk. I'll walk down to say hey to Fiona of the Kleenex. Fiona is in her front yard wearing green rubber boots up to her knees and leather gloves up to her elbows, clipping something. She's tall and embarrassed-looking and beautiful when she doesn't hide behind her glasses. She drags a leather-covered hand across her forehead and squints at me.

"Well, hi, Gentry."

"Hey."

"Are you up with your friends this weekend?"

"Yes. I, um, have a, um, dental appointment." Great, just great. Start umming, and talk about your teeth, why don't you. That's one fascinating topic.

"How are you?"

"I'm fine." And embarrassed by how beautiful you are, Fiona. And quite a conversationalist, as you can tell by these awkward pauses.

"Would you like to come in?"

"Um, no, I have to get back."

"Oh." She's puzzled. "Well, okay then."

God? Words?

"I just wanted to say thank you for that day."

She smiles. I smile back.

"Are you sure you don't want to come in?"

The day is hazy, mild. This state makes no weather sense, and I like it. "I'm, um, going to take a walk. Would you like to come with?"

"Excellent idea." She takes off the leather gloves.

"You look like a falconer in those," I say, and she bursts out laughing. I'm too embarrassed to say anything else, so we just walk.

Finally she speaks. "Those are actually falconer gloves."

"Really?"

"Really." We walk. Another long and awkward pause while I wonder why she has falconer gloves, but don't ask. "I'm glad you wanted to take a walk. I'm a writer and I forget that I need to move around sometimes."

"A writer? You write?" I wonder what she writes about? Maybe falconers?

"Yes." Ah, the pauses. "So, Gentry. What do you do?"

"I'm a teacher." Thank You, God, that I can say that again. Amen.

"What grade?"

"I teach high school."

She smiles. "I immediately assumed you taught grade school."

I keep my hands in my pockets. Fiona's boots scuff and her long hands fly around, pointing to fall flowers, fixing her hair, pulling at her sleeves, fiddling with a man's watch she wears. I watch her hands because they're beautiful.

We walk past Kathryn's, and then she stops talking.

I guess I'm supposed to talk, now. "I like this neighborhood."

"Why?"

"I like old houses."

She shrugs. "Most families up here only have one kid, and every house has at least six bedrooms."

"They would make fine rectories."

She smiles. "Yes, they would. Or embassies. There are a couple of former embassies in this neighborhood. They're the ones that look like funeral homes. You haven't gotten yourself another dog, I see."

"Another dog?"

"We have a friend who had a dog that was hit by a car, and he bought a puppy from the same breeder. He was really happy about how similar they were." That sounds ghoulish to me. She continues. "I thought it was creepy, but he was happy, so . . ."

"Bosco came from the pound. I asked for a dog for my birthday. My uncle was trying to get a full-grown dog and he accidentally picked out the world's largest puppy."

"Your uncle got him for you?"

"Yes. My uncle Mel. He got me Bosco when I was twelve. Then I went away to school and Mel had to keep him." I tell her the name of my school, the state, and she nods. "I was only twelve, and I really missed my dog. I'd wanted a dog since, well, my whole life up to that point, and I had to leave him. But Bosco liked the rectory."

"The . . . rectory?"

"Mel is a priest, so, that's where we officially lived, even though I was at school most of the time. But on my breaks and in the summer, I came home to the rectory. After I graduated, I went to college in Georgia and Mel retired to a monastery in North Dakota. And that was a great place for Bosco. And for me, too. I'd work on farms over the summer, and Bosco came to work with me almost every day. When I was done with my master's degree, we moved to Detroit so I could do Teach For America. Bosco came with. He was surprisingly okay in Detroit. We did a lot of walking around, seeing the city. Half of it is in ruins, and we'd poke into these old buildings. It was kind of like exploring castles. I mean, I think it was, but I've never actually explored any ruined castles. We moved out here in 1996 and stayed for one school year. He loved Oregon so much, I decided he shouldn't come with me to Oklahoma. He died up here while I was gone, but you knew that part."

Overcome with the strangeness of having told her Bosco's entire life story, I walk in silence for a good three minutes.

Finally, she speaks. "So. Priest, rectory, all-boys prep and monastery. I take it Bosco was Catholic?"

"Yes."

"I'm pretty perceptive, aren't I."

"Either that, or you're Catholic."

"My full name is Fiona Siobhan Wallace. Irish and Scottish. Catholic and Presbyterian. There was a holy war for my soul."

"And the Catholics won."

"The Catholics always win. I went to St. Thomas More and St. Mary's downtown."

"Gretchen says that's a great school. She thought about going there."

"It's wonderful. I do a writer-in-residence there every year. But I always wondered what public school was like."

"Chaotic and rewarding."

"Speaking as a teacher?"

"Speaking as a teacher. And as a student, I guess, for the first part of my life." It's nice out, but it's fall and it gets dark early this far north. Something happens in Oregon when the sun sinks below the cloud layer but hovers over the horizon. Everything is lit from below, with gold. I believe it's called gloaming. And she's lit from below, too, she glows just as golden.

She sighs. "Isn't that beautiful? The gloaming."

It's almost as beautiful as her knowing the word.

We turn back. "What's your last name?"

"Gentry."

"Oh. I thought that was your first name."

"I don't tell anyone my first name."

"Is it that bad?" I nod. She frowns. "Well, then. That's probably for the best." We're quiet until we're back at her home. Hugh is there, wearing the falconer's gloves and hacking at bushes. His face brightens when we approach. He remembers me, says hello, she says good-bye, and I go up to Kathryn's in the gloaming.

⁓

"Who was that woman you were walking with?"

"Fiona Wallace. May I wash up?"

"Of course." I wash up in the kitchen and drink a glass of water and walk into the dining room. The voice of Patsy Cline after all these years raises the hair on the back of my neck. But when I imagined sitting down at this table with Kathryn again, there was never a husband.

Jack rumbles a little phlegm around in the back of his throat and frowns. Without a word, she changes the CD. We sit, and Jack smiles at me. "Debussy. That's music to digest by."

Digestion to Debussy. Delightful.

She serves me chili. I always loved her chili. Normally, I would dig right in, but I have to let things cool these days. Jack complains about the menu throughout the process of sitting down, the serving of the bowls, my grace. "I can't eat this, Kathy, I'll be up all night."

She sighs. "I used Beano, Jack. It shouldn't bother you."

I can't help it, something about her saying "Beano." That word coming out of her mouth. "Beano." I clear my throat. "What is, um, Beano?"

"Beano neutralizes whatever it is in beans that causes gas."

Jack cocks a bushy eyebrow at her. Obviously Jack is not taken in by that balderdash. "Beano or not, I always fart."

I'm coughing, that's all.

"I could cook you something else, Jack. Would you like oatmeal with a sliced banana? That might settle better."

"No, I don't want you to go to any trouble."

"How about some Cream of Wheat?"

A sound escapes from me. She shoots me a look. Sorry, Kathryn. Chastened, I apply myself to the meal. Cornbread, too, with real butter.

"It's not just the gas, Kathy."

"Jack, please."

Maybe she'll say "Beano" again.

"It's the heartburn from all this chili pepper. I'll be up all night."

"Oh for god's sake, just take some antacid." Kathryn has clearly lost control of this conversation.

Jack peers at me from underneath his gray, bushy eyebrows. "Do you ever get heartburn?"

"Not very often."

"Well, I get it. All the time. And I hate it."

He sounds defensive. I nod. What am I supposed to say? Does anyone like heartburn? "I just, um, drink a little milk."

"I can't drink milk. I'm lactose intolerant. I can't digest dairy. If I drink it, I drive Kathy right out of the bed."

Well, then she could get in bed with *me*, Jack.

"That sounds, um, terrible."

"I guess it's worse for her than for me."

I'm just clearing my throat, here. We eat silently. Kathryn will skin me if I crack a smile, so I don't. "Kathy? Where's the Promise?" She sighs, rises, leaves the room and returns with a little plastic tub. He puts a dab of margarine on his cornbread. "What I hate most is when I'm asleep, and I urp up a little food in the back of my throat."

"That, um, has never happened to me." I sneak a look at Kathryn. She glares at me. It takes every speck of self-control I have, Kathryn, but I'm not laughing at your husband.

"Well, I thought I might have a hiatal hernia, but a colleague checked me out, and I don't. I just need to avoid spicy food, that's all." He turns his wrinkly eyes to Kathryn in an accusing glare, as if by cooking this chili I love so much, she's tried to poison him.

She looks as if she might like to.

I can't laugh, God, don't let me laugh or she will kill me. I stuff some food in. I'm enjoying her discomfort almost as much as I enjoy this chili. I eat hearty, I have seconds. I put extra butter on the cornbread. I drink a lot of milk. "Kathryn, your chili is the best."

She smiles. "I'm so glad you enjoy it."

Oh, I enjoy it. Almost as much as I enjoy the thought of you lying in bed next to your old, gassy, urping, sour-stomached husband tonight.

"Gentry? Why did you choose Oklahoma when you left here?" Nice direct question, Kathryn. To the point, succinct. Too bad my mouth is so full, or I could answer. "Swallow, and tell me."

I swallow. "I moved there to be near some friends. The Sandersons."

"They live in Oklahoma City?"

"No, they lived in Norman, south of Oklahoma City. But they moved to Colorado."

"But you stayed. Did you like it down there?"

"No."

"Well, you were there for almost, what, four years. Why did you stay if you didn't like it?"

That's a good question. I take a big bite of chili and consider how not to answer it.

"I've wondered if a dry climate like Oklahoma might be good for my knees. This one is killing me." Jack again. "My left knee. Tendonitis. It swells. Not much edema, but inflamed, and sore." For a doctor, he seems to have a lot of medical problems, what with stomach thing and those rickety knees.

"It's actually humid. In Oklahoma."

"Is it? Hm." Kathryn serves coffee, and he has something my wife liked called Mocha Mix in his. "Did you remember to make decaf? Kathy, I need decaf, is this decaf?"

"Yes, this is decaf, Jack."

"I hope so. I don't want to be up all night. I need my sleep. So if this isn't decaf . . ."

"YES. I told you it is decaf, what, Jack, do you want it in writing?" I will not laugh. I will not. I give Kathryn a look of fierce mirth, and she gives me a fierce look, but not of mirth, no, not at all.

The meal ends, and with it, Jack's litany of health problems. I offer to do the dishes, but I'm steered into the living room. I wish Gretchen were here. I brought a game that Danaia, my Detroit student who now owns her own game company, sent out to me. I would kick Gretchen's backside. But I have to sit here and talk with Kathryn while her kindly old husband does the dishes and sings. "Volare, whoooo, cantare, whooo . . ." She shuts a door. I can't laugh. Oh God, and when I say this, I really am praying, please, don't let me laugh.

She laughs, so I can, too. Thank You, God. We sit and laugh quietly for a moment, and then we settle down. She clears her throat. "When Michael came down to Oklahoma, he said you were drinking quite a bit. He was concerned. Gretchen, however, says you don't drink." She stares at me, calmly waiting.

I have suddenly found myself in a minefield. I have to step carefully. "I'm not drinking."

"I have friends at the coast if you ever want a sponsor."

"Can we change the subject?"

"Certainly." She gives me an appraising stare. "What exactly bothers you, as far as your teeth?"

"Pain from heat and cold."

"I wonder if things were loosened when you broke your jaw. I hope it's only fillings, Gentry. I'd hate for you to end up like Eve Mumford."

"Hey Kathryn?"

"Yes?"

"Can we talk about something else, now?"

"Well, I'm sure we can." Thank You, God. "Actually, I was hoping to hear a little about Miriam. I wonder what she was like."

She must have a list. "I'm beat."

"Gentry, it's seven-thirty. Jack might be beat, but you're not beat. You're avoiding the subject."

"Would Gretchen mind if I used her computer? I have a new game and I want to try it out."

"Gentry. I just want to *talk*." She sounds hurt.

"Leave him alone, Kathy." Jack has joined us. He gives me a kind, old man's pat on the shoulder. I pull away. "Women, they have a tendency to pester." And he sits down. "Well. What's the weather like down there in Oklahoma this time of year? I'm surprised about that humidity."

And we spend a very nice evening talking about the weather, and Gretchen's successful adjustment to the new school, and fishing, and the price of coastal real estate. We talk about work, mine and his. We even talk about the Cowboy Hall of Fame, which isn't actually called that, and I tell him everything I can remember about Jackson Sundown. Kathryn listens. We talk until ten, and then we go to bed. I hear nothing at all through the wall.

I like this Jack.

∽

"Sorry I caught your lip. Can you come back next week?"

"More?" I keep stanching it but bloody spittle tracks my numb chin.

"A lot more. I ground down the cracked tooth and put on a temporary, and I can put the crown on in two weeks. But you need two more crowns immediately, and there are three other teeth in here about ready to fall apart. That's six crowns. I need a few hours for each, and that's if you don't need any root canals."

Four hands in my mouth, that spray and suction, the taste of those rubber gloves, the whine of the drill and the smell of bone being ground away. I couldn't breathe, I kept gagging, panicking. He wanted to give me a little gas but I couldn't let him put the mask over my face, so I had to go back to panicking.

"I can't sit through this six times."

"I could yank them and make you a bridge."

"No."

"You want to hold on to them?"

"As long as I can."

He nods. "You take good care of them, I can tell. Healthy gums and bad teeth. Some of this is just the age of the fillings, and some of it was from the broken jaw. Those old fillings start to leak and you have decay no matter how you take care of your teeth. You didn't stay on top of things, did you."

"No. I didn't." I had other things to think about.

"I'll tell you right now. This gets expensive. I can use gold, so that saves you some money. And we can set up a payment plan."

"Fine. Just keep them in there."

I drive home, drooling, brooding. I have to send money to my in-laws, I had to wait to pay them for the funeral because I got less for the stupid house than Mike had hoped, and the stone, I have to pay for that, and now these stupid teeth. Six crowns.

I'll be broke for a long, long time.

But I have my job, my Jeep. I have a place to stay. I have a paycheck. I may not have my teeth after a few years, but if I have to get dentures I can always kill myself. Just a joke, God. I'd pray for money, but I'm afraid of the way You might answer that prayer.

I get to the house and walk upstairs and do the thing I want to, night and day. I strip off my clothes and slide into Kathryn's huge bed. But she's not in it, God. All right? Forgive me for wishing that she was, but she's not and I want to sleep in Kathryn's bed again. How can any bed be this big, pillows so welcoming, sheets so smooth? And I smell her. I allow myself to lay my stomach against the dusty, smooth, scent of her body.

I sleep.

Gretchen

A few weeks ago, Gentry gave me a box from my parents' old house. It had pictures and letters and certificates in it, some scripts with grey covers, an old journal written in a foreign language with sketches of people on board a ship. I took the whole box to Portland. Late at night, I go through it, putting it in order. I start with the pictures. I lay it out like a diagram, like a family tree, like a puzzle. I want to figure it out. I haven't yet, but I will.

This is a different box. He hasn't opened it. He won't even let me bring it downstairs. "Go through it, take anything you want, I really don't care, but keep it upstairs and don't make me look at any of it." He starts to walk out the back door, then turns back and stands there scratching his jaw. "Hey Gretchen? What are you looking for, anyway?"

"I don't know." That's a lie. I always know what I'm looking for. The first step in the scientific method is to formulate a hypothesis.

He won't even be in the house with this open box, so he cuts the grass while I cut the tape.

The oldest papers are in a manila envelope with a brass clasp. It feels very, very strange, seeing a certificate of live birth from a hospital in Great Falls, Montana with footprints in black ink. His feet were curved and tiny like any baby's. I trace a finger over his parents' names. Payton Cassius and Francisca Marie. Whatever's wrong with Gentry, these are the people who did it.

What I need is more recent. I find strong visual confirmation. I need a few more pieces, but I know I'm right.

∽⌒

I hear him washing his hands, making coffee, pulling a stool up to that island he hates so much in the kitchen. He's waiting for me.

He sees the pictures in my hand and starts to shake his head and I say, "Bosco."

His face lights up. He takes Bosco's pictures and lays them out chronologically. "You can see him grow up. Mel used to send them. I had a girlfriend who called me 'Dog Boy.' Everyone thought it was because I sniffed everything before I ate it, but it was because of these pictures over my bed."

"You had pictures of your dog up, not pictures of girls?"

"I had pictures of girls. I don't remember where that stuff is."

"Well, there's this one big envelope that says DO NOT OPEN on it."

His eyes get round. "Did you?"

"When someone seals an envelope with duct tape you kind of get the idea that it should stay shut." Since he handled the Bosco pics, I go back up and bring down more. I lay out a few of his yearbook pictures. Some from when he was in high school, some from when he was a teacher. I imagine him getting the packet when he was twenty-five and mailing them home to Mel, just like a kid.

He frowns. "I hate those."

"Why?"

"I don't really know."

I gather them up. "Can I take some of these?"

"You can take anything you want."

"Gentry? There are yearbooks from high school and articles from the school paper about your games and meets. You really were good at sports." He keeps his eyes on his cup of coffee. "There's a ton of stuff from college, all these old papers about poems. And some plaques, like, Greater Detroit Area Teacher of the Year?" He smiles a sad smile. "But there isn't anything from when you were little. No baby pictures. Nothing from grade school. No school pictures or report cards. I mean, there's some certificates and papers. Legal stuff. And this." I hold it out. She looks way too young to be getting married, but she has on a white veil and dress, and he has his arm around her. And I can tell they're his parents.

Gentry falls backward off the stool.

⁓

He's sitting on the floor with his back against the kitchen island, his knees up, his head in his arms. I know he's praying. I sit down on the floor beside him. "I'm sorry."

He pulls his head up like it's too heavy to lift. "I'm all right."

But he isn't. Gentry hasn't been all right for a long time. "Dad wants you to come see him. I'll be over there next weekend."

He shakes his head. "We have in-service Friday and I'm going fishing with Lorrie."

"No, Gentry, come to Portland. We have in-service, too, so the school will be open. You can come see it, then stay up at Dad's with me. Or over at Mom's."

"I can't take all that conversation up at your mother's. And I haven't seen that much of Lorrie."

"You see him every day at school."

"Gretchen . . ."

"Please, please, please."

Gentry

What a great school. A perfect school, and I know who pays for it. I'm supposed to stay at his house tonight. After the gracious hospitality I extended to Mike in Oklahoma City, I'm sure he feels indebted. He might even let me sleep in a bed.

I meet her teachers, visit the chapel. But Gretchen has more to show me. "We need to go over to the sports facility so you can see that."

"The sports facility?"

"It's really interesting, Gentry."

"I'm hungry. I want to eat."

She crosses her arms. "I want you to see it."

The saying "no" thing, God, I'll work on it. Tomorrow.

We pull in and she gets out, so I do too. "Gretchen? I want to go eat, so let's do this fast, all right?" She shows me the pool, the tennis courts. All nice but not particularly interesting. The soccer field. There's a scrimmage. I watch the boys and she watches my face. It takes me back almost twenty years.

There are some decent players out there, and one fearless young man who makes them all look sluggish. He's taller than I was, but just as fast. Okay, faster. Pass once in a while, kid, you're as bad as I was. But it's beautiful to watch him, that boy can run, but look at those tricks, too many stepovers, stop showing off and get it down there.

He raises his fists over his head and I laugh out loud.

"That forward has amazing foot skills. If he were in Europe, he'd have grown up in clubs." He takes off his shirt and uses it to wipe sweat from his face. I remember doing that. In fact, I still do that.

"He's only a sophomore. He made varsity in ninth grade. He's kind of a legend. His name is Tristan." Tristan? I think Tristan is right up there with Shelley, but she makes this name the most beautiful sound on earth.

The whistle blows. He sees her, waves. She waves back, sees me watching, blushes. "I'll be right back." She runs to him.

Hey God? Wait just a minute.

I go sit in my Jeep. I put on my cap, my sunglasses. If it were not so sunny I would pull up my hood because I want to hide, Dear God let me hide. I think of Mike. He's her dad. If it hurts me this much, how can he stand it?

I wish I could hide but I can't because they're here. He doesn't touch her, thankfully. If he touched her, I might have to rip his arm from his young body. I don't want to see him. I try to fix a normal expression on my face, a normal smile. But I keep my eyes forward because if I look at this boy I might take him by the throat and throw him to the ground.

"Gentry, this is Tristan."

I hang a hand over the side of the Jeep to shake, but I don't take off my shades and I don't look at him. I hear his voice. "It's nice to meet you, sir." I know that voice. "Gretchen talks a lot about you." I know that voice, I've heard that voice. Coming out of my own mouth. It's my voice.

I look down at his hand in mine.

It's my hand.

I look up into his face.

It's my face.

"I have to get back, G." He smiles at her.

He has my smile.

And he runs back. I run like that. He's fast, just like me.

He looks just like me from behind.

"Gentry, you're shaking. Are you cold?"

All these years I've looked for her face. Every crowd, I looked and looked and wondered if I'd even know it if it came before me because faces change. I was afraid I would look past it. And I've seen it on a boy.

"Are you okay? You're freaking me out."

Gretchen asked to see pictures of me when I was young. She asked me about my parents, about sports, everything. Gretchen knows something. "Have you seen his parents?"

"Just his mom. His dad died when he was seven."

We would have to have different fathers. But she's here. Where did she go, why did she leave, how did she come here? It has to be her. And she'd give him a name like Tristan, not as bad as the name she gave me, at least a person can say Tristan out loud, but he has a better name because he was good enough to keep. She didn't leave him, he's here and that's my brother.

I hold on to the steering wheel. "Gretchen."

"I'm here."

And so is she. She's here in Portland somewhere. Oh take me to her so I can tell her how it was for me. Let me tell her how it was for me.

Because I remember what happened to me.

I remember it, finally.

All the rest of it.

⌒

I ride beside her, wanting to throw myself over the side to escape it all sliding down on me. But there's no escape. If I hit the asphalt, this will hit it with me.

Gretchen drives. I shift for her.

Kathryn takes one look and puts me in a bed.

I sleep without nightmares. I don't need the nightmares any more. I lived them, God. The seals are broken. I remember all of it, now. And I find I can't cry. I can't pray. I won't pray to You.

But God, I'd like to say something.

I'll never, ever, get down on my knees to thank You or close my eyes and ask of You again. I've broken the commandment, I've taken Your name in vain, because when I was a child, every time I ever asked for You, God, every time I prayed, it was all in vain, there was never a time when it was not in vain. I called out Your name, God, for years. You never answered me, did You. I remember everything.

I know this, now. To pray is to sin.

To call out to God for help is to take Your name in vain.

Gretchen

"I don't know what you think you were doing, Gretchen. You should *know* how fragile Gentry is. What was your *point?*"

"He isn't fragile. Gentry's the strongest person I've ever known. And he needs a family."

Mom shook her head. "This is just a coincidence, Gretchen, just one of those strange things."

I'm afraid I really messed this up.

He was Spencer's best friend. His little friend who was always waiting on the lawn to run away with Spencer before Graham could catch up. I knew he was out there, but I'd never really seen him until the summer after eighth grade. Tristan would drop by, and they'd go off to the gym to lift weights together. I guess that was the year Spencer got tired of having skinny stick arms. Tristan didn't have stick arms. He was tall and thin, but strong. I'd watch the way he leaned back or forward, the angle of his spine, his neck. Every detail of how he moved.

I had no term for it. But looking at him made it hard to breathe.

Graham made ugly remarks about him that I ignored because I always ignore Graham. Spencer kept teasing me about him. "He likes you, Gretchen. I don't know why, you're so stupid and ugly and fat, but he does."

I laughed. I thought, right.

Spencer played soccer, too. Dad and I were at one of the games. Dad watched Spencer and I watched Tristan. At least I thought Dad watched Spencer. "I never noticed it before, but Tristan looks like Gentry." And of course then I could see it. He looked exactly like Gentry in that picture from graduation, right down to the brushy haircut.

I felt embarrassed, but it was already too late.

When Tristan finally spoke to me, he opened his mouth and Gentry's voice came out. But they're different people. Tristan never worries. I've never seen him flinch. He laughs more. Gentry's always saying, "Are you cold? I'm cold." Tristan's always saying, "It's hot in here." They don't like the same music at all, and Tristan loves to dance.

When I introduced them, I don't think Tristan noticed. Gentry almost passed out. Mom's mad at me for upsetting him. "Mom, they'd have to meet anyway, right?"

"Why, Gretchen? Why would their meeting be inevitable?"

"Because, Mom, eventually they'd have to. And they're brothers. I know they are."

She has the coldest eyes. "I don't know how you came up with this theory, but you need to let it go."

I got out the photos Gentry gave me from when he was in high school. I laid them down next to the school photos Tristan gave me from seventh, eighth, ninth and tenth. Year-by-year, side-by-side. "Look, Mom. Twelve. Thirteen. Fourteen. Fifteen. They look like the same person." I used my fingertips to shuffle them out of order. "Okay, Mom. Tell me who's who."

She had to sit down.

Gentry

I have to wake up and remember, but at least I slept.

I sit down at the little table. Kathryn puts coffee in front of me. "You slept so long. I was worrying." She strokes my hair. And I remember that my mother always stroked my hair. It was the thing I let myself miss. Her hand on my hair.

Gretchen studies me. "Gentry? If you promise not to do anything stupid, I can take you to his mom's house."

"You know who she must be?"

Kathryn puts a plate in front of me. "I don't think Toni Buchanan is your mother. She's my age. Gretchen said that according to the papers she saw, your mother would only be in her late forties." Kathryn sounds a little sickened by this fact. Sick little fact.

She was so young.

"I'm not hungry, Kathryn."

She takes my untouched plate and begins to eat it herself. Paige was always eating her kids' food. Am I your kid, Kathryn? I'm sure you're not my mother. My mother has eyes the same color as mine, she has my eyes and my hair.

And I look just like her from behind.

"Gentry? What do you want to do today?"

Today? I think I'd like to forget today. "We can do whatever you want to."

She smiles. "We can go to a soccer game."

"No."

Kathryn starts to talk with her mouth full. Who is this non-smoking, non-drinking, rounded woman with bad table manners? "Tristan's mother goes to every single game. And you'll know at a glance that Toni couldn't possibly be your mother."

This is not a bad idea at all, come to think of it.

❧

We go to the soccer game, where I park crooked next to Kathryn and Jack. Gretchen studies my face. "You look like the Unabomber. Take off your sunglasses and put your hood down." It is November in Oregon. The weather is supposed to be cold (I think), but this is Oregon and it's mild, and I don't need my hood. I do need my sunglasses.

I climb up into the bleachers behind Kathryn and Jack. We sit higher than Gretchen, who sits with friends, she has friends, this is good. It makes me feel better and miserable, because I want her near.

Kathryn, then. I cup her tiny hands between mine until they're warm. Jack seems stricken. Sorry, Jack. But today I have to touch your wife a little, or die.

Kathryn waves to a tall woman who climbs the bleacher stairs with steady, stately grace. "That's Toni." She waves at Kathryn. She's tall and strong and beautiful, with dark red hair and light eyes. "Well? Is that your mother?"

My mother. She was small and quick and sharp, with dark hair and eyes like mine. She laughed like a donkey. And kicked like one when they fought.

"No. That's not her."

Kathryn squeezes my hand.

I give up and watch Tristan play. He's far better than I ever thought of being. Oh, I was capable of falling into that state of hypnotic fascination where it was just me and the ball and what I could do with it, but not for long. Someone would get too close and I'd foul him. Hard.

I tried to control myself, because I loved my coach. Father Damien started every practice in a robe. He ran and cut with his skirts swirling around his legs. Eventually, warmed by the sun or frustration, he would strip to a pair of shorts, throwing the robe through the air. It scared me, sailing toward me like that, but I fought the fear and ran to catch it, to be the one who would put it away for him. He was a golden bear of a man. When I remember him, I remember my craven desire to please him, coupled with an unshakable conviction that I never would. I was always trying too hard.

Soccer is a game of self-control and sportsmanship. I'm grateful and amazed that they kept me on the team. Everything moving so fast, a foot, an elbow where it didn't belong, it was so easy and I always gave in to my worst impulses just to watch an opposing player fall. I would shrug, scratch my head, wander off, acting like it hadn't been intentional. It was always intentional.

There were yellow cards, the occasional red card, and my team couldn't win without me. Father Damien wanted to win. Coaches always want to win. Maybe I would have done better if Mel had been watching, but Mel never saw me play. That was just as well. I was a mean player.

This boy is not a mean player. He is the Platonic ideal of a player. He is so talented that the pitch fills with the rising scent of frustration coming off every other player, even those on his own team, because he's a one-man show.

He lets his body take over. I remember that. The mind falls back and the body does what it knows how to do. I had that in high school, but rampant growth knocked out my ease with my own body. This boy is as tall as I am but he's still sure of his body. And he's sure of something else. Whenever he scores, or steals, or makes one of his surgically precise passes, his eyes go to the bleachers. He doesn't look for his mother. He looks for Gretchen, for the radiance of her pride in him. She shines with it. He takes it in and it makes him even better. This is even more beautiful than the way he plays.

I have to put my hand over my eyes.

He doesn't run drugs on his father's fishing boat for a living. He couldn't smoke, not running that fast. He called me "sir." But I can't forgive his role in Gretchen's growing up. All those times she's come to stay with me, she could have been with him. She may have wanted to stay here more than she did, I see that.

I feel Kathryn's hand on my shoulder.

"Hey Kathryn? He's incredible, do you know that?"

"Everyone in the state knows that."

The coach makes a late substitution. Tristan comes out and watches intently while his teammates finally have a chance to play and his opponents finally have a chance for a point. He's already won this game. The pitch is empty of brilliance and full of glee because he's left it, and then the game is over.

His redheaded mother rises, graceful and tall. She has an amazing backside. Kathryn follows my eyes. "Do you want to meet Toni?"

"No." But I would like to take Toni to bed. Right now. Kathryn takes my hand and I decide I could take Kathryn to bed if Toni is unwilling. Either, both, I don't care, but at least one of them. Right now.

Kathryn leads me down the risers. I let her. I won't fall off the world, I won't.

At the car, Gretchen takes off my sunglasses so she can stare in my eyes while she argues with me. "You can't go home tonight. You never saw Dad."

"I'll call him and explain."

"No." She's upset. "You promised to stay a night at Dad's."

"No I didn't. I never promised to do that."

And here is sweaty Tristan come to get his girl, another one to take her away from me. I am almost physically sick over what a beautiful boy he is. Beautiful like a woman.

He smiles at me, stops, jerking his head back like he's taken a blow. "Whoa." He stares at me with a pair of puzzled brown eyes that could be my own. We study each other with each other's eyes.

What does it matter, I have an uncle and he has a mother and we're possibly brothers or maybe this is some joke, some strange cosmic joke, and we're both in the punch line this time.

I get in my Jeep and drive back to the house by the ocean, and I climb into Kathryn's bed and bury my face in the pillow that smells like her fine, dry hair. I wrap myself in her sheets. I won't have nightmares, now. I've lived through the worst of them. This has always been here, I remind myself, waiting to wake. Memory is demanding, ferocious, eating its way into me.

I refuse to drink.

Not that, too.

I fall asleep with the windows open.

A warm breeze wakes me. I pull back the sheet, open my arms to the gentle disturbance that flows over my body, pure and mild as beating wings.

The touch of air is innocent.

The phone's ring jars me like an electric shock. I stumble down the stairs, jerky and furious, and grab up the receiver. "What. I mean hey. Hello?"

"Did I wake you?"

"Hey Mike. I needed to wake up, anyway." What time is it? I missed Mass. But I plan to miss Mass for the rest of my Godforsaken life, so today is as good a day as any to start.

"Well, listen. I was hoping to see you this weekend."

"I was, um, kind of sick so I came home early."

"I don't like the sound of that."

"I'll be okay."

"Actually we were hoping you would come for Thanksgiving. Marci's going to make it down and Gretchen will be here. You can stay for the day, the weekend, whatever you want. We have plenty of room."

"Thank you. I have some, I don't, I mean . . . I'm not fit company right now."

"That bad?"

I clear my throat. "That lawyer called and the house closed, and he sent me a check. I'll have one for you soon." I stand naked at the back door, close my eyes and feel that gentle air washing over me, calming the storm. "Hey Mike?"

"Yes?"

"Thank you. For all of it."

"Oh hell, Gentry. Nothing to it. You're welcome."

"I, um, have to . . ."

"One more thing, Gentry. I understand you had a chance to watch Tristan Buchanan play some soccer yesterday. He's something, isn't he."

"He is." But what? Who is this boy to me? "Mike, I have to go."

"Just a second, Gentry. I want to apologize for something. I was supposed to let you know about your dog. When I flew down there. Kathy asked me to let you know, you know, while I was there, and I just couldn't do it. Your wife and all, it seemed like too much. I'm sorry you had to come back and walk into it like that."

Undone.

I hang up the phone and sit down at the table. I know if I lie down I will go back to sleep for the rest of the day, and possibly the night, too. I'm tempted. But that is not the plan for the day, is it.

All I have to do is remember. To sit at this table and remember. I look out the window at the ocean, brilliantly blue under a blue sky.

What did Isak Dinesen say? The cure for anything is supposed to be salt water. Sweat, tears, the sea. But I need something more to get through this and I'm so angry at You that I don't want Your help.

It is time to pick up the phone.

Mel

He picks me up at the airport. Heavenly intervention was required to get a seat on a plane this week. God must know, God does provide. He did need me.

I don't know why, though.

We drive to the shore in the Godforsaken vehicle he favors, the buckboard, I call it. "You don't mind that I came early? Before your school lets out?"

He watches the road. "I'm glad you came early."

"Gentry, you're not involved with Kathryn again, are you?" Because the two of them are fruits waiting to fall, and this would be a disaster.

"No."

I allow myself the briefest flash of hope. "Is there someone else you want me to meet?"

"No. No one." What is it? What has him like this?

I try a joke, something I used to ask him when he was still in high school. "Did you want me to come watch you play soccer?"

His head snaps back so fast I think his neck will break. He pulls over and grasps the wheel with both hands, and tells me. He has met a young man who reminds him too much of himself. "It's like looking into my own face, Mel. And hers." He means, of course, his mother. "I saw his face and it all came back. Everything. I remember."

I put a hand on his arm and he pulls away, the lonely boy I took twenty years ago, a boy who never heals. "So you know what happened to you."

He nods.

"Will you tell me?"

He shakes his head no.

Gentry was ten years old and almost catatonic when I took him to the hospital. When the doctor drew near, he turned into a spitting, snarling beast, fighting for his life. It took two orderlies, a nurse and me to hold him down so the doctor could set his shoulder.

No further examinations were attempted.

I thought Gentry's memories were lost because of trauma. And perhaps, at first, they were. But he remembered his neighbors perfectly, retaining his ability to speak to them in broken Vietnamese when English was beyond him. He remembered everything about his years in public school, his time at church, his religious instruction. He remembered me. The parts of his past he wanted to forget wandered outside like ghosts on the other side of a door he kept barred.

How they hammered at night, demanding to be let in.

His voice is empty, cold. "God is either cruel or useless."

We sit there with the engine running, the rain pelting the top of the Jeep, our breath curling from our nostrils like smoke.

I quietly give thanks that for Gentry, God might be cruel and God might not care, but at least God is not dead.

Gentry

It's been a wonderful week.

Mel watched me teach. He sat in the back of the classroom watching the kids draw on their shoes, rummage in their ears, pass notes, whisper, sleep. And he watched them learn. Mel said he wrote down some ideas for the CYO home page that he posts for Midwestern Catholic youth.

The kids were curious about the large man in overalls who observed them. Mel has the innate authority of a man of God, but as far as the kids knew, he was my uncle, here for the holiday.

"You are a fine teacher, my boy."

It's been a wonderful week.

And here we are, to give thanks with the Gilroys. Mel is round-eyed with admiration for the goose. We bow our heads. Poor Lorrie sits, rolling his eyes, sweating, feeling alone.

Deal with it, Lorrie. For every meal of my life, I do.

Mel says the grace. "HEAVENLY FATHER, I want to give a SPECIAL thanks today, to Victoria and Lawrence Gilroy. They have the GOOD GRACE to RECOGNIZE the bounty of their lives, and to SHARE that bounty. BLESS them, and BLESS their children, RENATA RENEE and WALTER GENTRY. BLESS the child within Victoria, as well, and grant them the PEACE, the LOVE, and the JOY that they SHARE with OTHERS. AMEN."

The kids are thunderstruck. Renata behaves during the meal, and that's a first, as far as I know.

I'm not sure what I've been eating, but I've been eating a lot of it. The goose is perfect, it seems to be all dark meat, and there are baked beans full of salt pork and rolled up pancake things that are not sweet and apple dumplings that are. "Vicki, this is the best. I mean it. This is the finest Thanksgiving meal, ever, anywhere."

She smiles back at me, her eyes dark and pleased.

Lorrie clears his throat. Vicki and I break our gaze. "So," he grumbles, "I s'pose you wonder about me and church." I'm certain this is the last thing Mel has ever wondered about. I've never even wondered about this. But there seems to be something about a priest that demands this conversation.

"Lorrie, you are a good man, I know that much about you. But if you would like to tell me." And Mel's eyes shine, because like me, Mel knows this is bound to be a good story.

"Well, I was raised south of here in Coos Bay. And I went to this stinky little church every Sunday of my life and I hated the place. It was some offshoot church, I know that now, some sonofabitching cult type church. Not regular. They spoke in tongues, and had fits, and all kinds of crazy bullshit. I sat through it for my folks, you know. I was just glad there were no sonofabitching snakes, I hate snakes. I hated that place.

"There was this point in the service where we were all supposed to stand up and say our sins out loud. I could not fucking imagine standing up and saying, what, I screwed some girl in the back of her dad's truck and boosted a tin of Cope?" He shakes his head. The children listen, rapt. Mel squeezes my hand under the table because he knows I'll laugh, and Lorrie is serious. Dead serious. "I just thought it was the most screwed-up thing imaginable. Saying your shit out loud like that."

"I can see that it might be difficult."

"Damn straight it was difficult. I could hear my brothers mumbling away about jacking their dicks or some such bullshit, and my sister, and my folks, I mean Jesus Get a Haircut Christ, I did not want to hear that. I just stood there."

I'm just clearing my throat, Mel. I'm not laughing.

"So, anyway, I never said a goddamn thing, I just stood there. Silent, like. And one Sunday, after we all stood up, and everybody said their deal, and we started to sit down, the preacher looked out over the crowd, about sixty people went there, and he said, 'LAWRENCE ELROD GILROY, REMAIN STANDING.'"

Elrod? Did he say Elrod?

"And he started in on me, who was I to stand without sin in the house of the Lord, did I have no shame, if I had the Lord in my heart I would join in with my brothers and sisters in Christ, Jesus knew that my soul was black with sin, and the flames of hellfire were waiting for me personally, damnation and hell and the lake of fire and Satan himself waiting to chew my flesh and gnaw my bones. All waiting for me, Lawrence Elrod Gilroy, the damned one."

He sits there a minute, white in the face.

Thank You, God, that I'm a Catholic.

"I stood there. I was fifteen, and I was what, six-four, two-forty? I listened to that little weasel for about ten more seconds, and then I started to laugh. I had a big laugh, even then. And then I said to that pale little Bible-thumping son of a bitch, 'Then bring him on. Bring Satan here, and bring him on. Because I would be happy to personally kick Satan's ass, almost as happy as I would be to kick yours, you goddamn twisted-up sonofabitch, feeling up my sister and screwing half the ladies in this church and you stand up there and talk about ME, you lying sack of holy roller shit.' And I walked out of there, and I never set foot in a goddamn church again. And the whole damn outfit fell apart after that, just so you know. Because what I said was true and somebody finally said it out loud."

We silently consider the bravery of it.

"I believe this calls for a toast." Mel raises his glass. He and Lorrie and Vicki have wine, and the kids and I have milk, of course.

"Lord, I raise this toast to Lawrence Elrod Gilroy, who belongs to you, Victoria, and not to any twisted up lying sack of holy roller shit!"

And we all say "hear hear" to that one, and we drink, to the finest man I know, next to Mel, we toast the man who has the worst name I have ever heard, next to mine.

⌒

After dinner, Vicki has the kids sing a song in French for Mel.

Mel is charmed. All children should be able to sing like angels. Like Gretchen.

"I need to take my walk." These may be the first words Vicki has spoken in the course of the day.

"I will join you, Victoria." She and Mel head down to the bay, and Lorrie and I take the kids outside to the swingset. The swingset is Lorrie's handiwork. He has strengths and talents, but he's not what I would call handy. The idea of his kids on this rickety structure, especially kids of this, well, density, these kids are hard to lift, it troubles me. The last thing I want to do is insult him, but I think we need to reinforce it. I'm trying to imagine a diplomatic way to talk about it.

"He's an okay guy, for a priest." Being an "okay guy" is quite an accolade, from Lorrie. "He's more normal than I would have thought, you know. I wonder if he ever got laid."

I suppose I could be insulted on Mel's behalf, but to be honest, I'd wondered that at some point, too. "I have no idea."

"You never asked him?"

"No. Too personal."

"Isn't he like your dad?"

"Did you talk about sex with your dad?"

"No, Gentry, my dad was a holy roller."

"Was he a *priest*?"

"I get your point." Lorrie sniffs. "But I bet you could have. Mel seems like a regular guy." I feel warm inside at the compliment to Mel. Being a "regular guy" is even better than being an "okay guy."

We watch them, far out on the spit, walking in long-legged strides, Vicki almost as tall as Mel, his belly much larger than hers, both in overalls and work boots. They are specks out there, but they are large in my mind.

He's absently pulling at a chain, and the timbers creak. Can't he see how rickety this is? Is he blind? "What are you going to do, little buddy?"

"About what?" About the swingset? I have ideas, but no idea how to put them forth.

"About women. Are you ever going to get laid again?"

"I'm waiting it out."

"Nothing doing with Kathy?"

"No."

"Don't bite my head off. I just don't want you to get all screwed over again. And if you wait too long, well, you know."

"I know." I'll starve, then blunder.

"When was the last time you had a good time, anyway?"

"A good time?"

"With a woman, Gentry, when was the last time you had an honest-to-God good time with a woman that included some first-class fooling around? When?"

"I guess it was on my honeymoon."

"And not since." He shakes his big buffalo head. "That figures. I told you, see, marriage for women is a sure-fire sex drive killer. She was hot on the honeymoon, and then . . ."

The kids get off the swings, and I'm relieved. How can I point out the need for a brace, concrete footings on this swingset? "It wasn't her, Lorrie."

"What the hell do you mean, it wasn't her? It's always the women. That's how women are." He watches Vicki. "Well, most women."

"It was me."

"Oh." He absorbs this, tries to think of the most insulting way to phrase his reply. "Well, that happens to everybody sometimes, I guess." He sniffs. "Except me, of course. You understand, I've never had any trouble that way, but if I ever had any trouble like that, and I'm NOT saying that I ever have, personally, I would bet that it might be from drinking too much."

"Drinking? Drinking will do that?" It started earlier, I know it was not just the drinking, but could that have been part of it? The poison?

"For Christ's sake, Gentry, they call it 'whiskey dick.'"

"Oh." I'm so stupid. I know nothing. Nothing.

"So, that could be part of that kind of trouble. If a person was to have that kind of trouble, not that I ever have."

This would be a review.

"And if I did, and this is purely on spec, Gentry, but if I ever did, because, you know, I'm getting up there, see, well . . ." He sniffs. "What the hell was I saying?"

"If you were hypothetically to have that kind of trouble, which you never have."

"Right. I remember. Okay, what I want to say, is, if a person was to have that kind of trouble, a good woman will help you. A patient, understanding woman. As opposed to a bitch."

"Vicki is a fine person."

And he fixes me with his eyes. "She is. She is one helluva fine woman. I would kill any man who touched her. ANY man."

"Lorrie."

"Oh, I didn't mean you, see, little buddy. Don't get all testy on me, now. I didn't mean you. Besides, if you ever had that woman, it would be the death of you. She's a tiger." And he leers. "What she has is good enough to kill you. But you'd die happy."

I'll hit him in the mouth for talking like that about Vicki.

No, I'll never hit this man again. But I want to.

He can tell. "Jesus, don't get so sore. I was just joking around." He shakes his head. "Look. I owe it all to you." He sniffs. "I thought about what it would be like if something happened to Vicki. But I'd have the kids, see. It's too bad you didn't have any kids."

"She couldn't have kids."

I feel his hand on my arm. "I'm sorry, Gentry. Christ, I'm an asshole. Shit, the things I used to say about it."

"I never minded. Never. Your letters . . ."

He gives me a hanky. His kids are wrestling in the mud, now. He doesn't seem to be noticing, but then he reflexively calls some advice on a hold to Walter. Is it fair for Renata to stomp him like that? They may drown in the mud puddle, but at least they're not in danger of dying on the rickety swingset. "Are you okay, now, little buddy? Since you stopped drinking?"

"I don't know." This is humiliating. And if I don't talk about it with someone besides my uncle the priest, I'll lose my only consolation. "Lorrie, I can't, I can't even, um, I mean, I don't know if I can because I can't even try."

"You can't even jack off?" I shake my head no. "Why the hell not?"

"I try, I start, but nothing is safe to think about. Everything I want to think about is wrong."

"You mean Kathy, don't you. Because she's married." I nod. "Well can't you look at a magazine or something?"

"Those magazines are an affront to God."

"God, you're a pussy. I just read the articles in those, anyway." Sure. Right, Lorrie. "Couldn't you think about your wife?"

"No. That would never work."

"It wasn't good?" I shake my head no. "Not even your honeymoon? Aw, you're smiling now, little buddy. It was good on your honeymoon, you said so yourself."

"It was good on my honeymoon. But not with my wife."

He puts his hands on my shoulders, fixes me with a face of pop-eyed, naked astonishment. "You screwed somebody else on your sonofabitching honeymoon?"

"I, ah. I did."

And a torrent of "Goddamns" and "shits," a cascade of "well I'll be damneds" and "screw me's" and "you little assholes," a river of "kiss my asses" and "you must be shitting me's" pours from Lorrie. "I love it. You screwed around on your *honeymoon*." He is congratulatory, proud. "Way to *do* it, little buddy. Well, think about *that*, then. Think about *that*, and take it out for a spin!"

But she was married. So was I, come to think of it. "Okay."

"You promise? You'll take it out for a test drive?"

"Yes. I will."

The children are shrieking, climbing the wobbly supports, near death. Lorrie is not concerned. How am I going to talk to him about this? How in the world am I supposed to talk to him about something like this play structure?

Renata knocks her brother to the ground and his face crumples.

Lorrie scowls. "Walter, you stop your crying! Take it like a man!"

"Don't say that to him."

"Say what?"

"No child has to take it like a man. Don't say that to him." I wait for the swearing, the ridicule.

"Okay, little buddy. Okay. I won't ever say that to my son again."

Help me, God. Take it away.

"Gentry? Are you there? Are you okay?"

I watch the children because children are always innocent. Walt is still angry at his sister. He has returned to the puddle, and she follows, taunting. She lands next to him with a splash. He takes off his boot, fills it with muddy water and pours it over Renata's head.

"Poophead."

"Walt, don't call your sister that. Jesus have a yard sale Christ, she is a little poophead, but don't you call her that, see." And Lorrie laughs.

We turn to watch Mel and Vicki, heading back to us. Lorrie starts to sing a song I remember from the radio in the garage in the house where I grew up. A sad song. It should hurt me to remember.

But I don't hurt.

Lorrie has the voice of an angel.

Mel

"Victoria Gilroy is a magnificent woman." Gentry and I sit in the kitchen, having tea. I have instilled a love of God in him, but not a love of tea. Ah, well, I have tried, Lord. "I spoke with her about the fragility of that swingset. She promises to fix it. I am sure that Victoria is capable, but it would be admirable, on your part, to assist her." I sip my tea. "She wants to come back to the church. Watch for her, Gentry, welcome her back to the church."

"I will."

"Lorrie will be less than pleased."

"Can you blame him? That church sounds like a nightmare."

I sip my tea. "Lorrie is aptly named."

Gentry's eyebrows fly up.

"A lorry is a truck, Gentry. Across the pond. You call them semis, here, the big rigs. But we called them lorries. Lawrence Elrod Gilroy. I wonder why he didn't go with Larry."

"The Three Stooges, he said."

"Ah. I remember the Stooges. But do you have any idea who the Three Stooges are, my boy?"

He shrugs. "I saw them a few times down in Oklahoma. They would hit each other and it was supposed to be funny."

As I recall, it was. "Drink your tea before it gets cold." He sips, makes a face, tries to hide it. I have tried and tried to get this boy to like tea. "Lawrence Elrod Gilroy. It takes courage to acknowledge a name like that. Some names are more difficult to carry than others. A burdensome name should be accepted or changed, in my opinion."

His face is hard. "Hey Mel? I don't want to have this conversation."

"You can choose another name."

"I'd like to choose another subject. Please?" He holds on to that mug for dear life.

His face is set, as is his mind. He will never accept his Christian name, and he will never give himself another. "What would you like to talk about, then? What, Gentry? The weather? Computers? We can talk about anything, anything at all."

God, take the edge from my voice. It is too sharp on him. Grant me patience. Help me not to badger the boy. Let me be calm with him. Amen.

We sit in the quiet kitchen and drink our tea.

"Mel? Why did you leave me there? When I was a boy."

Sweet Mary Mother of God. Never in my life did I think he would want to discuss this. "I have no answer good enough."

"Could you maybe try?"

"I knew who you were. You were a quiet boy, and so small. I would have taken you for four, but you were seven years old." A dirty, undersized, silent little boy, and astonishingly beautiful. "I didn't know your father. He'd stopped coming before I arrived, but you came with the neighbors. I thought that was his doing. People make these kinds of arrangements when they become angry at the church, they send their children anyway. You took your RE. And I guess I really noticed you when you came to confession. You didn't have much to confess. Mostly fights, as I recall. Do you remember?"

He nods.

"You never said one word about your father. And I realized how intelligent you were, Gentry, how very keen your mind was. You needed to go to a Catholic school. I was new to the parish, you understand. I'd heard a little about your father, the situation, and I didn't understand why no one was reaching out to the man."

Gentry stares at me, waiting.

"I was appalled that my brethren were content to leave him alone. So I made some tentative arrangements and went to see your father where he worked. He met me at the site and took me to an office. I told him you were ready for your

First Communion. Asked him would he be attending. He said no." And spat in the garbage can, but I decline to tell Gentry that detail. "I brought up your schooling, the value of a Catholic education, the grounding in both faith and superior education. He told me he couldn't afford it. I told him the church could help, but we preferred to do that for the truly needy. I was angry. He was a supervisor, a union ironworker. I said I had no idea how he spent his paycheck, but certainly tuition was within his grasp."

How he stared at me, staring me down with those fixed blue eyes. I told him I felt he had a moral obligation to properly school his son, it was a crime to waste a mind like that.

He said, *a crime*?

Yes. My voice shook with righteousness. A crime.

He stood over me, then. His violence was controlled, but just barely. *Hey Father? Leave. Now.*

"I left that office and went to the archdiocese to express my concerns. They asked, were you fed? Were you clothed? I said barely, just barely. They asked were you marked? I said no, but some marks do not show. They said to stay out of it. To attend to your spiritual needs and to pray. They said it was enough.

"I decided that prayer was not enough.

"I watched you carefully, then. You looked . . . untended to. I feared you were home alone, coming and going as you pleased. I started coming over. Do you remember that?"

He nods. I would bring him clothes, shoes, an excuse to have myself a look around. The house was immaculate. His father's room was spare, his belongings lined up with a t-square. Gentry's room was as neat as the proverbial pin.

"I tried to talk to the Nguyens, to get their impression of what life was like for you next door. They had next to no English, but they communicated, well, pleasure. Pride. They were proud of you. I called the school and they said you fought a lot, but that had to do with your size and age, because you'd been bumped up so many grades. Your behavior within the classroom was exemplary. And you never missed a single day. And I called the authorities. I spoke to social workers who were too tired to maintain their professional silence on your case. There was ongoing concern about his being a fit father from the very beginning. They checked on you twice a year, didn't they? Always, your household hit the marks for decent care."

He turns this over. Gentry is a mandated reporter, he knows. "No marks, fed and clothed, a clean house, school attendance."

"Exactly. You even came to Mass several times a week. I had nothing but suspicions, Gentry. Nothing to go on. When you were ten, you came to confession and told me what you'd like to do to little Tran. I should have taken you then."

"You took me."

"Oh, not soon enough. Never soon enough, my boy." I left him in that house, I left him with that father and I have to know what happened to him so I can finally forgive myself. I reach towards him. "Please tell me what happened."

He stares at my hands as if they will hurt him, and shakes his head no.

⸜⸝

We do other things, of course. We tour a cheese factory, an air museum. Gentry is fascinated by the planes, I am fascinated by the history. We take a short hike to a shorter lighthouse and gaze out over a cliff to rocks and waves that fill me with the heartfelt desire to pray.

Before I go to bed, I get down on my knees beside the obscenely large bed where Gentry has installed me for my visit, and give thanks for the restoration of his memory. Heavenly Father, You gave me a boy in pieces. I pray that he will finally be complete.

Amen.

Each night, I fall asleep alone, staring up at the Oregon rain hitting a pane of glass overhead. Such a strange idea, a window in the roof. When I wake from the burning pressure of my bladder, a sign that my blood sugar is up and my weight needs to come down, Gentry sleeps beside me, as he sometimes did as a child.

I am up and down as quietly as I can manage. When I ease myself back into this ridiculous bed, I study his sleeping profile. He never spoke a word about what happened to the social worker, the school therapist, to me. No one could get it out of him. Certainly, I told myself in those days, if the worst had happened, he would not seek me out at night. He would not sleep so profoundly beside me.

In the morning, he is always gone.

⸜⸝

We stand in the airport. I put my hand on his shoulder. "So what now?"

He shrugs. "Work. Mass. Friends."

"Mass?"

He shrugs. "God's always forgiven me. I guess I can forgive God."

"I am sure Our Heavenly Father will be greatly relieved."

He almost laughs.

I make him meet my eyes. "Who made you?"

"God made me." He reaches out and takes hold of me. My hands pat his back, his hair. My heart sings with welcome and joy. The Lord is never done with miracles, it seems.

God, this is the boy You sent to me.

This is the man he has become.

This is to give thanks.

Amen.

Gentry

Monday morning, and I'm talking to my English class. Business English. I teach this class for Phyllis. It's my penance for leaving her behind in that purgatory. I know plenty about English but nothing of business, so I email her occasionally for pointers, and she writes back, and I miss her.

I'm teaching Business English to students who are not sure of the difference between a noun and a verb. I'm teaching Business English to a few students who don't know English, one who only speaks a Russian dialect and another fresh from Thailand with her mother, who came over to marry a commercial fisherman. Occasionally her mother sits in, hoping to learn a little more English while she checks her email. They seem less confused than my English-speaking students.

"Can anyone explain to me the difference between active voice and passive voice?" I write the two terms on the board. The silence is deafening.

I can wait. I'm patient. Sometimes the largest part of teaching is alerting the students to their ignorance. Kids assume they know everything. Show them the void, they hate the void, they want to fill it up. I wait. The kids study the board.

"I know. Active voice is when you do all the work, and passive voice is when she does." Everyone is trying except Drew, of course.

"Drew is half right. Passive voice is when no one does any of the action. The verb has an object, but no subject."

Zeb raises his hand. "Gentry? What do you mean by subject?" Half a dozen heads nod, wondering the same.

I will start with the basics. Subjects. Verbs. Objects. We will get to transitive and intransitive a little later. Everyone pays attention, and five minutes later, we are all trying to apply this marvelous newfound knowledge that they should have learned in grade school.

Lorrie pokes his head in my room. "Hey, little buddy?"

I want to shout, please don't call me that in front of my students. They call us Gilligan and Skipper when you do that, don't you know that, Lorrie? "Yes, Coach Gilroy?" See, formal address. I accord you some respect. "Can I help you, Coach?"

"I was wondering if you took that test drive."

"What?"

"You know, that test drive we were talking about on Thursday?"

"I have no idea what you mean."

"That test drive? You promised you would take one. Did you?"

Ah. "Could we talk about this at lunch?"

"Oh, sure. But I wondered if you took that drive." He waits, smiling. "Did you?" The kids watch. They know something's up, maybe because of the grin on his face, maybe because mine feels hot enough to split. "Well, did you or not?"

"Yes."

"Yes? You mean, you test-drove it?"

"Yes." I will kill him.

"How did it go, little buddy?"

"It was fine."

"No problems with the handling?"

"No."

"Brakes weren't soft?"

"No."

"No flat tires?"

"No."

"Did you get any scratch?"

"Yes."

"Okay, just checking. See you at lunch."

I can hear him laughing all the way down the hall. And I know he can hear me, because I howl, Molly has to come thump me on my back because I laugh so hard that I begin to choke on my own spit, but I'll get him back, I will get him for this.

Scratch.

WINTER

Gentry

"I promised Mel I'd be there this year."

She refuses to give up. "You saw him twice this summer and you just saw him for Thanksgiving. We wanted you for Thanksgiving at Dad's house, and you stayed here. Please. We always come to the coast for Christmas. Oh, please, please stay and spend Christmas with us."

God, the "no" thing. I need to say no, don't I? Or could I say yes? Should I say yes? Guidance, please?

I've had many Christmas invitations over the years. People from school, work, neighbors, all wanting to take me in and show me what a real, old-fashioned, family Christmas is like. Every year, I'm invited. Every year, I decline. I always decline. Mel is only part of it.

There were no Christmases in that house. But there were trees at church, and songs. There was the procession of the nativity, awaiting the Christ child. His arrival. It was enough for me.

I saw how it was. There was always some kid who asked me questions. Some kid who pointed out to me what I was missing. I knew I missed out. You don't ask why when you're a kid, you just accept it.

After I went to Mel, we had our own Christmas system. The altar society decorated the church and the rectory, and our job was to give compliments. He would take me over to the church to watch the men set up the trees and string all the lights and climb ladders to hang the special banners. The ladies supervised. Everyone worked hard. When it was finished, Mel would announce that this was the most beautiful the church had ever been, ever, in all his years as a priest. And then, it would be my turn. I would say that this was the most beautiful the church had been in all my years as an altar boy. And the ladies would stroke my hair and thank me. I loved that. When they touched my hair.

I never gave Mel a present and he never expected one. But he always gave me something. He would hand me a bag or a box at some point during the Christmas visit, unwrapped, tags still on, and it was always way too extravagant and exactly what I wanted. That's how we did it, that was our system, and that's what I'm used to.

I have this mental vision of myself, strained, polite, unsure of how it's done, tree trimming and present opening. I don't know the systems for these things, and I would do everything wrong.

It was a relief that my wife wouldn't expect those things of me. We did have Hanukkah. Occasionally I would be allowed to perform some menial and repetitive chopping task in the kitchen as part of the preparations, but mostly I just had to eat. And listen. I loved listening, though I understood so little of it. "I wouldn't know how to act at Christmas."

"What do you mean, how to act? How do you act at the monastery?"

Hm. How to describe this. "I think what you need to remember about a monastery is that it's a bunch of older bachelors. Older bachelors who take cold-water showers and pray together and argue about religion all the time. At Christmas, they pray more than usual, and drink more, and they argue less, and they also eat quite a bit."

She thinks. "So, I guess you're trying to tell me that they don't exactly have a Martha Stewart Christmas there at the monastery?"

"Yes. That's what I'm trying to tell you. I guess. Because who is Martha Stewart?" That makes her laugh, but this isn't funny to me. "The monastery is what I'm used to at Christmas, and I like it, I love it, actually, that way of having Christmas. I love the food, the prayers, the Masses. And the conversations, Gretchen. I would miss the conversations."

She sounds dismissive and curious at the same time. "What *kind* of conversations?"

"So many intelligent people use their intelligence to think their way out of faith. The brothers use their intelligence to think their way into it. I don't get a chance to hear that very often."

"I don't understand your God stuff and I never will. And our Christmas conversations have nothing to do with God, but Christmas dinner is always excellent. My mother makes a roast pork that's incredible."

"Roast pork?"

"Yes. And Marci won't be here."

"She won't?"

"She's staying at Dad's this year."

"I have no idea about gifts."

"Dummy, I'll take you shopping."

I don't shop. I shopped with my wife because she loved to shop, and never in my life did I feel more sucked in and powerless than I did when I was dragging myself after her, making appropriate noises, my jaw clenching every time she got out the plastic. I think she just brought me along to hold her purse.

"Gretchen, you know I don't shop."

"Will you come along and help me?"

I open my mouth to say "no."

∽

And so, I drive to Portland, and Gretchen takes me to a mall. I hate malls. And the mall is just as awful as malls always are. There are crying children, and grumpy parents who look like they can't wait to get out in the parking lot so they can hit their crying children. There is canned music, Christmas canned music, most Sacred and Holy Muzak. There are women who look like they spackle their faces trying to spray innocent passers-by with acrid scents. Get away from me, that stuff makes my lips burn. There are booths set up in front of all the big stores, and the people there call out like desperate circus barkers. Open a charge account and get a free tire gauge or potpourri! I wish I had a big, scary crucifix to hold up to them, the vampires. There is store after store after store. Maybe it's the same store, over and over again, and we're on a Möbius strip and we only suffer under the delusion that we move. And everywhere, *everywhere*, there's weird stuff that no one could possibly need, like novelty slippers and electronic key chains and holiday socks and motorized coin banks and indoor fountains and all kinds of things that are for decorative purposes only and why do I have to be here, Gretchen?

"Gentry, could you relax, maybe? You look like a Russian tourist or something. Welcome to the Wonders of Capitalism!" She sounds like her sister.

It makes me hurt when she sounds like her sister.

"Here we are."

"This store doesn't make my lips burn."

Every woman with a fragrance sample has chased me down since we walked in here. I walked past a store that sold potpourri and I sneezed for twenty feet, like Bosco. But this store is different.

"These things are made with extracts and oils. Not chemicals."

"Hm." There's a rack of bottles of pure scents, and while she shops, I spend about ten minutes pulling up the stoppers, sniffing.

"Hey, Dog Boy. Why don't you buy something for my mom here? Maybe some lotion. I'm going to get Marci something here. Help me. What smells good? How about this one? It's supposed to smell like rain."

I take a sniff. "It doesn't smell anything like rain."

"Try this one." She holds out stopper after stopper. Finally, I shake my head. "It's giving me a headache."

"Of course it is. Let's go."

We walk up the mall, and I stop, frozen by a display of . . . "Hey Gretchen? They can put these things out here, and photos like this? They can do this in a mall?"

"Yes, Gentry, they can. It's the year 2000."

"At least you don't expect me to find something for your mother in this store."

"Oh please. Mom would rather go naked than wear this junk. She's a La Perla woman." Okay, whatever that means. We're halfway through the mall, and she hasn't found anything. "What should I get Tristan?"

"Buy him a Jeep."

"You're not being very helpful."

"Sorry." I stuff my hands in my pockets and keep my eyes on the floor. "I don't know why you would ask me for advice. I don't give presents."

"Except for a computer and a phone and a bracelet I still wear every single day." She flashes her wrist.

"Okay. But I've only bought three presents in my life."

"Seriously? What did you get for your wife for Christmas?"

"She was Jewish."

"What about birthdays?"

"She bought her own presents. That way she got what she wanted."

We pass another big store, another clerk with her stacks of mugs and stuffed reindeer trying to get people to open charge accounts. It makes me shudder.

"Do you want to leave?"

Right now, more than anything, ever, I want to leave, Gretchen. "Only if you're done."

"I'm done. I haven't bought one thing, but I'm done."

On the way out, we pass Santa, and the elf girls who help him are shaking toys in the face of a little hysterical girl whose parents are calling out encouragement.

Her face is red, snot running down her chin, fighting to get away from Santa, who looks tired. "Gretchen, why do people do this to their kids?"

"To celebrate the holiday, dummy." She smiles. "Gentry? Do you want to have your picture taken with Santa? I bet you've never done that before. Let's go over there and have your picture taken." She's laughing. "Come on, it'll be fun! You sit on Santa's lap, and you cry like that, be all scared, and I'll stand there and say, 'Come on, Gentry, please smile' while they shake toys at you." A fine metaphor for this trip to the mall and my approach to the holiday in general.

"I tried, Gretchen."

"Not very hard."

"No, but I tried."

We make the trek through the parking lot, fighting our way through the circling vehicles, being tailed at three miles an hour by desperate would-be parkers. Gretchen keeps pretending to go to the door of a parked car and then walking on, disappointing the hopeful driver waiting for her space. I make her stop that.

Somehow, I feel better about my complete mall failure.

I love this girl, God.

∽

This is a religious holiday?

I know, I'm not a pop culture kind of person, but I know what this holiday means to everyone else. I hear all of it on the radio. There's one man in particular with a conciliatory voice who calls himself my "personal friend in the diamond industry." He cozies up to my ear and pours in oily words about the perfect Christmas gift for Mom, that pair of diamond solitaire earrings. I feel violated, listening to that man. I don't have a mother, and if I did, I can't imagine buying her diamond earrings to celebrate the birth of the Savior. Who is that man? He's not my friend.

I've made it as clear as I can to Gretchen that I won't be giving or receiving gifts, so she had a small fit when a package arrived from Mel. "Why does Mel get to give you something, and I can't?"

"Because he's Mel."

"Well I'm putting it away so you have something to open. That way you won't feel all left out." My feeling "all left out" seems to be Gretchen's greatest fear.

I receive Christmas gifts. Every year, I get something from Mel. And then there are the items from my students, teacherly things. I use them for a while, and then I lose them, because how many book marks, coasters, desk statues, memo pads, pens, coffee mugs, magnets can I use? Especially when they have apples on them. Sometimes I get edible gifts from students, cookies I like, and candy I don't. The first year I lived in Oregon, I received an earring I still wear and a book on martial arts that my wife donated to the Goodwill. Since my wife was Jewish, we didn't have a Christmas gift "issue" in our marriage. That may have been the only thing about which we didn't have an "issue."

So I know about Christmas gifts. I just don't give them. I can't imagine it, sitting there waiting for everyone to open up the packages, hoping you got everything right. If you get a number of presents, one of them is bound to be wrong. The law of averages.

But Gretchen wants to give me a gift. I need to practice the "no" thing with her, and I'd like to start now, with this, because I truly don't know what to get for her and if she gets me something then I have to get something for her and we descend into the vicious gift-giving cycle, why can't she see that?

"No."

"But," she says softly, "you'll feel all left out."

"Don't get me anything, Gretchen. I mean it. No."

⟳

They arrive a week before the holiday to decorate the house. I'm allowed to observe without participating. To my relief, no one says, "Come put the star on the top of the tree, Gentry!" or anything stupid like that.

On Christmas Eve, Gretchen insists that I watch "The Grinch Who Stole Christmas." She speaks along with every single word. It's a sweet story, the "true spirit of Christmas" message is nice, and the tiniest Who reminds me of the Gretchen of old, and I will not cry, no, I will not become sentimentally unhinged.

When I go to midnight Mass, she comes with me. She seems to enjoy being there, and she sings. When I sit back down after communion, she yawns and leans against me. I put my hand in the cornsilk of her hair and whisper that we can leave. "I'm okay," she whispers back, and falls asleep against my shoulder.

⟳

I have to use the bathroom upstairs, and when I pass their open door, Jack and Kathryn are asleep. I think they're asleep. I don't hear any noisy sex, or any burping or urping or anything like that, either. So, yes. Sleeping. I've been sleeping in that bed since this fall, but three would be a crowd and Jack might not like being asked to leave.

When I come downstairs, Gretchen is in front of the fire with her blankets and pillows. "Marci and I always sleep here so we can catch Santa."

"Have you ever caught him?"

She points to her lumpy stocking. "Nope."

"You can have the couch."

"You're too old to sleep on the floor, dummy."

She's right.

I fall asleep thinking about that week of the ice storm. Those nights downstairs. How funny her sister was. And Bosco chasing popcorn when it exploded out of the popper.

I miss Bosco.

⁓

On Christmas morning, I'm allowed to observe from the safety of my sleeping bag. Jack and Kathryn come down in their robes, rumpled. They look like they just woke up, not like they just did anything else, and I think that's nice. For me, I mean. Kathryn sits by me, too close, and I guess that's nice. Between having to go to the bathroom and her proximity, I'm in agony, but I just think of it as Kathryn's Christmas present to me. Gretchen brings me a cup of coffee. Kathryn puts on the Messiah.

So far, Christmas is nice.

"Okay, stockings first. And since I'm the only kid, mine is the only stocking." She empties it out at her feet. I always wondered what people put in those. She has fruit, candy, and a clever little wooden box with a carving of a walrus on the top. "No Christmas Qtips? At Dad and Eve's, I always get Christmas Qtips. I guess Santa forgot this year. Sometimes we get Christmas cotton balls."

Kathryn snorts. Who is this woman? This woman who can hear the phrase "Dad and Eve's," this woman who snorts? Things have changed. "Remember when Marci got deodorant in her stocking at your dad's? Do you remember how angry she was?"

"That's nothing. Last year I got Christmas tampons."

I'm thinking, tampons? Really? Is she old enough? Well, she'll be sixteen in seven weeks. I teach high school, I taught girls younger than her who had babies.

But how did this happen?

"Okay! My turn!" Gretchen tears through a great many packages in a short amount of time. She gets clothes and books and software and new riding boots, which she puts on with her pajamas. She's happy. "Your turn!" Gretchen hands me my package from North Dakota. There's a great and mighty curiosity as to what priests send for Christmas. What Catholic mysteries lie within?

On top, there are some squares of the rough, sweet-smelling soap Mel used to send me before I was married.

"Open the *rest* of it!"

Lots of paper, and then a big tin. I pop the lid and smile. Loren knew I would miss these. I hand the tin to Kathryn, who pokes around, naming everything ("Korvapuusti! Vertebrod! I haven't had kanelbullar in years!") before selecting three treats and handing it to Jack, who can't have anything "because of the white sugar."

Gretchen stares at me. "Food and soap? Is that it?"

No. That's not all. There's a book in there, wrapped in butcher paper, and I can tell by the weight and heft and flex what it is. I tear away the paper to reveal the Bible Mel gave me when I left for high school. "I must have left this one at the monastery." I can hear my voice breaking, so I pull my bag over my head and close my eyes.

This is to give thanks. Amen.

When I finally poke my head out of the bag, Gretchen is staring at me, an expression of amused distaste on her face. "Are you done being overly religious?"

"For the moment."

"Great. Mom's turn!"

Kathryn opens a scarf from Gretchen, a sweater from Marci. She opens another box and she is confused. "What *are* these?"

Gretchen says, "Pass them over." She reads, then holds up an item at a time. "This is silicon kitchenware. These are silicon measuring cups. This is a collapsible silicon colander. This is a silicon cake pan. This is a silicon panhandle holder. I guess you're all set as far as silicon, Mom."

Kathryn raises her eyebrows. "Do you think it's a hint?" This must be a joke, because they all laugh. Who is Pamela? I wonder this as I drink my coffee.

Jack hands Kathryn a small aqua-colored box. "This is just a little something that reminded me of you."

"Jack. I thought we agreed the box seats were our present to each other."

"Just open it."

She opens the box and shakes her head. "Oh Jack, you really shouldn't have."

Maybe Jack is a personal friend of the man on the radio, I don't know, because the box holds diamond earrings. Kathryn smiles and puts them in. They're the size of her pinky nails and shaped like tears. The setting is the same color as her hair. They're almost as dazzling as her smile. Her hair, her eyes, her teeth and her earrings glitter.

The Snow Queen.

"Well, what do you think, Gentry? Did I do a good job?"

I nod, humbled by the idea of what those must have cost. I console myself with a little more coffee.

"Okay! Jack's turn!"

Jack opens a package and pulls out a plaid wool cap. He puts it on. Very jaunty. "Perfect, Gretchen. Right size and all."

I say, "Gretchen always knew how to read a label." She laughs with me, and it's Jack's turn not to get the joke, but he doesn't seem to care. He goes on to open one sweater after another. His nurse got him one, and Marci, and one from "Colin and Pamela," who I finally understand are his son and daughter-in-law. People must think he's cold because he's small and skinny.

Jack holds up the last one, a blue-green so dark and deep, you could fall into it. Gretchen narrows her eyes. "Nice color. But isn't that a little . . . enormous for you?"

Kathryn takes it and inspects the tags. "Leave it to Pamela to get you an XL." She passes it back. "I'll exchange it."

"I don't need three new sweaters, Kathy. Here you go." He throws it to me.

Well, I'm no fool. I pull it on. Nice and big. "It doesn't itch."

"Cashmere is goat hair, not wool." Gretchen tilts her head, narrows her eyes again. "That's too big. Do you even *own* a sweater?"

"Not since school, no."

"Well, he does now." Jack opens his last gift. A wooden box full of hand-tied flies. Jack stares at the flies, knits his generous grey brows and laughs until he wipes the corners of his eyes. Kathryn is laughing, too.

Gretchen and I trade looks. Why is this so funny?

Kathryn wipes her eyes. "Jack doesn't fish. He hates fish. He can't even stand to *eat* fish."

"Apparently Colin thinks I should start fishing and his wife thinks I'm still growing." He hands me the box. "Merry Christmas. I'll tell the kids you said thank-you."

I know very little of fly-fishing, but I recognize fine workmanship. "These are great, Jack. Thank you." Kathryn smiles, pleased. What neither of them know is that these flies are as useless to me as they are to Jack. I can't cast. I'm a bait fisherman.

I close the lid and sit back and drink more coffee.

How do people do this every year? Think of all these things, pay for it? But they're having fun. And watching, observing, what I didn't understand is that, yes, once in a while, a very strange gift appears, a gift that's completely wrong in every way. A good laugh is had by all, and then they move on. It doesn't matter. It appears to be part of what they enjoy.

"Do you want more coffee?"

"No thank you. Excuse me."

If I have any more coffee, I'll explode.

⌒

The phone rings as I pass through the kitchen. "This is Gentry." I hate it, I hate it, I no longer work in an office and when will I remember that I can just say "Hey" again?

"What the *hell* are you doing there on Christmas day?"

"Merry Christmas."

"Don't you 'Merry Christmas' me. Why are you at my house?"

"Hey Marci? Would you like to talk to your mother?"

"I can't *believe* this." Kathryn appears at my shoulder. I hand her the phone and get upstairs as fast as I can.

Merry Christmas.

She'll be here, I know it. Maybe not today, this week, but she'll be here eventually. As I knew she would. And pretended she wouldn't.

When she gets here, I need to make things right.

How am I going to do that, God?

Help. Amen.

⌒

Kathryn and Gretchen have worked in the kitchen for hours. I sit and starve while they decide that the pork is adequately roasted, the table adequately set with holiday china. I don't seem to be able to go into the kitchen to get myself anything to eat while Kathryn's here.

Jack pours himself a glass of wine. "Would you like one?"

"No thank you."

"You sure? It's non-alcoholic."

"Then what would be the point?"

That makes him laugh a little.

"It's time!" And then we sit, and I give great thanks for this day, and these kind people, and this food, Amen, and we dig in.

Kathryn laughs. "Don't hurt yourself, Gentry. You're eating the way you ate your first night here." I have no idea what she means, but I'll slow down. I've always fought this wolfing urge. Lately, eating alone, I may have backslid. I'll pause, chew, swallow, even make some conversation in an attempt not to eat so fast. I put my fork down, wipe my mouth. I drink some milk, wipe my mouth again. Let's see, conversation.

Weather!

"It's different. Not having snow. For Christmas." Gretchen turns a stricken face to me. "It's different but not bad, Gretchen. Just different." She brightens, good. I don't want her to think I'm sad.

Kathryn leans forward. "Have you always had a white Christmas?" She stares into my eyes. "Every Christmas?"

"Yes."

"So, you grew up in the north?"

"Yes."

"Where?"

I should pick up my fork, push in some food. I hold the handle tight. "Chicago."

"Chicago?" She repeats it with wonder and disbelief, making it sound as exotic as Bali or Antwerp. Her eyes gleam. "Is that where you were born?"

Gretchen looks up. "No."

Kathryn quiets her with a glance. "Gentry? Were you born there?"

"No." The last time I thought about where I was born was in Oklahoma, getting a marriage license. "I was born in Montana."

"Montana." Again, her wonder. "I wonder how you got from there to Chicago."

"I'm pretty sure we drove."

She smiles. "Did you have any family in Chicago?"

"No one besides my parents, no." And my neighbors.

"What did your father do?"

I carefully rearrange my cutlery. "He was an ironworker. He worked on skyscrapers." I loved that word, skyscrapers, when I was a boy. "He helped build the Sears Tower."

"And your mother?"

I shake my head. This has to be enough.

Kathryn smiles. "Detroit, Chicago, North Dakota, Montana. You come from such wintry places. When I was a little girl, we used to go to Minnesota at Christmas, and we always drove through the Dakotas. A vast plain of wind and white."

"Is that from a poem?"

"I don't think so."

"It should be." She smiles at me. I smile back. There are tears in the corners of her eyes. Her earrings flash. Jack clears his throat. Sorry, Jack. "The, um, air gets too dry there. I used to hate to get out of the Jeep because of the shocks. I felt like there was an electric fence up around me. It made Bosco jump."

"We thought about that for Bosco, you know. That invisible electric fencing." Jack interjects that, and Kathryn gives him a sharp look. Would anyone have done that to my dog, my Bosco? Shocked him? All the years I had him, he never even had a leash.

"Mom, can I go over to the Gilroys for dessert with Gentry?" Thank you, Gretchen. Because I don't want to cry on Christmas. I pick up my fork and eat, because I'm so hungry.

I'm always hungry.

∽

I'm so full, I may die. I don't remember ever being this full. I sit on the couch with my eyes closed and try not to groan. Oh, my stomach hurts. Help me, God. Send Your divine digestive intervention. Please.

I open my eyes and Gretchen stands over me. "What are you praying about?"

"How full I am."

"You ate like a bulimic."

"I don't vomit." Even if the idea tempts me. I'm in so much pain. I lift my arm and she slides beneath it. She puts her arm across my stomach and I move it away. "That hurts."

"I bet. I haven't seen you eat like that since you got back."

"I cook for myself, Gretchen. I never make anything that tastes that good, ever."

She's sad. "I don't like it that you cook for yourself. I don't like it that you order for yourself and you know how to cook for yourself."

"I don't like it that you have a boyfriend."

"Okay, so we both kind of grew up." She puts her arm back across my stomach, and I suffer the weight of it.

"Did you figure out what to give Tristan for Christmas?"

"I did. This huge Spanish book on soccer. Or 'futbol' as they call it. Powell's had it."

"In Spanish?"

She shrugs. "Tristan can read it. We took Latin together and after that he taught himself all the Romance languages. He gets the accents perfectly."

"That's remarkable." I feel a strange prickling of pride.

"He's remarkable. He's smart in all the ways I'm not." She sighs. "I saw a picture of his father." She shakes her head. "It wasn't the same man as in your picture." She sounds frustrated. "Things don't add up. Both his parents have light eyes. He has brown eyes, and those are autosomal dominant. So he has to be adopted."

She gave him away, too. "Don't ask him that, Gretchen. Don't ask him if he's adopted."

"Why? Maybe he really *is* your brother. Don't you want a family?"

"I have Mel. And you. That's enough."

༄

The Gilroy house has exploded. We're awash in a sea of paper, boxes, ribbons, and toys that require assembly. Walter cries quietly while Lorrie bangs at a vehicle

of some sort, and the stream of colorful language that issues from his mouth re-
duces Gretchen to repressed snorting.

All the Mumford women are snorters.

"Goddamnit, how does this sonofabitching thing go together? These crazy as-
shole Chinamen can't make directions that are worth a damn, do you know that?
They just do this to pay us back for Pearl Harbor. I should kick Vu's ass for this."
More tears slide down Walter's cheeks.

"Merry Christmas to you too, Lorrie."

We need to help, here. I relieve Lorrie of his assembly duties. And later I'll
give him some history and geography lessons. He stomps off to find Vicki. Renata
wanders, feral, through the boxes, grabbing, shredding, throwing, moving on.
Gretchen finds a trash bag and starts gathering up paper. She needs to do this
before Renata eats it all.

"Hey Walter? Would you like to help me, here?"

Walter stops crying, and we read the instructions together. He holds them up-
side down, but I was always good at this spatial stuff, and we get it figured out.
Soon, he flies through the house in a pedal fire engine, complete with a clanging
bell. I would have surrendered an arm or a leg to have something like that at his
age.

Gretchen asks me, "Do you think I should save the bows?"

"For what?"

"For next year. Some people save the bows."

I think we should just throw it away, the whole ridiculous mess. Half the toys
are already broken, or maybe they are just not put together. We decide to save the
bows just to be on the safe side. We hunt through the paper wads.

Gretchen is a little tired and pale.

"Are you okay?"

"Yes. It's just . . . poor Jack. Mom was really polite about those earrings, don't
you think?"

"Polite?"

"She hates jewelry. She doesn't even wear her wedding ring. Haven't you ever
noticed that?"

"I never notice things like that."

"Well, she'll probably take them back."

Poor Jack. He's not poor at all. But poor Jack.

Gretchen lifts Renata, makes a face, goes to find a new diaper. I do a little toy salvage work. I like toys. By the time Vicki comes in, we've restored some order in the universe of the living room. Vicki doesn't have on her usual implacably serene expression. I remember the scenes my wife and I treated people to, the wonderful public arguments, and I think we should leave.

Vicki comes over, gives me the nicest hug. We don't have to leave.

Lorrie lumbers in. "Where did your date go?"

"Funny, Lorrie. Very funny. Gretchen is changing Renata."

"Ah, don't get all testy on me. I guess I'm the official Christmas asshole. Vicki's mad at me, too. She thinks I went a little overboard on the toys. I say, what the hell, it's Christmas, right?"

I've seen your bait box, Lorrie. I don't blame Vicki. "Hey Vicki? These turned up at the Mumford house and they need a home." I give her the wooden box. She opens it and her eyes dance. Hug me some more, Vicki. I hug her back, oh, can we just go sit somewhere like this awhile? Can I touch your stomach a little?

He scowls at me. "Are you two about done?"

Well, no, Lorrie, but if it bothers you, then I'll let go. Vicki fixes me with her dark eyes and asks in that low voice, "Have you enjoyed your Christmas so far?"

"I think I have." I'm surprised at the truth of this.

She smiles so nicely. "I made you cherry pie."

I'm smiling back.

"Goddamnit, I'm in the sonofabitching room, you know."

I sigh. "Lorrie, what did you get for Christmas?"

He brightens. And we're off. I get a man tour out in the garage, with explanations, prices, comparisons. I make all the appropriate admiring noises, I mime envy. I ask for some advice, about nothing, tires, the like. He puts his hand on my shoulder and explains life to me, and I'm forgiven for patting his wife. "What did you get, little buddy?"

"Soap and a Bible."

The look on his face. He roars. "Jesus Christ, that sounds like what they send to inmates down at the county jail on Christmas!"

This was his Christmas present. Thank You, God.

One of the things he received was a new rod, and he wants to give me one of the old ones. He has seven. Vicki has eleven. I should say no, but I have to borrow one from them every time we go, and I would really like to have a rod of my own. I'm still so broke.

He hands me his old G Loomis.

"Lorrie. Give me a crappy one."

"I don't have any crappy ones."

"I wouldn't even know how to fish with something this nice." I could learn, though.

"Well, it's no goddamn yellow Berkeley ugly stick with a Zebco reel, but it will have to do, because it's the only one I feel like giving away. Merry Christmas, little buddy."

"Merry Christmas, Lorrie."

We return to the house. Gretchen put Renata in some sort of Christmas finery, and I have to laugh at the sight of her in all the ruffled stuff. She is a gum boots and overalls kind of a girl, like her mother. She has Vicki's PE whistle around her neck, and between her occasional blast and Walter's bell clanging, we have a real holiday din here.

I like it. I like it a lot.

We sit down to pie. I take a bite. "I've had cherry pie many, many times in my life, but I've never had any this good. What makes it taste like this?"

She smiles at me. "It's a Canadian secret."

"It's the best, Vicki. It's *fantastic*."

Lorrie throws down his fork. "For *Christ's* sakes." I'd better stop complimenting her pie before he hits me. And I eat two pieces, somewhere I find the room. We drink coffee and talk about school. Then, Vicki and I do the dishes, and Walter rams me with his fire engine, and Renata destroys her dress, and Gretchen and Lorrie watch football.

Vicki sends a pie home.

Jack peers at the pie, suspicious. "I couldn't eat that. Those cherries would just send me running for the bathroom, just running. Actually, that might not be such a bad idea, I have been stoppered up lately."

I pretend to be coughing.

Kathryn cuts herself a huge plank of a piece of pie. She takes a mouthful, closes her eyes. "Almond extract. Homemade butter crust, sour cherries, and almond extract. This is fabulous."

Almond extract? I preferred the mystery.

She has something to do for New Year's Eve. I thought she'd be here with me. Of course she's going home to be with Tristan.

I attempted not to look as pathetic as I felt when they all got ready to leave. Kathryn and Jack tried to make me come to Portland. Jack spoke up bravely. "I'll never make it to midnight. You could keep Kathy company." Oh yes, I could.

Bad, bad idea.

I never felt like an object of pity until I watched them pull away.

11:53

I watch the computer's clock tick off the minutes.

11:54

I watch for the magical moment when everyone in my time zone will have a celebratory drink. Everyone but me.

11:55

I remember there's a 24-hour liquor store in Astoria.

11:56

Astoria is a short drive.

11:57

I just want one.

11:58

God?

11:59

One more minute.

12:00

Happy New Year. So begins the true new millennium. I remember last New Year's, when Lorrie wrote me a series of letters asking me about computers. He was afraid that the entire national infrastructure would fail. What did he do with all that bottled water and dried food?

I'm going to bed.

The only hangover I have on New Year's Day is a television hangover.

This is to give thanks to You. Amen.

I watch television and pretend to care who wins. I clean the house. I call Mel and wish him a happy New Year. I make soup. I'm all right.

The phone rings. "Hey."

"She had the first baby of the goddamned New Year! It's like a Vegas Jackpot, the hospital gave us all kinds of sonofabitching crap, you name it, diapers, a car seat, all this formula that we won't use, but we can give that to the Food Bank, and they even gave us a rocking chair! Oh. And it's another girl. Ten pounds, twelve ounces. Geneva Leigh."

"She sounds *huge.*"

"Oh you bet. She's a whopper of a baby."

"Lorrie, you know how to ring in a New Year. Can I go see them in the hospital?"

"Hell, she's home already! Women like Vicki come home the same day!" I make the right noises, but I wonder what he means by "women like Vicki." Is there a special way for women of her fortitude? Does she chew on a piece of rawhide and drop the baby in a field, and then wrap it in the sleeve of her shirt and walk quietly on down the road?

I know nothing of birth. I will never know.

I glance up from contemplation of my self-pity to see Kathryn's Mercedes prowling down the drive. What? And what face is this in the window, nose to the glass? "Lorrie, I'll be over later. I, um, have to go. Bye." I hang up the phone and go outside.

Gretchen opens the car door. He jumps out. His hair fine like Bosco's but longer, and he's almost white. He squats for a little business, then sits down on my boots and leans against my legs, panting and smiling up at me. Gretchen's talking, but whatever she's saying about a neighbor bringing him over and her mother thinking it won't be all right and is it all right and all that, I don't really hear it as I drop to my knees. He stands on his hind feet, puts his big paws on my shoulders and wags his tail. I rub his chest and stomach, let him sniff me, lick my ears. He's going to be a big dog. Very big.

Hey, pup. Are you a good pup? What soft ears. What brown eyes. Oh, you want to lick my face? Puppy breath. Are you home, now? I think you're home.

"Gentry? You're sitting in the mud."

We don't care about mud.

Mud is fine, just fine.

⁓

Gretchen stayed with me for the rest of the break. I needed help with the pup. When Kathryn came to get Gretchen, I think they both felt better about leaving me, because of the pup.

I still felt terrible, seeing her go.

The night Gretchen left, I was trying to sleep. I felt pathetic and weak and alone. I hadn't cooked any dinner. I lay there and fed on my self-pity. My stomach started to growl. The puppy woke up and barked at my belly. I laughed out loud.

I felt better.

The puppy is too young for any sort of a sustained conversational effort. Mostly, he pulls at the edges of my clothing with his milk teeth and asks to go outside after he's already gone on the floor. Mel trained Bosco, and I call him for advice.

I take the dog to school with me. He sits in his corner and chews his pig ears. When classes change, he greets each student to exact the proper tribute. It takes most of a class period to greet each student, but he does it. He's calm and patient, and if a student doesn't pat him, he waits until the student rectifies that oversight.

I add a new rule. "Respect the dog." I make that rule number one. He never has an accident in the classroom. Okay, once, but only once. The kids vie to take him out, and they're full of suggestions for names. I won't name him Beavis or Doobie or Weezer or Spud.

What should I name you, fella? You need your name.

My pup. I like his sweet, puppy breath in my face at night, and I love to scratch his silky belly and hear his tail thump on the sleeping bag. We sleep on the couch so I can take him out easily.

We like the couch.

⁓

One Saturday morning I awake at dawn and take him outside where we water the roses. Steam rises because it's cold out here. Too cold to be awake. Come on, pup, we can sleep more. Come here. He burrows into the sleeping bag right next to me. We're warm.

We go back to sleep.

Gentry, she says.

Go away.

Look at me. Open your eyes.

I will never set my eyes on you.

Look at me. Wake up. I need to talk to you.

Never. I know what you want to show me.

Gentry, please, open your eyes.

I can't open my eyes, I won't, she's over me and I won't look, I won't do this, I won't see her again. Oh God, seal my eyes to her naked beauty. Save my soul.

Something tears out of me and I think I'm screaming, but it's her.

✺

Marci standing on top of the kitchen counter. She's stopped screaming. I quiet my dog, my poor dog, my dog is so frightened, but he'll be all right. He wet on the floor. Hey, pup, I don't blame you. Let's clean this up. "It's okay, this is Marci, and this is her house, come on, shh . . . Don't cry, you two just scared each other. That's a good boy." Tears fall from my eyes to the floor. Sam licks them up, then licks my face.

"I thought it was like *Alien*. I thought he was a chest-buster." I have no idea what that means. She climbs down from the countertop, shaking so hard that her teeth chatter. "What a horrible dog."

"You scared him. He's just a puppy."

"Are you even allowed to have a dog here? Does Mom know?"

"She brought him here."

She rolls her eyes. "Of course." She extends a finger toward my chest and I slam back into the cabinet. "God, Gentry, don't hurt yourself. I was just showing you that he scratched your chest. And your cheek is bleeding." She opens a cabinet, hands me a tube. "Put some of this on there." She watches as I apply the cream, look away, I can't stand it.

What to do.

I dial the phone and hand it to her. Marci shoots me a look of pure hatred. She smiles so the sound of that is in her voice. "Mom? Hi. Guess where I'm calling from. Just guess." The smile goes away. "How did you guess?" She is silent. "This is my house, Mom, and . . . Mom . . . MOM . . ." She might cry. She hands the phone to me.

"Hey."

"Gentry, I'm so sorry. She was supposed to let me know if she was coming."

"I can move to the little house. I don't mind."

She's quiet for a minute. "It's cold out there in January."

"I have a down sleeping bag."

"There's a lock on the door now. It's the key with the green sleeve."

"Okay, then. I, um, have to go. Bye." I hang up.

It's very quiet in the kitchen. I go upstairs to pack my few clothes out of Gretchen's closet, and she carries her bag into her stripped-down room. Her voice echoes out of its emptiness. "Who was in here?" She pushes open Gretchen's door. "Who slept in my bed?"

"I did."

"You slept in my *bed*?" Her eyes glow with outrage.

"When I was sick."

"Well, that was my mom's bed. You've slept in it before, right? So no big *deal*."

My mouth falls open. I can feel it, the visceral satisfaction I would take in shoving her right through the window to the paved driveway below, that driveway where she let him kick me almost to death.

Dear God, I am an animal. Help me figure this out. Amen.

I get my dog and go out to the little house.

Perfect. It's still perfect.

I sit down on the bed, the pup beside me. Gretchen sat here the first time I came in, like Goldilocks. I miss her. Oh, God. Why isn't she here?

The door swings open. "Knock knock." The dog growls. Marci stands there, a key in her hand. Several mental images occur, all of them violent. She is not safe around me. No one is safe around me.

I walk over and close the door in her face.

All right. Think. Figure it out. Come on, Sam. That's your name. Sam. Do you like your name? Sam's like Max, only backwards.

Sam, let's go for a ride.

Sam and I have a good time at the hardware store, depleting my small amount of money. We buy a few things. We bring in some tools from the garage and work on the door. A window blind, a new deadbolt and one of those useless brass chains, more for symbolic than security value.

There. This works, right, Sam?

My cast iron frying pan from Oklahoma is still in the big house. Her car is gone, so I go into the kitchen and get some pans, dishes, food, Sam's food. Sam is starving.

I go up to Gretchen's room and tear down the computer. I hate to do it because I just set it up, but I carry down the CPU and monitor, abandoning the peripherals. Those old printers weigh a ton. Let's set this up, boy. Good boy. The phone line is active. All I have to do is plug in the new phone.

"Fankhauser residence, Kathryn speaking."

"Hey."

"Are you all right?"

"I'm fine, just fine." Why does this make her laugh? "I'm calling from the little house. I was wondering if I could get DSL on this line."

"Of course. I'll call and authorize you on the account."

"Thank you. May I speak to Gretchen?"

"Well, she's out with Tristan. I'll have her call you when she gets home."

"Does she know this number?"

"No, but it's here in the phone, now. Are you really all right, Gentry?"

"I, um, have to go. Bye."

⌒

It's late. If I were asleep, I'd have been on the ceiling when someone rattled the doorknob and hammered on my door. But I'm still awake. Sam, on the other hand, is yowling, yipping in fear.

Come on, boy, calm down. Sh. Here, come here.

I open the door a crack. He presses his nose to it and yips in alarm.

Her hair is pasted to her head with rain and she has on running clothes. When did she start to run? "Where's the *coffee*?"

Sam starts to growl. "Pardon?"

"I *said*. Where is the goddamn *coffee*?"

"Do you mean, my coffee?"

She stares at me, her nostrils flaring. "That's not your fucking COFFEE."

"I wouldn't take it if it weren't."

"You're *lying*. You stole my mother's coffee, so just give it back because I'm *cold*."

I go get the bag of coffee. It won't fit through the gap. I unchain the door and hold it out. She stands there glaring, arms crossed, rain falling off the tip of her nose, staring at the bag. Which is getting wet. "Is this *decaf*?"

"Of course not."

"Then *forget* it." She turns on her heel and goes back to the house. I slam the door, lock it, chain it. That's not enough.

I need to hit something.

∽

I'm working on my computer late the next afternoon when there's more hammering at the door. I unlock the door. Gretchen bursts in. "What happened to your cheek?" She sounds as accusatory as her sister did the night before.

"Sam scratched me."

"I thought maybe she did it."

"No." I fold her up and hold her tight and smell her hair, which smells strangely dusty.

She speaks into my shoulder. "I'm going to cook dinner, and will you come in? Mom and Jack are here. Please? Don't just sit out here."

I want to say no to her. I never say no to her. "Give me an hour, okay?"

She slips away and back to the big house.

∽

I work for an hour until I have to go in there.

I knew, coming back, that this would be part of it. I came back prepared to face the worst. I have decided my crimes are forgivable. I pray to forgive hers.

Amen.

∽

It's a long walk from one door to the other. A long, long walk. I stop and wipe my feet. Sam and I walk in without knocking. The air is full of frying chicken. I almost stumble with how good the kitchen smells. Sam's mouth starts to run with drool. Gretchen is at the stove, Marci at the kitchen counter with Jack. I nod to Jack and walk to the sink, wash my hands, carry the towel out to the utility room. Marci smirks.

"You still do the surgical scrub!"

Kathryn calls from the dining room. "Gentry, will you help Gretchen?" I help Gretchen carry the food into the dining room. We sit at the same spots we always did. Gretchen across from me, Marci next to her, Kathryn at one end. Jack is at the other.

I do some chicken math. There are two birds, which means four thighs and four wings and four drumsticks. Gretchen gives me two of each. This is one of the many reasons I love this girl. We all take some of everything else. I experience a brief pang of nostalgia for Ruth Hirsch's jalapeño coleslaw, and then everyone waits while I say my grace.

Amen.

"Well," Jack announces from his new station of authority. "Thanks for sprucing up that deck furniture. And edging the driveway, that was good enough for government work. The place looks great, Gentry. You're really earning your keep."

Kathryn gives him a look so cold, I should check the windows for frost. "There is no need for Gentry to earn his keep." He drops his eyes, frowning. She gives me one of her encouraging looks. "But you have been busy, Gentry. You certainly have gotten trim again."

I nod. I chew. This chicken is great. I could get fat again on this chicken.

"What, was Gentry fat or something?" Marci wears an expression of pure delight. "Was he fat?"

"He wasn't fat." There's a long pause. "His stomach just stuck out a little."

Kathryn smiles. "It sure did. It was a nice little man-belly."

"Gentry, how much did you weigh?" Only Marci would ask this, of course. My mouth is full, so I shrug. "Don't you even know how much you weigh? That shouldn't surprise me, though. You don't know anything about yourself."

"Men never pay attention to things like that." Jack scolds the table. "I can't believe you women. Going on about this weight business. For Pete's sake, leave the boy alone."

"Well, he never knew anything about himself. One time Vu took him to get some boots and Gentry didn't know what size shoe he wore." She rolls her eyes. "I don't think Gentry even knows what his first name is. Does your wife know your name?"

"Marcialin," hisses Kathryn.

"What? I'm just curious. And by the way, where is she, anyway? Gentry, where's your wife?" She's smiling. "Or is that something else you don't know, like how much you weigh and what your shoe size is and what happened to your parents and your name?"

I set down my piece of chicken. I stare at my hands, palms down on each side of my plate. I study them. I do this so I don't stand up and use these hands to turn the table over on her. Dear God, deliver me from this table.

Jack speaks with the gentleness of a doctor delivering the worst news. "Marci, I guess nobody told you that Gentry's wife passed away."

"*What?*" She looks from face to face. "Are you saying she's *dead?*"

Kathryn

I tried to sleep, first.

No, first I suppose I spent an hour watching Gretchen pace the kitchen. "He can't go away again, Mom. He can't."

"He won't leave. Even though he probably wants to."

"Well, he *can't* leave."

"If he does, you can't blame me." Marci's features lapsed into the kind of adolescent face-making I'd thought she'd outgrown. "It's not my fault no one told me his wife is dead. You just let me sit at that table and make an ass of myself. It's your fault it happened. And how did she *die*, anyway? And *when?*"

"None of us know how she died, Marci. None of us. Not even Gretchen."

"That's crazy. Why doesn't anyone know?"

"Because he doesn't talk about it. Just leave him alone about it."

She threw her hands in the air. "What do you think I'm going to *do* to him?"

And I looked at her, and Gretchen looked at her, and she looked at us with rage and guilt in her young face. Jack looked at all of us like he'd rather not know what any of these looks were about.

Gretchen finally spoke. "I hate you, Marci. I honestly just hate you."

Jack spoke up. "Gretchen, honey, you need to calm down."

She ignored him. "If you drive him away again, I'll never speak to you again as long as I live. He has to be here. I *need* him here." She headed across the kitchen, and Jack moved in front of the door. "Get out of my way. I'm going to go see if he's all right."

He put a hand on her shoulder. I admired his bravery. I'd certainly never have risked touching her. "No you're not. You stay right here. He doesn't need anyone pulling the tablecloth out from under the china." Gretchen gave him a look so heavy with rage that I was surprised he didn't double up from the blow. But he stood firm.

Marci set her jaw in defiance. "He has no *right* to be here. He ruined *everything.*"

Gretchen was pale and trembling, but her voice was cold enough to frighten me. "He didn't ruin everything. You did."

"Enough, girls. Stop this *right now*. I mean it."

I sent Gretchen to bed. I made Marci some tea. And Jack went upstairs grumbling that he was old, too old, just too old for all this hullabaloo.

Marci sat at the counter and drank the tea. She sipped, and her eyes broadcast all the words she wouldn't say, all words that none of us have ever been able to speak aloud. I opened my mouth and she shook her head. "Don't you dare, Mom. Not after all the times I tried to talk to you about it. Don't you dare try to talk to me about it now, after you let him move back here and move in without telling me."

She went up the kitchen stairs to her empty bedroom. I finished her cold tea. Wished for a cigarette. Went upstairs, observed my expensive nightly rituals of repair and preservation, put on a nightgown and lay down next to my husband, avoiding contact with him because I was vibrating with anxiety over unspoken words and buried events. Jack laid a hand on my arm, the pressure sending a message to me as ably as Helen Keller tapping into a palm, waiting for him to speak it out loud.

"I'm here, Kathy. Tell me what's going on."

I rose from the bed and left him alone.

His light was on, as it always was at night. He'd put up a blind. I knocked and he looked through the slats before he unlocked the door.

"Hey." His voice was rough with sleep, his face confused and just a little alarmed. And so beautiful. The man was so unforgivably beautiful.

"May I come in?"

He scratched his head and glanced around the room, considering, then stepped aside. I sat in the only chair. He sat down on the edge of the bed. That bed was so old. It couldn't be good for his back, he wasn't in his twenties anymore, you have to watch out for your back.

Oh for God's sake, I'd started to think like Jack.

The puppy stretched and yawned before settling along his thigh. What a lovely place to settle. I watched his huge hand stroke the fur for comfort.

"A penny for your thoughts."

"They're not worth a penny."

"Gretchen saved you a plate. Piled high." He nodded, not as cheered by this news as I'd hoped. "Gentry, I'm sorry Marci said those things. But she had no idea about your wife's death. Marci talks to Eve more than she talks to me, and I assumed Eve had filled her in. My mistake." My stomach cramped with guilt, remembering my rage at the news of his marriage. Since hearing that she died, I'd been engaging in small orgies of self-recrimination, as if my jealousy had the power to kill her. "I'm so sorry about your wife."

He sat in front of me, a half-naked boy stroking his puppy. "Is that why you called me? Because you felt sorry for me?"

"I called you because I missed you. I missed you every single day, Gentry." My eyes dropped to the fine work of his collarbones and the muscular column of his neck, the point of his Adam's apple pushing out from it. His perfect, youthful maleness. "We all missed you. Even Marci, in her own bitter way, missed you very much."

He blinked. "Hey Kathryn? She doesn't want me here."

"You're right. But if you leave again, it will kill Gretchen. She waited like the little mermaid in the harbor, watching the ocean like you'd arrive by sea."

He pressed his hands to his eyes.

I rose with as much dignity and self-control as I could muster to take myself out of there. But for just a moment, I paused. I allowed myself the luxury of a hand on the heartbreaking fineness of his hair. He took his hands from his eyes and rested them on his dog. His perfectly arched nostrils flared, but he didn't meet my eyes, didn't touch me.

He was far too smart to touch me.

Gentry

G od, You brought me back here. You must have a plan. I submit to Your plan. But God? If this is Your plan, I could use an explanation.

Kathryn coming to me in the night, touching my hair, standing by my bed in a white nightgown. I saw her naked but I never saw her in one of those. God, You must know this, being omniscient, but a woman's nightgown smells like her bed, her sleep, her sex. Those mornings with Becca, opening her robe to see which nightgown I'd be removing. My little wife in her tiny nightgowns, stroking my hand across the softness to let it catch on whatever was covered. My wife's nightgowns were the softest traps.

And now, Kathryn. It took everything I had not to put my hands on her hips and pull her close, to lift that white gown to touch her scars, to see her faded butterfly, to know if she was silver everywhere. It took everything, everything not to ruin my life in this bed a second time by putting my mouth where it does not belong.

God, I will fall. I will. But I will not fall with Kathryn.

Amen.

∽

There were days in Oklahoma when I would have traded every last hour I had left to live for a single day here with them, just one ordinary day. But when they all went back to Portland and Seattle, I was relieved. My heart hurts and I miss Gretchen and I want Kathryn and I don't know what to do about Marci.

But I have work to distract me, and Sam. Sam is losing his milk teeth. My kindergarten teacher had a window club for all the kids who lost teeth. I was only in kindergarten for a few weeks, so I never joined, but I write "The Window Club" on the white board, and "Sam" underneath. One of the football players, Isaac, had a front tooth knocked out during practice, so I put his name up there until he gets his cap.

I go to the dentist as much as I go to church these days. I have anxious nightmares about my teeth shattering as I eat.

I don't want to join the Window Club, God. Amen.

Today is Friday. Fridays are free days. A quiet sophomore named Molly Butterfield is always here. I consider Molly Butterfield to be just about a perfect name, but she asks me to call her Rainbow. I manage to do that without laughing.

Molly dyes her hair with Kool Aid, which is something better to do with Kool Aid than drinking it. Her clothing is wound around her randomly, like burial cloth. Her garments are made from hand-loomed hemp, something like that, and she wears no leather because she is a vegan. I don't think I've known any vegans since I was in college, and they were always painfully thin. I consider veganism another kind of eating disorder, but Molly is a stocky girl, noticeably knock-kneed. The way she stands with her flat feet turned out makes it seem as if she's braced for an earthquake.

Despite being well-planted herself, she spends a part of every day gently lecturing me about walking lightly on the earth. I don't tell her my theory that the coal burned during the industrial revolution caused more damage than anything else, that we've already gotten to a place beyond repair and all the cloth tote bags in the world won't make a difference. But I try. I set up recycling containers and use the bond in the laser printer that makes it dusty. Every assignment I give out can be turned in electronically. I can't think of anything else to do. Still, I am quietly scolded on a daily basis for the heavy fall of my carbon footprint.

This is Oregon.

After she scolds, Molly works on her book. She comes in at lunch, before school, after school. She types away and carefully backs up her files on the network in direct violation of school policy against storing personal documents on district servers.

"Hey Molly?"

She has a Kool-Aid-hued braid in her mouth. She chews her hair, and the dye colors her lips. Today they are green. "Rainbow."

"Right. Rainbow. I was wondering what your book is about."

She blushes. "Dark urban fantasy. With steampunk overtones." I have no idea what she's talking about. It sounds like something Mike Mumford would say about a glass of wine. "Mm. Dark urban fantasy, with steampunk overtones." Still, I'm fairly certain this book is not about me.

She goes back to chewing on her hair.

Most of the kids spend their free time playing games, not writing. Some kids spend their free time being disgusting. Today, Drew keeps asking Zeb to smell his armpit. "Smell it. It smells like lunchmeat." He sniffs himself. "It's weird."

Zeb takes a whiff. "SICK. What did you eat?"

"Fritos?"

"Maybe that's it."

"Stop, you two. No more armpit talk." There's a limit, even on free days.

Zeb returns to the magazine that he pilfered from the backpack of a female classmate. "Okay, Gentry, it's time to find out 'The Right Prom Look For You.' Are you ready? When a boy comes to your door to pick you up for a date, are you most likely to be wearing..."

"I have no plans for prom."

Drew is reading over his shoulder. "Come on, Gentry, we need to figure out if you're a 'Tomboy Toughie,' a 'Romantic at Heart,' a 'Vintage Free-Spirit,' or a 'Slave to Sophistication.'"

"We don't need to figure that out."

"Well, can we at least use your pencil to fill it out?" Zeb's joking, of course. No one touches my mechanical pencil. They take the quiz for me.

"I think you're a 'Romantic, Vintage Tomboy.'"

I laugh out loud. They are so free, these boys. I rarely said a word in a classroom until I entered college. My mind wanders over to Gretchen, and then, oddly, to Tristan.

Who is he, God? What's he like in a classroom? Is he silent? Is he funny? Why do I care? Sitting in there with all the kids, I'm filled with curiosity for a boy I don't know. And more than that.

I am full of a strange longing.

Lorrie sticks his head in the door. "SHUT THE HELL UP!"

Lorrie

I hunt, see, and one of my buddies has this red tick hound, Monty, a good hunting dog, gentle mouth, you can fire a shotgun up his ass and he won't spook. He'd take on a bear for Emmett. He's that good of a dog. But if you say, "Monty," in a certain way, he tucks his tail between his legs and slinks away, like all the fucking sins of the world are on his back.

Gentry had that kind of shame on him. But he's a little better now. He's even starting to get pissed off once in awhile. Right now, he's real pissed off. We're walking to lunch. "I don't want you telling my kids to shut up."

"You're kinda cute when you're mad, little buddy."

"That's my classroom, Lorrie."

His classroom is right next to mine, and sometimes it gets so sonofabitching loud in there, I have to stick my head in and tell the whole outfit to pipe down. My little buddy gets a little testy with me when I do that. But he's right. They weren't noisy when I did it this morning. "I just stick my head in there because I'm so goddamn glad to see you, see, I have to check to make sure you're really in there. I feel stupid, I have to say something, so I tell the kids to shut up."

And he stops walking. He just stops. He sticks his hands in his pockets, kind of going on a little, he says he doesn't know what's wrong with him, he's remembering stuff these days, this stuff in his head, makes him touchy, it isn't anything he can talk about but it's hard right now, real hard, the last thing he wants to do is yell at me, he's sorry, looking at his big old boots and apologizing away. "I'm sorry, Lorrie. I don't know what's wrong with me."

I know what's wrong with him. Anyone who looked at Gentry could tell you what's wrong with him. He needs a woman.

༄

"He did it for me, Vicki. I need to do it for him."

I've been scouting the available mothers and I tell Vicki about a couple of them and she doesn't say a word, see, but somehow she gives me this look that lets me know that under no circumstances should we try to fix up Gentry with the mothers of his students. Then she pats my hand.

"Jesus I'm an asshole, Vicki. I'm so glad I have you." So then I'm trying to think about her friends, you know, her girlfriends, not that she has a lot of them but she does have a few and we could maybe find a candidate there. "He likes them short, I know that much," I tell her. "And skinny. He likes them skinny. And old, for some reason he likes them with wrinkles." Her eyebrows go up and there's a funny little smile playing around my wife's mouth. "And smart. He likes them kind of bitchy and smart."

"You're describing Kathryn Mumford."

Christ. What an asshole I am. "You better pick out the woman."

"Maybe Bonnie?" Matchmaking's not her thing, see, Vicki knows too much about people. But she says there's something about her friend Bonnie that might match up with Gentry. She says, "It's strange, but when I look at him, I somehow see her next to him."

Well, okay then, we're good to go. Bonnie is a nurse at the hospital in Astoria. She helped take care of Gentry five years ago when he was hurt and when we have her over for a drink so we can hatch up the plan, she remembers him. "He could hardly walk, but when we took the catheter out, he wouldn't use a bedpan. We had to help him to the bathroom so he could struggle around in there on his own." She starts to laugh. "He made me bring him an extra gown. He wore two, one backwards. He wouldn't let me give him a sponge bath. You bet. I'd love to have dinner with him."

And then the night he's coming over, the actual same sonofabitching night, Vicki shakes her head. "I just don't have a good feeling about this, Lorrie."

Ah Jesus Go Square Dancing Christ.

"Well, shit, Vicki, it's too late to back out now and besides where's your sense of loyalty and obligation in terms of getting Gentry hooked up with somebody so he doesn't make a complete asshole of himself with another bitch from hell, I ask you?"

She gives me one of those wife looks.

⌒

He pulls in, the guy has the dog with him, nice, bring a dog on a date, not that he knows it's a date because I kinda forgot to tell him about that part. And he's got a book for the kids, for some reason my little buddy has this idea that the thing to bring to the kids of a couple of coaches is books, he's always bringing the kids these damn books and then they want us to read them out loud to them, what the hell but anyway, we introduce them. Gentry's face goes all polite and bland like tapioca pudding, his eyes blinking. Vicki puts Geneva on the tit right there at the table and he stares at that like, well, you know, she's just nursing a baby, but still. That's her boob, he could maybe find somewhere else to look.

Then Bonnie says in her great big voice, "Don't you REMEMBER me from the hospital? I was one of your NURSES." Well I know that voice of hers is a little loud and but boy does he jump right out of his sonofabitching skin, his eyes are round like he saw a ghost or something.

Does he leave? No, but it might have been better if he did because he sits down at his place and opens his gob and puts in his French meat pie and green beans with Sam watching each and every bite but getting nothing because that's all the guy's doing, taking the food and putting it in his mouth, chewing and swallowing like he's in prison and afraid of catching the eye of one of those big butt pirates they have in there.

He doesn't say a word to any of us, not just Bonnie but me or Vicki or even the kids, Gentry always talks to the kids, but no, and Renata gets so fed up with being ignored that she calls him a poophead and he doesn't even notice. I tell her to knock that shit off, that's no way to talk at the goddamned dinner table.

And Walter's reading the book he brought at the table, which I don't agree with that either, see, where are these kids' manners, you'd think they were raised in a goddamned barn, see, that's like having a toy at the table, it's one of those Richard Scarry books with the worm that wears the boot, what the hell is that boot all about I'd like to ask you but Bonnie says, "Oh that's a GOOD ONE" in her loud voice, causing my little buddy to jump up in his chair so high that his legs connect with the bottom of the table and he makes a noise that lets us know he's kind of hurt himself over there.

She says, "I actually HAD this one as a kid. I DID, I read it when I was a KID!" So she smiles over at Gentry and asks, "Did YOU have this one as a KID, is that why you GOT it?" And he shakes his head all panicked-like, and she says, "Well what did you READ when you were a kid, GENTRY?"

He sort of gets a hold of himself. He pushes his hair out of his face and swallows a bunch of times so his Adam's apple is bobbing around, which always makes me kind of choked up because I remember when he got kicked there and almost died, but anyway, he thinks for a second, and he's really thinking by the way. "Um, engineering texts and fairytales."

Well Jesus on a rubber cross Christ, if he could have come up with anything weirder than that I can't figure out what the hell it would be. Maybe Penthouse and the Bible, that would be funny except come to think about it, that's what I read when I was growing up. But anyway, we all kinda go around it, you know, you recover and you go on and talk about something normal like your neighbors or the weather or something. He doesn't say another thing all through the meal. And here's the worst part. When we all finish he stands up and helps Walter clear the table, and then Walter asks him if he wants to play some Go Fish, which is what they usually do after dinner. He says "I, um, have to go. Bye." And bolts for the door, Sam at his heels.

Well now my kid's feeling bad.

Bonnie smiles and says "Wow. Do you think he LIKES me?" And I'd laugh because she's funny, but I follow him outside and he's over by his Jeep. He's pacing back and forth, all agitated-like, and then he says "LOOK" in a voice loud enough to make you jump and he tells me that Miriam was a nurse, and she was short and dark and had a loud voice and he knows it's not Bonnie's fault she's a doppelganger for his wife, so maybe could I please apologize to Bonnie for him, which I tell him I'm not about to do because a man should make his own apologies, so he says fine, he'll get her number and do it himself. And then he says he understands we just want him to be happy but he says in this voice like he's breaking up inside, "I don't expect anyone to understand this Lorrie, but I just can't *take* it right now, I can't *take* anything."

I put my hands on his shoulders. "Well Jesus Christ, Gentry, how the hell am I supposed to know what you can take? Why don't you give your friends some basic information once in a while? What am I, the amazing Kreskin, supposed to bend all the spoons in the lunch room and read your goddamned mind while I'm at it?"

The look on his face, all busted up, well, it lets me know I was an asshole right there.

Vicki comes out. And you know what my wife does? She hugs him, and she's patting on him and he's all moony like he is when he gets that close to her boobs. I go on back inside because it's just a hug but she's getting these wet circles on her shirt and I'm right on the edge at that point.

Bonnie has the baby. I take my baby girl, she's a nice baby, this Geneva. "He says he's sorry," I say. "You remind him of his dead wife. She was loonytunes." And she laughs, shakes her head. She's not taking this personal, I can tell that much. And Vicki comes back in and gives me the wife look and Bonnie and I sit down and play cards with Walter while Vicki gives Renata and Geneva a bath. After a while, the phone rings and I know who it is, I know what he'll say, I don't even need to answer.

But I do. "I already told her you're sorry."

"Thanks," he says. And there's this long pause and then we both hang up, because anything we'd say after that would leave us both sounding like pussies.

Gretchen

Gentry came to Portland for my birthday.

I told him not to worry, Marci couldn't make it. She was furious that he was invited. I could hear her smoking on the phone when we talked. "So, you want him there, and not me? Thanks a lot, baby sister."

"I want you both here. But only if you'll act like a human being towards him. It's your choice."

She hung up on me.

Tristan seemed confused whenever he looked at Gentry. Everyone else did, too. Spence kept looking back and forth from Gentry to Tristan. Jack noticed, and my mom kept frowning. Tristan talked with Spencer and Gentry talked with Dad and it sounded like the same two people were having conversations at each end of the table. Gentry ate enough food to kill himself. So did Tristan. Graham had something going on and he wasn't there and I was glad not to have to watch him chew.

I had a little trouble eating.

I'm sixteen, now.

Gentry

There was a break in the rain, so Gretchen and I are taking a walk as a concession to the huge amount of food I stowed away at Mike's expense. Sam's cold, but stoic about it.

Dinner was nice. I watched the ease between Mike and Eve and Jack and Kathryn, and I thought, when you have what you want, you can be easy with the ones who hurt you before.

God, I pray for that ease. Amen.

Spencer was there, grown up. A young man. Good manners. Very much like his dad. And this brother of mine has nice manners, too, he is unfailingly polite when dealing with the adults, and extremely funny when dealing with his peers.

Every time I glanced up, he was staring at me, frowning.

We all stood on the curb when it was time to go.

"That's a great Jeep," Tristan said. "CJ5?"

"Yes."

"Did you restore it yourself?"

"No, I didn't have a garage, so I bought the best one I could find."

"Yeah, you kind of have to have a garage." His gaze traveled the panels with a young man's longing. "But it would be cool to restore one."

"You'd have to buy three."

He smiled. "Two for parts?" I smiled, nodded. "Yeah, but wouldn't it be fun?"

I looked up and everyone was staring at us. And I couldn't stand this, everyone staring at me, staring at him, staring at whatever we are.

I watched him say goodbye to Gretchen, his arms around her in a proprietary hug. She loves him with that quickening, but she still loves me. He got in his mother's car and drove away, the car reverberating. I bet he's blown out those speakers and for some reason that made me smile.

I'm staying the night up at Kathryn's because I still can't face staying at Mike's.

I'm not as blind as I once was, God. Gretchen is sixteen, now. I'm a man and she's a young woman. No one will see it as innocent besides the two of us. But God? If it's in me, I can't find it. All I feel is love. Pure.

"What are you praying about?"

"You."

"Creepy."

"I won't tell you about it, then. If it makes you feel creepy."

She puts her arm through mine. "I'm sorry. I don't believe in God, but I'm glad you pray for me. Really."

"You don't believe in God?"

"No. I know you do, but there is no scientific proof for God, Gentry."

I consider this carefully, and dismiss it as crap. "God is as real and present and invisible as love."

She turns to me with fear in her eyes. "Will you always love me? Do you promise to always love me?"

"Gretchen. Come here." I pull her against me, stroke that white-blonde hair. "Always."

She speaks into my shoulder. "What if I did something incredibly stupid? Something that hurt everyone? Would you still love me then?"

"Of course."

"Will you always be on my side?"

"Yes. Always."

"Promise?"

"Promise."

She pulls back and finds my eyes again. "Will you do something important for me?"

"Anything." I will do anything for you, little girl, I will cut my way through the bramble, kill the giant, break the spell, sort the seeds and spin it all into gold.

"Could you go see Tristan's mom?"

"No."

"Will you *please* do it for me?"

"Why?"

"Because I want you to have a family."

I need too much from her. She wants me to have a family like the one that gathered tonight at the restaurant, a real family, not just one I hang on the edges of because I'm alone. I monopolize her, I make her feel guilty when she can't come to the beach and see me. She wants me to have my own. I drain her.

No. I'll do this for no one.

The next day, she shows me the way to Tristan's house.

They live up by Mike. Not as opulent, but nice, this street, this home. "Gentry? Are we going to go up to the door, or are you just going to sit here all day with that terrible look on your face?"

"I'm starving."

"We can eat as soon as we're done with this."

"I need something to eat."

"You ate enough last night to last a week."

"I want to leave."

She sighs. "You promised." I did. And I keep my promises. But I find that I'm physically unable to get out of the Jeep. Gretchen takes off my cap, gets a comb out of her backpack, fixes my hair, finds a band, pulls it back. We sit for a minute. "I love you."

"I love you back." I do this for her, God.

Gretchen knocks. The woman opens the door. "Gretchen, how nice. But Tristan's at practice." She has a soft, lilting accent, Georgia or maybe the Carolinas. She smiles. The hairs on my arms lift. "Hello there." She says it like "they-ah." So beautiful. A beautiful woman. Something in her face is familiar to me. Something . . . I study her, she's not my mother, she has blue eyes, her hair is not my hair, she's not my mother. But I see something. What?

I take off my sunglasses and look hard.

She goes white and grasps the doorframe to steady herself. "Come in." This is not a request, this is a command. We enter, and she leads us to a dining room table. "Sit down." She sits too, and she studies my face with horror and fascination. "Sweet Jesus. I can barely stand to look at you and I can barely stand not to. Explain yourself."

I open my mouth to speak, but my throat closes.

"Mrs. Buchanan, this is Gentry. He's a friend of mine, and he was adopted. He doesn't know anything about his parents, and we thought, maybe Tristan is his brother? Half- brother? Or his cousin? Or something?" Gretchen trails off.

"His *brother*? His *cousin*?" She shakes her red hair and gives me a look of poisonous hatred. "This poor girl, listening to your lies. Just drop this act and tell her the truth."

Gretchen's mouth hangs open. So does mine. "Mrs. Buchanan, he's just . . ."

"I *know* who he is." I want to tell her that she doesn't, she can't know me, but for some reason I know her face. Who is she? "What a coward you are." Her eyes blaze and her voice shakes with anger. "Get out of here. Right now. I want you out of here before my son gets home. Get *out*."

We stand, my chair falls behind me to the floor, and I can't stoop to lift it, I want out of here, and I move through this home that is not my brother's with the woman who is not my mother. Why do I know her face? Is this woman blind? Can't she see it?

I'm something to this boy.

I can finally speak. "I have to be *something* to him."

She studies my face for a long minute. "You finally want that, don't you. After all this time." The scorn in her eyes, the loathing. "You *had* your chance." She shakes her head. "She *warned* me you might do this. You were such a child yourself. She was sure of this once you grew up."

What's she saying? I don't know what she means, I feel sick.

Her eyes glow with how much she hates me. "She always said, when he grows up, he'll come looking. Well it took you ten years, but you got here and you didn't even look hard enough to *find* him. And now you're back and you think you can just waltz in here with this poor little girl and ask for a place in his life, pretending to be his uncle or something, his cousin, *lying* about who you are . . ."

Gretchen shouts, "What are you *talking* about?"

"She always *said* he would change his mind!" She shakes her head, raging, pushing me, shoving at me. "It's too *late*. He's *mine*. He's *all I have*."

She's so close I can smell the flowering of her hair.

I put my hand on the back of her neck. Her fists hit my chest but I twine my hand in her dark red hair and pull her to me, her face full of anger and disbelief and the smell of her hair, the vine that blooms at night, and both hands are in it, now, my hands, searching for the pins.

Oh. Come here.

I bury my face in those sunset curls.

⁓

Why am I on the floor?

"Gentry? Are you okay?" Gretchen's face is over me, her hair hangs down into my face. I was having the strangest dream about Becca.

This dream in which everything finally made sense.

"Gentry, wake up. I think you fainted. Can you talk?"

"Where am I?"

"At Tristan's house."

Dear God.

∽

"Can you hear me, son?"

"Hey, Jack."

"Gentry, I'm going to give you a shot, okay? And it'll help you. Let's get you fixed up here, just a pinch, and then hold this on there."

Ouch. I don't like shots. But this one helps immediately. I can get off the floor, now. And Jack and Gretchen help me to the couch, and I sit. I feel better. And then I stand, where is she, did she say that, where is she . . .

"Gentry, get back here! Sit down or you'll faint again!"

She's in the kitchen making coffee. She's pale, sick, she needs one of these shots, because I feel so much better, I feel wonderful, now. So wonderful that I can roar. "DO YOU KNOW WHO I AM?"

She nods.

"WHAT I AM?"

She nods.

"Say it now. Tell me who I am."

"You're his father."

God oh God oh God.

∽

They both help me up from the floor this time. I sit at the kitchen table and shiver, and Gretchen sits next to me, and I drink a cup of coffee because Jack says maybe the shot wasn't such a great idea. I feel sick, so sick, and I'm trying to tell this woman, I never knew, I never ever knew, she never told me, I never knew, if I would have known, it would have been so different, does she understand this?

And she has tears down her face because she wouldn't have had it any other way, because she loves her son and she's glad that I never knew. He's all she has, please, she says, he's all I have. I see, but please, I never knew.

"I thought you knew."

"I never knew."

She's Becca's aunt. "She said you were too young, she said she talked about getting married and you disappeared."

"I NEVER KNEW SHE WAS PREGNANT!" This shot makes me sick. I'm saying this wrong. "Please. I was sixteen. She was almost twenty. And I didn't want her to know, I mean, I was ashamed, I . . ." Oh God, what? What can I say? "I couldn't tell her what kind of a person I was."

"What kind of a person *are* you?" She seems horrified by what kind of a person might be the father of her son, what snakes and toads I might have in me. I have to explain this to her somehow. I was a good kid. I was an altar boy, a straight-A student, I played soccer and sang in the choir and wrote letters to my uncle. I was a good kid. But before that, I didn't want her to know about any of that. "I was sixteen, sixteen, doesn't anyone understand that?"

"You were eighteen."

"No. I was sixteen."

"You were eighteen when you signed the adoption papers."

"I never signed any adoption papers."

"You most certainly did. Daniel brought the papers back to us after you signed them. They were signed with your full name and notarized."

Daniel? Daniel is the only person who knew my name. "This can't be legal."

"Of course it's legal, are you trying to say that my son . . ."

Jack intervenes. "You move back, Toni. Give him some air or he'll faint again." She sits down. Jack's voice is heavy with concern. "Gentry, I know it's hard, but think about what you say. Everything you say right now is extremely important. Be careful."

Mrs. Buchanan sobs.

Oh, God. Dear, sweet God. "Please get me out of here."

And they get me out of there.

∽

Mike opens the door himself and sees my face. "What the hell?"

Jack says in an unfamiliar and doctorly voice, "He's going into shock. He needs a hot bath and something to eat. You take care of him. I'm taking Gretchen home."

And I see it, then, the grand second story of the Mumford home. It's magnificent. Mike almost carries me through the honeymoon suite of his room into a palatial bathroom. This bathroom cost more than the entirety of my awful little Okie house, I know it. Mike runs a huge, deep, hot bath and turns on the whirlpool. He pulls off my boots because my hands are shaking too hard, and I get the rest off and get in. He sits down on the toilet. "Will you live?"

"I'll live."

I have a son.

Eve brings me a sandwich and some coffee. She comes right in and plunks down the dishes on the rim of the tub and says "Enjoy!" like a waitress. I should care, but I don't. I don't even care if Eve smiles at me with those teeth of hers, just so long as she doesn't take her husband away right now, don't leave me alone, Mike. Please.

I gulp down the coffee and eat the sandwich. "Hey Mike? Tell Eve this was a good sandwich, okay?"

"Great."

"It was a perfect sandwich."

"Great. I'll tell her it was perfect."

"That might be the best sandwich I ever ate."

"Did you want another sandwich?"

"Please." He rises. "Don't leave, Mike." He sits.

"GRAHAM!" Graham is huge, hulking, sullen. "Tell your mother to make Gentry another sandwich." He lurks out the door.

I have a son, a beautiful son, far finer than this lummox of a boy. I have a son who looks just like me. "Mike? I have to go." Joy does that to me. Or maybe it was the coffee.

"You're not going anywhere just now."

"No, I mean I have to go to the bathroom."

"Pee in the water."

"That's filthy."

"Gentry, you're ridiculous."

"Hey, the shower, no problem. But not a bathtub." Not one I'm in, at least. "Please?"

"Well, do you need me to hold your dick for you?"

"No, but I need you to hurry." And he moves, and I get out, but Dear God I'm still so cold. I get back into the tub. I'm shivering again, what was in that shot Jack gave me?

Mike sits back down. He looks crushed. "You could require help holding that thing."

That thing? Oh, he's talking about my stupid penis. "Hey Mike? I'll trade you for this bathtub."

"Sorry. The tub's built in."

"This is too."

He laughs and adjusts the whirlpool. There must be some special thing about this tub that keeps the water so hot.

"Hey Mike? I have a son. I just found out. I never knew about him."

"You mean Tristan." Mike looks at me with something in his face that it almost hurts to see. "I've always known that kid. I hadn't really looked at him for a couple of years. But when I saw him again last year, I knew he had something to do with you."

"You knew he was mine?"

"Well, no. Not at first. But look at him. It's pretty clear if you just look at him." He shakes his head. "I need to go get something."

"Don't leave me alone."

"I'll be right back."

"Please, Mike."

Graham enters with the sandwich. "Stay with him a minute." Graham plunks my sandwich down on the edge of the tub, enthrones himself on the toilet. I wonder if he touched that sandwich. I don't care. I eat it anyway. This one is even better than the first.

He narrows his eyes at me. "Why are you in here, anyhow?"

"I was cold."

He smiles, revealing extensive braces and a cold sore on the corner of his mouth. "I remember you. You look like someone I hate."

He said that before.

He was talking about my son.

No, not going to pass out again.

Mike returns and he's got the phone. "There's no need to tow it. I'll have Graham walk over in a minute and get it. Calm down, Antoinette. It'll be gone when the kids get home." He picks up my jeans and finds my keys, holds them out to his son. "Graham, go over to Tristan's and drive Gentry's Jeep over here. And take this plate to your mom." Graham leaves, and Mike reinstalls himself on the toilet. "I'm saying sorry in advance, because Graham's a piss-poor driver. I'd have sent Spence but he's at practice with Tristan and she wants it out of there."

"That's fine. Jeeps were made for bad drivers."

That makes him laugh. He has a lighter in his hand. That lighter seems kind of interesting, I'd like to see it, but I don't want to get it wet.

"Hey Mike? Does Graham play sports?"

"Wrestling. He's good, too. He should go out for football, but Eve will never let him play it." Mike hands me something, all trimmed and lit and ready to puff.

"I don't smoke."

"I don't care. You're a daddy today, and the rules say you have to have a cigar." He demonstrates the proper technique, the system, and I study, and I mimic. I think I have it figured out.

We smoke for a minute. "Can this be enough?" He laughs. Thank you, Mike, for giving me this fine and phallic and appropriate symbol of potency and virility, but could you take this symbol away, and maybe open the window why don't you.

Thank you.

I love this bathtub. I sink down below the water so Mike won't see me while I pray.

God, I don't understand You. My heart will crack with what You showed me today. It will crack with joy.

This is to give thanks. Amen.

I feel a hand on my shoulder, pulling me up.

"Come up for air, Gentry. You scared me."

❦

"Mike?" I whisper, my hand on his shoulder.

"Watzit?" He was asleep, as I thought he might be at three AM, but I'm not and I need help. "What the hell is it?" He turns on the light, sees my face. Eve has concave cheeks and round eyes, but her teeth or their absence don't concern me.

"I need to hit something."

He rises from the bed and leads me down into the basement. I knew Mike would have something down here for me. Maybe some wives hanging on hooks, or a son even worse than Graham. But no, he has a kick bag. "You might need a lawyer, you know."

"Can I hit a lawyer?"

"No."

"Well, this is all I need, then. Thank you, Mike. Good night."

"Good night." And he returns upstairs.

I've been on the phone in his guest room. The walls here are thick. My conversation didn't carry. I called and accused and swore and vowed never, ever to forgive. I said words I wasn't even sure I knew how to say. Daniel pleaded for some understanding and compassion for Becca, for how it was for her, for what she thought I consented to.

What he told her I *wanted*.

I was told the most ridiculous lie, that it was done to preserve my future, to safeguard a life that looked so bright at age seventeen, when this was done to me and my newborn son, my newborn son I never got to see, never got to hold, never got to smell, never got to name because I would not have named him Tristan. And I was as honest as I could stand to be about how lonely my life has been. So thanks very much for the favor, but I would take a son any day.

He wouldn't let me talk to her. I heard her crying. He at least admitted it, he took responsibility. I listened while he told her that I never knew, that he'd forged my name on those papers and notarized them. I heard him say it, and I heard her wail.

I said, you let me talk to her. But he wouldn't.

I told him to remind her of everything we said and we swore to each other and we did together. How much we loved each other. I said, tell her I still love her. I listened while he did.

It's not enough.

I'll hit this until it breaks, or until I do. Whichever comes first.

༄

Gretchen eyes me at breakfast. I vacillate between a rage so intense it leaves me sweating, and blinding waves of euphoria. "What did you do to your hands?"

I was down there in the basement swearing, spit and tears and snot flying out of me. I did everything to that bag except throw it down and rape it. Finally I hit it so hard that it swung away and swung back so hard that it knocked me flat. I lay on my back in that dark basement and made a sound I'd never heard before. It was the sound of fifteen years missed with him, and with her.

"I'm fine, Gretchen. Just fine."

We're eating breakfast in a breakfast room. I have seen the dining room. I wonder if, somewhere in this vast home, there is a lunch room. A snack room. I wonder if Mike has a special room just to sit in and feel successful.

Eve's not smiling this morning. I need to get back to the dentist. I always think
about the dentist around Eve. "Do you need some hot syrup for your waffles,
Gentry?"

Oh, not just syrup, but hot syrup. Somehow I manage to keep an appetite.
"Um, no thanks, Eve, but some jam if you have it?"

She brings me eight varieties. But what are these? Quince Conserve and Black
Currant All Fruit Spread and Orange Marmalade and Marionberry Jam and Kiwi
Mango Chutney and Apricot Passion Fruit Preserves, even a jar of Three Alarm
Hot House Jalapeño Jelly. There's no grape jelly in here, of course. No strawberry
jam, either. Seedless Oregon Blackberry, then.

Spencer joins us and addresses Gretchen. "Hi, Stupid."

"Hi, Ugly."

He nods to me. "Good morning, Mr. Gentry."

"If you call him Mister, he gets mad."

"Sorry, Sir."

Gretchen rolls her eyes. "Sir is such an improvement over Mister."

"Sue me." They laugh.

He's a nice kid. He and Gretchen begin to discuss horses. Why have I never
seen how alike these two are? Because I've only seen Spencer twice, I think. She's
Kathryn and Mike's daughter, both, I can stand to see that now. But whose child
is Graham, I'd like to know?

He lumbers into view. He says nothing and his presence is not acknowledged.
But he smiles at me. "You're still here." Please, I was hungry and I need to eat, God.
His braces, I had those for six weeks, I know how difficult it is, but it doesn't look
like he even tries to clean them.

If I just look at my own plate, I can eat this breakfast.

Graham puts peanut butter on his waffles.

I take my coffee and plate into the kitchen. "Hey Eve? May I eat in here?"

"Oh, of course." I'll visit with Eve, then. I've never visited with Eve but it looks
like the plan this morning. I realize that she's a striking woman. She's not much
older than me. But the strange thing is, I find not one thing about her attractive.
And I'd put money on it that not one thing about me is attractive to her.

She's only having coffee. She watches me put away my waffles, keeps my coffee cup full. Gives me seconds. "Thank you. These are great."

"I'm glad you can eat them." She looks grim.

"I'm sorry I woke you up last night."

"Oh, that's fine. I never sleep very well anyway."

"Me neither. I have had, um, whole years where I hardly slept." I don't volunteer personal information very often, but I feel compelled to offer something.

"When I was first expecting Graham, I was up all night worrying, and then I fell asleep at my desk. Out like a light. Michael understood, though."

Well, I'd hope he would. "You still worked for him after you got married?"

"No. This was before we were married." She smiles, shrugs. "His divorce took forever. I was pregnant with Spencer before we finally got married." She has such miserable eyes. "Is Tristan really your son?"

"Yes." And no matter about my rage and her misery, I smile and beam with joy. Because he is, even if I never get to tell him, he's my beautiful, perfect son.

And Eve wipes at a tear. "He went to preschool with Graham, you know. But it was always him and Spencer who were friends. Spencer goes over there, but Tristan never comes over here. Remember the first time you came here and dropped off the girls? I said something to Michael then. I said, you know, he reminds me of Tristan Buchanan. Michael just rolled his eyes. He was only ten back then, so it was hard for Michael to see." She's trying so hard not to cry. "But then we saw him at a wrestling match. He came there to meet Gretchen. And he didn't look like you, then. He *was* you." Her face is full of compassion and regret. "I wish I'd said something to you way back then. I don't know what I would have said, it would have sounded so stupid, there's a boy who looks like you? But I wish I had."

My heart will break over what I missed.

"He's always been such a sweet boy, Gentry. The sweetest boy in the neighborhood."

"You have some good boys, Eve." She nods. "Spencer seems like a nice kid, a really nice kid. He and Gretchen are a lot alike, don't you think? And Graham, he seems . . ." Oh, what can I say here. Her misery over her other son is palpable, and my reaction to him shames me. I think of Graham's piggy little eyes staring through the crack in the door all those years ago and it still makes me recoil. I haven't felt so much distaste for a kid since Alex Fournier. "Eve? Kids change so much. Well, I guess, um, it's just what, um . . ." God, help here. Words, all right? "What was your favorite fairytale?"

"Cinderella."

"Mine was the Ugly Duckling."

She smiles at me. Those teeth. But she understands what I was trying to say. And though that's probably not a swan in the making, he might be something good someday. I hope so. "Oh!" She jumps a little, smiles. "I realized I have some preschool stuff you could look at."

"Preschool?"

"Group pictures and videos."

My heart will burst open.

I look at group preschool photos. He is tiny in them. Tiny, round cheeks, brown eyes and a big smile. She hands me a stack of preschool newsletters. "One of the moms always did a question of the month. His answers will be in there." His favorite color was green. For his next birthday, he wanted a little brother. He didn't have any pets, but he wanted a wiener dog because they're funny. If he couldn't have a wiener dog, then he wanted a little brother. For Halloween, he wanted to dress up like a pirate. For Mother's Day, he was giving his mom a little brother. When he grew up, he was going to be a soccer player. His most favorite thing was soccer. His least favorite thing was a nap. For Father's day, he was giving his father a little brother.

Eve finds a videotape. "We have to go into the blue guest room. It's the only VCR left in the house." She takes me upstairs to the room where I slept, and we sit side-by-side on the end of the bed and watch a Christmas program where he wears a construction paper hat with bells on it. He sings, shakes the hat so the bells ring. He sings loudly enough that I can hear him. I would give away everything I've ever owned if I could have heard him speak before his voice changed.

I search every frame for my perfect son. Eating a cupcake. Licking his fingers. Throwing the paper at Graham. Laughing. His mother and dad by his side. God, these were good people. Thank You.

"He was young for this class. His birthday's in September. I think that's why he was so little. Graham and Spence were always so tall."

"Like their dad." She smiles, and this may be the first smile I've seen from her that doesn't scare me.

I don't know why I lied to Eve. I hated that Ugly Duckling tale. I know she read it to me all the time, it must have been one of her favorites, but it hurt me to hear it. I preferred the blood, and the witches, captivity, like Fundevogel. Because it doesn't work like that. You don't spend your life at the edge of the pond and present yourself to die and then get called in to join the race of the chosen. You might try it, the stretch of the neck, the thunder of the wings. But you never belong. The truth of that tale is the kitchen, starvation, self-hatred. Your place is at the edge of the pond. Your place is not with the flock.

When they rise, you don't go with them.

I need to remember this.

~

"Mel?"

"Gentry! How are you, my boy?"

"Never better. Never, in my life. Mel, never have I been better. I'm the best I've ever been."

"Is that so?" He's laughing.

"Do you remember Becca?" Please remember, Mel, the one I made love to in her husband's bed, the one I tried to carry off, that one? "Becca in Georgia."

"She was your first love, if I remember correctly. And, of course, you saw her more recently."

"Yes. I made her pregnant, Mel."

He sounds alarmed. "You did?"

"No. I mean yes, but in college. Remember I said I met a boy who looked like me? That's him. His name is Tristan."

"Ah. I see."

"Do you understand what I just said?"

"You are telling me that you are a father, Gentry." His voice breaks. "Oh, my boy. Congratulations. Congratulations, my boy."

"Thank you."

"Is he Catholic?"

"Episcopalian."

"Well. That will do."

"Mel? You'll see this when you meet him, well, I hope you get to meet him, but he looks just like me, but he's taller than I was at fifteen."

"And do you see, now, my boy, how beautiful you are?"

"Yes." I see it. I finally see it.

∽

During lab, I put Zeb in charge. This is a guarantee of chaos.

I walk into Lorrie's classroom. He's browbeating his students over a pop quiz that everyone flunked. They are probably grateful for the interruption. I've tried to talk Lorrie out of this sneak attack approach to testing, but he believes in stealth, in terror, in the exposure of the soft underbelly of the academically weak. "May I see you in the hall for a minute, Coach Gilroy?"

He glares around. "Not one word when I'm out there, see. I mean it." I have a feeling they'll tie their clothes together and escape out a window if I take too much time. "This better be important, because I was kicking ass in there, and I hate to interrupt an ass-kicking."

"What's the educational value of intimidation, Lorrie?"

"Run your classroom like a damn zoo if you want to, but shut the hell up about mine. What the hell do you want?" Little beads of sweat rise up on his forehead, and he gets too close. I can smell his Old Spice. "Look, did you just haul me out here to insult my teaching?"

"No. I came out here to give you this." I stick the cigar in his mouth.

He takes it out and inspects it. "This is a nice one. But in case you hadn't noticed, Vicki popped six weeks ago."

"Say congratulations."

"Congratulations. What the hell? Did you get laid?"

"No. I found out yesterday that I have a fifteen-year-old son."

He puts a hand on each of my shoulders, his eyes drilling into mine. "Do not bullshit me."

"I'm not."

"You have a son?"

"I do."

"No shit, Gentry?"

"No shit." Don't kill me, Lorrie, don't crush me, My Dear God, this man will kill me, Please . . . "Lorrie, I can't breathe."

He lets go.

He stands in the hall and shouts, "GODDAMN" five or six times, then grabs a rough-looking kid and pats him down, relieves him of a lighter. The kid is afraid, because it's not too often that the teachers stand in the halls, smoking and swearing. The kids do it all the time, and maybe he's afraid of the apocalypse, now, when we join in.

I tell what I can, the bare bones of the story, and Lorrie punctuates the tale with a great many "Goddamns," and then we remember our classes and we agree to talk more at lunch. Lorrie extinguishes his cigar. "I'll finish this up with a good shot of scotch." He grimaces. "Sorry." It smells like cigar smoke all through the hall. On the way back to my room, I think of Lorrie's cowering, terrified students.

Those poor kids.

I pull the fire alarm.

SPRING

Gentry

Toni called me. "For Becca's sake, I'll have a conversation with you." She wanted to meet me for coffee at Papa Haydn's. I was surprised that she wanted to meet me at a place frequented by people she might know.

Kathryn ironed everything. "Let me do something for you for once." I stood by the ironing board in my shorts and socks and watched her iron, listened to the water slosh, smelled the steam. I closed my eyes and waited.

"Wake up," Kathryn whispered. I opened my eyes to see her holding out my shirt.

While I dressed, Jack cleaned up my boots. He did something with lit matches. "Learned this in the military." When he was finished, I could see my face in the toes.

I was ready too early. I stood by the door so I didn't get wrinkled. I could see my reflection in my boots. Gretchen came up, hugged me from behind. "You look so nice." She brushed my hair.

I felt like I was four years old, all ready for church. I felt like my first day of high school, my stomach in my throat. I felt like an idiot because none of these preparations would make any difference at all.

I stood in the entry of Kathryn's beautiful home and remembered when Becca took me back to Georgia.

⌒

I'd already been to Daniel's for Thanksgiving, so I had an idea what I was in for. But she wanted me to go, so I went. I would have done anything for her.

She had a car. I drove. I enjoyed the drive, especially when she let me put my hand up her skirt. She was anxious, and I enjoyed relaxing her.

It was a nice home, but it wasn't like the Shaws'. It wasn't a cathedral, it was a farmhouse. An enormous farmhouse with two stories, both with continuous verandas that wrapped the house on all four sides. The barn, that was the cathedral.

She pulled me to the front door, where everyone was waiting to meet me. I smiled and nodded and shook everyone's hand with my hand full of her, oh, what an idiot I was. Her grandparents were there, her grandfather suspicious and restrained, her grandmother a model of gracious welcome. Her mother was as tall and as beautiful as Becca. "My *goodness*. No one explained to me that my daughter was bringing home a work of *art*."

"*Mother.*"

I blushed. Her dad invited me to play golf. I couldn't explain to him that I didn't know how to play golf because I wasn't allowed to hit anything with sticks in high school, so I just nodded.

Everyone was kind to me. No one mistook me for domestic help. Daniel had shared a story about that with everyone in the fall, and I'm sure Becca's mother rounded up the staff and let them know that Becca was bringing home a ragged northern charity case and not to make him wax the floors or anything.

I had to bunk with her younger brother. Literally. I got the bottom bunk. He showed me to his room without a word. Everyone called him Young Derry. He turned out to be my senior by three months, but I was lying about my age so no one knew that.

I washed up for dinner and Becca came in, fussed with my hair. "Just try to keep it out of your face." I wore my church clothes, khakis and a white shirt. She put her dad's tie on me and asked Young Derry for a jacket. He loaned me one he'd outgrown. I walked down with Becca, and her mother looked at her son's jacket, looked at me. "I swear, young man, you're almost more beautiful than my daughter."

"*Mother.*"

I blushed again. We sat. We said grace and began to eat. I had good manners. The Jesuits don't hit you anymore if you don't, but they might as well, for all the shame they pile on. I behaved. I wanted to get through the meal without wolfing my food or answering any questions. And then I wanted to take off the stupid navy sport coat, because I had worn one every single day of high school and had sworn to never put on another. And then I hoped Becca and I could take a drive and I could bury myself in her, because I was as anxious as I'd ever been and I wanted to feel better.

The food was good. They poured wine, a glass for me because everyone was pretending that I was a grownup. I didn't drink wine and I was certain that I'd throw myself under a train if these people saw me drunk. I pushed my hair out of my face.

I never thought much about how I looked, except when people like Becca's mother looked at me. And she kept looking at me. "Where did you graduate from school, Gentry?" I opened my mouth, but nothing came out. Becca told them all where I went to school. The table sniffed some general approval.

Her dad, another Derry, spoke up. "I went there myself, actually. Becca's uncle and her grandfather went there too, you know. We wanted Young Derry to go there, but he chose Choate."

Young Derry hunched over his plate in a way the Jesuits never would have tolerated.

Her grandmother smiled at me, encouraging. "I think Derry Senior's younger brother knew a Gentry when he was there. That would have been the mid-sixties. Dash said he was a very bright boy. Could he be a relative?"

Everyone waited. And waited.

Finally Becca said it for me. "He doesn't know."

Her grandmother frowned. "Doesn't know? Well, Gentry, where are your people from?"

Becca spoke so softly. "His uncle is his only family."

There was the tinkle of silver on plates, the quiet sounds of food being eaten in the most genteel and restrained of fashions. Everyone ate. Everyone but me. I stared at my plate until a dark hand reached for it. I looked up into the eyes of a kind-faced woman who politely let her eyes pass over my face as she cleared my plate. But there must have been something in my eyes, some plea. She let her eyes skate back and gave me a barely perceptible smile that said, hang on, young man, you're doing fine and this meal is almost over. Just hang on. I smiled back. And I looked back at the table. All eyes were watching me supplicate the help. Becca smiled at me. Her smile was like her mother's.

Becca. Let's go away. Away from here.

Somehow, I lived through that week of polite dinners in her brother's jacket, that week when she showed me her town, her friends, her life in which I did not belong. Every night, we met on the veranda and went somewhere we could pretend it didn't matter. The pond, the barn, the base of a huge tree with branches that hung down to make a cave. We came together and it was violent and she cried. And though I hated to do it, I cried too, because everything about that week showed me how impossible it was.

We loved each other. But we always had to go back. She would go to her room.

I would lie in the bottom bunk listening to Young Derry talk in his sleep. I prayed, prayed to God that I would never be exposed, but I already was. We came back to our expensive private college that I could only attend with extensive financial aid, and I hid from Becca until summer.

But now, knowing what I know, I remember what happened as we left the farm, something I never understood. The leave-taking took forever because there were so many of them. I nodded, shook hands, nodded, my way of saying good-bye when my voice wasn't working. Her father and grandfather wished me well with open, hearty relief. Her grandmother wouldn't meet my eyes. I stopped in front of her mother to nod my head, and was brought up short by the hatred in her eyes.

"Young man," she hissed. "I should slap you across the face."

I thought she was insane. She wasn't insane, she was angry. They all knew she was pregnant and they thought I did, too. They brought me to that beautiful farm and offered me the opportunity to do right by their intelligent, accomplished daughter. And all of them, even Becca, thought I understood this. Why else would her mother want to slap me? No wonder they all hated me.

Oh, well. That lady who served dinner liked me, I think.

⌒

"Gentry? You don't want to be late."

Kathryn is gentle with me these days. She broke me once, and I appreciate the care. "Are you nervous?" I nod because my throat has closed, again, and speech is impossible. And I need my powers of speech to say the right thing. She straightens my collar. I buttoned my shirt correctly, I do it wrong sometimes and don't discover it until I take it off, but I was careful with this freshly ironed shirt. "You look very nice."

I might. I might not. The truth is that how I look doesn't matter. I could get dressed in Mike's closet, drive up in his car, and that would have nothing to do with how this all comes out. The passage of an iron over my clothes, a rag over my boots and a brush over my hair has changed nothing. This is not about how I look. This is about who I am. What happened in the past with my son happened because of who I am. What happens in the future, good or bad, will happen because of who I am.

And I know who I am.

I am Tristan's father.

She brought her lawyer.

He has a predatory smile and his clothes look like Mike's. He gives me a card. This lawyer's name is Lance Barnaby.

I think I'm in trouble.

We begin nicely enough. Antoinette introduces me by my first name.

"Please call me Gentry."

"Call me Lance."

"And everyone calls me Toni."

How chummy. Excuse me, but I've been blindsided. Mike warned me, Mike tried to warn me, when will I learn that Mike knows everything?

Lance smiles his sharky smile at me. "You go by your last name? Is that a coach thing?"

"No. It's a stupid first name thing."

He laughs, oh, put those teeth away, why don't you.

We order coffee. Gretchen felt that I needed to order something besides my usual "just coffee." She coached me. "I'll have a short double shot Americano. Please."

"Room for cream?"

"No thanks."

Lance orders a cappuccino, more foam than milk, one sugar. Toni asks for a decaf low-fat hazelnut mocha latte. That's enough to make me gag.

Don't get weird, just hang on.

"So Gentry. Where do you live, again?" I'm specific out of nervousness. I practically give him directions. He seems a little puzzled so I clarify. "I just stay there. It belongs to friends." Lance, don't worry, your initial economic assessment was correct. I don't own the place, I'm every bit the nothing you assumed I was the moment I walked in here.

Lance smiles at me. "How old are you?"

"Thirty-two. How old are you?"

He's a little taken aback. "Thirty-seven."

I consider asking Toni how old she is.

"Well, we all know why we're here." Lance produces some papers. "We have copies of the adoption papers right here. And you're claiming you never signed this?"

"My signature is not on there, and neither is my uncle's. And I was only seventeen. That adoption is not legal."

"That's what you say, Gentry."

"Pardon?"

He smiles. Stop smiling, Lance. "Well, Gentry, let me propose another scenario for you. Let's say, Gentry, that we have a scared, seventeen-year-old Catholic boy, and a pregnant young woman he doesn't want to marry. The boy begs his older friend, who happens to be a notary public, to let him be eighteen on some adoption papers so that his uncle, the Catholic priest, never has to know what the boy did. And because his friend cares about him, and because he cares about the girl involved, the older friend helps him."

"If I wanted to do that, I would have signed the papers myself. Here's my driver's license. You can see the signatures don't match. And you can see when I was born. Do the math, Lance."

He glances at it, pushes it back. "That's kind of tricky, Gentry, how you do the initials." And here he goes with the smiling again. "Signatures change. But if it's a forgery, that shouldn't be too hard for you to prove. Get a lawyer. Take us to court. Fight. You might get custody if the trouble you had in Detroit doesn't come up." He smiles. "But I think it might."

Does he think that's a threat? "I was cleared in that."

"Even so, these things take time, you know. If he doesn't turn eighteen before the courts have reviewed everything, you might get custody of him. And then he'll lose the educational trust that his grandparents set up for him when he was adopted."

Solomon. I taste metal. "I never asked for custody. I never, ever talked about anything like that. I just want to be able to see him." God, You give me some words, right now, Please, Amen. "If I were able to see him, you have my promise that I would respect Becca's privacy, I would never tell him a thing about her. If I could just see him."

Toni finally speaks. "Is it money you're after?"

What's *wrong* with these people?

"I want a chance to *know* my *son*."

She opens her mouth, but Lance puts a hand on her clenched fist. "There's another issue, Gentry, besides the money. Do you know Tristan? Have you ever stopped to ask yourself how he would feel about having someone like you as a father?"

"Someone like me? What do you mean by that?"

"Well, take a look at this." Lance hands me a sheaf of papers in a blue folder. I open it. "What is this?"

He smiles that shark smile. "A restraining order." He shuts his case with an authoritative snap. I sit there with my papers.

And then the coffee arrives. The waitress is flustered. "Are you all leaving? I'm sorry that took so long, the barista is having a, well, I'm sorry. Do you want anything else?"

"Just the check. Thank you."

She looks at me from under her lashes, almost shyly. "Gentry? I guess you don't remember me. I'm a friend of the Mumfords."

Ah, I remember her. "Your name is Kirsten, right?"

"Yes! I thought I saw you up at Michael's, actually, but then I thought, no, that couldn't be Gentry. But I asked my mom and she said that you live at the house at the coast now? She said you're, like, one of the family."

"Something like that."

She gives me a winning smile. "Well, when you see Marci, tell her I said hi. And you'll come in here and see me when you're in town, won't you?"

"Of course." I admire Kirsten as she walks away. She can't be more than twenty-two. I will definitely not be coming in here to see her. Forget it.

Lance sets his coffee down. "Ah, Gentry? You know Michael Mumford?" His face looks sick. I remember this look from grade school. The ironworkers' kids. We'd be getting ready to fight, and one would warn my opponent away from hitting me because the supervisor, the man who told their dads what to do all day, that man was my dad. Lance has that same sick look.

"Yes, Lance. I know Mike Mumford."

Toni explains, "Tristan goes out with Michael Mumford's daughter. Gentry is a friend of theirs."

"Ah, well." He smiles with visible effort. "I wish you'd told me that, Toni. Michael handles some things for the practice."

"He's good at that. Handling things." I think, and I remember the name of the lawyer Mike had helping me in Oklahoma. "He had a friend help me." I tell Lance the name and he visibly recoils. "I guess I should call him and get the name of someone up here to help me with all this mess. So you can expect a call. Here. This is for my coffee, and you can keep this." I put a five on top of the restraining order and push it back over to him.

Lance has finally stopped smiling.

⤳

Mike opens the door and holds up a hand. He wants me to wait while he finishes a cell phone call, but I have to talk to him right now. "I'd expect no less from you. No, I appreciate this. It will absolutely go no further. I understand." He's talking about something important, I can tell. "All right. Then it's taken care of? Because I'll make this clear right now, this had better be taken care of and taken care of immediately." He listens, nods, says "I'm counting on you," and shuts the phone without saying good-bye to whoever it is.

"Mike, I need some help. I . . ."

He steps out on the flagstone steps of his magnificent home and shuts the castle door behind him. "Listen, I did a little checking. I hope you don't mind. The thing is, that's an open adoption, Gentry."

"What's that?"

"An adoption that allows for visitations from the birth parents. And your name is on the original birth certificate."

"What does that mean?"

"It means you have the legal right to see your son according to an adoption agreement you supposedly signed. It means if they dispute those terms, you can dispute the adoption. They don't have a leg to stand on, and they're trying to intimidate you with that bullshit restraining order, which will be lifted on Monday. Don't let them do it, Gentry. The only person who can tell you to go away is Tristan."

I hug Mike, and then run back to the Jeep. I drive to Kathryn's. I hug her, and she hugs me back. I hug Gretchen, and she starts to cry. I even hug Jack a little, and he claps me on the shoulders.

And now I have to figure this out.

⤳

God, I was nervous when I made my first confession. I was nervous when I took my first communion. I was nervous when Becca took me home to meet her family. I was nervous when I stood up in front of a classroom of closed young faces for the first time.

I have never, ever been this nervous.

Gretchen said she would come along. I said no, for once. I don't want her here if he tells me to go away. Because he could do that, God.

Please, God. Not that.

We arranged to meet at Camp 18. I like to drive over here for biscuits and gravy with Lorrie, because Lorrie will explain the old logging machinery to me. I'm here early. The waitress brings me cup after cup of coffee. My anxious face alarms her. "Do you want to switch to decaf?"

"I think I'd better."

He's late, his mother lets him drive by himself, never mind it that Mel taught me to drive when I was twelve he still shouldn't drive here by himself he's not sixteen and he's late and he probably had an accident on the way and he died and it's my fault because he never would have driven here in this stupid weather if not for me Oh God I've killed my son because I'm a selfish man Forgive me Amen.

"Hi."

"Hey." I stand, we shake hands. We sit. The waitress comes, and she regards my son with admiration. "Are you boys ready to order?"

What a great smile he has, this boy. "Ma'am? I think I just want a Coke right now."

"Of course, honey. Whatever you want." And she smiles at me. "More coffee?"

"Please." Why did I not rehearse this? "How, um, was the drive?"

"Icy. Crummy."

"I'm sorry."

He shrugs a little. "The weather's not your fault, Mr. Gentry." We sit for a minute. "Could you please tell me why I'm here?"

It would be too much, I see, for Toni to tell him. She won't do anything to make this easier for me. "Do you have any idea why you're here?"

"Like, on the planet? Gretchen says we're here to propagate the species but I'd like to believe there's a little more to it than that." He takes a deep breath. "It's weird, Mr. Gentry."

"Just Gentry."

"Okay. Gentry. I found out yesterday that I was adopted. I never knew that, I never knew I was adopted. This is big news." He's trying to smile, but it's not easy for him. "And now I have to come here and meet you because there's more to it. And I'm so afraid you're going to say you're my father."

"I am your father."

He mumbles, "A Star Wars moment."

I don't know what that means.

"I knew it. I saw you the first time and I thought, whoa, is he a secret kid one of my parents had before they were married? I thought you were my brother." The waitress brings his Coke. He smiles, nods, but his face is white. "Look, I'm sure you're a great guy. Gretchen says such incredible stuff about you. But I had a father, you know? And he was great to me."

"I'm glad to hear that." I stumble up, reach for my wallet. "I'm sorry. I, um . . ."

He stands, puts his hand on my arm. "That's not what I meant. Don't go yet. Gentry, just don't leave yet." His pressure on my arm is strong. "Just sit down, okay? Just give me one minute, okay? Just one minute."

His hand is on me, and it's my hand. "You can have as many minutes as you want."

"Okay." And we sit. And I wait. "How old are you, anyway?"

"Thirty-two."

He does the math. "Wow. Seventeen when I was born? That's young. I guess people even younger than that have babies, though." He clears his throat. "So Gretchen says you teach high school? What subject?"

"Computer science and English. And you play soccer?"

"Yeah, and basketball. My parents put me in sports pretty early. My father coached all the peewee teams until he figured out what I was good at, because he knew I had to be good at something." He smiles. "He decided I was good at soccer and basketball. Soccer because I was fast and a showoff, and basketball even though I was such a shrimp, because . . ."

"You had long arms and big hands."

"Yeah! Did people say that to you?" I nod. "Didn't that make you feel like a gorilla?" He says in a voice, obviously his dad's, "You better grow into that reach, or you'll end up walking on your hands, Tristan." He scratches his head. "Did you run track?"

"Yes. Sprints, mostly. I wasn't much of a long jumper, though. No hurdles, either. I didn't grow until late. You're already as tall as me."

"Well, I was short until I was twelve. I always wanted to be as tall as my father. He never saw me shoot up. I mean, he died when I was seven." He looks away.

We work on those drinks.

"Tristan? He was always good to you?"

He frowns and smiles. "Oh yeah. He was great. He was, you know, right there."

He was there. Well, I would have been there, I swear. But I don't say this, I say nothing. When he died, Tristan, I want to say, I was living in Detroit. I got my master's when you were four, I think. I think, but I can only guess.

I don't even know the day my son was born.

I wish I could make a time line, and track every moment in his life and mine on it, where we were, what we were doing, running on parallel lines until that moment at the sports facility, when Gretchen performed her miraculous geometry and made us intersect.

"Are you okay?"

"I'm fine. Just fine."

"I guess what I want to say is that I only had him for seven years, but he did a great job. Not like some of my friends' dads. He wasn't just some guy in a suit."

"I hate suits."

Well, that was a stupid thing to say.

He smiles. "Me too. The last one I wore was to his funeral, and I told my mom, forget it, it'll never happen again." We sit for a minute, letting that suit hatred wash over us. "So, what was yours like?"

"My suit?"

"Your father."

Shut up and take it like a man.

God, get that out of my head. It will pass, it passes, it's over. Thank You.

"Gentry? Are you all right?"

"Yes. I'm fine." God, make it so.

"So, what am I?"

"What are you?"

"Yeah, like as far as French or Scottish or what. What kind of a name is Gentry? Is it English?"

"I'm not sure."

"You're not sure?"

"No. I don't have any family to ask."

He barks out a sharp laugh. "I can't believe this."

"I'm sorry."

"Would you *stop apologizing*?" And I open my mouth to apologize for apologizing, and then I laugh with relief, a sick, thin laugh, and he joins in. These are pained laughs, but neither of us can stop laughing at ourselves, at each other, at this strange meeting. It all makes no sense.

The merciful waitress comes to our table. "Ready to order?"

He wipes at his eyes. "I am. I'd like biscuits and gravy, please."

"How many?"

"Two, I guess."

"Oh honey, you can eat four."

"Okay, four." He smiles at her, and he has the most beautiful smile I have ever seen.

She turns to me. "And you?"

"Same, please. With two eggs over-medium."

"Add those to mine, too."

And she smiles. "You two are just *too* easy."

He snickers a little as she leaves, shakes his head. "You two are just *too* easy." His imitation of her is pitch perfect. His face gets serious again. "I guess I kind of wonder about my mother. But I'm not supposed to talk to you about that, right?"

"Right." That's the rule. I can't answer any questions about her.

"Was she pretty?"

"I can't tell you."

He nods, serious and disappointed.

"She was beautiful. And intelligent. And . . ." How to say it. "Gracious."

He smiles. "Thanks." He sips his Coke. "I wonder why you guys gave me up."

"I didn't give you up. I never knew about you."

He stares at me. "She didn't tell you?"

"She tried to. But I wasn't very good at talking. I mean, I didn't talk. I avoided talking. And she probably told me indirectly, but we didn't understand each other."

"So you really never knew about me?"

"No. Not until I saw you."

His face is stricken.

If I knew his birthday, maybe I could figure out when we made him.

~

Maybe the first time.

Daniel was gone for the weekend. And she said she'd come for the night. All night. I didn't dare to think it would happen, I didn't dare to hope.

She came to me, and we were alone so we took off our clothes. Well, I took off hers, and then I took off mine. She was long golden limbs, and her breasts made me shake, and her hair, shot through with gold, oh I wanted to touch everything, but first I wanted to see her. I turned her around, studied her, and touched her, soft, just a little, everywhere.

She looked at me. I had no bruises, nothing to hide. I wanted her to touch me and she did. I asked her if what we were doing was all right. She took my arms that shook with wanting to hold her, and pulled me over to a narrow bed. Then we touched. From our lips to our feet, we touched. And I kissed her everywhere, all over, because I wanted to taste her beautiful gold. I thought that was all we were going to do.

That would have been enough, God, it was more than I'd ever had. But then she said, I love you, Gentry.

Had anyone ever said that to me? In my life?

I love you. I'd never spoken those words aloud. I said it once and I couldn't stop, I told her I loved her, I'd always loved her from the moment I heard her voice.

I couldn't stop saying it.

She moved her legs apart, and I moved on top of her. I asked her if I should stop, and she shook her head. So I didn't stop. But then, oh, my God, into her, and I thought I would die, and she cried, she called out, Oh God. I hurt, I hurt more beautifully than I ever thought I could, and her hips shook with the pain. I tried to pull away, I couldn't stand to hurt her, I couldn't let her make this beautiful, painful sacrifice to me, and she put her arms and legs around me, wrapped herself so tight around me, and I knew, then, that she wouldn't let me go. We gave each other our bodies. We offered ourselves up and were consumed.

It could have been that time. It could have been any time. We were young and beautiful and Catholic, and there was never a time between us when he couldn't have been.

⤴

The waitress brings our food, frowns. "Are you boys all right?" She pats me. A patting waitress, why do I attract patting?

"I'm fine. Just hungry."

Then she pats my son's shoulder. I understand that. Who could see a face suffer like that and not give comfort to that fine boy? She sighs. "I wish I could just sit here and watch the two of you eat. But duty calls." She pours me some more coffee, moves on.

He smiles. "Duty calls." He's like a parrot. And then he frowns a funny, smiling frown. "Do people like to watch you eat?"

"They seem to."

"Me too. Is that strange or what?"

"Very strange." I give thanks while he waits, and then we take a bite, and we close our eyes, and I know that we're smiling, and chewing.

This tastes so good. I watch him eat. He lets me.

⤴

When I pay the check, the waitress asks us if we're brothers. He puts a hand on my shoulder and says, "It's complicated."

This is to give thanks. Amen.

At the Jeep, I introduce him to Sam. The three of us take a tour of the rusting logging equipment around the perimeter of the parking lot. I tell him what I can remember from Lorrie. We also inspect the chainsaw sculptures.

"Do you believe in Bigfoot?"

"No, but I have a friend who claims to have seen one. The same one who knows what all this equipment is for."

"Will you be in town next weekend? I have a game. If you're not doing anything better."

"I'll be there. What do you play?"

"Point guard."

"Me too."

God, this is to give thanks. Amen.

⤴

I stop at the post office.

Dear Gentry,

I think in just this one letter, I will dispense with the social niceties.

Before I left school to go to Portland to have our son, I sent you one last poem. I had Paige put it under your door. I found it in Daniel's papers last week. You never read it, Gentry, because he picked it up and figured out what I was trying to tell you. I find, of everything, this is what I hate the most. That you never read it.

I looked at a copy of the adoption papers. That is not your signature.

I won't pretend that it is easy here, right now. I sat there the night you called and tried to figure out how to make it all less monstrous. I wanted him to have misunderstood you, the way I did. But he told me the truth. He absolutely knew that you were in the dark. And he didn't enlighten you because he knew that I would never forgive you. He hoped I'd turn to him.

The morning after you called, I packed up Ariel and walked out the door. I thought I would punish Daniel for ruining my life, and yours. I would take his child away from him the way he took yours away from you.

I got to my father's house and told my mother what had happened. She pretended to think it was awful, but I could tell she was relieved and always had been. Her sister had a son and I had a suitable husband. No harm, no foul. I just wanted to kill her, Gentry. I looked at my daughter, who was so confused by all the anger flying around, and it was hard to make sense of it all. She told me she wanted to go home. I'm home again. With Dan. Where I guess I belong, because it's where God sent me, where God has me stay. Why, I don't know. But this is my life.

Women are trapped by the love we feel for our children.

Ariel is a miraculous girl. She will start kindergarten in the fall. And I have a son, as of last Thursday. And they are mine and I can't leave. Dan's practice is busy, and he has to travel quite a bit. Most first amendment law is practiced in LA, but I refuse to leave Georgia. So he's going to stay in LA for a while and let me figure things out here at home.

He is a lying coward and he has fled and I am so relieved, even though Walker is a long, nervous, fussy boy and I find I don't have enough milk for him. My neighbor has been a godsend. You probably didn't notice her while you were here. She's older, but she's wonderful with the kids.

Tristan knows me as his cousin. I need you to honor that. I don't want him to hate me for what I did, because I did what I thought was best and even with Uncle Doug's death, I think he's had a blessed, happy life. Aunt Toni has been generous to me. I pray she will be the same to you.

Life is strange, different. Gentry, I believed you knew. It was a fundamental fact that colored every decision I made. I look back at the last sixteen years and they are unrecognizable. And so is my husband.

Do you remember that long talk we had about how to judge a flawed man? We sat up and talked about all the great heroes of literature, trying to decide if a man should be judged by what he does right or what he does wrong. And I kept saying all the heroes were ruined by their flaws. And you kept saying no, the Greeks had it right, that a man couldn't be a hero unless he had a flaw. "Heroism requires overcoming. A flawless man has nothing to overcome." I wish you were here to explain it all to me again.

Daniel was my hero, Gentry. He helped me survive losing you and I guess that's his penance, that his job will always be to help me survive the fact that I don't have you.

We've decided that for the first time in our lives, we're going to be honest with each other. I don't think we ever have. Our entire marriage is built on lies. Not just his, but mine. But we are going to start telling the truth and see where that leads us. Maybe with God's help, we can salvage something. For the sake of these children, I hope so.

I made a life. I live that life. I look in my heart for forgiveness. I pray to find it someday. I pray you do, too. But Gentry, I want you to understand something. You will always hold me.

Yours,

Becca

The last page is the poem she put under my door. Her handwriting, round and slanted and somehow younger than the handwriting in the letter. Neruda.

Poems are puzzles, and easier to solve than women.

If I had read this poem, would I have understood?

Maybe it was a different time.

Daniel was gone, again. We spent Saturday in the room, all day. Exhausting ourselves. I was on my stomach, tired like a dog. She lay beside me, running her hand over my back, stroking that patch of hair at the base of my spine, what she called my vestigial tail. It felt strange and wonderful, like it was connected to the front by an electric wire, like when she touched my chest.

I groaned.

She laughed and called me dog boy, and then she started to stroke my backside. I liked that. It felt good but not so urgent. She said I felt like a baby, and I told her hush, I was no baby. She asked me, don't you like babies? I told her I knew nothing of babies. And she said, well, Gentry, you know how to make them. I dozed.

And then she stroked the backs of my thighs, she teased me and said I was getting so hairy. I was not hairy. I had less hair than her at that point, but my thighs were kind of hairy. She was brushing her hand across the backs of my thighs, I was falling asleep, it felt nice.

She sat up.

What are these? She took my hand and put it on the back of my thigh, and I could feel it like rows of grit under the skin. Scars. I turned away to the wall. She fit herself along my back but I kept moving away, leave me alone, get away, leave ME ALONE, I can't DO THIS

Weeping, she was weeping.

I turned around and we came together, crying. I knew she loved me, because for weeks she'd been talking about getting married. This boy with no name, no people, and she wanted to get married. Even with all the rest of it, all the pain and scars and damage, she loved me enough to marry me.

I couldn't stand it.

⌒

Was that when we made my son?

No. He was already in her. Because now I know what she was trying to tell me, and what she thought I was trying to tell her.

She was supposed to be mine.

If I went to her right now, if I got in my Jeep and drove to Buckhead Forest to her front door, she would walk through it and leave with me. I could finally get her back. I could have her and those children, that miraculous little girl with the curling red hair, the long fussy boy who needs more milk. I'd take them and raise them and love them and love their mother and I would finally have what I always wanted. The great mistake could be rectified. I could have her.

But then, I can't have Tristan.

God. Please help me. Amen.

Sam stands at the door, his nose pointed at the handle, his tail wagging, waiting, ready. The door opens. It's Vicki. She pulls me in close. We stand there in the kitchen for a long time, while the ocean pulls itself away from the shore and the sky hangs over like a grieving Mary over her son's body, pouring down rain. Vicki keeps her arms around me.

Eventually, she hands me a paper napkin so I can blow my nose. She keeps a hand on my back. She watches while I start a fire in the sink.

We watch it all go down to ash.

∽

The game has started by the time I find the school.

Toni sees me, and her face turns the color of her hair. I sit and sop my chin. I came here from a dentist's appointment and pain rocks my jaw, but I welcome sensation because it means I won't look like a stroke victim. Gretchen waves, I wave, but I want to sit higher than her so I can see them both. Oh, he's so good. He makes it look easy. And he's having nothing but fun.

Is that ref blind? How could he call that a foul? What an idiot.

The officiating in this game is a disgrace. Someone should sic some Oklahoma bill collectors on that ref. That would be a way to punish him for his ridiculous calls. Jerk. Thanks to that jerk, Tristan fouls out in the fourth quarter. I watch him, hear him call from the bench, feel his frustration. Still, they win. The basketball team is not a one-man show.

I wait in the stands. I'm studying my boots when I feel him plunk down near me. "I guess Mom left. Can you give me a ride home?"

"Sure."

"You probably noticed I fouled out. God, I hate that ref. The one with the bad knee?"

"What an idiot. I'd like to hurt his other knee." He laughs. I'm serious.

"It's weird. I never get called for anything in soccer. But I get called for everything in basketball." He sits next to me, radiating the smell of a boy's shower overpowered by sweat and sports and frustration. The smell of me at that age.

This warmth in my stomach, this growing fire. Like I feel for Gretchen. Grief and pain and joy, and the fierce glow of it. God, I feel it for *him*.

This is to give thanks. Amen.

⁓

I took Tristan home to his mother. It all showed in her face. How angry she is, how frightened. "Mom, can I take Gentry up to see my computer?"

"Your computer?"

"Yeah."

"I guess I don't see any harm in that."

We went up. Between his shoes and my boots it sounded like twenty people were climbing the wooden staircase.

My son had great equipment. "My grandparents gave it to me."

He had a picture of Gretchen tucked in the corner of his monitor. "I have that same picture taped to my monitor."

"That's cool."

He had a tidy room for a boy. "I'd take you to the basement and show you my drum set but Mom would probably lose it." His CDs filled a shelf with pure thug. He shrugged, smiled. "I'm all about the rhymes in P-town." Besides the usual posters of sports figures, he had pictures with Gretchen posed together in front of various artificial scenery. "Those are from dances."

"I know. I have a drawer full of these from students."

"Oh, right." He seemed a little embarrassed. "Yeah. We go to all of them. I like them more than she does. My mom made me go to dancing school."

What a fate. "I'm sorry, Tristan."

He laughed. "No. I liked it, can you believe that? I really like to dance."

Could he be my son?

I studied Gretchen as I had never seen her, dressed up, hair back. Like her sister at that prom. Tristan wore shirts, suspenders, ties. No suits. My son, after all. I saw another where they were not dressed up, at a game or somewhere, laughing.

"Can I have this?"

"That's my favorite."

"Thank you."

He laughed as I pocketed it. I wanted to walk across the room and bury my face in his hair, to fold him up in my arms and put him in my Jeep and take him away. I would teach him about Jeff Buckley and Michael Stipe and John Keats and Frank Stanford. I would show him how to rebuild an engine and fry eggs and catch fish.

First, I would get him a good dog.

"I, um, should probably go."

He studied the floor, kicked at the rug with his huge basketball shoe. "I wish you didn't have to."

"Me too. But your mom probably doesn't want to adopt me, too, so . . ."

We laughed, and that broke the spell. We thundered back down the stairs. He followed me outside and so did his mother, majestically seething along behind us as we walked to the Jeep. I jumped over the side and buckled up. We had to say good-bye under her bitter eyes. "Maybe, you know, I'll see you tomorrow?"

I felt that clear, fierce joy. "Sure. Just give me a call. I'm at the Fankhausers this weekend."

"Gretchen's at her dad's." He made a face. Half smile, half frown. "With Graham."

"Hm. Graham."

Toni's voice shook. "You two have exactly the same expression on your faces."

I made myself look at her. Really look at her. She was thinner, haunted, furious. I understood that I was destroying her.

She turned away, and I drove down the hill to Kathryn's.

⁓

Hey, Sam. Were you a good dog? You're a good boy here in the yard. Did you keep an eye on everything? Let's take a little walk before I go in to Kathryn.

Let's walk, Sam. Nope, wait. Let's try again. See? Right there. That's where you walk. Good boy.

"Hey, Fiona."

She puts down a box of plant food and comes to me. I smell something so fresh, so sweet. I think it must be whatever she was cutting. And then I realize, no.

It's Fiona that smells this sweet.

She smiles. "Hi!" She has on a grey sweater with holes in the elbows over a dress that isn't much longer than the sweater and those big green rubber boots. I see her bare legs rising from those muddy boots and I'm struck dumb.

My head itches. My skin is too small. I stare at her feet. "I wanted to show you the puppy." She leans down to pat him. I fervently wish I were standing behind her.

I'm an idiot.

He accepts her pats as his due. He sniffs his way through her tiny front yard, his hair floating around him. "I named him Sam."

"Oh, that's perfect." We admire him. Sensing this, he lifts his head in order to appear even more magnificent. "He isn't very hyper, is he?"

"No. He's a calm pup. Not like Bosco."

"Bosco was hyper?"

"Yes. A big, wild puppy. I wasn't very big when I was a kid, and I'd get a rope and he'd take it in his teeth and drag me all over the yard of the rectory." I remember, him tugging that rope, shaking me, and when I finally let go and lay there, he'd wait with that rope hanging out of his mouth. Begging for more.

She tilts her head. "What else did Bosco like?"

"Sleeping outside. I'd take a blanket out and we'd sleep in the yard. And he loved to go fishing. He liked to swim in the lake with me. And riding in the car."

"I understand dogs always love the car."

"Yes. Sam loves it. Especially when the top is off." I scratch my head and avoid her eyes. "I wanted to say thank you. But I, um, I never. I never thought about whether or not you had to pay for him."

She waves off that idea. "No, he was free. That little older lady asked me that, too. She was so suspicious. Is she your relative or friend or what?"

"Or what, I think."

Fiona laughs, a silly laugh, too loud, irresistible. I have to laugh, too, that little older lady, what a way to refer to Kathryn.

A tiny black dog has been watching Sam suspiciously through a fence, sniffing and staring. When we laugh, the dog sets up a yapping. It yaps and yaps, but its tail wags, too. Little dog, are you confused? Your back half doesn't agree with your front half. What's it going to be? Are you such a long little dog that your ends don't talk to each other?

Fiona rolls her eyes. "She won't stop barking unless you pet her." I bend down but she jumps back and keeps yapping. "And of course, sometimes she won't *let* you pet her. But she's a cute little thing." The yapping and wagging continues. This dog's person peers through a window at us. He looks confused and suspicious, as well. We're just laughing, okay? And make your dog be quiet.

Sam stares at the little dog as if he can't place what it's supposed to be, and then lifts his leg on a bush. The First Official Leg Lift. Sam is a real boy dog now. Kathryn was furious when Bosco watered her roses. "Sorry about that."

"Don't worry, he can pee on those roses all he wants. Hugh puts them in and he doesn't even choose the hardys or the antiques, he picks these scrawny, sickly hybrids with no smell to them, and I have to fuss with them. Roses are too much work."

"What kind of flowers do you like?"

"Antique pansies. Any violets. Snapdragons, lupines, cosmos. Fuchsias. And I love geraniums." She reaches down and snaps the stem of a flower, holds it to my nose. It smells so fine I nearly pass out. Everything smells so good lately. "Oh, and I love peonies, but Hugh hates them. I think peonies are vastly superior to roses." She launches into a discussion of "staking," "tight bud" and "aphid resistance," things of which I'm ignorant. Kathryn never taught me any of that. "Am I boring you?"

"No. No, I don't think you could ever bore me."

She blushes. I'm an idiot. The way she smells. Better than geraniums.

I don't know what a peony is.

I can ask Kathryn.

⌒

Of course, she doesn't like that question.

"Why are you interested in peonies?"

"I'm not, exactly. I just wondered what one was, and where a person might get whatever it is that peonies grow on."

"They're perennial flowers, and they grow on bushes, but they require staking." I see. Kathryn is anti-staking. "You might be able to get some at Midway. But why?"

"I thought I'd get something for Fiona."

"That person who gave Sam to you?"

"That person," what a nice way to refer to Fiona. Fiona isn't any better with her "little older lady." Why can't women call each other by their names?

"Her name is Fiona Wallace."

"Is she your friend?"

"I guess so."

"Hm. Interesting. I haven't found her too awfully friendly. But her husband seems nice. Have you met him? His name is Hugh."

"I've met him." I look at her, she looks at me. What? I can't even talk to Fiona, because of Hugh? "I'm going to bed. Goodnight. Come on, Sam."

⁓

In the classroom, Tristan is the new benchmark against which all these flawed, mortal children must be measured. I know my son had advantages. All genetic input aside, he had the best of everything from day one. These kids have not.

That's why I teach here.

"Gentry?"

"Hey, Rainbow."

She puts a dark pink braid in her mouth, sucks at it. I assume she eats her own hair because her body is starved for protein. I don't understand vegans. "Where's that dog?"

"I had to leave him at the vet." My poor Sam, he wasn't happy when I left him there. And if he'd known what they were going to do to him, I guess he'd have been even more unhappy.

"Sick? Is he sick?"

I shake my head. I feel pretty terrible about this, but I had to do it. Mel called and counseled me on it, and Kathryn scolded me about it, and Gretchen talked to me about it. Even Vicki brought it up. It seemed like such a terrible thing to do.

"He's getting fixed. They want to keep him until tomorrow."

"Good." She nods.

Mel took Bosco in when I was away at school, so I didn't have to think about that with him. And I know it's the right thing to do and healthier for him in the long run and the responsible decision to make.

I feel sick over it.

"You're sweet." She sighs, launches into an awkward invitation. "Sometime, would you? My mom. Have dinner? My house? Only if you want to."

That sounded like Haiku.

I receive these invitations every so often. Usually, this is a hopeful attempt on the part of a student to fix up a teacher and a parent. I know how excruciating these evenings are because I have gone, in the past, in Detroit. I rarely saw parents, usually just at funerals. But occasionally, the longing for a home-cooked meal got me over to a student's home. The hardworking African American women who cooked for me were polite and amused at the idea that I, with my youth, my hair, and what it is that I wear for clothes, was eligible for consideration. I said very little, ate an enormous amount, and thanked everyone with embarrassing profusion. The compliment to the cooking made up for the lack of conversation. The food was always good in Detroit. The idea of what I might be fed at Rainbow/Molly's frightens me. "Well, I'm pretty busy these days." Eating meat. "Um, I've been going into Portland quite a bit."

She nods her head. "Okay. Just wondered. My mom, single, you know." I know. I'm sure that at least half of the moms here are single. Lorrie keeps pointing this out to me. He keeps me posted on the marital status of all the mothers. He must have a spreadsheet ranking them by the characteristics that he considers desirable, things like large breasts, boat ownership, gainful employ. He's told me that Molly/Rainbow's mom is both divorced and respectably endowed. "No boat. Great boobs." I keep myself from berating him for talking about this in the lunchroom.

She walks around my desk, sucking on that raspberry braid. I want to give her something to eat, but I don't have any beef in my classroom. I follow my own rules. She studies the bulletin board. I never used to have pictures up, but I have pictures up of Lucy Rose, Byron Branwell, Percy Shelley and Emerson Gentry. "These kids. Yours?"

"No, these are the kids of friends."

"Do you have any? Kids."

It's a reasonable question, one I've been asked before. I found it inconceivable that a man would have children but there would be no perceptible trace of fatherhood in his life. What a sad idea. Of course, I just described myself. "I have a son your age."

"Do you have a picture of him? Your son."

I open the desk drawer, the drawer I open about fifty times a day just to see his face. I show her the picture of my son and Gretchen. She sighs. "Way too cute. Pretty girl, though." She frowns at the photo. "Wait. Gretchen Mumford? Such a dweeb." She shakes her head. "Beautiful now." She puts the photo on the bulletin board. "This belongs here."

Yes. It does.

⌒

I'm in Portland every weekend, seeing my son, seeing Gretchen. I go to his games, I watch her ride horses. I'm a little afraid of horses. Gretchen is beautiful on one, though. I stay with Kathryn. She feeds me, watches over me. I talk about weather with Jack, and Mike stops by and lectures me about financial planning. I stay away from all beautiful married neighbors. I don't go to Georgia. I go to the dentist. The Gilroys are understanding.

I've never been happier in my life.

And then, one weekend, Gretchen asks me to stay at the beach. "Don't come to Portland this weekend, Gentry, please."

"You want me to stay away?"

"No. I want to visit you, dummy. Have you all to myself." My heart is full. "I love you, Gentry."

"I love you back. And I always will."

"No matter what?"

"No matter what."

⌒

The one thing I can't seem to figure out no matter how diligently I apply myself to this puzzle, is how this came to be my fault.

This is all my fault.

Those who have decided I'm to blame include Kathryn, Mike, Antoinette, and of course, the peripheral but equally accusatory spouses, Eve and Jack.

They called me to this meeting. I thought they might have called me here because I'm a parent to one of the two people involved in what Mike refers to as "this situation." I was mistaken. I'm not here for any other reason than to take the blame.

We meet at Jack and Kathryn's home. There was probably a war of the westside living rooms to determine in which of the three palatial Portland homes we would meet. I would have voted for Mike's because he has the best view and if things got bad, I could always go take a bath. But Kathryn won, even though Toni's rugs are nicer, and Mike's view is better, because Kathryn has more of that expensive crystal stuff on shelves in here.

God, I'm sick of not having any money and having to be around people who do. So sick of it. It's not even that I want money, so much as I don't like looking at theirs.

They're all staring at me.

It's my fault. I mentioned that. It's my fault because Gretchen came to me a week ago. We sat at the kitchen island in the big house, and she cried. She held both my hands tightly as she said it out loud. She wasn't sad, God. She cried because she was afraid to tell her parents, but she wasn't sad about it.

I was undone.

"I knew you'd smile, Gentry. I knew you'd smile."

She came and sat on my lap, let me cup the roundness of her belly with my hand. I held her and whoever that is growing in there, held them both with heartbreak and disbelief and reverence for the future and gratitude to God. I put my head in Gretchen's hair and prayed and cried and rejoiced.

Then, I made her call her mother.

Gretchen told me first. No one in this room will ever forgive me for that. Gretchen told me and Tristan told his mother and now I sit, surrounded by betrayed eyes. I haven't suffered glares like this since I went to Miriam's funeral. Ice eyes, granite eyes.

Kathryn, please. Your eyes hurt.

I recognize the gravity, here. I'm not an idiot. They're children. I realize what this will do to their lives. But this is a baby, not a situation.

Mike starts. "Well, we all know why we're here. I just want to make sure we're all on the same page." I add that phrase to my vocabulary aversion file. "I want this understood. I only want what's best for our children."

"What's best."

"Absolutely."

"Of course."

"No question."

All eyes are on me. I nod, is that good enough? I don't know how to say this bland and stern and general stuff, so can I just nod?

Nodding seems acceptable.

"The problem, of course, is that she's so young."

"A child."

"A baby herself, really."

"She just turned sixteen."

"Absolutely."

Eyes on me, again. Yes, that's how old she is, I can agree with that. She's sixteen. I nod again. They're satisfied.

"And Tristan's only fifteen. He has a fine future ahead, if he stays on track."

"I know what you're saying."

"It would be devastating."

"Absolutely."

"We can't forget that."

Eyes on me. My son has a future, we all have a future. I wonder if we are still all "on the same page." But I nod.

"I think we all agree that, at her age, she has to have an abortion."

"Absolutely."

"There's no other choice."

"None."

"I agree."

All eyes on me. I knew it would get here, so . . . "Why is that the only choice?"

"Oh Gentry . . ."

"I'm only asking."

Mike roars. "She's *sixteen*, for God's sake!"

"Michael, don't." Kathryn sighs. "You knew we would have trouble with him."

"With *him*? Do you mean *me*, Kathryn?"

"I don't care for that tone, Gentry." Jack fixes me with flashing, wrinkle-enshrouded eyes. "You have absolutely no legal rights in this. None at all."

"Hey Jack? Neither do you, as a matter of fact."

Kathryn pats him. "Jack. Calm down. He's just upset."

He sure is. "Could someone explain to me why abortion is the only choice?"

A chorus of groans.

"Because she can't have a *baby*." This is Toni, who used to be a Catholic, Toni whose husband died, who wants to kill her son's child.

"Keep in mind how far along she is." Kathryn shakes her head. "I shudder to think what type of abortion is available to her at this point."

Mike cuts her off. "Don't even go there or he's going to start quoting Knights of Columbus literature at us."

"Hey Mike? Shut up."

"Why don't you make me, you self-righteous Catholic dickhead."

"All right. Stop it, you two. That doesn't help anything." Kathryn sounds so tired.

Eve pipes up. "Well, what's she supposed to do if it's too late for abortion?"

Toni's tone is frosty. "She could have it and give it up for adoption. There are *thousands* of couples waiting for a . . ." She swallows. ". . . baby like this."

Eve stares at Toni, who is going to start crying.

Mike says the stupidest thing of all. "I don't understand how the hell it happened." They all sit in their beautiful, expensive chairs, looking comfortably mystified. Obviously these people need to go to the library.

Every single one of them turns to stare at me.

"Don't look at me. This didn't happen while she was with me." Kathryn winces. Toni shifts in her chair. Mike glares. "What do the kids want?" It might have been nice to have them here so they could tell us themselves, but since that's not the case, I have to ask.

Toni sighs. "He wants to marry her."

I love my son. He's no coward. God, if I had known Tristan was in her, I would have taken Becca off to North Dakota and married her and made a living custom combining. Tristan would have been a poor kid with a funny accent instead of the perfect, glorious boy with a college fund that he is. My own mistakes have taught me very little, but I have learned that pregnancy is not a good reason to get married. Still, I admire my son's bravery.

"Well, that's ridiculous. That's not even worth discussing." Mike neatly dismisses my son and his ridiculous, idealistic desires. Mike happens to be right, but it still rankles. "I think it's a case where we just need to bring the right kinds of pressure to bear."

"Hey Mike? What do you mean by pressure?"

He speaks clearly, as if speaking to a stupid person. "I *mean*, Gentry, that we need to make it understood that there will be some . . . *consequences* if she resists having an abortion. I won't keep her at that school, for one thing. I don't think they would let her stay, anyway."

"It would be so awkward for Tristan." Toni clucks when she says this. I see. Gretchen is pulled out of the wonderful school, but Tristan gets to stay, unembarrassed.

"Gretchen loves her school." I point this out. In fairness.

Toni says, "She can go back once she gives it up."

It? It? Toni, It? I'd like to break some of that expensive crystal. But I make myself calm, and ask the obvious question. "So those are the choices? She can have an abortion, some kind of abortion that's even worse than the regular kind of abortion . . ." Mike groans and I ignore him, ". . . or she can quit school and have the baby and give the baby away?"

"Yes, Gentry. Those are the choices."

"The only choices?"

"The only choices."

I shake my head. "There has to be at least one more choice."

Mike slams a fist onto a table, making crystal knickknacks and all of us jump. "Oh for Christ's sake, Gentry. You don't honestly expect them to get married at their age, do you? This isn't the Ozarks, or wherever you come from."

You know where I come from, you jerk. "I don't think they should get married. They're too young."

"Congratulations. That's the first thing you've said today that makes any sense." You know, there is a limit. And I've reached it.

"Why did you all ask me to come here? It can't be any big mystery what I think, what I'm going to say. As Jack pointed out, I don't have any legal rights in this. So why am I here? Why did you ask me?"

They look at me, and I understand. I'm here because years ago, in the glory of my ignorant, innocent, Catholic youth, I laid down with a beautiful girl and made a baby. He has brown eyes and plays soccer and likes computers and he got a beautiful girl pregnant, just like me. He did what I did all those years ago. And somehow, I'm supposed to answer for this.

You know, I've had it.

"I'm not Gretchen's dad, and I hate to think what would have happened if I'd tried to talk to her about any of this, what you all would have said about it. This was your job, not mine. And as far as Tristan? I'd met him once, one time ONLY before it happened. I'd seen him up at the sports facility for about two minutes. So I'm pretty sure talking to him about sex was not my responsibility."

Unfortunately, I seem to be shouting.

"Not that I COULD have talked to either of them, because no one ever told ME about any of it. I didn't even know what to call my PENIS until I was eight years old. I was raised by a PRIEST, do you people understand that? A PRIEST. A Catholic priest took over my raising when I was eleven years old and I'm almost thirty-three and guess WHAT? I've NEVER used birth control. I don't know ANYTHING about it, I've never even SEEN any birth control, so I'm pretty sure this was NOT my job and NOT my fault, and I'm SICK of the way you're all LOOKING at me."

They look at me in that exact way for a long moment.

"Really? Seriously?" Mike sounds awestruck. "You didn't know what to call your penis? You've never in your life seen any birth control?"

Kathryn speaks through clenched teeth. "Michael, be *quiet*."

I wish this floor would open up right now and suck me into the basement.

"Can I just say, um, one more thing?" They all stare at me, waiting. Transfixed, really, by the spectacle of idiocy and ignorance I present. "I, um, well, it's just that, um, well." I refuse to um. But I'm not going to shout, either. "There are six of us in this room. Six grandparents." Oh, flinch at the word, but I will say it, I will give it a name. "This is huge, what they're facing. And they have to face it. So instead of sitting around figuring out how to pressure these kids into doing what you all think they should do, I think they should figure out what they want to do, and we should help." Mike starts to interrupt, but I hold up my hand. "Because we could, you know, we could help. All of us. I don't have any money, but I have summers off. And you all have more than enough money, and we all have time, and this is our grandchild we're talking about, this is a baby, a baby just like those kids were babies, that kind of a baby, like we were all babies. And if they don't want to kill their baby, or give our grandchild away to strangers, I think we should help them figure out how to do this."

It's quiet for a moment.

Jack says, "He's right."

Mike and I both stare at him. Which one, which of us is right, please, Jack?

"Gentry is absolutely right." Jack clears his throat. "Regardless of who's to blame, or who's not, that's all beside the point, isn't it? What's done is done. Now it's time to figure out what to do. And the kids have to do that, not us. They have to live with this decision, so they'd better be in on it."

Jack, I do like you. I do. I hate Mike, though.

"Oh for Christ's sake, I won't listen to this. You're letting your religion get in the way of *reality*, Gentry."

"No, Mike, I'm not. The reality is, that this 'it' you keep talking about is a baby.

And if they want me to, I can take the baby. If none of you want to help, I'll do it by myself. All of it."

Kathryn bursts into tears. Everything is quiet, except for the sound of her sobbing, this sound that tears my heart out of my chest.

When Mike speaks, for once he isn't yelling. "Kathy." He speaks to her in a voice so loving that I want to slam a fist into his mouth. "Kathy, talk to me. Why are you crying?"

"Because, Michael. Because he has nothing, and we have everything, and he's offering more than *any* of us."

Mike stands. "I've had enough of this." His voice is cold and furious. "I want you all to KNOW this. I will NOT help. And YOU, you pious asshole." He charges towards me and I stand to meet the blow, but he stops himself, just jabs a finger into my chest to punctuate his words. "You're ruining my daughter's LIFE, do you understand that? You're ruining Gretchen's LIFE."

I bat his jabbing hand away. He gets me by the throat. Kathryn calls out "MICHAEL!" as my head hits the wall, my jaw rattles.

I'm back down in the chair.

He stands over me, staring down. "You know what, Gentry? I wish I'd never helped you. I wish I'd let you sit in that crap hole in Oklahoma and drink yourself to death over my ex-wife."

I let him have it in his mouth.

He staggers back, swaying. "You little fuck. You dirty little fuck." He presses the back of his hand to his mouth, stares down at the blood, glares down at me. "If you ever hit me again, I'll have you arrested."

He leaves.

～⌒～

Jack shines a light in my eyes. "No concussion." His hands, surprisingly strong and deft, travel my jaw. "As far as I can tell, your jaw is fine. Your larynx is fine. And I'm too damn old for this tomfoolery." His eyes shine. "But that was a nice punch, Gentry. A very nice punch." He prescribes an ice bag and goes to bed, exhausted.

I sit on the couch for a while, icing the back of my head. Then I ice my hand. I worry that my temporaries are loose. I feel sick.

Sam, here you are with Kathryn. Is that a new ball? Did Fiona give you a ball? Yes, this is an amazing ball, but we can't play with it in the house.

Kathryn brings me some coffee and sits beside me. "Well, Gentry. A penny for your thoughts."

I shake my head. "Does anyone think my thoughts are worth a cent?"

She closes her tired blue eyes. "Just drink your damn coffee."

I drink my coffee.

Kathryn pats the couch. "Come here, Sam." Sam jumps up and settles next to her. "You're such a good boy." She pets him. They have similar hair, those two. Sam seems tired.

She reaches up and pushes my hair away from my neck. Checking for bruises. "If you disagree with Michael, he feels attacked." She strokes my cheek with a touch so painfully tender that I want to cry. "He also feels attacked if you punch him in the mouth."

"I think he deserved it."

"He did." She puts her hands on Sam. "You know, I keep thinking that none of this would have happened if only Bosco had been here. Isn't that silly?" She sounds defeated. "How could a dog do what I couldn't. Keep her safe. But you would have kept her safe. You're so protective."

"Kathryn, I was here and it still happened."

"I mean, with her. If you were with her all the time." Tears roll, one by one, down her cheeks.

I'm on my knees before her, holding her cold hands. "I'll help any way I can."

"Of course you will."

"I mean it."

"I know you mean it. Why do you think I'm crying?" She shakes her head. "But a baby is not a dog."

I rise up. "Sam, come here." I leave her there alone and go up to bed in the room where I throw off my clothes and go to the pink room and climb into the pink bed, where I can't sleep, because I'm too angry.

I know the difference, God. A baby is not a dog. But a person who will keep a sick dog alive, or cry over abandoned puppies on the news, or write letters to a congressman pleading for the life of a dog that bit someone, that same person will expect a girl to abort a baby.

God, help me to understand. Help me to understand so that I can forgive. Because some things, I can't understand.

Some things, I never will.

◠

I'm surprised to wake up, because I never thought I'd sleep. Something is wrong. I get up, go to the window. Sam's not in the room.

I run downstairs.

There you are, Sam, did someone take you out?

"He's been out. He did both." Kathryn is at the table, staring at a coffee cup. She looks up and raises her eyebrows. I look down and notice that I forgot my pants. She waves away this awkwardness with her dry little hand. "Don't get all incensed when I tell you this."

"What happened?"

"There was a confrontation last night up at Michael's. The kids made it clear that they're keeping the baby and Michael didn't take it well. He threw her out. Gretchen walked home at one in the morning. Down that hill. Across Burnside in the middle of the night."

She's not exactly describing a war zone, but the idea of it. "She's pregnant, Kathryn."

"I know that. And Michael knows that. He called me this morning to let me know he won't pay for Gretchen's college if she keeps the baby. He won't even pay her high school tuition."

I've paid off the funeral, paid off the stone. I'm still paying on my teeth. My credit is shot, I have no assets, I have nothing. Nothing to offer, no way to help.

God, this is impotence.

"Toni called, too. She was up all night thinking. She can't do anything about the baby, but she does have some control over his trust. If they keep this baby, Tristan loses his college money, too." Kathryn is going to cry again. "Don't worry. Jack will pay her high school tuition, Gentry. He's happy to do it. Michael knew he would, and he just wanted to make a stand. He knows she isn't going to abort. Not at this point."

Jack is old, but Jack has money. I'm young and I'm poor.

"Gentry? Jack went to the store for Mocha Mix. It might be better if you had on some pants when he got back."

I go upstairs and fall on my knees by the bed. God, I have nothing. But whatever I have, God, whatever there is, I'll sell it.

Just show me a path. Show me how to help.

However You answer this prayer, I will submit. Amen.

⌒

She would have a male secretary.

"Gilbert and Vranizan Literary Agency how may I help you."

He could speak with some pauses. "May I speak to Ms. Gilbert?"

"I'll see if she's in whom may I say is calling please."

"Gentry."

"Last name please."

"That's my last name. Tell her Mr. Gentry."

"One moment please while I see if she's available." I should just hang up now, just hang up and figure out something else. Right now.

He comes back on. "Mr. Gentry what is this in reference to."

"We had a discussion last summer about a book, and I, um, wondered if she'd like to continue the discussion."

"One moment please I have to put you on hold." I don't see it as being on hold, I see it as one last opportunity to hang up and salvage my self respect. "Mr. Gentry Ms. Gilbert doesn't seem to recall any discussion."

"Fine. Good-bye."

"WAIT I mean just a moment Mr. Gentry Ms. Gilbert indicated that perhaps if you told me what your name was your full name perhaps that would ring a bell."

I sigh, but I say it for him. My full name. I give it the flourish it deserves. "Does that refresh her memory?"

"Gentry? How interesting to hear from you." And there she is. Conferenced in. "You're interested in talking about the book? Could I ask you why?"

"I need the money."

"Money. I see. You need money?"

"Yes, I need money."

"I see. You need money."

"I said that. Hey Brooke? Are you at all interested in talking to me? Or am I wasting my time and yours by making this call? Because I'd be more than happy to hang up right now if that's the case."

There is a silence. This woman doesn't want me to have one card to play against her. "Well, I have a small amount of interest in speaking with you. I'd rather do it in person, though. How about this. I have to go to Atlanta today. I could change my route."

"I moved to Oregon."

"Oregon?" She says it like orry-gone. "Did I say Atlanta? I meant Los Angeles. I'm flying out to the coast today and I have a . . ." I can hear typing. ". . . a layover in Portland. We could meet at the airport around . . ." I hear more typing. She's checking flights online. "Four PM. We could meet at that main restaurant and talk. I could see if the book is still of interest to me."

"We could do that."

"Here's my cell." She gives me the information, and I write it down.

I feel sick.

Dear God, give me some help.

~

She opens the door wearing a plaid bathrobe and a big hat with ear flaps. She snatches off the hat. "Hi, Gentry!" She sees my face. "What is it? Is something wrong with Sam?"

"Hey. No. No. Sam's fine, he's up in Kathryn's yard. Um, no, I'm, um, I, um, could I, um . . ." I lose it entirely.

"Would you like to come in for a cup of coffee?" I nod and follow her into the house. I say nothing while she makes me some coffee, sets the cup on the table, sit down across from me. I drink coffee and think. She plays with that wool hat and waits.

She has to wait a few minutes while I figure out what to say.

"Hey Fiona? My wife wrote a book."

She stares at me. "You're married?"

"Not anymore. My wife died."

"Oh my gosh, I'm sorry."

"It was about a year before I moved back here. But she wrote a book. This terrible book. Someone wanted to publish it, this agent or whatever she is, and she came to see me, and offered me a lot of money. I said no. That's how bad the book was. And now I need that money, so I called this agent or whatever she is, and she's coming to talk to me out at the airport, and I'm scared, Fiona, I'm scared of this agent or whatever she is. I need the money but I hate the book." I hold on tight to the coffee cup.

"Gentry? What scares you the most?"

"Seeing the agent or, um, whatever she is."

"Your agent is supposed to work for you. My agent is wonderful."

I never ask personal questions but I have to ask this one. "What do you write?"

"Mostly romance novels. Listen, Gentry, I talk with these people all the time. They aren't that bad. You just need to play the game. I can come along."

"You'd do that for me? You'd come with?"

"Sure. I'll come along."

"Thank you."

She smiles. A beautiful smile. And then she reaches over and pats my arm. "Don't worry, Gentry. I'll kill the whatever she is, if that's what you need."

We need to play the game. That's what Fiona said. But I only like to play when I win. Something tells me I won't win with Brooke Gilbert.

I pick up Fiona at her house. She steps out with no blanket, no boots, no falconer's gloves, no wool hat. She smiles. "I know, I'm wearing real clothes. Think of it as drag." I'm too nervous to laugh. Or talk.

I drive.

When we get to the airport restaurant, I introduce the two women and they smile. Women always smile when they meet and they rarely mean it. I think of dogs, the sniffing and the posturing. Me when I met Mike.

We take a booth. I sit down first out of stupidity and a need to hide my lower half, because for some reason the instant I saw Brooke this is what happened. Brooke slides in next to me, great, proximity, that's going to help, plus I can't get away unless she leaves first. Bad planning.

She orders from the waiter without even glancing at him. "Bring us a pot of coffee."

Fiona's eyebrows go up, but she keeps smiling.

There's a card thing. They exchange cards. They discuss the cards. They both give their cards to me. I have no card. Fiona's agent's card figures in, here, and Brooke lays down an editor's card to up the ante. Brooke mentions her other clients. I've never heard of any of these writers, but Fiona has. Fiona mentions three different names, and I realize she's talking about her pen names. She talks about the books she's "doctored." Brooke mentions the New York Times bestseller list.

Fiona's been on it quite a few times. They both seem impressed after all this swapping of names and cards and contacts and lists and so on. I become extremely preoccupied with putting their cards in my wallet.

They talk about money a little. I wish I knew how to talk about money. All I know how to talk about is weather, computers, fishing, sports. Oh, and my teeth. I've added my teeth to my fascinating conversational repertoire. They talk, though, and their smiles seem less suspicious, more genuine. And then, finally, after the cards and the talking, Brooke turns her attention to me.

"This is a good story, Gentry. This is a seller. I mean, it needs cleaning up, but the book is interesting, timely, commercial. And if we had you out there promoting it?"

"Me?" For the first time, I look in her eyes. "I wouldn't do that."

"Why not?"

"Because I would never do anything like that. And I'm not offering you that book. I'm offering you a revised book."

Her eyes narrow. "What if the original book is the only book I'm interested in?" There's a moment, then. A moment when she looks at me and I look at her and all the things I wanted to apologize for no longer haunt me.

"Then there's nothing to talk about. Because I'm only offering you a revised version."

"Well." She frowns. "I think the publishers would be interested in a revised version only, and I mean only, if it were revised in a way that made it as interesting as the original."

"What does that mean?"

"Meaning you're welcome to add anything you want, but they don't want you to take anything out."

I make a noise. She waits.

"Well?"

"That book is not the truth."

"That depends on how you define truth."

"I define truth as 'that which is true.'"

Fiona laughs out loud. Brooke smiles a patient, condescending smile. "Truth is subjective. That book contains your wife's truth. You're welcome to put in your own."

"My own truth?"

"Yes. You remember. All those things you told me. Don't you remember what you told me?" She smiles. I swallow. "You have about forty thousand words to play with. You can use them to tell the truth. The truth about yourself. For instance, your bisexuality."

Fiona's eyebrows go up.

"Yes, I'd like to hear the truth about that. And your drinking. And those affairs, I need to hear the truth about your affairs. And you used to beat up your wife, didn't you? I think it would be so refreshing to read an abusive man telling the truth. You could give us the true story behind your time in jail."

Fiona's mouth is hanging open.

"And there's the whole issue of the abuse you suffered as a child. Because after all, that's the real truth, isn't it. What happened to you as a boy. The root of things, I guess." She tilts her head, thinking. "Actually, I wonder if forty thousand words is enough. Because after this book was written, you drove your wife to suicide. Are there enough words to tell the truth about how you did that, and how you live with yourself?"

Brooke glances over at Fiona to make sure she's heard it all.

She has. Fiona has heard it all.

"There's one more thing."

I set this up.

"About your impotence?"

I walked into this.

"Are you still impotent?"

I did this to myself.

"Because I know the truth about that, firsthand." The waiter brings the pot of coffee. He's surprised when Brooke rises to leave. "I have a plane to catch. Call me and let me know whatever you decide. Nice to meet you, Miss Wallace."

Over her shoulder, she calls one last goodbye to me.

She calls me by my first name.

Fiona

I think he's going to sit there with his hands pressed over his eyes forever.

"Gentry? She's gone." I take out my moleskine, jot down a few notes. Quite a story here. The trouble is, I don't believe any of it could be true. And was that his name? Really?

Could that honestly be his first name?

"Her plane might not have left yet. I could still catch her. I always wanted to figure out how to plot murder mysteries. She had on a very expensive scarf. I could strangle her with it and call it research."

Nothing.

The waiter flutters over, curious. "Is everything all right, Miss?'

"No. Take this coffee away and bring us two hot teas. Right now."

"I'm sorry?"

"Well you should be. Now get this stupid coffee out of here."

"Yes, Miss." He takes away the coffee, returns with the tea. I work on my notes. I drink my tea. Gentry maintains his eye-hiding posture. I finish my notes. I doodle a little.

The waiter again. "Miss? I can see the gentleman is upset. Was it the coffee?"

"He's not upset. His eyes are tired. And if he was upset, it wouldn't be over the stupid coffee."

"Is the tea all right, Miss?"

"His water's cold. Get him some more hot water, right now."

"Of course, right away."

"Bring me some more, too. Please." He fusses away, fusses back over with the water, and he stares at Gentry. "That's fine. You can go away now." I drink more tea. I put away my notebook. I clean out my backpack. I find a cough drop, and I suck on that in a loud, slurpy way. He sits there. If I couldn't see his chest move a little, I would assume he was stuffed.

Not this waiter again. "Would you care for anything else?"

"Yes. More tea."

"Yes, Miss, I'll bring it right over. Would the gentleman care for more hot water? His water seems to be cold again."

"He likes it cold."

"Miss?"

"Just bring me some more tea."

I find a newspaper on the table of the booth next to us, and I do the crossword and the Jumble. "Gentry? Do you know a four letter word for a German river?" It's Elba, everyone knows Elba. "How do you spell Mort Sahl's last name?" Everyone knows that one, too, but no answer. I get the puzzle about two-thirds done and abandon it to ponder the man across the table, wondering if he's had mime training.

"Miss? Is the gentleman all right?"

Why does this waiter keep bothering us? There are plenty of other people in here, can't he just stay away? "He's just thinking, that's all. Go away." My feet hurt, so I kick off my shoes under the table.

Gentry's wallet is sitting on the table. That would be pretty sneaky, snooping through a catatonic person's wallet. Unless I ask first. "Do you mind if I go through your wallet, for research?" I pick it up. "I'm researching your wallet now." Nothing. "Don't you even care if I go through your wallet?" This is low, unfair. I do it anyway.

An Oklahoma driver's license, issued and signed with his initials. Almost expired. "Nice picture. If Jesus had a driver's license, it would look just like this." No movement at all. Oh well.

Does he weigh this much? He doesn't seem the type to lie. Or, let's see, get drunk and beat up his wife, or sleep with men, or drive anyone to suicide. But you never know. He certainly looks younger than he is. I thought he was more like my age.

Proof of insurance. A little stack of business cards that includes mine, now. An older picture of the tall blonde girl. Pretty. Seven dollars. Okay, I'm an insufferable snoop but this is enough, even for me. I put his wallet back on the table. He doesn't stir a mite.

The waiter comes. "Here, keep the change."

"THANK YOU, Miss!"

"You earned it. I'm sorry I was such a bitch." He fusses away. I think he liked being bossed around. "I paid the check. We need to go." Nothing. "I was mean to that waiter, wasn't I. I gave him a twenty-dollar tip."

No movement at all.

Well, five cups of tea and the voyeuristic excitement of going through his wallet have certainly done the trick. "Gentry? I'm afraid all this tea has made me a little desperate. I really have to find a bathroom, right now." No response, no response at all.

Okay, enough. I stand by the booth, holding my shoes. "Come on, Gentry. I really have to pee and it's getting late and Hugh will be wondering where I am. I leave the house so infrequently that he thinks I won't be able to find my way home." Finally, a little movement. "Should I just call a cab or get the light rail?"

He takes his hands from his eyes and my breath catches in my throat, remembering when he lifted his head up from the steering wheel to reveal those brown eyes, tears streaming down over those cruel, beautiful cheekbones. I knew at that moment he was sharp rocks and dangerous waters, the kind of man who wrecks women by loving them.

Clearly I was right.

I pull myself out of my romance novelist reverie as he stands up, refusing to meet my eyes. "Don't forget your wallet." He walks through the terminal with his hands in his pockets. Not speaking. I pay for the parking and pocket the receipt so I can write it off. "Are you okay to drive?" He stares ahead.

He drives just fine.

~

The amazing thing is this: Brooke wants that book.

She knew better than to call Gentry. She called me that next morning, and emailed the manuscript. She called again three hours later. "Did you read it?"

"I scanned it. It doesn't seem very plausible."

"Plausible?" Her voice was scornful. "How well do you know him?"

"Actually, I hardly know him at all."

"Well, listen, Miss Wallace, he admitted to me that it's all true. This man has a huge amount of hostility toward women. He takes it out sexually. I think he might be dangerous." She's practically panting. "You need to know that before you agree to work with him. Can you keep him in line?"

"I'm sure I can handle him." The whip and the chair and that sweet, mild man.

Sure thing. What the hell is she talking about? I've had a night to think about it. Who am I fooling? I'd like to think Gentry is the dangerous romantic creature I imagined him to be at first sight, a man who could drive women to suicide and inspire the lasting wrath of literary agents. But the truth is he's much more the awkward, bumbling man who shows up at my house to talk about his dead dog.

I need to stop thinking like a romance novelist.

"Well, talk to me again before you start. I'm having a little problem with the house. The editors are disappointed. They wanted an attractive couple that would go out and do book tours, and now they're getting this creep who won't even have his name on the book."

"I don't think he's a creep."

"He's a handsome creep, and he would have shot well on TV, that's the problem. The cameras love a handsome creep."

"He's not a creep."

"So, the house has very specific guidelines for revision. You'd be rewriting her part, which we always knew needed rewriting, and adding at least forty thousand of his words. And this story has to be juicy. I want you to think about it before you commit. I want you to know what you're getting into. Why don't you to talk to Miriam's sister before you agree to anything? Evelyn Hogan." She gives me the number. I hang up.

I think Brooke Gilbert is a creep.

⁓

Evelyn had never read the book, but she was anxious to help. "I think my sister's story deserves telling." She had an obnoxious voice that softened whenever she spoke about her sister. "MIRANDA! Put that BACK. Sorry. She's into everything these days."

"Can I ask you your general impression of Gentry?"

"Let's see. He's very tall."

"He's six feet tall."

"I know! Huge." Where, in the Land of Oz? Evelyn went on. "He used to work for my husband Ben, who gave Gentry a good job after he got fired from that vo-tech school."

"Do you know why he got fired?"

"You know, I never knew at the time but Miriam finally told me what it was and what it was is that she had a miscarriage and it sent him into a breakdown which is just like him." That sentence could send me into a breakdown. "MIRANDA! I SAID TO PUT THAT BACK! Sorry."

"He had a breakdown because his wife had a miscarriage and he couldn't go back to work?"

"Exactly. It happened right after they got married."

"She was pregnant when they got married?"

"Yes. BEN COULD YOU COME IN HERE AND GET MIRANDA! Yes, she was pregnant. I think that's why they got married. Him so Catholic and all."

Well, that's interesting. That wasn't in the book.

"I'd have to work with Gentry closely. What do you think it would be like to work with him?"

She thought for a minute. "As far as work? Boring, probably. I think working with Gentry would be pretty boring."

"He's boring?"

"Very boring. Ben always said that it was just like working with a ghost."

"He's not violent or anything?"

She brayed. "Violent? Gentry? This is Gentry we're talking about? He's about as violent as a house plant."

"Is he an alcoholic?"

That bray of a laugh. "Oh no. I ate dinner with him every Sunday for three years. He never had a single glass of wine. He got drunk at my sister's funeral, but we all did. Aside from that, no. He never drank."

"As far as you know, was he ever arrested?"

"Arrested? For what? No, I don't think he was ever arrested. Arrested for what?" And then I hear her calling over her shoulder. "BEN, DID GENTRY EVER GET ARRESTED?" I hear a male voice in the background. "JUST ANSWER THE QUESTION ALREADY, DID GENTRY EVER GET ARRESTED FOR ANYTHING?" She waits. "BEN I'LL TELL YOU IN A MINUTE BUT JUST ANSWER THE GODDAMNED QUESTION ALREADY."

My ears. I let them recover while she listened for a minute. "Ben says not that he knows of. And employers generally know. I'LL TELL YOU WHEN I'M OFF THE PHONE, WOULD YOU JUST SHUT UP."

And then I tried to find a diplomatic way to ask her the worst question of all.

Which was impossible for me, because I'm not what you'd call diplomatic. So I just blurted it out. "Do you think he's sexually dangerous or anything like that?"

She brayed again. "What, do you mean like a *sex maniac*? Not according to my sister. She bragged at first, you know how it is in the beginning. She bragged and bragged about what he was like. But then after a year or two she admitted that she had to twist his arm to get him to even sleep in the same bed with her."

Well. "Did he have affairs?"

"Affairs? Gentry? Not that boy. He's so Catholic. Miriam loved that about him, how faithful he was. Her first husband was nothing but a CHEAT."

"There's nothing about a first husband in the book."

"Well he was a leech and a cheat, which is why she quit nursing. She made so much more money than he did that he went after her for support. Can you IMAGINE? This GROWN MAN, going after a WOMAN for support. So after he left her, she declared bankruptcy and let the house go into foreclosure so the creditors would go after HIM, and then she quit nursing and lived like a PAUPER while it all dragged through court. That man was RUINED, let me tell you. And he deserved it." She sniffs a little. "I thought for SURE she'd go back to nursing as soon as David couldn't get his hands on her paychecks, but she was together with Gentry by the time everything was final and she wouldn't go back to it because she always blamed all those KNIGHTS."

I am so confused. "Knights?"

"Nurses work a lot of NIGHTS. She thought that was one reason David was such a cheat, the OPPORTUNITY, you know. But she didn't have to worry about Gentry. Ben said he never even looked at anyone in the office, and let me tell you, if he did, I wanted to know. Miriam was my sister. But he never even looked at anyone. Even after she was gone."

"Gentry was faithful to her?"

"Oh yes. He's just that kind of guy. Before she died, and then, I swear, he was still faithful after." I could hear the pain in her voice. "If you could have seen him in that hospital. He was not going to let her go, we begged him but he was not going to let her go. Night and day, right there, and she was, you know, already brain dead. He was so sad. You've never seen anyone as sad as Gentry after my sister died." She took a deep breath. "BEN I'LL BE THERE IN A MINUTE."

My ears rang. She continued. "He was always quiet, you know, he never had all that much to say. Miriam never shut up. Opposites attract and all that. But when she died, he went completely silent. I don't think he said a word to anyone for a year. I've never seen anything like it." I could hear her sniffing. "And then at the unveiling, he seemed like he might be coming around, turning back into his old self again. Because he was a really sweet guy, you know. The way he put up with my father. My father thinks he's being funny but mostly he's not, he's just being awful and thinking it's funny. You would not BELIEVE the things he used to say to Gentry, trying to get a rise out of him. Gentry never got mad, though, he put up with all of it." She takes a moment to blow her nose. "So there Gentry was at the unveiling, talking. So sweet with Miranda, that's the first time he saw her. He's got a way with kids, you know. And out of the blue, his people just showed up and took him away. I don't think we'll ever see him again. He was my sister's husband, and now he's just . . . gone. Isn't that the strangest thing? People just go like that. They disappear."

"Do you blame him for what happened?"

"Of course not. How can I blame him for an accident?"

"An accident?"

"Yes, JUST A SECOND HONEY, MOMMY'S COMING. BEN CAN'T YOU EVEN GIVE HER A SNACK? I swear, she's the most impatient child ever born." I heard her blow her nose again. "Miss Wallace? I need to go, all right? But you can call me for anything. I'd be glad to help. This book meant so much to Miriam. Once she found out she couldn't have kids, I think it meant EVERYTHING to her. Well, this book and Gentry."

We said good-bye and hung up.

I sat there thinking.

⤸

When Hugh came home, he could tell I was in a mood. "What's wrong? Let me guess. You heard from Miki, right?"

"No."

"Good." I scoffed a little in honor of his empathy. He just smiled at me. "Nice hat."

"I'm cold. It's always so cold in here. And my ears hurt. It's this book."

He frowned. "The book made your ears hurt?"

"No, no. Listen. The weirdest thing happened."

"Wait." He set down his briefcase and loosened his tie. "Do I have to listen to weird stuff about this book all the time, now? Is that how it's going to be?"

"I'd think you'd be grateful not to have to listen to weird stuff about Miki all the time."

He sighed. "You have a point." He sat down at the kitchen table and listened to me rant away about the volume of Evelyn Hogan's voice and all the weird inconsistencies while I put some Spanish tuna and Pierre Robert and water crackers on the table. He gave the food a sideways glance. "Is this dinner?"

"Sure. Here. Here's the vegetable."

"Olives. Nice."

"Would you just open the wine?" While he poured me a glass and I stuffed my face with triple cream, I told him the money was great, but apparently Gentry was some kind of a wife-beating impotent homosexual altar boy psychotic ax murderer. "He seems like such a nice guy, though." Hugh had to set his glass down because he was laughing so hard. Which made me laugh. Which made me forgive him for never being properly sympathetic. "Now, listen. Stop laughing and listen. So, that horrible agent said he admits to being all of the above, right? And she had me call his dead wife's sister to confirm all this."

"And?"

"And I called her. And the dead wife's sister says that none of it's true. *None* of it. Isn't that weird?"

"It's weird. And so?"

"So I'm confused."

"You're always confused."

"I am." I took off the hat and set it on the table. He picked it up and put it on his head. He fastened the chin strap. At least when I wore it, I didn't fasten the chin strap.

"This is the guy with the Jeep, right? That dog guy?"

"Yes. That dog guy."

Hugh picked up his glass and swirled his wine before he sipped, which struck me as pretentious. We were in the kitchen, not a tasting room. However, the wine had legs. "He seems like a nice enough guy. And personally? I don't think he's gay. Or bi, even."

"Like you actually believe anyone is bisexual."

Hugh shrugged. "I'm just saying he doesn't seem gay."

"Well, who cares what he is, it's not my business. But if this book is true, he's a horrible man."

He rolled his eyes. "Right. He seems really horrible." He popped in three olives and talked around them. "You're manufacturing intrigue. Don't make it complicated. It's simple. Before you decide whether or not to work with him, take a walk."

"A walk?"

He spat the pits into his palm and studied them, verifying that he'd removed every last little bit of olive. "Yes. Take a walk up the street to our haughty little neighbor's house and ask her some questions. You know you love to snoop. Wear the hat." I do love to snoop. So after I ate all the cheese, I took a walk.

I didn't wear the hat.

⌇

The first time I took a walk to this house, it was New Year's Day. I had a killer hangover, the best of intentions, and a puppy.

The night before, Hugh and I had gotten roaringly drunk at the home of a friend named Mitch. Mitch has an apartment near Cinema 21 on 23rd Avenue. He lives his entire life for his beautiful Golden Retriever, Milly, a very sweet, mannerly dog that he's too paranoid to spay, so she was bred by a big white dog one day up at Wallace Park. It was a purebred show dog but I can't remember the breed. Milly waved her tail at him and they both broke free from their leashes and like that, it was all over. Mitch described the mounting in graphic detail, including his attempts to pry them apart. Hugh, empathetic as usual, kept laughing and saying, "You needed to spray them with a hose!"

Mitch got a little emotional. "It was too beautiful to stop them."

"Dogs humping in the park was too beautiful?" I was laughing but I also understood, possibly because I was so drunk.

Mitch loved Milly too much to have her spayed while pregnant. He found homes for all the girl pups, but there was one boy that no one wanted. No one wants male dogs anymore. This pup was getting leggy, but he was so sweet and calm. Somehow over the course of this New Year's Eve, I ended up convincing myself that I needed to take this dog to Gentry. "That DOG GUY needs a DOG," I kept shouting at Hugh. Hugh kept laughing at me.

Nothing like drunken logic, is there?

In the light of day I was less convinced. I woke up and there he was, sitting next to me, staring at my face like, "Okay, lady. What next?" I wasn't used to pets, my father was allergic to dogs and cats, so I didn't really know what to do with this puppy. And he'd piddled on my floor. But he gave me a kiss, so I forgave him.

I took some aspirin and walked him up to the blonde girl's house. She got right into the spirit of the enterprise, but then her mother came out and I knew by her icy eyes that I had walked into her territory. "We can't make this kind of a decision for Gentry."

"Mom, come on. He needs a dog. He'll be fine if he just gets another dog, Mom."

"Can't he pick out his own?"

She shook her head. "He'd never even think of getting another dog besides Bosco."

I didn't even know where he lived, but I offered to take the dog to wherever it was and bring him back if Gentry didn't want him. Mitch would take him back. The look this older woman gave me. "I don't want Gentry disturbed." But the blonde girl kept begging, and the puppy kept running around the yard, wagging and panting and smiling, taking off on some long-legged puppy business, leaping around the yard and chomping at bees and tripping over his own big feet. And then he ran over and leaned against her muscular little legs and gave her hand a lick. She tenderly set a small hand on his lovely white head, and cooed something I couldn't hear.

She looked up saw us watching her.

Caught.

"Oh for heaven's sakes, Gretchen. Just take the dog and get in the car." The blonde lady went in her house and got her purse. She came out rummaging for her wallet. "What did it cost?"

"He was free. But he needs his second set of shots."

"Fine. We'll stop at Dove Lewis and get them on the way." She got in her Mercedes, slammed the door and drove off in a clatter of diesel engine ticks and fumes. The puppy put both his paws on the window, smiling out at me. He knew he was on his way to that dog guy.

That was January first.

Here I go again. It's almost summer, but the air is still chilly because it never warms up here until the Rose Festival is over in mid-June. I knock on her door. She opens the door looking older than she usually does. "Hello. You are, oh, I'm sorry, I'm so bad with names."

"Fiona Wallace."

"Fiona." She waves me in and offers me tea, which I accept. Then, silently, she lets me know that I'd better get to the point quickly because she doesn't want me in her house.

It comes bursting out of me in an awkward rush, the way so much tends to. "I'm sorry to bother you but I have to do this to put Hugh's mind at ease, and I guess mine, too." Does she have to be so icy and poised? Poised people bring out the worst in me. I blunder on. "Well, you probably already know this, but I met with Gentry and an agent about that book."

"Book?" She squints at me. "Was this the meeting at the airport?"

"Yes."

"And it was you, him, and an . . . agent?"

"Yes. I've done book doctor work before, and he asked me to work on the book with him if they can make a deal, and . . ."

She holds up a hand to halt me. "Do you have a copy of this book?"

"On my computer."

She clenches her jaw. "What's this book about?"

"He never told you about it?" She shakes her head. "His wife wrote it. It's her account of their marriage."

"Is it, now." She looks down her nose at me, hard to do because I'm so much taller than her, but she manages.

Well, this isn't going well. "Yes. The editors want me to edit her part, and they want his version of the story in there. Her part is awful, I mean, it's not what you'd call a flattering portrait of Gentry. So I just want to know, woman to woman, if you think Gentry would be safe to work with on a project. Because the agent seems to think he's a dangerous psychopath."

She gives a haughty little chuckle. "Why in the world would she think that?"

"Because of the way his wife died. The agent seems to think it was Gentry's fault."

"His fault?"

"Yes, but her sister says it was an accident. The stories don't match."

Kathryn sighs and picks up a spoon, one with a long, thin handle. She holds it between her thin little fingers like a cigarette, caresses it, regards it. She sets it down with precision and firmness. She is absolutely done with that spoon.

"Gentry was in Oklahoma for almost four years. He met and married his wife down there, and she was dead a year before he came back. He's refused to talk about any of it with me. I know nothing." And she regards me with something like pity in her eyes. "I can tell you one thing. You will never, ever get him to tell you one thing about himself."

I feel something inside me rising. Rising to the challenge. "Really?"

"Really. You'll never find out any information on him at all. I've known him since 1996, and I don't even know his first name."

"I do."

She stares at me, such hard, cold eyes. In them, the desire to know wrestles with the desire to maintain dignity. Dignity wins. "You might know his name, but you don't know him. I do. And to answer your question, I trust him. I trust him with my daughter. He always kept Gretchen . . . very . . . safe." Unshed tears hang in those crystal blue eyes. She's human after all. "I'm sorry. I can't talk anymore today."

She draws herself up, I stand on command. Since I'm many inches taller than her, she has to stop looking down on me. She shows me the door. "What was your name again?"

"Fiona Wallace."

"I'm sure I'll just forget."

I'm sure she won't.

Gentry

I get it on the third ring. "Hey."

"Hello, Gentry. Thank you for trying to sell your wife's book."

"Hey Kathryn? How did you hear about that?"

"That Fiona person came up here and talked to me. She's trying to decide whether or not to work with you. Gentry?" Her voice is sharp. "She asked me questions about your wife. I had nothing to offer her, of course. What could I say? Michael's never told me a thing, and neither have you." She sounds hurt.

When I think about Mike lately, I think about his Jag that's so unreliable that he had to buy a Suburban for when it's in the shop. I think about all that money he has and how he uses it to make people feel insignificant. I think about what he did to his wife and what that cost his girls. I never think about that week in Oklahoma. So tell me, God, why does his loyalty hurt so much?

A knock. "Um, Kathryn? There's someone at the door."

"Stop trying to avoid talking to me, Gentry. I've had it with this. I have strangers knocking at my door asking questions about you and I want to know what's going on."

"No, there's truly someone at the door." I check the window. "It's Tristan." I let him in. "Hey." I hold up a finger, he nods.

"Gentry, I thought we were friends."

"We are friends, Kathryn."

"Will you ever talk to me about Oklahoma?"

"I, um, have to go. Bye." I hang up. "So, um, hey."

My son has the saddest eyes I've ever seen. "My mom doesn't know I'm here. And I need to talk." And he chose me. Thank You, God.

∽

We go to the beach to walk. It's a nice day. I throw a few sticks for Sam. Sam is fussy about what he will put in his mouth, and he'll only fetch a certain type of stick. He finds a smooth one of the correct diameter and insists on that. I have a fussy dog. He's pretty, though.

"What did you do when you were fifteen?"

"What did I do?"

"Yeah. Like, with your time."

"Ah, my time. I had no time. I was a senior in high school."

"At fifteen?"

"Yes. I spent that year finishing school. And growing. I grew so much that year, I quit sports. I grew all summer, too." My body rearranging, stretching, changing into something manly and unfamiliar. Fitting itself out to make this young man walking beside me.

"Is that all you did that summer? Grow?"

"My uncle got me a job at the Cenex. Sort of like a gas station? I was trying to save money so they let me work twelve-hour days. That was what I did that summer, I pumped fuel and grew. And ate."

"You didn't hang out with anyone?"

"That was the first summer I stayed at the monastery. So I hung out with the brothers."

"The Dakota brothers." He smiles. "I bet girls came out and knocked on those big wooden doors, huh."

"No. Well, a few tried to talk to me at work, but I was too shy."

"Shy, huh. I guess the last thing I am is shy." His hands are deep in his pockets, as are mine. "My mom probably never thought of sending me to a monastery. I bet she wishes she had." He scans the water, watching for something. "How old were you the first time you had sex?"

"Sixteen."

"Did you like it?"

I clear my throat. "Yes."

He glances over at me. "Can I tell you about it? I mean, really tell you about it?"

He needs to talk about this. But can I stand to hear it?

I'm his father. "Of course."

"My mom was at a retreat. For church. And I stay home alone, you know, I mean, I'm fifteen, I don't need a baby-sitter or anything like that." And we both sort of chuckle, because that's supposed to be a funny idea. Kids needing supervision. "Gretchen told her mom she was spending the night with Reese. And I was ready, you know. Prepared. I bought condoms."

"Okay."

"So, we fooled around." He shoots me a guilty glance. I stay calm.

I'm calm because I've prayed about this, gone over this, accepted this. I've spent too much time trying to resign myself to the fact that Gretchen was always going to grow up, always, not just when she showed up in Oklahoma as a young woman, but before that. The first time she brushed my hair, or when I walked in the little house and she was sitting on the bed like Goldilocks, she was going to grow up. Even before that, before I knew her, when she started kindergarten knowing the basic ecosystems of each of the continents, before that when she was a child in diapers, back when she was born from Kathryn, when she was growing inside her, even when she was no more than God's thought, she was going to grow up. Tristan didn't cause her to grow up. It's not his fault and this was God's plan for Gretchen, that she would grow up and fall in love and make love and make a child and I accept that, God. I accept it. Amen.

And please don't let me hit my son.

We walk. "You know, we both wanted to. Okay? It wasn't just me."

"I believe you."

"Okay. Because that's true. And so I went to put it on. And it didn't fit."

"They fit?"

"Well, I didn't know that, either. I went to the drugstore and got something and left before the clerk asked how old I was. I didn't know about the sizes. But it was so hard to get on, and it kept rolling back up, and then it . . ." He makes a desperate set of hand motions, ". . . disintegrated. And then, there's that rolled-up part?" I can sort of imagine what he's talking about. "And that ring part got stuck about a third of the way on there?" Now he starts to laugh, so I let myself, finally. We both laugh. "So, I was trying to get that off, but it made me stay hard. I couldn't get it off. And I freaked out, I thought it was going to get rolled up in my foreskin. So Gretchen found some scissors."

We both stop laughing.

"Gretchen was really nice about it. Just calm, like she is. I felt like a freak of nature."

"You're not a freak of nature."

He glances over at me again, checking to see if he's lost me. "I felt like it. So then we kind of, calmed down. You know. We were laughing about it. I thought, okay, well. Maybe another time or something. But we started to fool around again. She said it would be okay, she said she still wanted to. So we did."

His voice shakes. And I don't hit him.

"It hurt her. It really hurt her. And I tried to pull out, but I didn't, you know, in time." I nod. I was never very good at that. I mean, when a woman asks you to, you try. It's almost impossible, but you do it. "I knew she was pregnant."

I don't feel violent. I just feel sorrow. My poor kids.

God, why did You make it so awful for them?

"See, this is all my fault, Gentry."

"How is it all your fault? You tried two different ways to keep her from getting pregnant. Neither of them worked, but you tried."

We walk a little, and he thinks about that. "Okay. So maybe it's not all my fault. Just maybe like three-quarters my fault."

"Bad math."

"Okay, half. Okay? Half my fault. But here's the thing. I thought it was supposed to be *good*." His eyes are full of disappointment. "I need you to talk to me about how it's supposed to be."

How it's supposed to be.

"Hey Tristan? I don't have any experience talking about this stuff. I probably won't be very good at it."

"I don't care. That's why I came here. You're, uh, this is weird but you're my dad, right? You're my dad and I need you to talk to me about it today, right now, whether you're good at it or not."

"Okay." We have to walk while I think. Everything I've ever said out loud about sex has been stupid. But I'll try. For my son. "When I was a kid, whatever I heard about sex was from other kids, and it seemed . . . wildly improbable."

"Bellybuttons and buttholes."

"Exactly. So I ignored it. And then I skipped up some grades, but I was too young to really understand what they said in Health class." I scratch my head. "I didn't want to understand it, to tell you the truth. I was happy being the world's most uninformed kid when it came to sex. I didn't want to know any of it."

"You weren't curious?"

I shake my head. I almost can't talk, but I have to. "All I really knew about girls was that they couldn't throw, which made them useless at recess as far as I was concerned."

"Why do they throw like that?" He scoops up a rock and throws by pushing it away from his chest. "Classic girl throw." He finds another rock and does the wild crossover that invariably sends a ball to left field. "And then there's this one." He gives a rock nice wobbly underhand pitch that lands ten feet in front of us. "I call that one the arc of failure." We're laughing. Sam watches us thinking, a stick, idiots, why don't you throw a stick? We walk more.

"I went to live with my uncle around the time I turned eleven. He's a priest. He's a very good man but he probably wasn't sure how to talk about sex and girls."

Tristan stifles a laugh. "Because he was, like, a priest."

"Yes. And then I was never around girls after that, anyway."

"So you lived with a priest? Like, where the priests live?"

"No. Mel wasn't a working priest that year. We lived in an apartment right by the church until I went away to school." I tell him where I went.

"Mom wanted me to go there but I said no because I'm not Catholic and there are no girls. I mean, no girls?"

"No girls. And Sex Ed wasn't a big part of the Jesuit curriculum." He nods. "I went off to college when I was sixteen. And then, there were girls. Everywhere. Girls. I was with a lot of girls in college. I know it was a sin, but it didn't feel like it at the time." God forgive me, but I was so young. "When I was twenty-two, something happened. I've never talked about it with anyone."

"Never?"

"Never." We walk, and I remember an angry man's voice saying, *the wages of sin is death*. "I went off with this girl. Her dad tracked us down. I was sure he would kill me."

"That's scary. That's very scary."

"Has Mike threatened you?" If he scares my son . . .

"No. Not very much. Don't worry about it, Gentry, just tell me what happened."

"Well, I put it all away. I did nothing. That lasted until I was twenty-seven."

"Five years?"

"Five years."

"Was AIDS part of it?" He sounds nervous. "I mean, you don't have to worry if you use a condom, right?"

"I don't use those."

He frowns. "Because you're Catholic? What are you supposed to use, then?"

"Luck. Self-control. Prayer."

"Do any of those work?"

"Probably not." We walk for a while. Tristan waits for me to continue. "When I was twenty-eight, I met the woman I married. We were together for three years."

"And she died, right? Gretchen said."

"Yes. Almost two years ago."

"And since then?"

I shake my head.

"You don't do anything?" He sounds worried.

"Not with anyone else. Besides myself." Well, that sounded stupid. Thanks for those brilliant words, God.

"Oh." He's relieved. "Well, everyone does that, right?"

"I think so. I think everyone does that."

"All the time?"

"All the time, Tristan."

He smiles down at the sand. "I am not alone."

We walk for a while. When he lifts his head, he isn't smiling. "Here's the thing. I don't ever want to have sex again. Because I'm scared."

"I know how that feels." I study his haunted face, searching for words, and I find the question someone asked me last week. "What scares you the most?"

"I'm scared to hurt Gretchen. Have you ever had sex be bad? I mean, terrible?"

"I don't think it will be that way for you the next time you try. The first time is…" My first time was overwhelming and beautiful. I shake my head. We walk for a while. Our strides match. Our feet are the same size.

This boy is my son.

"Gentry?"

"Hm?"

"This is probably stupid, but well, I'm doing the math. So I wonder. Was your first time, maybe, with her?"

This is the rule of seeing each other. He's not supposed to ask me anything about her. I'm not supposed to tell him anything about her. We both know this is the rule.

"Good math."

"Was she just one of those girls?"

"She wasn't just one of those girls. I loved her and she loved me. But I was too young to know how to do anything right."

We walk for a while, our hands in our pockets, heads down. Sam walks beside us, ignoring the water, the gulls, the other dogs. Trotting beside us, proud and quiet.

We'll turn around, soon, and walk back and climb all those stairs up to the house where I live. He'll drive back to Portland and I'll call his mother to tell her that he's on his way. She can yell at me instead of him. I can't do much for my son, but I can bear the brunt of that anger for him. But for now, I'm walking by the ocean with my son, God.

I love him.

Amen.

ANOTHER SUMMER

Gentry

Gretchen won't come with me to the store. Because she shows. I'm choosing my eggs. Zeb is rearranging the dairy case and bothering me to buy tickets to a community theater production. "Come on, Gentry, you have to."

"Sorry. Not me."

"Please? Come on."

"I never go to things like that."

"Why not? Too faggy?"

I hate dramatic tension unless I can close the book on it. "Are brown eggs healthier than white ones?"

He speaks low. "The white ones are fresher, that's for sure."

I get the white eggs. On to the cheese and butter, no decision there, I support the Tillamook Cheesemakers. Are all these types of margarine necessary? "Does this really taste like butter?"

He checks my cart. "You have butter."

"For toast. I need margarine for cooking."

He gives me an expression of pure supplication. "Come on, Gentry. Forget the margarine. Learn to cook in olive oil because trans-fats will kill you. Are you coming to my play or not? I sing."

"You sing?" He's proud. This is important to Zeb. "What play is it?"

"The Sound of Music."

"I thought that was a movie." I have some vague awareness of this movie. Singing? The Alps? *For a limited time only* . . . I need to give up television. "It isn't violent, is it? I can't go if it's violent."

"It's not violent. No one gets hurt." He smiles. "Do you want two or four? They come in pairs." His apron pocket is full of tickets. I get out my wallet.

Maybe Gretchen will go with me.

⌒

The phone rings as I'm putting away the groceries. "Hey."

"Hi, Gentry, this is . . ."

"Fiona?" I'm stunned. She *called*.

"Yes. So, will you do it? The book?"

"Yes, of course. I need the money."

"Gentry? What do you need money for?"

"Something important."

"Oh. That explains everything. Listen, I've gone over the book. It's awful but I think we can fix it. You're off for the summer, right? Can I come work with you a few days a week until we're done?"

"Here? Where I am?"

"Yes. There. Wherever it is you are."

"I'm at the beach. I mean, the coast."

"Oh. I was going to stay in a motel, but there won't be any rooms this time of year. Well, I guess that's out."

I'm a long time in answering. "I have room for you."

"Really?"

I scratch my head. "Yes. You can stay in the little house. It has a great view."

"The little house. That sounds cute."

"Yes." I'm quiet, thinking. "Hey Fiona? Won't Hugh mind?"

"Hugh *never* minds when I get out of the house. He throws parties to celebrate. You have a computer, right? My laptop's fried."

"I have a computer." I give her Man Directions, and then I have to go.

Kathryn is going to hate this.

Gretchen

Gentry's spent the morning bouncing around the kitchen, taking mysterious phone calls. I have no idea why he's so happy.

I'm too sick to be happy.

The doctor says I'm not supposed to be sick at this point, but I am. I thought it would be interesting to be pregnant. I didn't realize it would feel like having a big parasite inhabiting my body, rearranging my internal organs and leeching my nutrients.

Imagine, women do this on purpose.

I told no one but Tristan. We went to the Lovejoy Surgicenter, carrying my clean catch. And we listened to them say I was pregnant. They started in on the counseling, and we sat there. And when they finally let us leave, we stepped out the doors and he said, *Whatever you decide, I'll do it.*

I want to have it. And he turned to me out there on that sidewalk full of screaming baby savers, and he picked me up and kissed me and twirled me around. *We're having a baby!* The baby savers cheered. Tristan said, *Don't you wish you had a machine gun sometimes?*

They gave us great information at the Lovejoy Surgicenter. I knew exactly how long I had to wait to tell my parents. No one would expect me to have one of those saline procedures.

Dad did.

I spent four months sleeping day and night, secretly barfing. And then I came here and told Gentry. He made me tell Mom, and Mom made me tell Dad. And then I sat up at Dad's house with Tristan while they had this meeting where they decided how mad they were going to be. Dad came home, picked Tristan up by the neck and threw him out the door.

Dad's going to be really mad.

I'll live through this because I have Gentry. Tristan feels the same way. Sometimes he just sits beside me and repeats himself. *I can't believe that's my dad. I can't believe it, you know, G? Do you know what I mean? That's actually my dad.* I know what he's trying to say.

When Gentry jumps around like this, he reminds me of Tristan. "Have you had too much coffee?"

"There's no such thing as too much coffee."

"I can't drink it now. Heartburn." I'm so sick of everything that's wrong with me. "I want to go take a nap. Can I sleep in Mom's bed?"

"Of course."

I want my mom to be in it. I want to curl up next to her in the nest. But she's so mad at me, so disappointed and distant.

"Gretchen, what is it?"

"I want Mom."

"Come here." I go over there and he holds me close, puts his face against the side of my head, smells my hair. "It'll be all right."

"No it won't."

"It will, Gretchen. It'll be all right."

I'm so tired I could cry, but I go upstairs and barf instead. I can hear Gentry talking on the phone. I curl up in Mom's bed and the stupid baby kicks me in the ribs and I wish I could punch it back.

I wonder why I ever thought this was a good idea.

Gentry

I hear Kathryn's voice ice up when I mention Fiona. "Gentry, are you telling me she'll be *staying* there? With *you?*"

"And Gretchen. In the little house. Is that all right with you, Kathryn?" I want to beg, please, don't be cold to me, Kathryn. "Hugh's going to help me with the money. From the book. He, um, works with investments." I see Fiona pull up outside. Great, the Man Directions worked. She drives a Honda minivan. Hondas don't stink, as far as cars go, but a minivan? They don't have any kids, they don't even have a dog. Why a minivan?

"Oh, her husband's helping you? That's wonderful! He seems so nice. They're such a lovely couple. They're one of those married couples that resemble each other. They seem so happy. Compatible, too."

All these ringing matrimonial endorsements. "Yes." What am I supposed to say? "He, um, I, yes." I'm an idiot, but I wish she weren't so aware of that fact. "I, um, have to go. Bye."

I watch Fiona get out of the car. She stands there for a moment, enjoying the view, her arms wrapped around her ribs. She drove here barefoot. She has on that sweater with the holes and a dress from another time. The breeze picks it up, blows it around her thighs, and her hair is down and it whips in the wind and look at her, just look at her, oh God, she is strange and beautiful and perfect and it hurts me to look at her and she's right, Kathryn is right, I'm going to be an idiot and I'll do something stupid and everything will get messed up and I won't be able to help the kids.

No, God, not this time. I wait for Your plan. I submit. I wait. If I were a perfect man, Yours is all the love I would need. But I'm just a man. So send me what I need. Soon.

Fiona goes into the little house.

This phone has a speed dialer. Here's a number I need to dial, speedily. "Michael Mumford here."

"Hey, Mike."

"What the hell do you want?"

"Nothing. I called to tell you that Gretchen will have a college fund again. So, she doesn't have to choose between this baby and college."

"I don't believe you."

"I don't lie."

"You little asshole. Where the hell did you get it? You broke little asshole, you have nothing, nothing at all but a fucking Wrangler and a computer. You camp out in a house I gave away because I don't NEED it, you're NOTHING, and that's ALL you are. I don't believe you. You LIE. Where the hell did you EVER come up with the kind of money it takes to put a kid like Gretchen through the kind of a college she deserves?"

I swallow, hard. "You told me to identify an asset and sell it. So I did."

"What the hell did YOU have to sell?"

"Myself." I hang up and think what I'd like to say. I write this out on a piece of paper and take it out to the little house.

She's doing that thing with her hands. "Gentry! I'm sorry I didn't come to find you but I had to check this out! I love this little house!"

"Great."

"This is the fastest computer I've ever used!"

"Great."

"I even love the tea kettle!"

"Hey Fiona? Would you read this out loud for me?"

She takes the paper and scans it, frowns. "Mike Mumford can go fuck himself?"

"Could you say it again? Louder? Maybe with some expression?"

She gives it some gusto. "Mike Mumford can go FUCK himself!"

"Thank you."

She laughs out loud. "Anytime, Gentry, anytime."

I feel better, somehow, as I go back to the big house.

Fiona

What a sweet, strange man. He comes over briefly to have me swear for him, then he comes back a little later bearing a huge turkey sandwich and a tiny pickle on plate. Sam tails him everywhere he goes. Sam is getting huge.

You know, I've read the book carefully. I wonder how in the world any of it can be true. He's beautiful like a prayer card, a pretty, holy picture, far prettier than, say, me. This is simplistic of me, reductive, but the truth is I don't understand how anyone so beautiful could be so bad.

He comes out to retrieve the empty plate. "That house is so big and this little house is so perfect. Why don't you live out here? There's Internet, right?"

"Yes, there's DSL on this line. But it's erratic." He casts a longing look at the machine. "Hey Fiona? I need about an hour on the computer every night."

"Okay. I go through this with Hugh. Just tell me and I'll let you on."

He nods. "Bosco's buried on the bluff right under this window. So if you see me out there, please . . ." He puts a hand on Sam.

"I promise not to think you're a peeping Tom."

Gentry nods. "We should work."

"Are you anxious to get started?"

He sounds sad. "No. I'm anxious to finish."

Gentry

I snoop over her shoulder. She's stored the files correctly. I appreciate that. She opens a browser. "Let me find this email. Brooke sent an itemized list of what the editor wants. She bulleted it."

"Bullets seem appropriate." I won't ask You to kill me, God, I think the idea of what's on that list will kill me without any heavenly help.

"She wants the same things she talked about in that, I guess we would call it, conversation. Do you want me to read it to you?"

"No. But go ahead."

"'Fiona, Gentry should add his perspective on the following issues: Spousal abuse, jail time, alcoholism, financial troubles, marriage counseling, infidelity, religion.'" She stops and clears her throat, frowning at the screen. "'Childhood trauma, nightmares, Catholic sex abuse, bisexuality, impotence.'" She blinks a bit, then continues. "'I need Gentry to tell the story of his wife's suicide, including why she did it, how she did it, and how it affected him, including why he ended up in a mental hospital. I know the infertility was not handled the way it reads in Miriam's manuscript, but infertility sells and I don't want it changed.' In other words, she doesn't care if that part is true."

"Hey Fiona? I don't think she cares if any of it is true."

"Well, I write fiction, too. So we can add some of that."

"We're going to have to." I study my knees.

Her voice is sad and gentle, like she's saying a prayer for someone. "I don't want you to hate me for the things I have to ask you. That's important to me, Gentry. That you not hate me."

"I won't hate you." I gaze into her eyes. "I could never hate you."

She blushes. God, save me from my stupidity.

Her hands fly up like startled birds. "Well! Good! I had this idea. That maybe you could try me out with something that isn't on this list, something embarrassing that happened to you. See if you can talk about it, and I'll just listen."

"Why would telling you about something that wasn't part of the book be any easier?"

"Well, I would listen differently, for one thing. I wouldn't see it as material. I'd just listen."

"Something embarrassing?" If I have to be humiliated, can it at least be useful humiliation?

"Something that you wouldn't normally talk about." Does she have any idea who she's talking to, here? My entire life falls into the category of something I wouldn't normally talk about. I could talk about my grocery list and it would be a revelation, compared to the amount of personal information I generally volunteer. "Try me, Gentry."

I think about it, and what amazes me the most is the idea that the most humiliating moments of my life happened in groups. My marriage was a four-year humiliation campaign. The Oregon group seems to center on Marci. I search through those. Hm. "Gentry? Are you there?"

"I have to think before I speak, Fiona. I have to think about what I say."

"So you don't stammer."

"I think of it as 'umming.'"

"Have you always done that?"

"I don't know."

"Do you ever do it on purpose?"

I wonder how she knows this. "Sort of. Sometimes when I don't want to talk, I start to blurt and I know I'll 'um' and I do it anyway." And that reminds me of something I can tell Fiona, something embarrassing, but funny. I tell her all about my Thanksgiving visit to Daniel Shaw's home my first year of college. He insisted I come home with him.

I walked into his ancestral home and it was as big as a church and ten times more grand. I thought I might start accidentally smashing family heirlooms by bumping into everything. That was happening that fall because of the growth spurt, I was still thrashing, lurching, flailing around.

Daniel was embarrassed when we entered his home. It wasn't the clumsy young scholarship boy who embarrassed him. I think it was how much he had. He carried my dirty duffel bag up to a guest bedroom the size of a classroom. When he left me in there, I fought the urge to go hide in a cabinet until the weekend was over. But I washed up and combed my hair in a bathroom that was larger than our dorm room.

I went to find him, tripping over priceless rugs and bumping into fragile tables all the way. The halls were hundreds of feet long. The stairs went down into an enormous foyer that had archways going off in all directions, like transepts and naves. Had this house formerly been a cathedral? I was baffled as to where I should go.

I went out the front door because the one thing I knew how to do was leave.

And the gardener saw me and came up yelling about what was I doing using the front door, he expected me an hour ago, get over here and get to work, and he took me over to a mower. I had no idea what to say, I opened my mouth and all that came out was umming, babble mixed with um's, so . . .

"You cut the grass?"

"Well, some of it, until Daniel came out and found me. The look on his face. I pointed to the gardener, and I said, 'He made me do it.' And then we both laughed, and then he took me in and got my bag and put me in his room with him. He never left my side. He was afraid that he'd come into the kitchen and find me peeling carrots if he left me alone.

"And after that, every time we saw each other doing something stupid or strange, one of us would point at the other and say, 'He made me do it.' It was our joke. I said that to him when I got married." He made me do it.

Daniel made sure I got married.

Fiona is staring at me. "Are you cold? You're shivering."

"I'm fine, just fine."

Fiona has a thick folder of information. She pages through it and frowns. "Do you have any pictures of your wife?"

"I gave them all to her mother."

She clears her throat a little. "Okay. Well, what drew you to her? Was she pretty?"

"Yes, well. No. She was . . . cute." I wonder if Fiona hates men who call women "cute." But that's what my wife was. Cute.

"What did she look like?"

"Small and, um, fit. Dark hair. Wavy. Her eyes were a different color."

"Different? Like, from each other?"

"No. They were amber. Sometimes they had an orange cast to them."

"That sounds weird."

"It was beautiful, like fire." I stand up and go to the window, thinking about those eyes glowing with anger. "She had a nursing degree. She could be funny when she was talking about work. She was very political, she had strong opinions. We didn't have common interests. But she was different, Fiona, she was different than . . . it seemed like things could be different with her."

"And were things different?"

"Yes. Things were certainly different." I bark out a laugh.

"What was best about her? Her best trait."

"She was an excellent teacher."

Fiona tilts her head. "And the worst?"

I think of her temper, her foul mouth, her suspicion, her sharp nails and hard little fists, how she treated my friends, the disposal of my stuff, the relentless critique of everything I said and wore and ate and did, down to which size spoon I used to eat cereal. What was the worst thing?

"Her cooking."

"Just tell it to me like a story. Start with when you met her. If something's hard, leave it for later. Give me some idea of how it all began."

I can do this. I can tell a story.

"Once upon a time, I threw up in a driveway."

∽

The next morning, I wake up when Fiona knocks on the kitchen door, setting Sam off in that funny puppy yelp. "Sam, hush. Come here, boy. Hush." I have a television hangover. I stumble over to the door, let Sam out, let her in. "Hey. Please don't knock. He always barks at knocking. Please just come in from now on."

"Really? What if you're sleeping?"

"Then I'll wake up." I scratch my head and smile at her.

She smiles back. "I wonder if you have any tea?"

"Sure. Just sit there for a minute." I go out to find Sam and relieve myself. Kathryn would kill me if she knew I went on her grass. All the time. "Sam, in the house. Come on. Let's go find Fiona."

Time to wash my hands.

I make tea for her in a pot so she'll stay. She waits for it with sleepy eyes. This is nice, seeing her in her plaid bathrobe across the counter like this, drinking her tea. I make myself some coffee. I hate tea.

Sam jumps up on the couch to go back to sleep. He's tired. Last night Gretchen came in and lay down on the bed and cried for all the things she's too brave to cry about during the day. I held her until she fell back asleep. I couldn't, so I ended up on the couch.

Gretchen comes down the stairs to the kitchen.

"Good morning."

She scowls. "There's no such thing as a good morning. Morning equals puke." She stares at Fiona, and Fiona stares back. They dip their heads at each other. Gretchen walks over and leans on me. "The only thing I can stand to smell in the morning is you." I put my face in her hair. It smells as dry and sandy as her mother's, now. She pulls away, takes a package of crackers from the cabinet and goes in to watch cartoons.

"When is she due?"

"The end of July."

"How old is she?"

"She turned sixteen in February."

Fiona throws her tea in my face and slams out the door.

⌒

I go out to the little house and open the door. She's jamming things into her suitcase. "Hey Fiona?"

"That girl would have been FIFTEEN when you did that to her."

"Listen to me."

"You're a TEACHER?"

"Could you *listen* to me?"

"Her mother said she TRUSTED you with her."

"Fiona."

"How COULD you? You seemed so NICE. Brooke was RIGHT. You're a CREEP."

"Would you listen to me?"

"NO. Let me OUT of here."

I'm so angry that my hands are shaking. My eyes water from some flowery spice in that tea. I'm afraid I'm going to hit something. "I refuse to shout. Please listen to me for one minute and then I'll get out of your way." She hates me, but she holds still, her arms crossed. "Gretchen's baby is my grandchild."

"Your *what*?"

"Gretchen is pregnant by my son."

"Your *what*?"

"My son."

"You're too *young* to have a son."

"He's fifteen. I was seventeen when he was born." Seventeen. Fifteen. Maybe this baby is a boy, and he can be a father at thirteen. My eyes are watering, that tea, that's all, and I'm not angry anymore, I'm just tired. Exhausted. "I need the money from this book to help the kids. Their parents are angry because they won't abort the baby. I have to be able to help. I have to have some money, Fiona."

She stares at me. "*That's* why you're selling this horrible book?" Her grey eyes are wide with something I can't name. "You're doing this for *them*?"

I nod.

She smoothes her dress, clears the anger out of her throat, notices her suitcase. She starts to put her clothes back in the closet.

Gretchen

I'm trying to eat, and Gentry's trying not to watch me. "Stop it."

"I'm sorry. I thought you liked soup."

"Don't be sorry, and don't watch me, and don't worry." Everyone is always worried. No one understands how terrible it is to eat. I'm full to the top with this kicking thing, and I don't eat tomatoes, beef, spices, citrus, anything like that anymore, and I still get the worst heartburn. "It's impossible to eat. The gastric acid just bubbles up and burns me."

"Oh, so you have the urping problem, like Jack? Maybe you have a hiatal hernia, Gretchen. Better have a colleague check you out."

"At least I'm not stoppered up."

"And your knees are good. No edema."

"Have you seen my feet lately? I do have edema. And I have hemorrhoids, too. I'm not joking, I really do." He looks like he could have gone his entire life without knowing that, but I have terrible hemorrhoids, and it's not what you would call fun. That's part of what makes eating so hard, the pain at the other end of the digestive process. "Why don't you eat too? Maybe it will help me eat if you eat."

Even though I brought up hemorrhoids, Gentry will eat if I ask him to. He washes his hands, gets himself a bowl of soup. He must be nervous, because he washed his hands before he cooked, before he dished me up, and now again. He's like a raccoon. I watch him say his grace and start to eat. He eats in a way that people like to watch, just like Tristan.

Oh, I don't want to think about Tristan.

"I'm so fat."

"You're skin and bones."

I look down at my arm. "You're right. I'm skinny and ugly."

"You could never be ugly."

"I am. I don't know how Tristan can stand to look at me. Everything on me is gross. I have stretch marks all over my hips. Look at my breasts, Gentry. I always wanted breasts like Marci and now look at them, they're huge and I'm getting stretch marks on those, too. Northern Europeans don't have enough elastin in their skin. I won't ever be normal again. Everyone else is normal and thin, not stretched out and ugly. Tristan should just find someone else."

Gentry takes my hand and holds it. "Tristan loves you."

"He's going to ruin his life. He'll quit soccer, Gentry, he won't get a scholarship without soccer and I know him, he'll want to help me and he'll stop playing."

"No one is going to let that happen. Because we're going to help you."

"My dad is *not* going to help me. He won't even *speak* to me."

He holds out his arms. "Come here."

I sit on his lap, even though I'm too old to sit on his lap. He puts his arms around me, rocks me, smoothes my hair. It feels as good as it did when I was ten. His voice is low and firm. "Listen to me. I'll help with the baby. I'll have money. I'll make sure you both go to college. Everything will work out."

"Everyone hates us."

"No one hates you."

"It seems like it."

"I know. But babies put people in a forgiving mood. Everyone will come around."

"Even my dad?"

"Even your dad. Trust me."

"And you won't ever leave me again?"

"No. I will never leave you again as long as I live. I promise." He's trying not to cry. And something about the catch in his throat relaxes mine, stops me from hurting, stops me from crying. I wipe my nose on his shoulder, and it makes us both laugh.

"I still think I'm gross. I don't know how Tristan can stand to look at me."

Gentry sighs, one of his big deep sighs. "He's a lot like me, yes?" I nod. It's embarrassing, but the truth is Gentry and Tristan are almost exactly alike. "He loves you like I loved his mother. He can't even see anyone else because he loves you so much."

"But you stopped loving her."

"I've never stopped loving her, Gretchen. She was my first love." He breathes this into my hair like it's a secret. His hand feels warm, rubbing my back where it always aches.

I sit there for a minute, remembering riding at night in the back of his Jeep, his voice telling Mel about the girl he loved in college, the beautiful redheaded woman in Georgia. What was her name? He went back to find her when he left Oregon, and she was married and had a baby.

Named Ariel.

The hair on my arms stands up.

Gentry smiles and frowns at the same time. "Feeling better?"

"I am." My blood sugar must be all over the place, because I'm suddenly starving. I sit on his lap and eat his soup, and after it's gone, I eat most of mine.

Fiona

I called Hugh and told him what happened. "This is why I should never leave the house." I was almost crying, but all he could do was laugh.

"Classic, Fiona. Nice job. Was this something you got from Masterpiece Theater? I bet you called him a cad, didn't you. You called him a cad and a scoundrel, and dashed your tea in his face!" His voice softened. "Come on now. He'll forgive you. You mess up in such entertaining ways that everyone always forgives you."

"I hope so."

"Trust me. So, speaking of unforgivable, you'll never guess who came by the house today. She dared to darken our door. I wouldn't let her in." I think about this, feel those cold shivers of longing that go down my arms when I think about her. "Fiona, honey? Are you okay?"

"I'm fine. Just don't give her any information. All right? If she comes to the door, don't let her in, and if she calls don't tell her anything about me. Don't tell her where I am."

"I could tell her you joined the Foreign Legion."

"Tell her nothing. Please, Hugh."

"Sweetie."

Everything hangs there, his care, my heart, her name. I can't talk, so I hang up and put my face down in my arms.

I like being alone, but this would be a nice time to be around other people.

⌒

I don't knock, because I'm supposed to blithely stride into the kitchen. What if he's sitting on the couch spanking the monkey or something? Maybe he doesn't do that.

I walk in. They're at the kitchen counter, eating soup. I need to tell him I'm sorry, but I won't be apologizing in front of her. Imagine how humiliated she'd feel, knowing I thought a thirty-two-year-old man was the father of that baby.

How can a girl that age be pregnant?

He smiles, miraculously glad to see me. "Hey. Do you want some soup?"

"Yes, please have some soup." Gretchen rolls her eyes. "Have a gallon."

"I'd love some. But just a bowl, please."

"Great." He jumps up. "Okay, sit down." I do, next to Gretchen. Gentry washes his hands and dishes me up out of an enormous pot. Apparently they plan to eat soup for a long, long time. I take a bite and close my eyes. It tastes like the soup my mother made from whatever was left in her garden. It was always my favorite meal. "This is delicious."

He blushes. "Thank you." He gets busy eating.

She glances up from her bowl. "We need a DVD player."

He clears his throat. "I thought we just . . ."

"No. We need a DVD player because Marci bought me a pregnancy yoga DVD. According to my sister, it will help me retain the muscle tone in my pelvic floor."

"Your pelvic floor?"

"You know, the muscles I'll use while giving birth. She's worried about my vagina."

He looks absolutely mortified. "I can't get one until I have another payday. Which will be in September."

"Well, dummy, that's after the baby's born." Gretchen shakes her head. "Never mind, I'll ask Mom."

I speak up. "I have a spare player at my house. I could bring it. Really, we don't use it, Hugh bought a better one. I'll bring it back with me." He nods, still embarrassed about the pelvic floor, I guess. There are two tickets to a community theater production of "The Sound of Music" on the counter. "Are you two going to a play tonight?"

"No way." Gretchen sounds grumpy. "That show is so lame. Mom watches that movie all the time." She sings a little, making a mocking face. "The hills are alive, with the sound of music . . . aah aah aah aah . . ." What a voice, incredible. And she's utterly unaware of what a gift she has. She shakes her white-blonde head. "I'll pass."

He sighs through his nose. "Well. I won't go either, then."

"Fine. Don't go."

"I guess I won't."

"Don't."

"Great. I'll stay home."

"Fine. Stay home."

"I will." He gets himself some more soup. "Zeb will be disappointed, though."

"Gentry? Why are you telling me about Zeb? He was such a dick to me in grade school, so I really don't care if Zeb's disappointed. If you care about Zeb, then go by yourself." Gretchen is pregnant, sixteen, and very grumpy.

Here goes.

"I love 'The Sound of Music.'"

"Why don't you go, Fiona? Why don't you go with Gentry, then? Because I'm not going to go, and I don't want to have to feel guilty if Gentry doesn't go. So just go."

So we go.

∽

Here we are at the theater.

Before we left, I went out and put on a dress and let down my hair. Yes, I'd packed some pretty sandals.

He was waiting for me in the living room when I rushed back. "Ready!"

He looked me up and down, blinked. "Excuse me." He ran upstairs and came down three minutes later in a pair of khakis and a tucked-in oxford shirt with no holes in the elbows. He'd put his hair in a ponytail.

He said hardly a word on the drive.

∽

Gentry has no idea what part his student is playing. He's never heard of the Von Trapp family singers. In trying to understand his sexuality, I should probably take his lack of background in musical theater as an indicator. But who knows? Anything can happen these days. A man can be gay and never have seen "Evita."

Everyone in the auditorium says "hi" or "hello" to him, and he says "hey" back. People stand there and smile at me until I introduce myself. He must not date very often. Not that this is a date.

Maybe he's forgotten my name.

We sit down. They have a remarkable orchestra playing. There are a lot of artistic types that live here on the coast, I think. They have a darling Maria. She trills and lilts and emotes on some well-constructed living hills, but I can't help thinking that Gretchen sang it prettier, in her mocking, pure voice.

Maria heads back to the convent.

They have some talented older ladies to play the nuns. As a graduate of Catholic schools, I can vouch for their authenticity. Very nun-like. They converge on the stage in their habits and wimples, singing about the Maria problem.

Gentry grabs my hand in a death grip. His hand is ice cold and shaking. He's trembling all over. When the Mother Superior comes on the stage, he puts his head down and presses my hand against his mouth. I feel his shuddering breath in my palm. He keeps his head down until Maria leaves the convent.

"Gentry?" I whisper. "They're gone." He sits up slowly and peers at the stage. He starts to breathe normally. Eventually, as Maria takes charge of the many Von Trapps, he relaxes, but he still holds my hand. He knows all the kids onstage. I know this because whenever one comes onstage, he leans over and whispers the name in my ear. Which makes me blush, for some reason. But it's dark and he can't see. Zeb sings very nicely during his sappy duet with the eldest Von Trapp girl.

Intermission. The lights come up and he lets go of my hand.

We go to the lobby. He looks longingly at the beer and wine concession but gets some mineral water, instead. "Is that brand good?" He hands it over. I was only making conversation, but I drink it because I'm thirsty. He looks at the floor, at the program, at the door. Anywhere but at me. We don't speak. The few people in the auditorium who didn't come over to find out who I was before the show do so now. I introduce myself. I start to feel a little strange because he hasn't introduced me once. They flash the lights, and he looks longingly at the street door.

"It's time to go back in."

"Oh. I though maybe the power was failing."

"No. That's just a warning. Intermission is almost over."

He sighs, one of those deep sighs that starts at the floor and moves up, leaving me a little weak. "Okay."

We walk back in and take our seats. "There's one more part with the you-know-whats. Don't worry, just relax and enjoy the show, and I promise I'll warn you, okay?"

He nods. He watches his student morph into a Nazi. His treachery breaks my heart, as well as the heart of the little Von Trapp strumpet. When they flee back to the convent, I nudge him. "They're coming." He puts his head down. I put my hand on his back. He only trembles a little, and pops right up after all the scary penguins leave the stage.

The music festival starts. "Gentry?"

"I'm okay," he whispers.

"It's just that . . ."

"I'm really okay."

"I think that maybe . . ." And then all those nuns start to pop out of the holes at the sides of the stage, singing "Climb Every Mountain" in their warbling old voices. Gentry leaps from his seat. He looks like a wild horse, his ponytail flying out behind him, vaulting over seat backs and theater patrons as he bounds out of the auditorium.

Gentry

"There were NUNS. You KNEW there were NUNS in there. Why didn't you TELL me?"

"What's the problem with *nuns*?" Gretchen thought I was crazy.

I was embarrassed, then, too embarrassed to tell her that I'd just lettered in track getting out of there, winning some kind of World's Oddest Idiot Award.

Fiona spent the ride home trying not to laugh out loud at what an idiot I am, and I have to work with her today. I take my coffee out, and she's typing. She doesn't comment on last night. "Here, sit down and read a little. I've revised the courtship, but we have to work on the wedding." She gets up and tends to a tea bag.

I read through the revised courtship, scan the wedding. "This reads like a parody."

"Brooke loves it."

"As long as Brooke is happy." As long as she doesn't take away the money.

In the book, I'm officially married, and Sandy and I are on her parents' queen-sized bed. What exactly were we supposed to be doing? "What does this mean, he was 'poised above' me? What was he poised to do?"

She shrugs. "Maybe he was just . . . poising."

"Okay, for one thing, her parents slept in twin beds. And Sandy wasn't even my best man." She sips her tea. I clear my throat. "Hey Fiona? What kind of a moron would get married in the living room of his in-laws' home and then go into their bedroom and have sex with his best friend in a house full of relatives?"

"A sexual thrill-seeker?"

"Oh, that's me."

She stifles a laugh. "It isn't very plausible."

"What happened is that he came in the bedroom when I was changing, and he hung up my suit and hugged me. She walked in when he hugged me."

"That's it?"

"Yes. We were standing up, we were dressed." I shake my head. "He did compliment my shorts. You know those shorts Gretchen had on yesterday? He said, 'great shorts, Grasshopper.' And that was it."

"He calls you Grasshopper?" She stifles another laugh. "Okay! Well, Brooke says I have to leave this whole part in. You can refute it, though. Move, please." I move and she seats herself. "Let's see." Fiona thinks, and then she lets go in a burst of inspiration, like electricity flows out of her fingertips. She types like a madwoman.

I sit down on the bed, wait, pet Sam. Wonder silently if she is laughing at me. And try not to think about nuns.

Finally, she reads. "How about this. 'On the day of my wedding, I knew that my desperate bargain with God to give us children would not work,' blah, blah, blah, some more religious stuff here, praying, bargaining, that kind of stuff. 'I knew in my heart that I had made a mistake, but I am a man of honor, and I knew I would stand by the woman I had pledged to honor and love.'"

"You used honor twice there. And 'pledged'? It sounds like dusting."

"What?"

"You know, that stuff you dust with. Pledge."

"I never dust."

I feel manly today.

"Gentry, please stop critiquing and listen. 'My friend Sandy counseled me, consoled me,' blah, blah, blah. 'My fiancée's dark suspicions had swelled in the year before we married. I stood accused of infidelity at every turn. According to her, no glance was innocent, no word uttered to another woman was uttered in friendship, and as much as I tried to reassure her, she remained convinced of my guilt. But to stand accused of sleeping with my best friend at the wedding left me broken and despondent, unable to find the words to refute her ridiculous charges.'"

"Hm. It has a kind of judicial feel. Standing accused, pledging, plea bargaining, honor, suspicion."

She laughs out loud. "Don't bother analyzing it, it's only crap!"

"I have a friend in Oklahoma who could write this kind of crap."

"Give her my agent's name. Crap sells." She types away, happy, cheerful. How can she step in all this and still be happy? "Infidelity is on the list, for some reason. Was Brooke thinking about this episode?"

Hm. I have a distinct moral dilemma here, in Vu's words. On my honeymoon, I kept myself true to the woman who understood my despair. Unfortunately, that woman was not my wife. I managed to make it through the entire week in Paradise without sleeping with my new wife. "I know she was suspicious before we got married. But I don't think she was ever suspicious later." A lie of omission, God, forgive me.

Fiona types away. "So, the only affairs were hers."

"Excuse me?"

"Her affairs."

"She never had any affairs."

She shrugs. "There are a few in the book."

"I read nothing about an affair."

"Gentry, I think there might be a few things that weren't in the copy you read."

I see. I got the Bowdlerized version. "Like what?"

"Like three affairs."

"Three? Who?"

"One of them doesn't even have a name. Some student she turned to 'in despair.'"

"Was she broken and despondent?"

"She was." She arrows through the document. "Here's the second one. A neighbor kid named Erik who approached her when she was sunbathing in the front yard. She slept with him while you were at the store. And the last one. A younger man with a big nose named Arthur Fillmore."

"Arthur Fillmore?"

"Yes. An adjunct faculty member."

"That has to be Ardis Fillard." Ardis has written me steadily since she died, boring me with bland recipes ("It tastes so much like something Miriam made") and detailed descriptions of traffic intersections ("They really need to time that light differently"). He lives in Yakima, where he teaches at the community college. "She never had an affair with Ardis Fillard. She made fun of his nose all the time. I never understood that, because she had her nose fixed."

Fiona is quiet for a moment. "Evelyn said they both had perfect noses."

"Miriam's didn't start out that way."

"I have her entire medical history." She thumps a stack of folders. "I've been through the whole thing. No rhinoplasty. Miriam must have lied."

"Hey Fiona? She told me she had it fixed. What would be the point of her lying about that?"

"I don't know. She was your wife. Why don't you figure it out?" Fiona is irritated with me. Her hands dart around, cleaning up my computer table, which is good because she's the one who messes it up.

Fine, then. I'm good at puzzles. I'll figure it out.

Miriam told me she had her nose fixed, and our kids might have big noses. She wondered if I would mind. That was the second year we were together. She must have been thinking about noses because that was the year Ardis started hanging around. He had a big nose, and that must have made her worry. That if she did get pregnant, the baby would have a big nose.

I lie down on the bed.

"Gentry? Are you all right?"

"I helped Derek *rebuild* that car."

She stares at the screen. "Well, what do you want me to do? Take it out, leave it in, or change it?"

"Leave it in there. All three of them. Put mine in there, too."

"You had an affair."

"I did."

Her eyes are not wide with concern. They're wide with something else. She returns to the computer and types.

"Hey Fiona?"

"Hm?" She types furiously. Fiona is all of a sudden not very talkative.

"Hey."

"Hi."

"No, not hey, hi. Hey, I want to explain something. It was not an ongoing thing."

She keeps her face carefully blank. "It's none of my concern if you cheated on your wife. You don't owe me any explanations. Your marriage isn't my business."

"Right. Except for the part where you have to write a book about it."

She shrugs. "It has nothing to do with me." And she goes back to typing.

"I'll be right back." My coffee is cold. I go back into the house to get a refill. I think I need to wash this cup out, really well. Twice. I pour myself a hot cup and go check on Gretchen. She's watching television.

She frowns. "You have a really weird expression on your face."

"Thank you."

"Is everything all right out there?"

"Fine. Just fine." I fight the urge to get in the Jeep and drive to, oh, I don't know. Maybe North Dakota. I go back out to the little house. She's still sitting at the computer, typing and ignoring me. "Hey Fiona? Could you look at me? Just stop typing and turn around and listen to me for a minute?" She turns and gives me a polite stare. I sit down on the bed and decide the artificial nature of her expression is the most heartbreaking thing I have ever seen in my life.

All right. I might be overreacting, but it hurts me. Badly.

"When I got married, I thought I was doing the right thing. I thought I had to do it."

She stares at me without blinking. "Because she was pregnant?"

I have to take a moment, I'm so surprised. "How did you know that?"

"Just go on."

"After the wedding, we were in Hawaii and I had what my uncle calls a dark night of the soul. I, um. I turned to someone else."

"Oh my GOD." She turns back to the keyboard and starts beating it up again.

"Hey Fiona? That's a new keyboard."

She stops typing, hangs her head. Shakes it. "You cheated on your pregnant wife on your honeymoon."

"I'm sorry."

"Don't apologize to *me*, I'm not personally affected by this. But don't accuse me of flowery language when you try to cloak the fact of a one-night-stand on your honeymoon with a phrase like 'dark night of the soul.' Because honest-to-God, that's bullshit."

She is so angry. And so right.

She shakes her head again. "Please just go on."

"With what?"

"With whatever else you have to say about infidelity."

I have to take a minute to figure out what I want to say. And whatever I say, it has to be honest. This woman can see right through me.

"I was with her longer than I've ever been with anyone else. Three years. And that was the only time. I tried to make it work with her." How to say this. "I want you to understand that I tried to make it work. I even went to counseling."

"You went to counseling?" The expression on her face is, yes, it's amazed. Okay. Amazed is an improvement over profoundly disillusioned or artificially calm. "I thought she must have made that part up, because I can't imagine you in counseling, Gentry. Well, I can. And it's funny."

"It was probably even better than you imagine."

She laughs. Laughter is a definite improvement. "Well," she says, "it's in the book. You're supposed to talk about it. Let's go." And I don't know how, or why, but she asks easy questions and I find myself telling Fiona about the counselor, his shoes, his questions. I tell her all of it, all the picking and the pecking and the pestering and the harping. Fiona listens and laughs and hoots and squawks. I tell her all of it, my clothes and my job and my weirdness and my DEFENSIVENESS. I even tell her about the mayonnaise question. I finish up with me yelling about that hairy spot, my vestigial tail, and she holds her stomach and leans back in her chair. Finally. Someone who understands how terribly, awfully, horribly funny the whole thing was.

"Can I see it?"

"See what?"

"Can I see your hairy spot? I want to see it."

"No."

"Oh Gentry, please."

"No."

"Please. I'm so curious." She waits. So I stand up, and lift my shirt and hitch down my jeans, just a little, not that low.

What's wrong with me?

"It's not that thick. It's really fine." She speaks in a wondering voice. "It looks so soft." Her fingertips drop to my skin and play across my lower back.

The noise I make.

I'm out of the little house like a gunshot, Sam at my heels.

Lorrie

You know, this guy is supposed to be my friend. And since Gretchen holed up there to drop the kid, I haven't hardly seen him. School gets out and he disappears. A person gets damn tired of that sometimes.

So I go up to see him, see, and some woman I never seen before in my goddamn life answers the door. I ask where he is and she says in Portland, taking Gretchen to the doctor. But as far as knowing who this woman is, I have not one sonofabitching clue.

So I call him up. "Who the hell is that? I stop by your house and some broad comes to the door. Who the hell is that?"

"Her name is Fiona."

"Nice legs. Are you knocking boots?" That's a perfectly okay question, but he gets all testy with me.

"She's married."

"So? Answer my question."

"No, Lorrie. She's helping me with a project."

"What sonofabitching project?"

"I don't want to talk about it."

Little asshole never wants to talk about anything. A person gets damn tired of that sometimes. "Screw you, Gentry. Do you want to go fishing or not?"

"For what? What could we fish for right now?"

"Oh hell, I don't know. We're leaving for Canada pretty soon. I thought, hell, you know . . ." Well, I just want to go fishing. With him, to tell the truth. "Gentry, I want to get out of here, see, I'm sick of wiping up baby shit. This baby of mine shits every time she eats."

"Hm. What does the doctor say about it?"

"It's nothing, it's just because Vicki nurses her. Something about the milk. I'm telling you, that milk is different but Vicki swears by it. She likes having a little one on the tit. She's always got Geneva on there, always. A person gets damn tired of that sometimes. Once in a while I'd like to pay those tits a little attention myself, you know. Jesus Christ, they're round and big as cantaloupes, and the nipples? Stand out there like thumbs. But no, I can't touch'em."

I expect him to get mad, but he says, "I, um, have to go."

"Don't you want to fish?"

"No. I have to work on something."

"Screw you, little buddy."

"Bye, Lorrie."

Forget him. He can sit up there in that house and get all huffy at me and have all the sonofabitching secrets he wants. I have to go change a diaper.

A person gets damn tired of diapers sometimes.

Fiona

Hugh nearly died laughing. "Is it really a tail? How long is it?"

"No, Hugh, it's a patch of hair."

"And you *touched* it?"

"I couldn't help myself!" I still can't believe I did it. He's probably never been more affronted in his life, me putting my hand on there like that. That soft, silky hair. As soft as Sam. I'd better straighten up or Gentry will bag this project.

Gentry is, by the way, sitting on the bed, reading one of my magazines. "I gave you new names."

"Hm?" He glances up.

"Names. I named Miriam 'Mavis' and some big guy dropped over here looking for his little buddy, so I named you 'Buddy.'"

He shakes his head. "Mavis and Buddy. She was always after me to choose a different name. I wonder what she would have thought of Buddy."

"Why don't you choose a name you like?"

"I like Gentry. I like it just fine." Well, I'm learning to recognize that tone, that "ask me again and I'll run away" tone, so I don't push it. His name isn't on the list.

But the drinking is. I read out loud. "'From the beginning, his drinking was out of control. Many was the morning when I went to find Buddy, collapsed in his own urine and vomit, totally passed out on the floor of the bathroom. My life turned into a total masquerade, covering for him at work, hiding his drinking and my shame from our family and our friends.'"

What friends? Did this woman have any friends?

I should talk.

The expression on his face is incredulous. "Collapsed in my own urine and vomit?" He shakes his head. "We were together for three years. I didn't drink at all for the first two."

Drinkers always know when they started, almost to the day. "So no urine and no vomit?"

"No. Well, I did throw up at my bachelor party."

"Well, good. I'll put that in there, in case Brooke has her heart set on some vomit." He laughs. I love it when he laughs. "Gentry, how bad was it?"

"Oh, um, bad."

"How much did you drink per day? Or do you even know?"

And he gives me this look. "Of course I knew. I had to plan for it so I didn't get sick."

He sounds like a very organized drinker. "How much did you drink per day?" He tells me exactly how much. "That's not all that much, Gentry. That's actually not all that much to have in a day."

He shakes his head. "That was after a year of cutting down."

"Cutting down?"

"Yes. I couldn't drink anything cheap for some reason. It started to make me sick. I had to buy nice poison and it cost a fortune. So I was drinking as little as I could by the time Mike Mumford came down there."

"Mike Mumford? The guy you had me swear about?"

He's embarrassed. "Yes. He came down the week before I left Oklahoma and upset my whole system."

"Your drinking system?"

"Yes."

"How?"

"I drank all the time, but I was never drunk. One of the nights he was down there, I got drunk. And then I couldn't drink in the morning in front of him, that threw things off. So then I was sick. Once I was sick, the system no longer worked. When he left, I quit."

"You just quit? Wasn't that hard?"

"It was as easy to quit as it was to start."

"I've never heard this described as easy."

His eyes are hard, angry. "Well. It was. Except I was sick." He stands up and starts to pace, and then he sits back down and stares at me in a vaguely accusatory way, as if I'm supposed to know something. "That was the only time in my life I ever drank like that. Usually I just drank to have fun. But in Oklahoma, I set up a way to live in it. It was what I had left."

"Did you miss her that much?"

"Gretchen? I missed her so much, I thought I might die of it."

"I was talking about Miriam."

He shakes his head, and stands up again and paces. "I need to go take a shower or a walk or something."

This is hard to watch. "Gentry? What does it feel like?"

"What does *what* feel like?"

"This. What you're feeling."

He stops. Takes a breath. Calms down. "I'm not good at describing things."

"Just try."

He swallows. "I have this dry ache in the back of my mouth. Like a pang, like a lust? It fills my whole body."

An ache, a pang, a lust. I'm intimately familiar with those. "So you still miss it?"

"Every day. Some days more than others. I feel . . ." He has his hair in a ponytail today, and his neck is so strong. He angles his head on that strong neck so he doesn't have to face me. "I feel lonely for it. It's always felt like there's a room, and inside there's this part of me I only get to with drinking."

Karen G. Berry

"A part of you in a room?"

"Yes. A part of me that's waiting in there."

"What does he do when you don't drink?"

"He sits. He waits." He shakes his head. "I need say good night."

"Good night, Gentry."

He walks away through the night towards the house, where all the lights are on. I work for a while, thinking about drinking and systems and sickness, imagining a small room where a lonely drinker has to live.

When it all gets too sad to bear, I get up and walk out the door of the little house, and stand where I can see into the kitchen. The ocean is behind me, black and loud and too deep. He's talking on the phone, nodding. I stare at his neck. A woman's neck is beautiful when it's slender, and a man's neck is beautiful when it's strong.

His neck is strong.

Gentry

It's June. Her dad hasn't spoken to her since March.

Fiona brought a DVD player (apologizing for the lack of a manual, "we never save manuals," almost dropping it, blushing and stammering until I took it away from her) and I hooked it up. Gretchen does the yoga every morning, watching the screen. The soft voice of the instructor, her long limbs, her concentration, all gathered around her round stomach. Posed and holding. Waiting.

Her arms and legs are sticks. I cook when she's out of the kitchen and then air it out before she tries to eat. Kathryn suggested this. It helps, but only a little. She takes four or five bites to please me, then gives up.

Gretchen took away all my funny boxers and sewed the flies shut, and she wears them. I actually see my own underwear in public on a sixteen-year-old girl. Kathryn offered to take Gretchen shopping, but she declined.

One weekend, Kathryn presented me with six pairs of sweats. I know these are to share. And then she asked me, "Do you need underwear?" Of course I didn't need underwear. I had Gretchen to buy my underwear, why would I need Kathryn to buy my underwear?

I share the sweats with Gretchen. She wears my T-shirts, too.

I drive her in for her doctor's appointments. Tristan meets us. I come to all the appointments because Gretchen wants me to.

At first, the nurse was confused. She thought we were one and the same, Tristan and I. I want to shake people, there is no way I look as young as this boy of mine. He's fifteen years old. And what about the hair? He has short hair. Sometimes all three of us go in and listen to the baby. The heartbeat is strong, like the baby who kicks her.

The doctor lectures Gretchen about her weight. "The baby takes what the baby needs. It's you we need to worry about." She crosses her arms and nods, watching the doctor with her scared blue eyes.

"She eats. She tries hard to eat."

"I believe you, Gentry. But she has to eat more because she's probably not even done growing herself yet."

Gretchen rolls her eyes. "How much taller am I supposed to be?"

"With your dad? You could top six feet."

Everyone knows Mike Mumford.

This doctor is a good man. He's very patient with me. He returns my calls, and I blurt out some anxiety I have, and he tells me that she's fine. Other than the fact that she hasn't gained enough weight, she's healthy. The baby is big, he says that every time.

At first, he wondered about the date of conception. He asked about that twice. When he asked a third time, Tristan blushed and blew some air out of his mouth. "That's the only day it could have happened, Doc. It's the, uh, only time."

One time. One time and their lives change this way. God, why did You do this to them? They're so scared, so brave, so sad. I think of Becca going through this without me and I want to break furniture.

⌒

Gretchen's skin is dry. The baby takes her water away. I try to get her to drink more but she says it gives her heartburn to drink water. I make her herbal tea, and I put sugar in there, and she drinks that, but the skin on her arms is like parchment.

She says the smell of lotion makes her sick.

I drive to Portland, go to that store at the mall and find a clerk and explain the problem that my pregnant friend is having. I try to explain without umming. The clerk is helpful. "Let's avoid almond and vanilla, and all the florals. Those seem to bother the pregnant women."

She helps me find a nice smell, one that won't upset Gretchen's stomach. I think it smells clean. I buy her five bottles of lotion, and a little pot of something for her lips, she breathes through her mouth at night and her lips are so dry, and some stuff for her hair, because her hair is dry and it keeps breaking.

This clerk is as young as Gretchen, and she reminds me of how girls of sixteen spend their summers. Working at the mall. She puts in samples, free things. "Your girlfriend is very lucky."

"Pardon?"

"Your girlfriend is lucky that you care so much."

I don't explain. I'm tired of explaining.

∽

She's already in her bed, propped up and reading when I get back from Portland. She sets down *The Panda's Thumb* and smiles when she sees what I have for her. "You went to the mall? For me?" She takes off a cap, dips her nose to it, wary. "This smells great." She sits up and rubs the lotion into her hands and arms, then pulls down the covers and rubs the lotion into her legs and feet. She pulls up her shirt and rubs the lotion into her stomach. She pulls down her shirt and smiles at me. "I can't believe you went to the mall."

"Neither can I." I am exhausted, and I fall into bed without undressing.

∽

She lies back on the sand.

I want you to see, she says, the breeze playing with her hair, the sun warming her blue eyes until they glow silver. She tries to lift her shirt and I stop her. Don't, I say. I object to your having breasts.

No, dummy. I want you to see.

She lifts her shirt. And where her belly is, there's a pool of salty water. The baby is there, attached to the side of the depression, part plant, part animal, part boy, part girl, some of both and in between, transparent and beautiful and waving with long red hair that branches like a coral reef.

Hey Gretchen? This is amazing. How do you know all this?

She smiles. I cry.

⌒

I wake, wipe my eyes. I can hear her breathe. She's in the big bed with me and Sam. She comes in here every night. I reach over and touch her hair, my hand wet from tears. She sighs, settles.

God, tell me it's all right for her to be in here.

Please let this be safe.

Amen.

⌒

She kicks in her sleep. It's like sleeping with a colt. She kicks and kicks, and then wakes up yelping.

"Let's stand. Come on. Up you go, come on." I help her stand by the side of the bed, she's whimpering until the leg cramps subside. "All gone?"

"For now." Her voice sounds so hopeless. "They'll be back."

"Maybe they're done with you tonight." She carefully lies down, so scared of the pain. I sit at the foot of the bed and rub her calves so they won't get stiff. And then we both lie there. Neither of us can sleep.

"Gentry?"

"Hm?"

"What's lust?"

I think for a minute. "I've always thought of it as strong physical desire that's not tempered with love and commitment."

"Is that how your church defines it?"

"No. My church just defines it as physical desire."

"Any desire? And it's a sin?"

"Yes."

"Your church shouldn't blame people for desire."

"Why not?"

"It's a necessary part of biology. Without it, no one would ever do this. The propagation of the species would be over. Because this is the worst thing in the world."

"Come here." I lift my arm, and she moves in close to me. She puts her hand on my heart. She likes to do that. She likes to feel it beating, she says.

"Sex is stupid, Gentry. It's awkward and painful. And being pregnant is horrible. And I'm so afraid I'll hate my baby."

"You won't hate your baby."

"I won't?"

"No. You'll love your baby."

"Do you promise?" Tears in her voice.

"I promise."

She sniffs. "Well, if you promise."

"Hey Gretchen? I promise you'll love this baby. And I think someday, you'll have another baby. On purpose."

"What an amazing idea. Having a baby on purpose. Do you promise that someday I'll be stupid enough to do this on purpose?"

That makes me laugh. "I promise."

"Okay. If you promise." She wipes her nose with the sheet. "You know what, Gentry?"

"What?"

"I think someday you'll get to have a baby on purpose, too."

My arm tightens around her shoulders, my heart tightens in pain and longing. I put my face in her sweet, dusty hair.

She sleeps.

∽

Her school friends visit when their families are at the coast. There's a girl named Chelsea, a girl named Devon, a girl named Reese, and twin boys named Kyle and Ryan. They drop by, pick her up, take her away. They sit in the living room with the television on and talk over it, loudly, they talk about everything else in the world. They let her laugh and forget.

Reese makes fun of me. "You're Tristan's *dad*? What, were you like, *five* when he was born?" She reminds me of someone.

The boys ignore the fact that Gretchen is pregnant, they avert their eyes and avoid the whole topic of her straining stomach, but the girls talk about it. They tell Gretchen that she is "so brave," they are "so jealous." I try to stay out of the way. I try not to lurk, alert to any slights or hurtful remarks directed at my Gretchen.

Tristan isn't allowed to visit.

It's odd not to work. I have never in my life had a summer off, unless I count the summer after I left Oregon when my mouth was wired shut and I was too weak to work. Mel understands. It's been five years, after all, but he had a full summer of work lined up for me just in case. I could have used the money.

Mel has been kind. If I had known about Becca, telling Mel would have been the hardest part. But he's good about this, the man is a priest, he's heard it all. I forget that. He told me once that he'd heard things in confession that made him want to kill. "Only God has infinite patience, my boy. And priests are only men." When I told him about everything, he told me to "hold my position." He told me not to "fly with the pixies," no matter how tough it got. But I rarely want to drink because Gretchen is here.

I assume that Becca gets her news through Tristan's mother. She has to care, yes, God? As part of seeing Tristan, I agreed not to reveal his existence to Sandy and Paige and our other mutual friends. In my messages to them, in my chats with them, I stay off any subject that I fear will lead me to blurt out the truth. Gretchen is now one of those subjects. So no one knows I have a son. No one knows I have a grandchild on the way. No one.

Oh, Dear God, if I could just tell Paige. If I could just look into her eyes and see what would be in them when I said the words, "I have a son."

The friends here know, of course. Vu stops by and flirts with Gretchen. "I have to say those are some amazing breasts you've grown there, Gretchen. They put your sister's to shame."

She shakes her head. "You're such a perv."

"I know." He wiggles his brows. "I've always liked pregnant women. They're juicy."

"That's just my hormones keeping my mucus membranes ready to disgorge an entire human being." He cringes, she laughs. He says obscene things, vulgar things, but never profane things. I like to hide around the corner and listen to them laugh.

The Gilroys visited before they left for Canada. The kids, including Gretchen, ran off to the water with Sam. Lorrie stayed in the kitchen with me. He advised me gravely on all sorts of grandfatherly issues, based on all his grandparenting experience. He managed to swear while being patronizing. I held Geneva, who is silent like Walter and Vicki. I'm thankful for whatever Lorrie gives me, God, whatever it may be.

I told Vicki about Gretchen's leg cramps. Vicki told me about calcium, darkly cursed the doctor who did not have Gretchen on calcium already. They left, then, for Canada. I called the doctor, and I got somewhat out of control on the subject of calcium, and he told me that she got extra calcium in her vitamins, and I apologized.

I'm trying to stay calm.

Fiona visits with her, makes her laugh. I love to hear that laugh like bells. Marci calls her, and there is no fighting. Thank You, God, for that.

Kathryn comes during the week. When Kathryn's here, Fiona goes home to Hugh. I take Sam fishing. I take my Jeep out and try to get it stuck, but of course my Jeep never gets stuck. I drive the coast highway and play my music too loud. I relax.

I come back to the house, deliver the catch, eat too much of Kathryn's cooking. Gretchen falls asleep sitting on the couch, watching television.

I like to sit and drink coffee with Kathryn, but I miss the kitchen table. "She's so happy when you're here."

Kathryn shakes her head. "She's miserable."

"She misses Tristan, and she's alone."

"She's not alone. She has you."

"And you."

Kathryn shakes her head again. "I've let her down. I've done every single thing wrong." She blinks back tears. "I need to go to bed." She gives me a hug goodnight and the other thing she always gives me before she goes upstairs.

I make a point of not going upstairs.

I wonder if Gretchen sleeps with her. I hope so.

⌒

I hate working on this book. I'm talking some of this over with Mel on the computer, trying to sort out how I feel about what I'm doing for money. Mel never minds typing into the night.

The door opens. Fiona. "Hi." Sam trots over to her, licks her hands. "Hi Sammy! I saw your mommy this weekend, yes I did! I saw Milly!" He hops around and she ruffles his fur, gets him all wound up.

"Hey? I thought you were coming back tomorrow?"

She's embarrassed. "I'm back early. Hugh was in a pissy mood so I just left. And you're ready for bed. And Kathryn's still here, isn't she. I can get a room at a motel."

"This time of year?" All our little towns are full of strangers. "No, no. I can sleep on the couch. I need to say good-bye to my uncle and send a note to my son."

"Okay, no hurry. But I have to pee like a racehorse." Fiona runs into the bathroom. She shuts the door. I say good-bye to Mel and begin my daily email to Tristan.

When Fiona comes out, she puts the kettle on to boil. "I did some research this week. I checked on a few things." She gets her tea bag picked out. "Can we talk about a difficult thing?"

"Isn't that all we ever talk about?"

She smiles. "Well . . ." She sits down on the bed. This is strange, to have me sitting at the computer typing and her sitting on the bed. "Brooke is really pressing me on the issue of your sexuality."

"Of course she is." So she can humiliate me. Of course she's pressing that.

"Gentry, I'm trying to think of a diplomatic way to say this. Miriam says in the book that you had no experience. With other women. Besides her?"

"I don't talk about that stuff, Fiona."

"Well, that's fine. That's gentlemanly of you, Gentry. And you have a son, so obviously there was at least one other woman. But I guess what I'm trying to say is, it's hard to be good in bed when you don't have any practice. And it doesn't mean you're gay. It just means you're bad in bed."

What?

I was with a woman who wouldn't let me touch her, let me KISS her most of the time, a woman whose idea of foreplay was to hit me in the face with her briefcase, and I'm bad in bed? I should go in there and get Kathryn, I should march her out here and have her verify that I'm not bad in bed, I fight an urge to go over and show Fiona that I'm not bad in bed, give me an hour, one hour. I'd hold her down and make her cry with it, by God.

I just swore there, but I am NOT bad in bed.

The teakettle whistles.

"Gentry? Did I hurt your feelings?" I ignore Fiona and concentrate on the twin activities of breathing and typing. She gets up to make her tea and lays a hand on my shoulder. "Listen, I don't believe what she said, I really don't. I bet you're just . . . *great* in bed. Really."

I am overcome with a surging urge to show her, but I ignore it.

She makes her tea. I send the last of my mail.

I can't stand up.

Fiona

Well, I have the biggest mouth in creation, I guess.

How many stupid things can I say to one man? Gentry slammed out of here last night, furious. But he never actually said he wasn't gay.

I called Hugh and described the conversation. I got to the part where I patted Gentry on the shoulder and told him he was probably *great* in bed, and Hugh said to stop, his stomach hurt from laughing at me.

∽

I went to the kitchen door for tea this morning. Through the window in the back door, I saw him and that ice queen smiling at each other over coffee. They appeared to be working on the crossword together.

I came back out here.

I don't care for that brittle little lady. Maybe it's how haughty she is. I'm very happy to see her car drive away right before he knocks at my door.

"It's open!"

When he opens the door, he's absurdly happy. "Hey."

"Hi! Ready to work?"

And his face falls. "Um, sure." He sits on the bed.

"Well, did you and your friend have a nice breakfast?"

Just like that, his face brightens again. "We did." He's annoyingly happy. "Why didn't you come in for breakfast?"

"I peeked in the window and you were talking away, so I left you to it."

His expression crosses the line from annoyingly happy into stupidly happy. "I finally got Kathryn to read Denis Johnson. She didn't think she would like him, but she did."

"Oh, Denis Johnson." Whoever *that* is.

I clear my throat. "So. Did you read the pages I printed out?" He nods. "What do you think of the book so far?"

And his face moves from intellectually stimulated into plainly embarrassed. That's right. He's embarrassed. "I think it reads like a romance novel." And probably nothing like Denis Johnson, whoever the hell that is.

I try not to, but I glare at him. "Gentry, have you ever even read a romance novel?"

He thinks. "I don't believe so."

"Have you read *Jane Eyre*?"

"Of course. One of my degrees is in English."

One of his degrees. La-di-da. "*Jane Eyre* is the grandmother of all romance novels. And it's my second favorite book."

"What's your favorite?"

"Guess."

He thinks, scratching his chin because he hasn't shaved. The faintest dusting of dark whiskers shows along his jaw, his upper lip. "*Wuthering Heights*?"

"Of course."

"I read that too." He makes an apologetic smile. "It didn't speak to me so much."

"That's because you're a man. Romance novels aren't meant to speak to men. They're all about miscommunication and men don't like miscommunication. But women love it."

"Why?"

"Because women want to believe that men who don't love us actually do. The entire genre is about that. These seemingly remote men bursting with secret thwarted love, turning away from the true contents of their hearts and broadcasting their frustration as anger or aloofness. But a man isn't really like that. A man is straightforward. If he wants you, he comes to your door." He nods, but doesn't meet my eyes. "Except, of course, in a romance novel, where the doors are barred with obstacles that don't matter to men in real life, like social standing."

He frowns. "But there are obstacles. People are married, for instance."

"No, no, in modern romance the obstacles are usually social, not legal. Ethnicity, economic class, social standing. Sometimes religion. A difference in social standing is the biggest barrier. No one in a romance novel is married, that's too insurmountable."

"Catherine Earnshaw was married. Heathcliff was, too."

"Only after they miscommunicated."

"Rochester was married."

He really did read those books. "Gentry, if she'd written that novel today, Charlotte Brontë would have had to fix that. Her editors would have insisted. Because you can't have your heroine going after a married man in a romance novel. Marriage is the holy grail of all these books, right? It's the point, the prize. It has to mean something. So the big obstacle would have been the difference in their social standing. That's why I'd rather write so much historical romance. I like using love and sex to subvert those oppressive social hierarchies."

"So you think your work is subversive?"

"Not really, because I work within the commercial boundaries of my genre. And in my genre, the relationship paradigm is so restrictive that nothing ever gets overthrown. I get tired of it. It's like brainwashing. I start seeing the world that way. I have to take a break and write something else."

He scratches his head for a minute. The man is itchy this morning. Then he smiles a smile that makes my whole body warm. "Well, then, Fiona, let's do it. Let's overthrow a restrictive relationship paradigm."

"Let's! Let's subvert oppressive hierarchies with love and sex!"

He laughs out loud, and gives me a look I can only describe as tender. Tender? I haven't taken enough of a break. I'm responding in a romance novel way, imagining him brimming with unspoken words and denied emotions.

I need to remember that when a man wants you, he comes to your door.

Gentry

God, please tell me that I have not been wrong.

I see my Gretchen, God, what this does to her, and I feel as wrong and as low as I can imagine feeling. The only person who feels worse is my son. Tristan looks at her and the guilt in his eyes, God, please allow him to forgive himself.

We meet him at the doctor, and they want me to go to the birth class with them. I don't want to go to the birth class. But I can never say no to Gretchen. So I accompany my kids to the birth class. I see all the people my age there to have their babies and for once I'm not incapacitated with envy, because my son sits in this class with me.

My son.

I just watch, really. The job of panting all over Gretchen, pretending to help, that will be Tristan's. I pay close attention to Gretchen's anesthesia options, because this sounds like the only way to go as far as I'm concerned.

I don't like the curiosity of the other couples. I can see the heads shake, the eyes flicker. No one thinks this was a good choice. Not for these kids. They went around the circle the first day, everyone told who they were, what they did. There were doctors and lawyers and investment counselors and accountants and a weaver and a plumber and a respiratory therapist. Gretchen spoke up in her high, clear voice. "I'm Gretchen, and this is Tristan, and I know you're all wondering so I'll just tell you that we'll both be juniors in the fall."

The pain on that instructor's face. "Juniors in college?"

"High school."

The instructor asked what school they went to, and Gretchen told her. And then the teacher asked who I was, could I introduce myself and tell people what I do.

"I'm Tristan's father. Gentry. I'm a teacher."

"You teach *there*?" This was spoken in a tone of disbelief. The idea that I might teach at such a fine, expensive school seemed to alarm everyone.

"No. I don't teach there." Everyone nodded, satisfied. And I thought, why do these people care who I am, what I do, where I do it? And I figured it out. My kids were what every couple hoped were growing inside each belly in the room. Something went wrong, though. They saw my bright and shining kids, and they saw the tired man behind them, and they knew that the inadequate gene came from the man who taught at a poor little school, the man who entered fatherhood too early himself, the man with the ponytail and the beat-up Jeep, the man with the archaic religion, the man with no money. And they felt better. This wouldn't happen to their kids because they were not me.

What were they pretending to themselves? That it was possible to purchase a life without mistakes? A woman came up to me after that first class and said, "I think those kids are so brave."

I find that I'm angry in the class.

The information is interesting. Some of it makes me dizzy, but the basic information is helpful to someone who received his basic knowledge in a fifth-grade health class. Someone who read about human sexuality in the library after he'd already had sex. I needed the review.

I tell the kids that I understand the general idea after a few classes. And that I would rather sit on the lawn of the hospital and read on those evenings. Because I'm tired of being the bad blood.

I sit in the hot evening sun and read my library books, catching up on this boy wizard series they love so much. I spent years at boarding school and it was not this fun. I differ from this magical boy in that I would have pounded the blond kid with fists, spells and heavy objects until he was dead or I was expelled.

After the classes, they sit in Toni's car. I ignore them so they can kiss. Gretchen climbs out and sits down on the grass and cries a little, "because it's so stupid that the only time we get to see each other is at this stupid class about the stupid baby," and then we go home to the coast.

And even though this is not how I thought it would be, God? Those words, "home to the coast," are a miracle, and I thank You.

Amen.

◦◦◦

I call Antoinette. "It would mean a lot to Gretchen if Tristan could visit her."

"He sees her at the doctor." They have such a nice time there, between the weighing and the measuring and the helpful nurse and all the curious people who stare at my kids in the waiting room. "And they go to birth classes." Oh, and that's fun, too, being stared at by pompous couples who think she should have had an abortion.

"Hey Toni? Gretchen is having a hard time waiting this out. I think she could use a little time to talk to Tristan when she isn't having her blood pressure taken or learning about cervical effacement. This is hard for her."

"It's hard for him, too." She's silent for a few moments, and I have no idea what to say so I let the silence stand. "I don't want them alone together."

I want to shout into the phone that this is a little after the fact. I want to say, why didn't you make sure back when it would have mattered? But I want to see my son, and I want Gretchen to be able to see him.

I try to imagine what Mike would say. "I respect your position on this, Toni. We're on the same page. We have to keep caution top-of-mind."

"Good. Well, then I guess he can drive up Saturday." That crap works? "I expect him home Sunday afternoon. And I want them supervised. They can't sleep in the same room."

"I understand. Tristan can sleep out in the little house. It's, um, a guest house."

"You'll make sure?"

"Absolutely."

⌒

Thank You. Because it makes her smile, this news. Dear God, thank You for making my Gretchen smile. And her face when she sees him, and his face when he sees her. Thank You, God.

They go down by the water and take a long walk. They're back in time for lunch, and then they go off to Main Street. They come home laughing. I feed them dinner. Soup of course, I'm getting tired of soup but it's all she can eat.

They do the dishes, then sit on the couch and watch television. I sit on the chair Kathryn had delivered out here a few weeks ago. I watch them. They like the same shows. My son keeps his hands on his child. His voice is a low croon. "Hey, little one. Give your mom a break." He moves his hands. "I think this one is a striker."

Her face is relaxed and pleased and young, and so is his.

I stand. "I'm beat."

"It's eight-thirty."

I clear my throat. "Tristan, you're supposed to sleep in the little house."

"Mom told me."

They continue to watch me with young, impassive faces. They're waiting for a lecture about trust and responsibility. Waiting to be told how badly they've fallen down in both areas.

"I have some stuff to do on the computer. Lesson planning. I may be on there late. So, um, I'm going to sleep out there. I'll see you both when I get back from church. Good night."

God, forgive me this. But they were so happy.

⌒

We're eating at the Pig'n'Pancake.

The kids surprised me earlier today. Tristan galloped out when I was getting in the Jeep. "Wait! We're going to church with you."

Gretchen came out and gave me a hug. "Did the brothers wake you? Happy birthday. You're officially more than twice my age."

"Thank you."

"Happy birthday," said my son. "Let's go to birthday Mass. Let's wear big party hats, like the Pope. Have some communion party snacks." My son made me laugh, too. Their baby, their child. Would this baby grow up and make me laugh?

Gretchen stared at my face. "What is it? What?"

I couldn't even say it out loud. I was too happy.

We went to Mass. Though he only sang the Lord's Prayer, I did get to hear him. He sang beautifully.

I introduced him to Vu's mother. I introduced him to the priest. I introduced him to a colleague, three former students, two current students and their families, a woman who lives next door to the Gilroys and one of the checkers at Fred Meyer. I guess I must have looked sort of idiotic, there, chasing down people I hardly knew in order to introduce my son, but my fellow parishioners were patient. People can be very kind to idiots. And my son Tristan was respectful and courteous and all around perfect, I think.

And now, breakfast.

I'm relieved that Gretchen has an appetite. Tristan, being my son, stows away an enormous amount of food, but that's just part of his perfection. He keeps his arm around her shoulders. He pats the baby, proud. "Fill up for my little forward, here." She smiles. He whispers in her ear and she blushes. He looks at her, touches her hair, her cheek. How could she ever think she was ugly? When Tristan looks at her, she should feel beautiful, because she is.

She looks up and behind me and drops her fork. I look at her face. She looks at me, shakes her head. What is it? Her blue eyes plead with me.

She doesn't want me to turn around.

The hair on the back of my neck starts to rise. No. I've been back, what, a year? I thought You might spare me this, God. But You spare me very little. Gretchen picks up her fork deliberately, begins to eat.

Maybe this moment will pass.

I look up when he brings himself to stand by the table. He has no hair. And I'm thinking, skinhead? But no, Vu said the Navy. He looks at me, at Gretchen, her belly. He looks at Tristan the longest. He looks back to me.

"Hey, faggot."

Tristan starts to stand as Garret walks away, but I'm already on my feet. Her sweet young voice rises like a siren. "Gentry, don't, don't let him make you mad . . ." Mad is not the word for what I feel as I stand and follow and catch up with him, yank him around by his shoulder and look down on him because this kid is short.

He stands before me, radiant with failure. *My* failure.

The restaurant seems quiet, suddenly, for a Sunday morning. Very quiet. He stands facing me, his fists clenched. I wait. I wait, and the restaurant waits, and he waits. His face goes from white to red.

"You don't fucking scare me. You don't."

But I do. I always have. And I have always done it on purpose.

I study his flinching eyes. I lean down. I used to do that to show him how small he was, how insignificant. I speak softly, so that no one will hear but him.

He blinks in confusion.

I turn my back on him and walk to the table, where I sit down across from the round eyes of my kids. The noise of the restaurant picks up, the buzz and clatter.

I bow my head for a moment.

Amen.

The smallest acts are huge, today. Finding my fork is a tremendous undertaking, lifting food to my mouth a feat of cutlery and coordination. Chewing seems foreign, something I have heard about but never actually done. Swallowing won't happen for quite some time.

But my food is still warm. It's still my birthday. I'm still with my kids. I'm still in Oregon. And I've given Garret what I owe him.

Fiona

I got here early, and no one was in either house. I'm cold and tired and lonely, and I funnel all that into work until the Jeep pulls in.

I can't help myself. I stand to one side of the window in the door and spy as they climb out, watching with a curiosity that feels like hunger as they hop out, an easy move where they grasp the side of the Jeep and move over the side, eschewing doors.

The glorious boy is a bit taller and thinner than his father, but his face isn't quite as lovely, lacking some of Gentry's hollows. His hair glows chestnut when the sun hits it, and roses bloom on his emerging cheekbones. His mother was probably fair. But he is his father's son. The way they walk, stand, rock back on their heels, laugh. Exactly alike.

This is the kind of child he would make.

Gentry goes into the big house and leaves the kids in the driveway to hug and kiss good-bye, two children clinging to each other in a strong wind. The boy gets into a BMW sedan and backs out. Gretchen stands and watches, sad and ashen and far too thin. Despite this, and despite the disturbing bulge of her middle, I'm trying to figure out where to use her in a book because the set of her shoulders is tragic. I make myself look away.

I'm back at the computer when I hear a tap. "Come in!" He has the dog at his side and a book in his hands.

He smiles. "You're back."

"I can't stay away." And the truth in that makes me so shy I can't face him, I can't stand it, I go home and prowl around the house and bug the hell out of Hugh and count the minutes until I can come back.

He smiles again. "Here." He puts it in my hands. *The Throne of the Third Heaven of the Nations Millennium General Assembly: Poems Collected and New.* Denis Johnson. I feel a blush start on my neck, feel it heat and rise, especially around my ears. I'm sure my face is the color of a strawberry. "I'd be glad to read it." When I can force myself to look up, Gentry is at the window.

"Why didn't you come out to meet my son?"

"I was too shy."

We watch the blonde girl in the driveway, standing there alone, staring out at the water. I don't know anything about teenage girls except how lonely, painful and hollow it feels to be one. Gretchen finally goes into the house, walking like she's cracking apart. "Don't you need to take care of Gretchen?"

He shakes his head. "She wants me to leave her alone." Like Gretchen, he wears his emotions on his back. They're squared up under the weight of an enormous grief.

I turn back to the computer. "Let's see. I need to update you on our progress. You've waged a heroic battle against the bottle with Mavis by your side. 'Work pressures led me to the bottle around the time that Mavis and I decided to formalize our life commitment by getting married. Mavis was understanding, compassionate, but my secret drinking took its toll.'"

"'Took its toll'?"

"I'm on a cliché roll. So far I have 'took its toll,' 'broke the bank,' 'paid my dues,' and 'paid the piper.'" I type a little more. "I even worked in 'pound of flesh,' Listen to this . . ."

"Don't."

"What?"

"Don't use 'pound of flesh.'"

"I'm sorry, I didn't think, I . . ."

"Just take it out, please."

He hates me. I'm the stupidest woman who ever walked the earth. "I forgot. I don't have an English degree, Gentry, and I forgot."

He turns and looks me up, looks me down. "What are you wearing?"

I'm wrapped up in a vintage black dinner jacket that smells like moth balls. "I found it in the closet. Should I put it back?"

He studies me, a small smile playing at the corners of his mouth. "It's okay. I forgot about that. It looks nice on you." He walks over and sits heavily on the bed. Sam hops up beside him, his plume of tail waving in happiness. "Hey Fiona? Let's do the next thing on the list. Let's get this over with so I can get the advance and never have to think about it again."

I forget that I've been paid and he hasn't. His first payment won't be disbursed until Brooke approves a draft. Which is ridiculous. That book is already sold. She's supposed to be his agent, not the house's agent.

He lies back and pets his dog. I work for a while, taking out my ugly misstep and sticking in some other hackneyed phrase, cleaning up the misses, cutting and adding and moving. Editing reminds me of gardening. While I trim, he talks so softly. "Hey, my Sam, are you tired too? Have you done dog work this morning? We're dog tired, aren't we. Are you dog tired? Don't lick my face, Sam. Yuck. Don't." He lies there while Sam licks his face.

It's so tender.

I'm awake a lot at night, and I see the kitchen light go on, I see the glow of the TV through the window. I know Gretchen wakes him up because she apologizes for it almost every morning when I go in for tea. And he always tells her not to worry, he doesn't mind, and then he comes out here and answers my questions and talks to his dog and naps, because the man's exhausted. He doesn't sleep.

"Well, the bottle is done. Why don't you tell me about the jail."

"Jail?" He sounds beaten. He pets Sam with both hands. "She called the police because I hit her."

"Did you hit her a lot?" I sound absurdly conversational. Like, oh, how was your drive over and do you like cream in your coffee and did you hit your wife all the time?

"No, just one time."

"Was there something specific that took you over the edge?" He stares at his feet. "I need this for your part of the book." He turns to stare out at the water, and his face sets like rock. The soft grey light coming in the window could be lighting up a monument.

I wish I could touch him. But he would hate that.

"Why don't you think of it as a story? Something you can tell."

"A story. Like a fairytale," he says softly, staring out the window. "Fairytales are always so grim." He keeps his eyes on the ocean. Only the set of his mouth betrays him. "Once upon a time, I came home from work, and my wife had given my computer to the Goodwill. And when I told her to get it back, she said no. So I hit her. And then I did it again. And then I picked her up and dragged her up the stairs to the phone, and I made her get my computer back. She did, and then she called the police and I went to jail." He turns back to me. Looks me in the eye. "The end."

I wrap myself tighter in the tuxedo coat, feeling sick. "Okay! Thank you. That's all I need as far as that." He stares at me like I'm insane. And I probably am, but the important thing is to stay calm. "So. She says in here you were in jail for one night."

"Yes." He shrugs. "That part is true."

"So you told her about what happened that night?"

"No, we never talked about it."

"Then how did she know what happened in there?"

"She didn't."

I keep my voice steady and calm. "What exactly happened to you in jail?"

"Hey Fiona? Have you ever been in jail?"

"No, just prison."

He gives me a look that I'm stupid enough to misread as affectionate. "Well, when you go to jail, they, they do this processing stuff, fingerprint you and take your photo and search you and take away anything you might use to hurt yourself. So I did all that. And they put me in a holding cell full of other men. Mostly drunks. I sat down on a bench and leaned up against a wall and fell asleep."

"And?"

"And whenever someone yelled or threw up or fought or got too close to me, I woke up and contemplated self-destruction until I could get back to sleep."

"And? That's it?"

"That's it."

"That's all that happened in there?"

"Yes. I wasn't charged or even formally arrested. Just detained. In the morning she came and got me, and we went home."

"And that's all that happened to you in there?"

"That's it."

"You'd better read this." I make him come over, sit down, read the screen.

He looks like he wants to throw up.

When he stands, the chair hits the floor behind him. He picks it up carefully scoots it back in place. "Hey Fiona? Get it out of there."

"Brooke likes it. She thinks it's hot."

He shakes his head. "Brooke likes anything that humiliates me. Just take it out." He sounds so exhausted.

Brooke will be angry if I do. According to Mavis, "Buddy spent the first part of that night on his knees in the corner of the jail cell." A lot of really graphic detail, gagging and so on. Then, she had him bent over a bench and liking it. "This fulfillment of his darkest fantasies didn't help him in his quest to establish a masculine identity." But what if someone found out that this anonymous book was supposed to be the story of Gentry's marriage? What then?

I've juiced things up. I've exaggerated the "overwhelmingly intense physical passion that drew them together," I've let Mavis be "the instrument of his physical awakening," I've talked about the way "the flames of their passionate sex life were extinguished by the icy advance of the fertility battle," I've written some fairly good sex. There's more that can be said about jail without violating him like this.

Brooke will have to deal with it.

I see him sitting there, his face grey. He's tired. I'm tired, too. Tired of doing this to him. But I have to.

There's a knock on the door and a dark-haired girl Gretchen's age steps in. "Hi."

He frowns. "Hey Reese. Where's your car?"

Her face lights up with disbelief. "Where's my *car*?"

"Yes, I didn't see your car."

"It's parked on the other side of the *house*. So now that we've located my *car*, can I *talk* to you for a second?" She frowns. "Who are you? The writer?"

"Yes. I'm Fiona."

She's done with me. "Gretchen's in the kitchen trying to cook your birthday dinner and she's crying so hard that she threw up in the sink." He leaps to his feet but she holds out her hand. "I know it's your birthday, but . . ."

He runs his hands through his hair in desperation. "I don't care about dinner, I didn't expect her to cook, I'll go . . ."

She holds out her hand again. "Don't go in there. I'm taking her over to my house to see my mom." He opens his mouth to argue, but there's the flat of her hand again. Reese is not having it. "You're a great friend, but tonight she needs a mom." She nods over at me. "Take *her* out for your birthday. She's very pretty." We watch through the window as Reese goes back to the big house.

When I turn to Gentry, his hands are pressed to his eyes.

Gentry

I take her to the Blue Sky Cafe. I come here with Gretchen. They offer a mix of the type of food I love and the type of food I hate. Fiona has to like one or the other.

Tonight, we have one of those intensely encouraging waiters. His arms are like windmills, and there are beads of sweat on his forehead. "Let me tell you about tonight's specials."

"Do you need to hear them?"

Fiona gives her head a little shake. "No. I know what I want." The waiter clenches his fists and smiles an angry smile. He has possibly been practicing, and we take it away from him like this.

He sneers at me. Oh, he remembers the last time I was here, when the old ums bubbled up and Gretchen had to intervene. I take a deep breath. "I'd like the rock shrimp, please."

"Great choice. Salad or chowder with that?"

"Chowder."

Fiona brightens. "That sounds great. I'll have the same, but I want a salad with vinaigrette." She smiles. "If I can have a bite of your chowder, you can have some of my salad." I don't want any salad but I nod, imagining the moment when I get to hold out the spoon across the table and watch her take it into her mouth.

Okay. That's bad.

She eyes the waiter as he walks away. He has on cargo shorts and gum boots and a tweed sports jacket with patches on the elbows. "I have that same outfit."

"I hope you like the rock shrimp. There are, um, big hunks of bacon in it."

"I like pancetta."

"Oh." I'm a little disappointed. When Gretchen had it, she picked out all the pancetta and put it on my plate.

I sit with this woman day after day, talk about whatever I have to talk about with her, and right now I can't think of one word to say. So I just look at her. Fiona is so nice to look at.

Stop, stop, stop.

But I like her grey eyes, and the way she waves her hands around, and the way her hair falls into her face. The way she pushes it back, impatiently. With her hands.

Get a grip. Right now.

The waiter, with his barely veiled edge of hostility, brings our food all at once. She takes her own bite of chowder. And that is for the best because I want to fall face first into any dish that tastes this good.

"So your son's name is Tristan? That's a beautiful name."

"It's not a name I would have chosen."

She tilts her head. "Who chose it?"

"I don't know. I wasn't there."

"For the birth?"

"For any of it. I didn't raise him."

We're quiet for a while. I decide I would rather eat than try to explain the sad facts of my life. I expect questions, but not the one she finally asks. "What would you have named a boy?"

"Max."

"Just Max?"

"Max is enough."

She smiles. I have to smile back. But I don't want to talk anymore, I want to eat, and people keep stopping by the table. I have to interrupt the bliss of these shrimp in my mouth to swallow, use my napkin, smile, stand, be told to sit, speak. Parents come over, talk to me, appraise Fiona. When I remember names, I introduce Fiona. When I don't remember names, I sit, mute, until they introduce themselves. That's my system.

The doctor is here with his wife. They come over and start to talk about the play with Fiona like old friends. This woman seems relieved that I'm out on what she takes to be a date. She clutches at her little purse and smiles at me. "It's so nice to see you out, Gentry." The doctor shakes my hand and smiles, hearty. If his wife is encouraging, he's congratulatory. "How's the jaw?"

"Fine, just fine." He claps me on the back. He seems as relieved as his wife that I'm out here with Fiona. Why is everyone so relieved? Why would anyone care if I have a date?

The play was not a date. This is not a date. But the word spread like the flu after the play, "The computer teacher finally had a date!" Kids came up to me for a week asking questions. This evening's sighting will probably show up in the town newspaper, or on the high school's home page. The entire string of coastal communities will know I've been seen twice with the same woman.

The doctor and his wife leave.

"Hey Fiona? I'm sorry. This is a small community."

"No, it just makes me embarrassed for myself. I live like a hermit. I know about ten people. I sit in the house and type."

I shake my head. "I don't know that many people."

"Well, a lot of people know you, Gentry."

It's quiet between us for the rest of the meal. I watch her tending to her plate in her careful way. The way she sits, curved in her chair, her long legs twined around each other under her chair.

Everything about her makes me hurt.

∽

We are arguing a little.

"Let me treat."

"No, you can't treat."

"Gentry, please. I promise to write it off, even."

"No, I'm paying."

The owner, Carla, has a daughter in my class and knows Kathryn fairly well, because she's always asking after Kathryn when Gretchen and I come in here. She stands there watching us argue over who's paying.

Fiona makes a sound of impatience. "It's your *birthday*."

Carla smiles. "It's your birthday?" She takes the check from my hand and rips it in two. "Happy Birthday."

Fiona laughs out loud. "Well, I guess that's settled."

I don't know what to say. I look from Fiona to Carla, too embarrassed to speak. And then I remember what you say. You say thank-you.

Like I said to Mike.

Fiona

I suggested that he drive because the thing about the check obviously shook his masculine pride. Maybe taking the wheel of my late mother's minivan would restore it.

"Thank you, Fiona."

"For what? I didn't even pay for dinner." I reach over and pat his arm. He still seems sad. Time to cheer him up. "So, I have some news. The legal department is concerned. Brooke tells me that because he's a priest, I need to take out all that about Mel. They're concerned about getting embroiled in all the lawsuits going on. So it's out."

"Good, since it's all lies."

"All of it?"

"All of it."

I'm relieved beyond words.

But there's something about Gentry. Something that's wrong. I think about what she wrote. She claimed that she told him about her own past to, and I quote, "heal the total scorching shame he felt at becoming sexually active, finally. He listened eagerly to all my stories of other men, pressing for detail after detail. He wanted to hear about the sex organs, the techniques, the details of all my previous lovers. Little did I know that he was aroused by those details, because all his private thoughts were totally of other men."

His private thoughts. What a woman. But I have to admit that it's weird of me to have memorized that particular passage.

"Can you tell me anything about before you lived with Mel?"

"Hey Fiona? I don't remember."

"Don't remember, or can't remember?" He drives along, not saying anything. "You understand the semantic difference. So which is it?"

We ride in silence.

Gentry

We get to the house. "Tea?"
"Tea."

Sam, where's our girl? I thought she would be home by now. I push the message machine button. "Hi, dummy. I'm spending the night at Reese's. Don't worry, and don't call, but since I know you'll call, the number is . . ." And she leaves the number, and I call.

She answers. "Hello, dummy. I knew you'd call." She tells me that she's fine, that they have videos and pizza and some male prostitutes with AIDS to keep them company, and she laughs at me, and I get a hold of myself. She sounds happy, she sounds sixteen. She can sleep somewhere else. Gretchen is safe. Reese's mother is there, so I can relax. I can't relax. That is my Gretchen, and my grandchild in there, too.

"If you eat pizza you'll get heartburn."

"Then I'll get heartburn."

"Do the milk and soda cracker thing."

"Okay, Gentry, I'll do the Saltine system."

"Do you want me to bring over your Tums?"

"No, I'll be fine."

"I could bring you something to sleep in."

"I wear your pajamas all day. I guess I can sleep in them."

"Well, do you want your pillow?"

"They have pillows here."

"Oh."

"Goodbye, Gentry."

"I'll drive over to get you if you change your mind."

She starts to laugh. "It's been a few years since I got scared at a sleepover."

"I just meant if . . ."

"Goodbye, Gentry."

"Bye."

"Hang up, Gentry."

"If you . . ." She hangs up. Well, fine. I hang up.

Fiona's face looks like she's going to cry, probably from laughing at me. I get tired of this, God, I get tired of being this hilarious to the world. To women. To her. She comes over and puts her arms around me. "You're the dearest man who ever walked the earth. You're sweeter than Jesus." She kisses my cheek and leaves without any tea.

I watch her walk into the little house and close the door.

Fiona

He's controlled and precise, whatever he's doing, cooking or cleaning or computing. He gets embarrassed if his stomach rumbles or he accidentally lets a burp escape. Other times, he's easy. He runs down to the beach and throws himself on the sand when it's warm. He never uses the door of his Jeep if the top is off, he vaults in and out. He's always free with Sam.

That's what they're doing when I come into the kitchen of the big house. Playing. And I know I have to wait.

Sam stands in front of Gentry, puts his head down, yelps his "I want to play" yelp. Gentry pushes at the dog's head, and Sam makes a funny "rrr-ing" noise, and Gentry pushes him around by his muzzle, his sides, his rump, turning the dog around and getting him all wound up, talking to him in this low voice, "Oh Sam, here you are, Sam, move it, Sam, you're a wild boy, are you a wild boy . . ." And then, when Sam is all spastic, they run around, all through the house, jumping over furniture and through every room, up and down the stairs, Gentry's big boots clomping, Sam's toenails skittering on the wood floors, taking turns chasing each other, barking, because when Sam barks, Gentry barks back in a perfect imitation. And then, Gentry falls to the floor, and Sam puts one paw on each shoulder, and Sam licks his face. "Oh, Sam. Not the face. Ick." Sam licks his entire face, and when he gets to the ears, Gentry rolls away and Sam chases, fighting to get at those ears. They tussle a little more. "Not the ears, I have limits."

And when all of that's over, all that pushing and romping and barking and licking, Gentry looks up like it didn't happen. "Hey. What are we working on today?"

It's time to explain his life to him a little bit.

I was up most of the night with a box of files. I've gone through the records, read all the reports. I've been on the phone with Evelyn for a few hours, listening to the story of the last month of Miriam's life, hearing about how she actually died. I've called a doctor in Oklahoma, spoken with the medical examiner.

I'm as angry as I've ever been in my life.

I sit down at the kitchen island with some tea and remain calm. "Can you talk a little more about when she did it?"

"Did it?"

"That day. The day she went to the hospital."

His eyes say no, enough, please. "I have to talk about that?"

"Yes, Gentry, yes, you have to tell me what actually happened. Because there's nothing in here about it for the book. I have to have something to go on."

"Something to go on." He sits down, staring at the floor in front of him. "I was at work and she called me and told me she'd written a book. And someone wanted to publish it. I asked her what it was about. I kept thinking it was a cookbook."

"Wasn't she a bad cook?"

"Yes. I don't know why I thought it was a cookbook. She explained that it was about us, a book about everything we'd gone through with her infertility. I was confused by that. I'd gone to the doctor a couple of times with her for tests, but we hadn't actually done anything. I didn't understand how she could have written a book about it. The idea was as ridiculous as her writing a cookbook." He sits there staring at the floor.

"I had a bad feeling. A bad, bad feeling. I knew it was probably going to be bad. So I asked if I could read it. She sounded happy that I wanted to. I could tell she was proud. She brought it to my office. I'd worked there maybe eight, nine months, and it was the first time she'd come by. All the people I worked with, they were very, you know, curious. They all came to reception to meet her. I wondered why they all stood there staring at us. She said she had to go. And I couldn't do it."

"Do what?"

"I couldn't pretend. That everything was all right. So I didn't hug her, and I didn't kiss her."

"And you regret that."

The pain in his face. "Yes. I regret it."

"Gentry, do you actually think she committed suicide because you wouldn't hug her?"

"I don't know. I mean, no, I talked to her after that. After I read the book. I called her and told her to forget it. I mean the book, but us, too. I told her I wouldn't let her publish it. She said, if you don't let me publish it, I'll kill myself. I said . . ."

He presses his hands to his eyes.

"I said, then kill yourself, Miriam."

I want to go over there and put my arms around him, but if I say anything, anything at all, he'll stop. He takes his hands away from his eyes, gets up and paces a little.

"I was going to leave, Fiona. I told her I was leaving. I came in the front door and stood on the landing and I couldn't hear her. I went up to the bedroom, she was in her bed, sleeping. But her face was wrong." He sits down, strokes solemn Sam. "She always looked angry, even when she slept. She had those lines." He points between his own brows. "She looked calm. So I knew something was wrong. I took her by the shoulders and she felt limp. She was quiet and calm and soft and she wouldn't wake up. She smelled all wrong.

"I called my uncle. He called the police. The ambulance came, and then the police came. The note and the bottle were right there by the bed. I don't know why I didn't see them. They asked me questions, and I asked them to call her parents. Then they took me to the hospital."

He presses his hands into his eyes, and when he takes them away, his eyes are still dry. "I sat there with her. I wouldn't go home. Evelyn brought me clean clothes. I sat and waited and prayed. Bargaining. God didn't listen."

"God listens."

He shakes his head. "We finally let her go. Her family was afraid to leave me alone. They asked me if I would stay in the hospital. Her mother cried, she said 'if we lose you too, I can never forgive myself. Gentry, please let them take care of you.'"

"Were you out of control?"

"No, not at all. I was quiet. I could barely speak." He looks up. "That's why I called Mel when I found her. Because my throat closed. It closes sometimes and I can only talk to him."

If Miriam knew that, how could she ever think Mel molested him? But Miriam didn't know anything. Miriam didn't know one thing about this man she was married to.

"So they committed you?"

"No. I committed myself. I signed some paper, but I thought I was going to stay in a regular hospital room to get some sleep. I hadn't slept much for a month. They said they would give me something, and I wanted to sleep."

"When did you realize where you were?"

"Well, I had my suspicions when they took my shoes. But I knew for certain the next morning, when they made me go do some arts and crafts. I had to make a trivet. I didn't even know what a trivet was. Everyone was mad at me because I had all the red tiles, and I sat there and I thought, I can't, I just can't. I *won't* make a trivet, whatever that is. I went up and argued with them. I thought, I signed myself in here, I can sign myself out. But I had to stay for forty-eight hours."

"Two days?"

"Yes, and then they made me wait another day while they tried to get a doctor to make me stay longer. They gave me nothing to help me sleep, nothing. They made me go to group therapy, and everyone yelled at me because I wouldn't talk about my wife, and I couldn't sleep because there was this man who crawled around on his hands and knees all night. He was afraid to sleep. They left the doors open and that man crawled into my room. By the end of three days, I was ready to kill him, but they finally let me out after Mel called. I think everyone was afraid he would bring down divine retribution. And they needed to have the funeral. I was terrible at the funeral. I'd never been to a funeral before, Fiona, but I've been to a few wakes. So I did it Catholic style, with a lot of drinking, a little singing. I offended everyone I possibly could." He shakes his head to an almost violent degree.

I'm going through all of this, figuring out what to use. By her side day and night for a month, that's good. I'll use that. Mental ward, also highly usable. Trivet, probably not, even though it's my favorite part. Funeral drinking, absolutely.

"The suicide note?" He recoils as if he's been struck. "I need to know what Miriam said in it."

Gentry recovers his composure, goes to the sink, carefully washes his hands, washes the dog spit off his face. "I don't have it."

"Then I need to have some idea what it said."

He sighs. He dries his hands and his face, and he carries the towel out to the utility porch. He's out there for a minute. I hear the washer start. He finally comes back. "Are you hungry?"

"No. Will you sit down here a minute?"

He gets himself some coffee.

"Gentry? What did it say?"

He takes his coffee cup in both hands and turns around to sit backwards at the island and stare out the window. His voice has that particular choked quality I recognize. "She did it because she was married to me."

"Because you made each other unhappy?"

He stares out the window, suffering. "Yes."

"She could have left you, Gentry. She had a career, she had a family. If you were so terrible, leaving was easy to do. What exactly did she say in the note?"

"Just write it. Make it up."

I'd like to shake him. "Gentry, she was a nurse, right? She knew about medications, dosages, things like that?"

He nods. "She taught the certification courses the nurse's aides had to take so they could hand out meds."

"Well, Gentry, if she was such an expert on medication, then I wonder why she didn't take enough to kill herself."

"She did kill herself."

How can such a smart man be so stupid? I try to be patient, I try to be careful. "She only died because she metabolized this medication extremely well. She was so small and so healthy that she reacted at an accelerated rate. They did a very thorough autopsy because the amount she took shouldn't have killed her."

He frowns, shakes his head, shrugs. "She left a note."

"No one but you even saw the note, no one in the family. It says in the reports that her parents kept insisting it wasn't suicide because of the amount she took, so they investigated it. They eventually ruled it an accident because whatever she said in the note was 'inconclusive.' No one thinks she meant to kill herself."

He shrugs. "It affected where they could bury her. So maybe . . ."

"You thought the coroner said she didn't kill herself so she could be buried in a certain cemetery?"

"Yes."

"Gentry, coroners don't work that way. They don't care where the dead bodies go once they're done with them. They only care how the bodies came to be dead."

He swallows, getting pale.

"I need to know what she said in the note, Gentry."

He stares down at the coffee cup. "I never read it."

"You never read it?"

"No. They took it that night and they never gave it back."

"Well, I can't believe you didn't ask to read it."

"I didn't need to read it to know it was my fault."

"Oh *stop* that." He stares at me, a little round-eyed. I need to calm down. "You told her you wouldn't let her publish the book, right?"

"Right."

"And then she threatened suicide, and that still didn't move you. She knew you wouldn't change your mind unless she got to you somehow. So she wrote a note, but only took enough to knock herself out."

"Why would she do that?"

He's so blind. "I don't think she ever meant to die. I think she meant for you to feel guilty enough to let her publish."

He shakes his head. "No one would do that."

"Why not?" He's silent. "I can see what you're thinking, Gentry. I see what you want to believe. But didn't you tell her you were leaving her? Is that it? Isn't that what happened?"

He opens his mouth to speak and nothing will come out.

"I want you to *look* at it, Gentry, the *truth* of it. You weren't going to let her publish and you were leaving. This was all just a way to force your hand, but it backfired."

He keeps shaking his head.

"She wanted things her way and she knew she could make you do anything if she made you feel guilty enough. And what better way to get to a Catholic than suicide? She did this to manipulate you and she accidentally killed herself. And you keep taking the blame like a martyr."

"It doesn't matter, Fiona, it doesn't matter if she meant to or if she didn't. She did it because of *me*. It's still *my fault*."

"What bullshit."

"Shut UP." He stands, and he's reeling, falling back like I'm pushing him but I haven't touched him. He drops the cup, his arms thrash out to his sides, flailing, trying to catch himself on the counter like the floor is tilting under his feet. He finally gets his balance and bangs out the kitchen door. Sam follows, barking like crazy.

Gretchen is getting out of a car in the driveway. "What's going on?"

He pushes past her and stumbles to the steps and down to the beach. I stand there feeling like I've violated everything here. Gretchen runs to the top of the stairs to the beach. "He's in the water!" She turns back to me, one arm around her belly, the other raised to point down the driveway. She stands there, tall and furious, her hair streaming in the wind. She's elemental, a spirit of wind and water. "You get *away* from here. Get *away* from him. And *stay* away."

I have been banished.

Gretchen

"**W**hat are you doing?"

He's sitting on the sand. Sam walks around him in circles, worried.

"Gentry?" He peers up at me. "It's too cold to swim in this ocean. You need a wet suit to swim here, you know that." He stares out at the water. Sam brings me one boot, then the other. What if he'd worn his boots in, what then?

I won't cry, I won't.

"Let's go up to the house. Come on." I take his arm. I pull him up. He's shaking. He stops at the base of the steps to the house, groans. "Come on. Forty-four steps. If Bosco could do it, you can do it." Sam leads the way and we go up the steps. Sam and I carry his boots. He moves stiff, slow. I have to keep pushing him. We finally get to the back door. "Wait here. I'm going to get a blanket." I run up and start the tub, and then come back downstairs and get the throw off the couch.

He's still standing there when I come out. Teeth chattering, lips blue. Sam is near him, trying figure out how to fix it.

"Take your clothes off or you'll ruin Mom's floors." He pulls off his shirt, then turns around before he pulls down his jeans so I won't see the front. I put the blanket around him. "Okay. Get inside." We go in and he stops at the foot of the kitchen stairs and groans again. "Get up there. Just get up there." We climb, and I push him into the bathroom. I test the water, turn it off, cover my eyes. "Get in." I hear him falling into the tub. I open my eyes and his are closed, his head tipped back, and he's still shaking. But he looks alive.

I'm going to kill him.

"Your lips are blue, Gentry, and you look half dead, and if you ever do that again, I'll kill you. I will. That water is 58 degrees and that's hypothermia cold. Do you have to do this stupid book thing when it upsets you so much? Do you have to do it right now when I need you? I *need* you, you stupid *dummy*. I'm going to *lose* you again."

I feel his icy hand on my arm, feel it shake. "You won't."

"Do you promise?"

"I promise."

"Listen to me. It's not just me. You're really a dad now, Gentry. You can't be stupid, you can't go freaking out and running away. You don't get to do that anymore. Tristan already lost one father."

He folds up, ashamed.

I go beat the sand out of his clothes against the side of the house, crying and swearing, before I put them in the washer.

Gentry

Fiona left. She left without talking to me. She wrote me an email. She said she'd work in town for a couple of weeks, and then be back.

I'll live through this. Not just for Gretchen. Tristan, too.

∾

Gretchen has to go to the doctor every week, and he has to check her. The first appointment like that, she said she needed me in there with her. I said I had to leave. She pleaded with me in front of the doctor who looked at the floor while we talked. She said she hated it, she was embarrassed, it was the worst to be alone with the doctor for it.

I couldn't do it. I had to leave. I made the nurse come in and hold her hand.

Gretchen wouldn't look at me on the drive home. She wouldn't speak, and she wouldn't eat. I've promised to always be there whenever she needs me. I failed her. She slammed the door to her room and didn't come down for dinner.

I gave up and went to bed.

She's in the water. I'm not supposed to go in there. She has me by the hand and she's naked, and I can't bear how beautiful she is, the curve of her breasts and the arch of her back and the length of her legs and the rise of her belly, hard and high and holding the future. Everything about her breaks my heart.

I'm not supposed to go in. Especially not with all these clothes on. I have on every article of clothing I own, and my boots. I know I'll drown.

It's all right, she says. It's okay to go in if I'm with you. They won't hurt you if I'm with you.

She pulls me in.

I wait to die from the water, but the water is warm in my lungs if I'm with her. How does she do it, what is her magic, how does she make everything around her safe. This is her magic. I can live anywhere, through anything with her.

Look, she says, there they are.

They balance on their tails and dance across the water in sheer joy at the sight of her. They fly and flip, calling and laughing, and she laughs back in her laugh like bells, pealing across and then under the water.

They're here for her, I know that much. They belong to her and she belongs to them and they'd never come here for me, only for her with that white dryad hair that streams behind her. She is the most perfect sight my eyes have ever known.

Like this, she says, and I watch how she does it. I put my a hand on each side of the long body that feels like it's made of pure muscle. She smiles, do you feel the hair? People don't expect them to have hair, but they do. It's like bristles. They're us, you know. They're the other humans.

I hold that column of muscle between my palms, and I'm carried along by the strength of it. She's doing the same. I never knew it would be this easy. And I look and there's a third along with us, holding on in the same way, so small, and white and strong, and too small to be so beautiful.

She smiles. It's okay, she can be out of me down here. She still breathes water. She's an in-between thing, Gentry.

She's safe.

"Gentry?"

I shake off the dream. She's sitting on the edge of the bed with my Becca pillow in her arms, tears on her face.

"Come here."

She curls up under my arm. I hold her while she sniffles. Where is my fearless girl who swims with the dolphins, who always saves my life? "You'll be there when I have the baby, won't you?"

"In the room?"

"Yes. I want you with us in the delivery room."

The thought of that.

"Promise it."

I put my face in her hair. "I promise."

I will keep this promise.

∽

July was the month when the baby would come. Sometime in July.

We spent July waiting.

Kathryn and Jack came for the Fourth. Tristan was on a camping trip with friends. We made a fire on the beach and watched the fireworks. Gretchen fell asleep with her head on her mother's lap, looking up at the stars. While she slept, Kathryn lay one of her hands on the bump of Gretchen's belly that rose like a dune on her young body. The fire made their faces glow gold and orange, and the flames lit Kathryn's tears, her white hair, her cold little hand.

It was a moment. Jack ruined it by saying, "Well if she's just going to sleep, why are we out here risking chilblains? Let's go up." We went up.

We waited.

∽

Fiona stayed in Portland and worked on research. She had a lot of research to do, she said. All the infertility medicine, which she'd be researching up at the medical school. I called her every few days and asked her when she was coming back. "Oh, soon, Gentry. I'll be back soon." She didn't come back. But I knew she would.

We waited.

⌒

I walked on the sand with Sam, throwing sticks and wondering when Fiona would be back. Sometimes Gretchen walked with us. She still liked the tide pools, but found it hard to get up and down to study them with her belly like that. Her belly was enormous. She kept her shirt pulled above it, and her belly got as brown as her face.

One afternoon she said, "I guess you miss Fiona."

There was no point in lying to Gretchen. She always knew the truth. "I do. But she'll come back."

"How do you know?"

"We have to finish the book." But it was more than that. I knew in a way I'd never known anything that Fiona would come back.

We waited.

⌒

Gretchen spoke to Tristan on the phone every morning and every night. She cried after every conversation, locking herself in her room. I would knock and be told to go away. I finally called and asked him what they were talking about that upset her so much.

Tristan sounded shocked. "Like, soccer camp? Stuff like that? Not really anything. Whatever movies I've seen?"

"And that's it?"

"I swear, Gentry, I don't say anything that would upset her."

"I didn't mean to accuse you, Tristan. I'm just trying to figure it out."

"Yeah. I guess sometimes I get kind of, you know, uh, like, focused on how much I love her and how much I wish I was with her right now. But I don't say anything to upset her." I apologized for asking him and went to knock on her door. I could hear her crying.

There was a long pause, while I waited. "It's just because I love him so much, okay? I miss him. Now go away and leave me alone."

"Okay." I went away.

We waited.

⌒

It's August. She's overdue. The doctor says don't panic, it's normal for first babies to come late. Tristan came to get her this morning to take her in for this week's appointment. I haven't been able to see enough of my son, and I wanted to take him somewhere, talk to him, make sure he was holding up.

But they need to go to the doctor, and I need to get ready for the fall.

I call Kathryn. She agrees to meet them at the doctor's. "You have to be in there when they check her," I explain.

Sam and I go in to work for a while in my silent classroom, where I belong.

It feels so still and uncomplicated and calm. I move the keyboard, put my head down on my desk.

Oh Dear God, thank You for sleep.

⌒

I walk in to an empty house and a ringing phone.

"Hey."

"Hi, Gentry. I've been trying the house for a couple of hours."

"I fell asleep at the school. I thought you'd have her back here."

"I'm not bringing her back. The doctor says she's close."

"How close?"

"Maybe a week."

"Another week?"

"We've only known she was pregnant for four months."

"She's been pregnant for at least two years."

Kathryn laughs a little, that small icy laugh in my ear. "She needs to stay here, now."

"It's hot there."

"It's always cool in the house."

"There's pollution."

"There's no advisory right now. There's a breeze. She'll be fine."

"She doesn't have her lotion."

"I have lotion, or we can go to the mall."

Is she laughing at me? I don't care. "She didn't take any clothes."

"She can wear Jack's clothes."

I want her to wear my clothes. "Can I talk to her?"

"She's too upset."

"Did she talk to Tristan, is that why she's upset?"

"No, he's actually upstairs with her right now, trying to calm her down. She's upset because she can't come back to the coast."

They should bring her back to me. "Will Mike see her?"

"No, Gentry. He won't see her." I want to hit him. "Gentry, Marci called. Her internship is over and she's moving back to Oregon. She wants to be close when Gretchen has the baby. She's too angry to stay with her father and she and Jack fight all the time. I want things peaceful for Gretchen."

"Well, where will she stay?"

"She plans to stay there."

"Here?" I am trapped by the kitchen walls. "You mean this house?"

"Listen, Gentry, I've argued enough about this with her. Will you please just figure it out? There are three bedrooms and the little house and a couch. That's five different places to sleep. Work it out. Gretchen is the priority."

She is. But I wish Fiona were here.

⌒

God, Marci will be here, soon. I need to pray about that. I need a plan. I decide to be nice. That's the plan. Be nice, and avoid certain topics, like her mother and what happened between us, any combination of love, pain, betrayal, her, me, her mother. And be polite. I have to be polite.

This is not the best plan I've devised.

Help me, God. Just help me out, here. Amen.

I hear a knock, I think, the doctor was wrong and Gretchen's back but she wouldn't knock, it must be Marci but why would Marci knock at the door of her own home?

It's Fiona.

God, she's been gone since June twenty-third and it's August eighth and thank You that I didn't frighten her away permanently.

She waits on the threshold, scared. I'm scared I'm going to kiss her so I cross my arms and rock so far back on my heels that I almost fall over. "Hey. You're not supposed to knock."

"Well, forgive me then."

"I can do that."

"You can? You can forgive me?"

She rushes up and hugs me briefly. I leave my arms crossed so I don't slip my hands around her neck and angle her face just right and . . . she moves back and puts a paperback on the counter. "Here's your book. He's great."

She smells so sweet. "Can we talk about it?"

"The poetry?"

I can't stop smiling. "Yes. Please?"

"In a minute. I want to talk about something else, first." Sam celebrates, turning in circles of puppy joy. He loves her, kisses her, leans on her. We missed her, didn't we, Sam. "Are you sure it's okay for me to be here?"

"Yes. I'm sorry I scared you."

"I'm the one who should be sorry. I talked to Hugh about it and he reminded me that this was your life, not some episode of Law and Order."

I hated that show. And parts of my life did resemble an episode, come to think of it.

"Gentry, I keep asking myself if it can possibly be okay to do this to another human being for a stupid book. We're almost done. I could just work from Portland, now."

I think, during the forty-four days she was gone, I missed Fiona more than I've ever missed anyone in my life. Even Gretchen. Even Becca. Even my mother. What I feel for Fiona is the most beautiful and terrible thing I have ever felt in my life.

"Hey Fiona? I'd really like it if you stayed here."

Oh God, God please let her stay here.

Amen.

She smiles. "If you want me to stay, I'll stay." She reaches over and puts her hand on my heart. And there's a singing somewhere inside me. It's a stupid thing to let a heart sing like that, a stupid, stupid thing.

Help, God.

She takes away her hand. I get myself under control.

"Well, if I'm here to work, then let's work." She sits down at the counter and takes a notebook out of her backpack.

"I'll make you some tea. Would you like some tea? Would you like, I don't know, some cookies?" I hunt through the cabinets. I think there are cookies, where were those cookies? Did Marci eat them all? I find a package of cookies with a French name that Kathryn brought here and set them by her teacup. What else would I like to put by her teacup? An armful of peonies, a Bible, a newborn lamb, a million dollars, my heart. What is *wrong* with me? I shut the cabinet.

"Thanks." She's scanning her notes. "I have all these notes for the infertility part. That's the core of the book, according to Brooke, so I have you two doing it all, including unsuccessful in vitro. I was up at the medical school all month with a friend of my dad's learning about this."

"Your dad?"

"Yes. He's retired, but a couple of his friends still practice. One of them is a fertility specialist. We hung out at the medical school, watching couples get their hearts broken and talking zygotes."

"Hm." Did I know her father was a doctor? Do I know anything about Fiona, besides her religion and where she went to school and how great she smells?

"I can't believe what they can do. I know you hate all this, but it is really a miracle, Gentry. I'm actually writing an article about one of the couples who let me follow along. I'll finish it after their babies are born. Except, it doesn't work in the book, of course. It's awful what I make you two go through, and incredibly expensive, and I never let the two of you get pregnant."

"Thank you for not requiring my participation."

"It doesn't sound like you were ever too excited about participating."

"I refused to participate."

"Why?"

It takes me a while to say it out loud. And when I do, I'm aware of how much I sound like Mel. "Because children are meant to come from God."

She eats cookies and sips tea. "I think we need to talk about God."

"Hey Fiona? I'm as comfortable discussing God as I am discussing sex."

"Well, we're going to have to talk about that eventually, too. So let's practice with God, okay?" She laughs a little and I smile.

"Okay."

"Have there been times when God didn't work for you?"

"Of course. But I always go to church and I never stop praying. I pray reflexively. I have an involuntary prayer reflex."

"I like that." She writes it down. "Did you grow up going to church?"

"Yes."

"So your parents were religious?"

This is the strangest part. It's like finding more rooms in a house you have lived in for years, rooms and rooms, some full of horror, but most of them full of the basic stuff of life, the banging of pots and pans, her small, worn shoes by the back door next to all the books that had to go back to the library. Her listening to the news on the radio. The way she smiled when she combed my hair. *I should sell you to the wigmaker.* Folding the laundry. Refolding the newspaper after reading it so he wouldn't be bothered that it was out of order. She was so quick and small and familiar. But on Sundays she came out of that room looking like a beautiful stranger. *What do you say, little man, I clean up pretty good, don't I.*

These are the first memories I put away, because they hurt so much.

I shake my head to clear it. "They both went to church. She talked about angels."

"Angels?"

"Yes. I think she believed in angels. But that doesn't necessarily mean she was religious."

She gives me a curious stare. "You don't think so?"

"She liked fairytales. When she talked about angels, it sounded like another kind of fairytale."

"Well that's kind of interesting. I can do something with that." She makes some more notes. "How about him? Was he religious?"

"I have no idea. I hardly saw him. He drove the car and sang the hymns."

"But they were both Catholic?" I nod, because they knew the Litanies, the Creed, they made the right motions and knelt on the prayer rail after communion. "What did you think about God when you were little?"

"He lived at the church and I've always loved church. But I wasn't so sure about Him."

"What made you start loving God?" She reaches over and touches my hand. And I know I can do it.

"Communion. That was when I started to love God. Taking God's body into mine. I had this small body, and I felt very weak. But God's body was infinite, and infinitely strong. He came into me and made me strong. He filled the places where

I was empty. He surrounded the things I couldn't stand and held them separate so I could go on. He held that all for me until I was strong enough to finally hold it myself. God saved me, and I don't mean the sacrifice, even though I'm grateful for that. I mean that He saved this life. The one I have to live every day. And He keeps saving it. So how could I not love God?"

"Do you believe in angels, Gentry?"

"Me?" I can't help it, I laugh out loud.

She's embarrassed. "Not even a little?"

"I don't believe in heavenly angels. I believe . . ." How to put it. "I believe the love of God pours through us. That we all have the capacity to be vessels for grace. Haven't you ever had a person come into your life for the express purpose of saving it? People like Mel, and Gretchen. I believe God's grace makes angels of all of us."

"You should talk about God more. You should talk about God to everyone." She wipes her eyes on the sleeve of her tattered sweater. "Will you pray for me, Gentry?" I nod.

She gathers up her notebook and leaves.

She wants me to pray for her. I'll pray on her behalf, yes.

But I know better than to pray for her.

Marci

I was mad enough to hit someone, if there were ever anyone around to hit. "Let me get this straight. You're telling me that I can't go to my *own* home at the coast because Gentry's there, suffering. And I'm supposed to *care*. Well, listen, little sister. I'm done with school and my internship and I'm coming home and there's nothing you can do about it."

I could hear her sobbing away. "You can't GO there, you can't DO this."

"What do you think I'm going to *do* to him?"

"Shut up, you know."

"Don't be gross, Gretchen."

"Look. I have to stay in Portland and have this stupid baby, so you have to be careful with him. It's this book he's doing. It's killing him. He's worse than he ever was back then. Swear to me that you won't make things any worse for him. Swear to me that you won't make him go away." She was crying so hard. My baby sister was desperate.

My dad is also desperate. My dad has bullied and charmed his way through life to this point, and Gretchen won't be bullied, and she refuses to be charmed. He's furious at her, furious at Gentry. Most of all he's furious at *"that asshole's little clone."* Tristan, the kid I watched grow up without ever noticing him. Gretchen has her very own Gentry, now. My baby sister, about to become a mother at age sixteen. A mother to Gentry's grandchild.

The word is "heinous."

∽

When I first heard he was back, I called Mom. I tried to be polite because you could murder someone in front of my mother, and as long as you did it politely, she'd raise no objection. My voice strained at the edges but stayed in the range of courteous. "Eve says Gentry is staying at our place at the coast. Can I ask why Gentry is staying at our place at the coast?"

"Marcialin, you never come to the coast. So why does it matter?"

"Why does it *matter*? That's my *house*, Mother."

"It's *my* house, and I've given him permission to stay there for a while."

"How can you let him come back, after . . ."

"After what?" Her voice was ice. "Is there something more you need to tell me, Marcialin? Something I don't know about?"

I closed my eyes and remembered standing next to her in the dark, watching her cigarette flare as I told her it was all my fault. I swallowed. "No. There's nothing."

"Then there's no reason for him to stay away. And right now, he needs to be left alone." I hung up on her.

My dad called. "Honey? Are you doing all right? I haven't heard from my favorite girl in a while." I thought, good, Dad cares. At least one member of my family would be on my side. But I was wrong.

I told him Gentry was back and I didn't like it. But Dad was a member of the "poor sad Gentry" club, too. "Gentry was having a hard time of it down there in Oklahoma. I'm sure he won't be at the house forever."

So I told my father about those accusations against Gentry in Detroit. "Dad, I don't think he should be around Gretchen. I can show you footage of when he was investigated, I have tapes . . ."

"Honey, I ordered the clips too. I checked it out. That was a media feeding frenzy. Anyone could see that Gentry's not the kind of guy who would do something like that to a student."

Dad and his piercing insights.

Gretchen was fifteen years old and they let them stay alone together at the coast. I called her and reminded her he was not the saint everyone seemed to think he was, and she knew that. My little sister told me to fuck off.

It was like those weeks when they all hated me, when I was invisible. It's none of your business. Leave him alone. My mother's angry face. "Don't you dare go anywhere near that man, Marcialin. Don't you SPEAK to him." It was like that all over again.

I couldn't sleep. It was bad again, like it was when I heard he'd gotten married. My roommates in the big U District house didn't like me much in the first place, but they liked me even less when I spent all night in the room with the TV, watching and rewatching the tape the clipping service put together for me. The tape of Gentry in Detroit.

Gentry being ambushed by reporters in Detroit outside his apartment house, him and Bosco walking away, not saying anything for over a block, just walking, his face grim, while people ask him questions like, "*Why won't you speak in your own defense, Mr. Gentry?*" "*How many other girls have there been?*" "*Do you only prey on black girls, Mr. Gentry?*" Finally, Bosco starts barking, and they leave him alone.

Gentry going into a courthouse, grey-faced and miserable, his lawyer shoving away microphones, saying, "*No comment.*" Gentry coming out of the courthouse, just as miserable as when he went in, the lawyer saying, "*Of course my client is very relieved that this situation has been resolved, but he has no comment.*" Finally, Gentry at a news conference, his lawyer reading a statement about how his client just wanted to go back to work and get on with his life, Gentry sitting silent beside him. And then, for reasons I don't understand, he had to answer questions. Was he angry at his accuser? Was he going to stay in Detroit? Had this in fact ruined his life?

He had the same answer for every single question. "*I have nothing to say.*"

They never showed the girl. All I knew was this: she was black, underage, and she recanted. Maybe she lied, too.

Dad told me the secret to successful lying. He says you pick a lie, you keep it simple, and you stick to it. The trick was to keep it simple.

Dad should know.

∽

I went to college on another planet, really. That's how far away Colby was. I wasn't the smartest girl, or even the meanest. But Gentry was right, I did like college, and I was good at it. I avoided all conversations about my life before Colby, and with the exception of one stormy affair with a professor and one small nervous breakdown after I heard that Gentry got married, I was almost fine. I arranged my internship with a Seattle paper, so I didn't walk in my commencement.

Back in Oregon, Mom stopped drinking. She got sick and got better and married Jack. Gretchen grew up into the beautiful young thing I always knew she'd be. I visited as little as I could. We put our family back together, such as it was.

But Gentry was *back*. Back in my *house*.

I sat on the futon in my Capitol Hill apartment and tried to make some sense of all of it. How could Gentry be back in my house? How did that happen? Where was his wife, why was he there without her? Did he leave her? Why did he come back?

Who did he want?

I was sitting there watching the tape one last time, and I heard a funny flapping sound. The screen fuzzed up and I knew the tape had worn out and snapped. Something inside me had snapped, too. Whatever it was that kept me wrapped up on the futon in my shitty little hole of an apartment, it had broken. I was free to go.

I got in my car and drove south.

I thought about what I wanted to say all the way there. You ruined everything, Gentry, you ruined my life, so just get out of it. Or maybe I'd say, my mother is married, now. She chose what she wanted. So choose me, Gentry. Have me.

One or the other.

∽

It was almost daylight when I got to the beach. And there he was, asleep on the couch with the TV going. He was zipped into his sleeping bag. One arm stretched out, hanging off the side of the sofa. The other arm curled up and around his head, showing the tender underside of his arm.

The word was "vulnerable."

I tried to wake him gently. He kept mumbling. I'd say "Gentry, open your eyes," and he'd mumble back, and I'd say, "Gentry, I need to talk to you," and he'd mumble again. I thought, I didn't go to all that therapy and figure this all out and drive all this way to hear him mumble.

"Gentry. Look at me."

He opened his eyes and scrambled out of the bag and something horrible and white flew out with him, snarling and snapping, barking and biting at the air behind me as I ran into the kitchen and climbed up on the counter, shaking and screaming. Gentry was right behind me, silent and fast but when he got to the middle of the room, he snapped to a stop like there was an invisible rope tied around his middle and he'd reached the end of it.

He fell forward at the waist and hung there for a moment, just hung there on that invisible rope. He jerked up straight and threw back his head. A sound came out of his mouth, a sad, wild sound that echoed in the kitchen.

And then he woke up.

Blinking, calm. He knelt to the horrible white animal by his ankles. "Hush, boy. It's okay. Hush." Crouching on the kitchen floor, speaking so softly to that cowering thing. "It's just Marci. She lives here. It's all right. You're all right." It put its big paws on his knees and gently licked his face.

It was only a puppy. And Gentry was only a man.

I saw his chest, his cheekbone and thought, he's bleeding again, and it's all my fault. What I told my mother was true. It was all nothing. And it was all my fault. But I can't stand to think about it, especially when I know I have to go face him again. Because my sister is going to have a baby, and that means I need to come home.

⌒⌒

You can only mentally rehearse something so many times before your brain starts to hover at the surreal level. By the time I pull up beside his Jeep and some minivan, I'm almost hallucinating with alternative versions of how it might be to

see him again. I can see him through the window sitting at the island. He's reading, maybe a book, maybe the paper. His hair's long again. I always hated his hair, so I don't understand why I'm relieved that it's long again. He sees my headlights, opens the door and stands on the step with his hands jammed in his jeans pockets. He looks exactly the same. I can't do this. But I have to. Get out of the car. Smile. A nice big, fake smile. "Hi!"

"Hey."

I take my overnight bag and a backpack out of the passenger door. He walks over to take them away from me. There's this awkward tugging while I resist, then give in. He sees that the car is packed to the top. "You brought a lot of stuff."

"I'm moving back here."

"Oh." His eyes pop a little, but he recovers. "I'll, um, help you with the rest of it in the morning."

"That would be great." I guess we've both decided that our only hope is to be extremely polite. We enter the neutral territory of the kitchen, the part of the house where he was always allowed. "Whose minivan is that?"

"A friend's." He moves past me to carry my bags upstairs, so I follow. He enters my room, definitely not neutral territory, and sets them on the floor. Home again, home again. Ugh. The new wall looks too white and the room is too small. Mom took four feet off the end of it to enlarge hers, and she said she was going to open up the closet to get the space back but she hasn't. The bed is freshly made. I've decided that this time, I won't say anything about him and my mother having sex in that bed. That's probably best for the mental health of everyone involved, right? "Who put the TV up here?"

"I did. There's cable."

"Don't you want the TV downstairs? Gretchen said you were a TV addict."

"I decided to kick the habit."

"I guess you'll have one of those 'One Day at a Time' stickers on your Jeep, now. In the shape of a television." And he smiles, a small smile, but a real one.

That stupid dog circles me. He's calm, but I can see the hair up on his neck. I hate that dog.

"Sam. Come here." He immediately trots to Gentry's side, as perfectly behaved as Bosco always was. "Hey Marci? Are you hungry? There's soup."

"No, but I'm thirsty." We walk downstairs to the kitchen, single file. His boots are insanely loud on the kitchen stairs. I seat myself at the island and look down at what he was reading. One of the Harry Potters, like Gretchen. The word is "juvenile." He puts on the kettle, takes out three cups. Then he takes out the decaf loose leaf and Mom's teapot. "Gentry? Seriously? Tea?"

"A friend told me it might help my insomnia."

"Your minivan friend?"

He nods.

Tea and a minivan. Wow. Whoever this friend is, she's probably really hot.

The back door opens. The smell of the ocean blows in, that full, salty smell of home. Someone beautiful blows in with it.

She can't be much older than me. She might even be younger. Her hair is darker than Gentry's, and it must be long because it's twisted up haphazardly on the back of her head. Her ugly hipster glasses can't hide her light grey eyes or her arched brows that almost meet in this intense Frida Kahlo way. Her clothes are ridiculous, a Mr. Rogers sweater over a vintage dress and green Hunter boots. Her legs are as long and perfect as Gretchen's. Everything on her is long, her neck, her hands, her hair. Like a Modigliani. My guess is she's never plucked her brows, dyed her hair, worked out, been on a diet, bleached a tooth, had a professional haircut or a manicure.

She sees me and stops short.

The expression on Gentry's face tells the story, even more than the tone of his voice when he says, "Hey." Like, Hey, where have you been? Or, Hey, what took you so long? Or maybe, Hey, I love you.

Like that.

She wafts in, airy and vaporous. The dog runs to her, panting. "Hello sweet Sam. How is my sweet boy?" He dances with joy. She bends to pet the dog, fresh as a tree branch that's never been bent. The word is "willowy."

My creative writing professor accused me of melodramatic metaphors. She said I was always comparing my feelings to things I'd never actually experienced, so everything I wrote rang false. Well, I've never actually been stabbed in the stomach with a knife, but my guess is it would feel exactly like this.

"Oh, um, Fiona, this is, um, Marci Mumford. Marci, this is, um, Fiona Wallace."

She smiles at me, a shy smile that hints at her perfect teeth. "It's nice to meet you." For God's sake, even her *voice* is perfect, sweet and reassuring. She sits down beside me and nervously fiddles with a piece of yarn trailing from one of her elbows. She studies her elbow, Gentry studies her, and I can't think of anything to say.

Except the obvious. "How did you meet Gentry?"

"We ran into each other in the neighborhood. I live by your mom."

I wonder if Gentry understands that she must have money.

"The, um, tea is ready." He sets the pot by the cups. She twists her head on that swan's neck and her hair falls, a glossy river spilling down her shoulders and back. She deftly twists it up again, and Gentry watches her arrange her hair as if it's the most mysterious, beautiful act a woman could ever perform.

I can't stand this.

She angles her head. "Marci? Can I pour you some tea?"

"Sure," I say, sounding as disbelieving as I feel. She pours me some tea, then she pours herself a cup, this woman who has dared to offer me tea in the kitchen of my own home. I get up to find the Splenda. I feel her watching me move around my kitchen, in which I know where everything is because did I mention that this is *my* kitchen and *my* home? What is she *doing* here?

"Can I ask why you're here?"

"Well." She says that like, well. Now I understand what kind of a person I'm dealing with. "Gentry and I are working on a project."

"A project?"

"A writing project."

"The book Gretchen talked about? The one she says is killing Gentry?"

"Yes," Gentry murmurs. "The very one."

I look over at Gentry's love-stunned eyes. This woman is his perfect match. They will stumble into love and marry and have the most beautiful children that anyone, anywhere, has ever seen unless I *do* something.

This is no longer about my mother. My mother made her choice, and she's married.

So this time, I have a chance.

Gentry

I make myself drink this tea while they talk. I don't like tea, I've never liked tea, but after listening to me talk about my insomnia, Fiona gently explained to me that maybe one of my problems might be too much caffeine.

I told her I didn't think so. I'd been drinking coffee by the bucket since I was sixteen, and I'd never had insomnia because of it. She smiled at me kindly. "You're older, now. Things change. Try decaf tea before bed, just try it." So I drink this stuff at night. I don't like it, but I drink it. I do sleep better.

Marci is exhausted. "Gentry? Be quiet in the morning, all right? Don't bang around, don't sing in the shower, okay? I can hear everything in that stupid giant tub." There are rings of fatigue around those mocking green eyes. "I'm hoping being here will help me sleep."

"You should leave your window open. The noise and the cool air helps."

"Right. I grew up here, remember? So that's not exactly a new idea to me."

Ah, a flash of the sharp-tongued girl I remember. "Sorry."

She's embarrassed. "I'm sorry. Thank you for the suggestion. Goodnight. Fiona, it was nice to meet you. Good luck with the project." She goes up the kitchen stairs. I hear her door close, the mumble of the television.

Fiona stares at her teacup for a while. Say something, Fiona, I want to hear your voice.

She rises. "I need to get back to work."

That was not what I wanted to hear her say. I resist an impulse to beg her to stay in the house. "Sam, stay here." He likes it out there, but Sam needs some rest. Fiona leaves. I finish my tea. I hate tea.

God. This is a mess. Good night. Amen.

‿

When I walk barefoot down the stairs at seven-thirty, trying not to wake her, I find Marci awake and seated at the counter, reading my library book. She smiles an apologetic smile. "You didn't even take a shower, did you."

"I can get one later."

"I made coffee."

"Thank you." I'm not used to talking to anyone but Sam in the morning, and my voice sounds rough and strange. I tie on my apron and wash my hands. "Do you want some breakfast?"

"I heard a rumor about that. You can cook?"

"I can fry." That makes her laugh. "How do you like your eggs?"

"Poached." I don't know how to poach. In Oklahoma, I had a little machine for that, but I gave it to the Goodwill. I must have a funny expression on my face, because she smiles. "How about over-medium? Can you do over-medium?"

"I'm the over-medium expert." I get busy because I'm starving. But first, some coffee. Mm. "You make good coffee, Marci."

"Anyone in the Pacific Northwest who can't make good coffee is escorted to the Idaho border by armed guards."

I roll olive oil around the pan. "They have to go live in North Dakota. The land of Folgers and Maxwell House."

But she doesn't laugh. Maybe she's never tasted bad coffee.

"I was pregnant when I was sixteen."

I drop an egg. Thank you God, that she can't see my face as I clean this up. Sam licks his chops and smiles. Sam, ick, don't eat raw egg.

"I had an abortion at that place we saw that day. Do you remember? With the protesters? That's why I was so hard on Tiffany. If there was ever an argument for abortion, it would be the offspring of Garret and Tiffany."

Even that child deserved a chance. I don't say that, though. I stand up and nod, because to do or say anything else would be cruel. "Could you, um, butter the toast?"

"Sure." I watch her, trying to understand how it is that women can butter toast without flattening the bread. "I did the right thing, Gentry. I've never doubted it."

God? Why do women tell me about their abortions? I'm no priest, I can't absolve anyone. This started in college, hearing about it. They tell me about abortions and they bite me. Maybe I should start operating under the assumption that all women have had abortions. And they all bite.

She puts more bread in the toaster and depresses the lever. "Why didn't Gretchen just have an abortion? She's so scientific. Wouldn't that make it easier to have one, knowing a zygote isn't developed enough to be a human being?"

Is she asking me to explain, or is that rhetorical? I wish I had the right words. I'm archaically Catholic and I'll never know the right words to say about abortion.

She goes to the fridge and pours herself some juice, pours me some milk. I set up the plates and take off my apron. We sit down in front of our eggs. I made myself four. I'm starving.

I lay my hand over hers. "Hey Marci?" Her hand is small and cold, like her mother's. "Will you teach me how to butter toast?"

"You can't butter toast?"

"Not without flattening it."

She shakes her head and smiles a tight, crooked smile. "I'll show you the trick."

I keep my hand over hers while I give thanks for this meal, Lord, to lend her the grace of my small prayer. For these thy gifts we are about to receive. And thank You for this chance.

Amen.

I open my eyes. She's regarding her plate with that same small, sad smile, but her hand still sits under mine. She waits for a moment, then picks up her fork with her left hand and moves the egg onto the toast. She sets down her fork and lifts the toast, takes a bite. She makes a moan of pleasure when that yolk hits her tongue. "This is perfect. *Perfect.*"

"Hey Marci? Don't talk with your mouth full." I dig in. She's right, it's perfect. Under mine, her hand warms.

Fiona

Yesterday, I was mooning around my kitchen feeling bored and useless, and the phone rang. I stared at it for a moment because I hate answering phones. I used to stare at the phone and will Miki to call. It occurred to me that I'd stopped expecting to hear from her. And then it occurred to me that it might be Gentry.

I snatched up the receiver. "Hello?!"

A broken girl's voice sobbed. "Fiona? You have to go *back* there."

"Gretchen?"

"You have to go back to the coast *right now.*"

My stomach sank, him in the water, my fault. "Is he all right?"

"He won't be if you don't get over to the coast *right now*. He's in *trouble*."

"Trouble? Gretchen, are you sure? I don't know if . . ."

"You don't *understand*, I have to have this stupid baby now and Tristan has to stay here with me and the Gilroys are up in Canada and Mom won't let me call Mel. So go *back* there. *Please*." She hung up.

I threw my things in the van. I drove too fast, jerked to a stop next to his Jeep, ran to the door and pushed in. There he was, sitting on a barstool, drinking coffee and calmly working a Sudoku puzzle. He glanced up at me and smiled. "Hey."

I thought, what's the trouble?

I felt like I'd called the fire department screaming that a restaurant was on fire, and they arrived to find a busboy on a cigarette break behind the kitchen. But, I reminded myself, it wasn't me who overreacted. It was Gretchen. So I took a break from feeling like an idiot and felt relieved, instead. He was fine. And he was, miracle of all miracles, happy to see me.

We had a nice talk about the progress of the book, a very professional discussion of what I'd been doing, because I really had been busy. And then he talked about God, and the words he spoke were so sad and beautiful that my heart broke. I gathered up the pieces and went out to the little house to put them back together and unpack. I fiddled around on the computer, let Hugh know where the hell I was and loaded the latest version of the book on the hard drive. I managed to get my heart put back together.

When I came back later for tea, trouble was perched on one of the barstools.

∽

I was going in for tea this morning, but saw the two of them through the window, sitting side-by-side at the counter, holding hands and eating breakfast. Cozy. Not that it's any of my business, no, not at all. But still. Very cozy.

I came back out here and made a cruddy cup of teabag tea.

My stomach is growling and I've been working really hard this morning, by the way. Gentry's here going over what I did while I was gone, and he frowns a little at how hard I'm typing. Maybe he fears more keyboard abuse.

"Gentry, can I ask you something?"

"Ask me anything."

"That girl? Marci?" That gorgeous girl, so petite and groomed with her streaky blonde hair and round breasts and prominent hipbones? With the powerful little legs of an ice skater and the perfect butt to match? Who sat at the counter last night, glaring at me like an interloper she needed to warn off with her ridiculously large eyes the color of good jade, that Marci? "Who exactly is she?"

"Gretchen's sister. Kathryn's other daughter."

"Who is she to *you*?"

He's confused. "Is this for the book?"

"Never mind." I've been back less than a day, and I'm already messing it all up again. "It's none of my business. I'm sorry I asked."

"Marci was my student." He stares out the window, looking tragic. This is a hint that I might be dealing with only a partial truth. "She wasn't excited about a teacher living here."

"You seem like you're friends now."

He smiles and frowns at the same time. "I made her some breakfast this morning. She ate it, so maybe there's hope."

Breakfast. Maybe that's all I saw. And maybe he hasn't noticed that she looks at him with starving eyes. Maybe he hasn't noticed that being around him is a torment for that girl. Maybe he's sort of an idiot about women.

I might be a recluse, but I'm no idiot. I've noticed that all these women act like they own him. Kathryn with her beautiful, lined face, waving me away. Gretchen with her proprietary care of him. And now this devastated Marci. "I think she probably had a crush on you."

"I think she did."

"Students probably get crushes on you all the time."

He nods. "I'm old, now, but it still happens."

Oh, right, he's so old. "You're thirty-three? You don't look your age."

He holds up a hand. "Don't."

"You don't like getting compliments?"

"Not about how I look."

"It bothers you?"

"More than I can say."

"Oh, I can relate." He nods, taking me seriously. "Gentry, I was joking. All right? No one ever talks about my looks. But I can see how, hypothetically, if a man were remarkable enough to invite those kind of remarks, that it would be embarrassing to have people talking about how pretty you are."

He shakes his head. "I'm not pretty. Sam's pretty."

"Yes he is. Pretty boy. Sam, you're a pretty boy." Sam smiles and pants and thumps his tail because unlike Gentry, Sam likes a compliment. "While we're on the subject . . ." I have a stack of pictures in an envelope. "Evelyn sent these to me."

He goes all wide-eyed. "I need to go do the dishes."

"Dishes can wait. Just look." I sit down with him on the bed.

He scoots next to the wall. "I'm tired."

"You woke up an hour ago."

"I want something to eat."

"You ate a half hour ago." Next, he'll tell me he has to go to the bathroom. No, he would never say that. Gentry probably doesn't even go to the bathroom. All bodily wastes evaporate into some pure essence that he surrenders to heaven once a day. Via prayer. "These are just pictures, Gentry. Two-dimensional representations of people who are not actually in the room with us." That makes him smile in spite of his panic. Good, this works. I put my hand on his arm. "Will you please look at them with me? Tell me about this one." He has long, long hair in this photo, so long it hangs into his lap. He's seated and Miriam's standing next to him with her arm around his shoulder. He has his arms crossed over his chest.

He studies it carefully. Nothing happens. The woman in the picture doesn't jump out and bite him, and he doesn't jump up and throw himself off a cliff. "I think her dad took this the first time I went over there to meet them."

"You look uncomfortable."

"I look like an idiot."

He doesn't look like an idiot. But he does look uncomfortable. She's cute, as much as I hate to admit it, she's cute. She looks so much older. "You were so much . . . taller than her."

"Yes. My height was an issue."

"Did her family like you?"

"I don't know. They were polite to me. They included me in everything. They forgave me for acting like a jerk at the funeral. My brother-in-law kept me on the payroll." He shakes his head. "They were decent to me."

"Well, I'm glad for that. How about this one?" They're sitting at a table wearing leis and he has his arm around her shoulders. He's barely smiling and she's outright scowling. The picture's in a folder with the name of a hotel on it. "Let me guess. You went to Hawaii on your honeymoon and this was part of the Hawaiian Honeymoon Experience."

"Yes. What a racket. What do you think they do with the pictures people won't buy?"

"Throw them away."

"What a waste."

"That's quite a platter of ribs. Is it an entire pig's worth?" I hate it that he has his arm around her, but I remind myself that she's dead. "Miriam looks angry."

"That was just how she looked." He studies the picture, a couple sitting in an overpriced restaurant, palm leaves and tiki lamps, the vaguely out-of-focus faces of the couple behind them floating like ghosts over their shoulders. And he smiles the softest, sweetest, saddest smile, as if he's gazed on the face of something too rare to describe.

Well.

"How about this? Was this a special occasion? Or maybe an infomercial testimonial?" They're standing up together in front of some disturbing drapes. She has on a little ladylike lavender suit with a short enough skirt to show her great turbine thighs. Her shoulders jut out like a swimmer's, and her arms are so buff that they strain the fabric. Gentry looks like a mild-mannered job applicant, with short, brushy hair, a grey suit and a tie. He looks younger in that get-up than he does in his baggy jeans. "So, what's the occasion?"

"The occasion? Hm. That would be . . . adoption applications."

"You both look very nice."

"Nice?" He studies the picture. "She kept telling me to look normal. That made it impossible."

"You don't look abnormal. Just a little tense. You look good with short hair." He does, he looks sweet, shorn, naked. And so young. It looks like a mother and son before his Bar Mitzvah.

"Can we burn it?"

"Evelyn wants these back."

"You talked to her?"

"Yes." And listened to her cry, describing Gentry's vigil at Miriam's bedside for the month he's never told me about, a month when he wouldn't let her die.

"I wonder how the baby is."

"As far as I can tell, naughty." That would have been his niece. This bothers me for some strange reason, so I return to the photo. "Miriam certainly was in great shape."

"Yes, she worked out to those, um, tapes. She had everything of steel." I feel him shiver. We need to move on. I give him another picture of him and her and a group of somber people dressed up and grief-stricken. Maybe a funeral. He has on a big brown suit. He has a swollen eye and his hair is still long. Miriam has on another tight little suit, peach colored. Looks like a size one. "Nice shiner. Who died?"

"Oh, that was when we got married."

"Are you *kidding*? This is the *wedding*? Look at your *faces*. Who are all these sad people?"

"This is Daniel Shaw. He was my best man. He's married to Becca, who didn't come to the wedding. And these are the Sandersons. Paige and Sandy. He actually went to high school in Subiaco." He waits for me to react, so I make an exaggerated nod, as if I have any idea at all where Subiaco is or why going to high school there might be impressive.

Gentry goes on. "This is Kevin Montrose and his wife Parker, she's a Protestant, and over here, you can only see his arm, but this arm is Dexter Hamilton. He didn't get to be in the picture because he's a technical virgin." He studies his friends and the sweetest smile plays across his face. Strange how there are no smiles in that photo, though.

I point to the man who looks like Gentry but older, taller, with long wavy blond hair and blue eyes. He has the kind of lethal good looks that make me uncomfortable. "This is Sandy? Sandy of the broad, wide bed and the poising? Is he really this handsome or is this just a good picture?"

"This is not a very good picture of him."

"Are you kidding?" His shoulders are three feet wide and I can't see his chest, but I bet it would look great peeking out of a white shirt open to the waist. "He should take up modeling for romance covers. I'm serious. He could make a little extra money."

"I'll tell him that."

"Have you told him what Miriam said in the book?"

His voice is hard with anger. "I will never tell him." Why does this allegation bother him so much more than the others?

Maybe it's his name.

I lay a hand on his forearm, which is as strong and solid as a young oak. "Gentry. You know your first name used to be a man's name, don't you?"

He pulls his arm away. "That's not a man's name."

"Well, originally, it was."

"You didn't grow up with it. He hated it, he said it was a girl's name, and he would . . ." And he stops, swallows down whatever he was going to say. He's suddenly so far away.

"Gentry?"

"Hm?" He comes back. "What?"

"Did you believe him?"

He frowns. "Who?"

This is eerie. He's doing it right in front of me. Not remembering.

"Did kids make fun of your name?"

"Well, yes. Kids make fun of everything. But I'd fight anyone who did."

"You fought?"

"Of course. A name like that guarantees you'll fight."

"But did anyone call you gay growing up?"

"No."

"Are you homophobic?" I'm nearly holding my breath, asking this.

"I don't see myself as homophobic. Unless it's about me, and then I get angry. So I must be."

Is that logic? "Gentry? Have you ever, you know . . ."

He glares at me, like, oh no, not you, too. "No. Never."

"Many people who identify as heterosexual have had homosexual experiences." I sound like an educational pamphlet. "Experimentation is normal."

"Well then, I'm not normal."

It's like watching a windshield crack, that slow but inexorable break spreading across his face. He tries to stop but he can't, it's throaty and painful and pulled out from a place he doesn't want anyone to see, a wailing wall of pain.

I wasn't supposed to do this to him again. I'm as fascinated as I am guilty.

He cries and cries and cries. I remember the first day I met him. He was torn up over the death of his old dog. He sat at my table in the throes of grief, and I couldn't even pat his back because he was a complete stranger. But I sat beside him, because life is full of terrible solitude and sometimes, you just need to be near someone when you're cracking into pieces.

The door swings open on this beautiful spectacle.

"Knock knock." Marci looks from me to him and back to me, her eyebrows lifted in suspicion. "What the *hell*? What's going *on* out here?"

He lifts his shirt to dry and hide his face.

"He's having an allergy attack."

She fixes me with her angry green eyes. "I'm going to the store. I wondered if you *need* anything." She waits, arms crossed.

"He needs you to leave."

She stands very still, gathering her dignity before she slams out. I watch through the window in the door as she carries piles of clothes on hangers into the big house.

She's not going to the store at all.

He puts his hands on the back of his head, curls up and breaks down all over again.

I return to the computer table and type a bit while Marci empties her car into the house. I carefully organize the photos by his hair length and put them back in the envelope. Finally, I hear her car door slam, the engine, the sound of it going up the drive.

"I guess she really was going to the store."

Without a word, he stands up, drags his sleeve across his face and walks out.

Gentry

G retchen is only eighty miles away. If I need to see her, I can get in my Jeep and go. I know where she is. I'm allowed to see her.

This calms me.

Here's your stick, Sam. Let's walk. We'll walk and think. Let's solve our own puzzle, one we never wanted to think about. About going off to the Jesuits with Band-aids on my thumbs.

When I got there, there were other boys with Band-aids on their thumbs. At night, we probably all took them off and had a field day. We didn't get into each other's beds. We lay there and tried to be brave. I would pull the sheet across my mouth, tight, and pray not to be a baby, a sissy, a girl. I would pray not to suck my thumb. Eventually, I learned to sleep on my back with my arms out, off to the sides of the bed. Gretchen calls that my Jesus pose. I never told her why I sleep like that. That way my thumb stays out of my mouth. Maybe once a year, I wake up and it's in there. I have always forgiven myself for this.

All those years, accused of a name.

Sam, find me that stick. I'll throw it.

When Gretchen was eleven I wanted to fly kites with her. When I was eleven I went to live with Mel.

Mel is the oldest of fourteen children. He has seventy-two nieces and nephews, and most of them have children. They live all over in Australia and New Zealand. One sister lives in Hawaii, so there's family there that I could have visited on my honeymoon, if I'd known. That probably wouldn't have gone over very well with my wife.

Mel didn't have any children, but he knew children. And he knew what I needed. When he reached for me, I shrank away, but he kept reaching.

Finally, I let him hold me. It felt so good. His arm around me.

A few times that year, when I was outrageously angry and had lost all control, when I'd flown at him kicking and biting and hating, he had to restrain me in a way that wasn't kind. After, he put me in his lap. I was too old for that, I was eleven years old. But Mel sat me in his lap and let me suck my thumb.

He never said a word about that, not one word.

When I had nightmares, he came to me, patted my back, stroked my hair. He said the psalms for me. His small hands on my head, his voice in my ear, until I could sleep.

Sometimes when I couldn't sleep I went to find him. He slept on a pullout couch in the living room of that little apartment, sprawled out on his stomach like he was embracing the mattress. I'd climb up and sleep on his back. The warmth of his big body in the night. How that felt. The sound of his snoring.

Other people had touched me over the years, women mostly, pulling me in for hugs, stroking back my hair. That was bliss and agony. Little girls would kiss me, chasing and teasing and then their dry, sweet lips that tasted like candy or gum or toothpaste would brush mine, leaving me angry and blushing. My neighbors gave me little shoves and pats, steering me around with their rough, loving hands. They only touched my head to cut my hair or check for lice.

I never touched anyone. Oh, there was that one day on the swing. After that, I never got close to another girl. I never touched anyone after that unless I was fighting. I never touched anyone gently. Never reached for a hand, never rested my head on someone's shoulder, never hugged anyone. Until Mel. Mel was safe.

I was a busy kid, always running around, taking things apart, finding games in the street, headed somewhere. But I had to check in with him. He insisted that I learn to do it. That was new for me, having to be accountable for where I was, and it was the only place we had a conflict. I had no idea why anyone would care where I was.

So after I learned to check in, I'd take that as a time to touch him. I would take his hand. If he was seated, I'd hop into his lap, very briefly, just put myself on his knees for a second, tell him what I was up to, and then jump down. If he was busy, writing or engaged in conversation, I'd run up behind him and lean against him. He'd hold still, waiting, and I knew he was smiling. I was completing a circuit, charging up with a current only he could give me. And then I'd run off again.

When we sat at the rectory table, working on declensions, I'd hook my leg over his and let my boot bump his calf. It helped me concentrate. When we camped, we'd lie outside by the campfire and look up at the stars and tell ghost stories. When I got scared, I'd move my bag close to him. I'd set a hand on his stomach, which rose so tall it seemed like a mountain to me.

So that was a secret. That I could touch someone, safe like that.

When I was thirteen and drunk and he did what he did in that alley, Father Peter told me he'd seen me. How I was. What I wanted.

I would never touch Mel again.

⁓

The first time I saw Sandy standing in the campus ministry vestibule, I recognized him. I knew how he would walk, how he would run, the exact manner in which he would kneel to tie a shoe. I knew how he would laugh and swear and cough and sing, how his hands would sweep his hair back from his face, and how those same hands would feel hitting me.

I wanted to hit him back.

I followed him around for three weeks, putting myself near him, waiting, every hair in my body rising in alarm and anticipation. He sent the occasional remark my way, assessing my youth, my innocence, challenging my opinions, watching me. And I watched him. I was right about how he talked, laughed, sang. I was right about every single part but one. When he finally raised his arm to me, he put it across my shoulders and said, *You have much to learn, Grasshopper.* He burst into a laugh that roused something so fierce and strange in me that I have never had a word for it.

I was a boy and feared the worst.

I hit him once. He didn't hit me back. He just made me pierce my ear. I took him every question I ever had about women, school, life, God. He answered every one. He counseled me, teased me, threw me on the ground, held me down and laughed at me. I went from wanting to tear him apart to wanting to lay down my life for him. Only by dying for him could I show him what he meant to me. Because I did love him and that was fine. He was older and wiser and smarter and bigger than me, and he took care of me like a brother, and we loved each other.

I never knew where Sandy came from or why You sent him to me. Like Mel, he is a gift. Thanks be to You for Your wisdom, mercy and grace.

Amen.

Marci

He comes in with his dog, just like he always did. He goes to the sink and washes his hands, then bends over the sink and scoops up handfuls of cold water to bathe his eyes.

"You must have terrible allergies."

He leans down under the spigot and drinks. He straightens up and shakes his head. Water flies out from his hair. I have the funniest thought, that it's holy water and now he's blessed this new kitchen. Things are getting too Catholic around here.

He trudges up the kitchen stairs, the dog behind him. I hear him go into my mother's room and close the door behind him.

◦◦◦

I'm seated at the kitchen island reading when he reappears at dinnertime, rubbing his eyes and raising his head like a dog to sniff the air. "Lasagna?"

"Lasagna."

He smiles. Good. He nods towards his library book. "Are you enjoying it?"

"What's not to like about magical snacks and dangerous creatures? And Quidditch?"

"Gretchen says the next one is even better."

"Wow. I can't wait." Barf.

We carry in the food like we always did, and sit. He crosses himself and starts eating. "You still pray."

"I do."

"I used to torment you at the table. How did you stand it?"

"I was hungry." That makes me laugh. He shovels it in like he always did, he has good manners but he's still so hungry. "Hey Marci? For five years, I've expected lasagna to taste like this. And it never does. You put something extra in the cheese part, don't you."

"Oh, just some spices. Nothing special." I sit there smiling. All across my cheeks, my arms, my heart, I feel small, hot waves of pleasure. This is utterly ridiculous.

He stops eating, his face so grave. "I, um, borrowed some CDs from your room. I burned them all for myself."

"You could have taken the actual CDs, you didn't have to burn them."

"I should have asked."

"You have my retroactive permission."

"Thank you." He is so relieved.

"I'm taking it you don't do Napster."

"No. I don't like the idea of someone downloading files from my computer. Plus it's going to be illegal."

"It's not going to be illegal, don't be so paranoid." I actually do make good lasagna. Why don't I ever make this anymore? "So what happened to all your CDs?"

He blinks a little. "How's your internship going?"

Oh. So someone does mention what I do once in a while. "My menial internship at the community newspaper is over. I'm a college graduate." That gets a smile.

"Did Gretchen call while I was upstairs?"

"She called and cried. Dad's being such an asshole."

He looks back to his plate. "He's concerned."

"Dad isn't concerned, Gentry. Dad's pissed and he's being an asshole."

"Maybe he needs more time to get used to the idea."

"He's had months."

"In some ways, your dad was right. I had no idea how hard this would be on Gretchen."

I stare at him. "I'd really like to know how you can sit there and defend my father, considering what he says about you and your son."

"My son?" He sets down his fork. "Tristan is . . . he's *fifteen*. He's doing whatever he can. How could he say anything against my son?"

He just doesn't get it. "Gentry, it isn't personal. But my brilliant baby sister is pregnant. She's supposed to be finishing high school so she can go to med school and cure cancer. But she's sixteen years old and she's having a baby. My dad's not ever going to like the boy who did that to her."

He sits there for a minute, taking that in, then stands up and carries his plate to the kitchen. I hear him start the dishes. Do I always have to say the wrong thing? The worst thing, the thing that hurts him?

I leave for the bar.

Gentry

S *he sits beside me. I'm naked.*

I'm lying in her front yard, naked, and she's sitting cross-legged beside me. In her lap is a pot of geraniums. She has on an old dress, her ragged sweater. Her long feet are bare.

And we're talking, but there's no sound. She's telling me a story with no words, no speaking, no sound. My unspoken story.

She snaps a leaf off the geranium. She stops after she snaps the leaf, and puts it to her mouth, carefully licking it. She fixes the wet leaf on my bare skin like a stamp. She snaps another, and then another, snapping, licking, pressing. The smell of the broken stem fills my nose. Fresher each time I smell it. The smell of her.

I am covered, leaf by leaf. Once upon a time.

⌒

Fiona's sweet smell, her breath. I open my eyes to her face over me.

She smiles. "Hi."

"Hey." I sit up fast. My book slides down from my chest and hits me hard where it hurts. I make some noise of pain and set the book on the floor. "What time is it? Where's Sam?" Sam comes up beside me and puts a paw where it hurts, ouch again. I move his paw. "There you are." We touch noses. I love my Sam.

Fiona's trying not to laugh. "You're pretty cute when you wake up. It's nine o'clock. Do you want to go back to sleep?"

"I've slept most of the day." I try to stand up, I'm too tired, someone filled me up with lead. I sit back down. Hard. "Since Gretchen left, all I can do is sleep." I close my eyes, remember. "I dreamed about you."

Her voice is soft. "About me? What was I doing?"

"Fixing me." I open my eyes. "I need some coffee or I'm never going to wake up."

"I'll make you some tea."

"I want coffee."

"Tea, Gentry. It's nine o'clock. Where did Marci go?"

I stand up. "I'm not sure. She left while I was doing dishes. Are you hungry? There's leftovers. It's really good." We walk into the kitchen, well, Fiona walks in, but I sort of stumble.

"Are you all right?"

"I'm fine, just fine." I'm still asleep. I stand and go to the window. I love these long summer evenings when I can take a nap and still see the sunset. The sun gets so red as it sinks, dark and heavy with it. Like blood.

I close my eyes and see Becca sitting naked on my bed in the dorm, talking about running away to Oregon, to the coast, where the sun fell into the ocean like a blood orange. *If you don't want to get married, let's run away to Oregon.* Her gold-shot red hair cascading down, so long that it curled with her other hair, falling like a river and my heart falling along with it, plummeting into love for her.

I look over at Fiona and feel my heart falling that same way.

Hey God? I'm in some serious trouble, here. It's her hands, the deft movement of her long hands as she cuts herself a piece of the lasagna. I want to hold those hands, to kiss the tip of each slender finger, to watch those hands comb the hair of our children.

Help me, God.

She smiles in happy anticipation. "This does look good. Do you want some more?" I wash my hands and sit as an answer. She serves some up for me. We give thanks and eat at the counter. She doesn't speak. She just eats. There's an exquisite concentration she brings to the basic tasks, like eating, typing, putting up her hair.

I have to get myself under control.

God. Now. Amen.

When we're done, Fiona puts the dish in the fridge and washes the plates. Then she sits down with her notebook.

We always have to work.

"I wanted to talk to you about all these aversions you supposedly have. Miriam has you down for so many things that I've already seen you eat that I thought I'd just come in here and find out the truth." She has her notebook. She frowns. "I forgot my pencil." I hand her mine. "Thanks. This is a nice one. It's vintage?"

"I think it's older than me."

"Well, I like it." She moves the lead up and waits, pencil poised. "Tell me something you hate and why."

"Something I hate and why?"

"Sure, like I can't stand to wear shoes because my father's a podiatrist."

"A podiatrist?"

"Yes. A podiatrist. And he believes that everything about a person's health is determined by his feet. The shape, the arch, the way a foot sets on the ground, it's all very important to my father. As a result I had to wear the ugliest, weirdest shoes you've ever seen. So I stopped. I only wear them for special occasions. It drives my father crazy. But he's living in Arizona, so he doesn't have to worry about my feet in person. He just worries about it over the phone." She smiles. "Okay, so tell me something you hate and why."

"I hate sweet drinks. Like pop? Juice? Sweet tea?" She appears to be baffled. "I had rotten teeth when I was a kid. Sweet drinks always hurt my teeth. See?" And I hook my fingers in my mouth and pull back my cheeks and let her see.

She whistles. "Like a rapper. But your grill's in the back."

"I never eat ice cream for the same reason. Or candy. Or peanut butter."

"Peanut butter? That's not all that sweet."

My stomach rolls, but I wait it out, let it pass. "I got sick on it once."

"Oh. Like chemo."

"Chemo?"

"Chemotherapy makes people nauseated. Cancer patients have to be very careful about what they eat because they develop aversions. My mother couldn't eat anything." Grief falls across her face, and it's like when the sun leaves the sky. I want her in my arms. I know how to make her feel better.

Okay. Stop. She's married.

She is calm again. "Why did Miriam make such a big deal over this? She made you sound so, I don't know, defined by all these things. She said you were phobic." She's staring at me.

"Hm."

"Well? Do you have any real phobias?"

I shiver. "Besides nuns?" I think. She's waiting. "I don't like flying."

"But you did it, right?"

"Yes. But I didn't like it."

"Give me more. Give me something weird. I'll take notes."

"Okay." I have to give her something. Something besides guns and teeth and spit and belts and blood, and the horrible, sinking way it feels when a man puts his hands on me. "Certain colors make me feel sick. Pentecostal Christians. Pornography. Workshops and seminars. Any type of therapeutic situation. AA. And I guess I have a problem with wearing clothes that fit me."

"Oh, they're fine, your clothes are fine. For Heaven's sake." She frowns, reading the list she's been making. "Isn't there anything else?"

"Not really."

"Nothing?"

"Well, words. I dislike certain words and phrases. Like indicate, issue, defensive, private industry, top-of-mind, sense of urgency, bookworm, computer geek, sole breadwinner. I hate being on the same page and thinking outside the box. I refuse to do anything on a go-forward basis. I hate the word 'boundaries.' And I don't like the words people use when they talk about their, um, backsides."

"Do you ever swear?"

"No."

She's thinking, knitting up her eyebrows. Her eyebrows are wispy and soft at the edges, and they lay above her eyes like feathers and I want to touch them. "You know, Gentry, I hate certain words, too. But I collect what I hate, and incorporate it into whatever crap I'm writing at the time."

"Like what?"

"Like, 'fulfilling lifestyle.'"

"That's a bad one."

"Right up there with 'dysfunctional family.'"

"Or 'fear of intimacy.'"

"Organic."

"Win-win."

"Process."

"Hey Fiona, did you know that I'm an 'internal processor'?"

"I would never have guessed!" And we both laugh. "I guess you should be prepared. I use so many of those phrases in the book. But don't worry, I have one phrase I despise too much to use, even in my writing. It would be perfect for this book, too." She's smiling.

"Is it 'recovering Catholic'?"

"Of course." She smiles. "I'm going to go work on this."

"By yourself?"

"By myself. You're barely keeping your eyes open. Good night." She kisses me on the cheek and hands me my pencil and goes off to work on my weirdness. I do the dishes and let Sam out for a minute and then I decide to go to up to bed, because I can't seem to get enough sleep.

Come on Sam, my good dog. Let's go back to sleep up here on the bed, come on up on Kathryn's nice down comforter and make yourself at home.

Let's dream of sweet Fiona, because Mel said a long, long time ago that dreams don't count.

Marci

This room spins a little.

I just want to see him. He still sleeps with the light on. I bend down and I breathe in that sweet breath he has. His lips are parted. His face is so peaceful, it's peaceful like, well, like something peaceful. The word is "peaceful."

I'm so drunk.

The dog growls. Be quiet, stupid dog. The word for you is "mean."

Gentry's eyes open. "Get out of here." He scrambles out of bed and stands with his arms crossed over his chest. "Get out of this room."

"This is my mother's room, not *your* room. You should *never* be in here."

"You need to leave."

I raise up my hands, see? Hands up. No weapons. Harmless. "I just want to talk. I think we should talk. We never talked, Gentry."

He's using a teacher voice. "You can talk to me about whatever it is in the morning." The stupid dog, he stands up on the bed. He starts growling.

This room is starting to spin too much. I stare at the cross he hung over my mother's bed, I focus on that, but I still feel dizzy. "I feel sick."

"Then go to bed."

"Is that an invitation?" But the dog is there, growling.

Gentry points to the door. "Marci, get out right now." He's dismissing me. I'm too old to be dismissed. And he's not my teacher anymore.

"Gentry . . . did you know that in college, you can sleep with the professors?"

He shakes his head, hard.

"Oh come on. You used to laugh at my jokes. Don't you think I'm funny anymore? Because Garret still thinks I'm funny." And his eyes get wide. "Oh, don't freak out, I had a drink with Garret, so, big deal. We didn't fuck or anything. He's in the Navy. I would never fuck anyone in the Navy."

The dog shows his teeth. And the stupid thing stands there on the bed and snarls at me, barks at me, barking and barking and Gentry doesn't say a word, he lets that dog bark at me.

I have to shout. "Fuck you. Just FUCK you, Gentry. Fuck your DOG, too." I go into my room, and I leave the door open. I see him close his. I hear him throw the lock.

I hear him say, "Good dog, Sam. Good dog."

I stand by the door and shout as loud as I can. "I WAS LYING! I DIDN'T EVEN REALLY HAVE A DRINK WITH HIM! HE WAS AT THE BAR BUT I DIDN'T EVEN TALK TO HIM! I WOULD NEVER TALK TO HIM! GOD! I WAS LYING JUST TO PISS YOU OFF!"

He calls through the closed doors, "Just go to sleep, Marci."

"NO! I WON'T! BECAUSE I HATE YOU TOO MUCH TO SLEEP!" I do. And I hate this BED. Because he was with my MOTHER in this bed. I can't forgive either of them for that. They can both forgive me all they want to, but I will never, EVER forgive them. NEVER. I can't believe I tried to KILL MYSELF over him. He's an ASSHOLE.

The room spins and spins and spins.

I never had a chance against my mother.

I'm so good at lying. I told my best lie on the night I graduated from high school. I didn't want to go to that stupid all-night party where my mother was volunteering. I asked my dad to take me home and he wouldn't, so I asked Garret. That's all I wanted from him, a ride. He drove me home without saying a word. I went upstairs and got in Mom's shower because that bathroom door had a lock on it and mine didn't. I stood in the shower and cried, because once he drove his old Jeep out of town, that was it. Gretchen would never survive, my mother would never forgive me, it was all my fault and I'd never have a chance and that would be my life.

The word was "hopeless."

I got out of the shower so the hopeless part of my life could begin.

We'd bought Mom two robes that year, a pink fuzzy acrylic thing Gretchen found at a store in town, and a navy blue wool robe we found after Christmas at Nordstrom's. I bought it with one of my gift cards. I wanted to wear one of Mom's robes. When I opened her closet, the intense reek of Chanel, whiskey and smoke made me gag, but I found the navy robe on a hook. I lifted it up, and underneath hung his brown terrycloth robe. There it was, confirming everything she screamed at him that night. I'd wanted to believe that she was drunk, out of her mind, raving, making it all up. He was her lover, I *hate* that word but that's what he was, her young lover who kept his robe in her bedroom and slept in her bed with her, probably sneaking in after we were asleep.

I started to shiver. I wrapped that old robe around me, belted myself into its scent. Sandalwood and sweat.

When I came downstairs he was standing in the kitchen, looking like Jesus with a cardboard box. He opened his mouth to say something. I've wondered over the past four years just exactly what he was going to say. Maybe, *Thanks for ruining me, Marci. I'm driving my Jeep off the bluff.* Or maybe, *Come with me, Marci. Let's just leave.* Maybe he was going to say, *It's you I want, not her. It was always you.* Or maybe even, *Go to school and come back in four years. I'll be right here waiting.*

Whatever it was, he choked it back. He handed over that box and walked out the door. I carried it upstairs like it was full of shattered glass and broken hearts, and set it gently on my bed.

When I came back down, Garret was still sitting on the couch staring at the TV like the moron he was. "Garret? Would you please leave?"

He was confused. "What the fuck, babe?"

"Would you LEAVE?"

His face got hard. "Why, so *he* can come in here?"

Again, the word was 'hopeless.' The word for my entire life.

That's when we heard it, the sound of shattering glass and wood on metal, everything cracking to pieces. Garret didn't even move. His precious short box was being beaten to death, and he just sat there because he was afraid of Gentry.

The truth is, I goaded him.

"You're afraid. You're afraid of him. And he's always known that, hasn't he."

He stood up and went out the front door that no one ever used. He left it open, I'm sure so he could run back in as soon as the fight started. Because it was clear to me that they'd be fighting. I thought, good. Garret wasn't a student and Gentry wasn't a teacher anymore, no one would be fired or expelled for it, they were just two stupid males who wanted to fight, so let them have their stupid pissing match.

I could hear Gentry. "Don't ever touch her again." How dare he talk that way about me. In that special protective way like he was my father. I was shaking, furious.

And then Garret laughing, sneering, "I don't have to touch her. She can't keep her hands off me. You should go ahead and fuck her." Laughing at Gentry. "You should've fucked her, you really should've. She's *great.*"

I thought, all right, it can't get any worse than this, can it? And I can live through this. I can live through Garret standing outside my house yelling that at Gentry. I haven't died of shame yet, and it can't get any worse.

I stepped outside and Gentry said, "You stay away or I'll tell her what you did to Tiffany."

What could Garret have done to Tiffany? What?

There are phrases meant to express what I felt, like "dawning recognition" and "flash of insight." These phrases are not equal to the job of expressing what it's like when you suddenly understand every aspect of a complicated situation. It's a physical sensation, like you've been lit from within and truth shines into every corner of you and illuminates what a blind, deluded, ridiculous fool you've been.

It wasn't Garret I hated, then. It was Gentry.

The look on Gentry's face, like he felt sorry for *me.* I turned away and went inside and closed the door on all of it.

I sat in the kitchen, staring out at the ocean. I was almost too angry to cry.

Almost, but not quite. The sobs came ripping out of me. I wanted to act like my mother, to swear and scream and break something. I'd already broken my little sister, so maybe I could break all the new glasses, or beat up Gentry's Jeep because Gentry had known all about it, he let me go on walking around this town with Garret after he'd gotten her pregnant. Standing up with him at prom, expecting to win.

I hated him for letting me be a fool.

The truck tore around the house. No lights at all left in it, so it was like a ghost vehicle, only located through the roar it made. It raced up the drive and onto the highway and I knew it would never come back again. All those nights in the little house, in the truck. The taste of beer and pot and cigarettes in his mouth, the feel of his hard arms around me, the muscles in his back, the tarry smell of his hair. His bowed legs and crooked smile and mean eyes and cruel, beautiful face.

With Tiffany.

I stared out the window, howling my betrayal at the dark. For the first time in my life, I understood my mother's rage. I wondered how my mother had kept herself from killing my father.

And then I thought about Gentry, his sad eyes and low voice and the way it felt when I made him smile or laugh, when he took my hand, when he held me in his arms that day in the attic. He made me so safe. I loved it and hated it because it was a wall. And then when I got around that wall, the brush of his mouth against mine, the heat of his breath on my neck. Thinking, now, yes, mine. It's finally going to happen.

And then, what he said. *I have ruined my life.*

I started to argue, to beg, feeling him move, push away my arms, pull my legs from around from his waist, disentangling himself from me on the bed, leaving me with only the horrible sinking recognition that he was going to make everything calm and safe and proper and right. It didn't matter that Gretchen came in. It wasn't her. He'd regained control before she ever opened that door.

No chance.

You'd think I'd have understood. But I took another pointless chance when he stayed late at school, asleep behind his computer in the lab. I groveled to him, I told him I loved him because I thought somehow if he understood that, it would change things. I thought it would matter. He slammed me against that blackboard, holding me away instead of holding me down. No matter how he felt, no matter what coursed between us like electricity, I knew he would never do it.

Because he loved my mother.

Garret had betrayed me, and betrayal left me stripped and hurting. But my skin would grow back if I let it. I could get over Garret. But the way I hurt over Gentry was like the ocean. It would take me and roll me and grind me to sand for the rest of my life.

I'd stopped crying. It was just me and the moon, and the constant roar of the ocean. But Bosco wouldn't stop barking. I'd never heard Bosco bark like that. I went out the kitchen door, and heard this thumping, banging. He was throwing himself against the door of the little house.

Why didn't Gentry let him out?

I walked around the side of the house. Gentry was on his back, his eyes closed, his mouth hanging open. It had never occurred to me that he might lose the fight.

All around him, the ground sparkled with broken glass.

I leaned over him. I saw the strange set of his jaw. "Gentry, open your eyes."

He didn't. He refused to open his eyes. I wanted him to open his eyes. I wanted to have him on that glass bed that would cut our beautiful bodies to pieces. Gentry on a bed of diamonds. "Wake up. Look at me."

His eyelids gently parted to let me in. I opened his robe and showed him what he wouldn't see for himself, that I was young and perfect and his. I watched his eyes roll back a little, the dark lashes fluttering, settling, closing. A dark bubble formed at one of his nostrils. It hung there, swelling, then broke. A trail of oily blood fell down his cheek.

I realized he couldn't move.

I didn't panic. I rolled him on his side so he didn't choke on his own blood, and went back in the house. I picked up the phone and dialed 911.

Dad always told me, choose a lie. Stick with it. Keep it simple.

The dispatcher was nice. She asked if I wanted her to stay on the line until the ambulance got there. I said no. I hung up the phone and looked around the kitchen. There was a glass in the sink. I didn't know who'd stood at the sink for a glass of water, whose fingerprints were on it, whose DNA was on the rim. I washed it carefully, dried it and put it away.

I hadn't ever been alone in my house at night. Not once. But I wasn't really alone, was I. Gentry was dying out in the driveway, and it was my fault.

I was afraid to go upstairs, but I had to.

The box was still on my bed. I shoved it in the back of the closet. I took off his robe and hid it behind the box. My clothes were on the bathroom floor. I put on the same pair of underwear, my lavender bra, my commencement dress. I slid my dirty feet into my shoes and did up the buckles. I dabbed on lip gloss and brushed my hair.

I walked carefully back downstairs, afraid I'd fall in my heels, and dialed the ugly yellow phone. He answered. He listened while I explained what he and his father needed to do with the truck. I made Garreth Blount Junior repeat what I'd said back to me before I hung up. The exact words.

I heard sirens.

Gentry was still on his side, a pool of darkness under his head. I didn't know if he was dead. I thought maybe he was, I thought, maybe Gentry is dead. I wanted to put my hand on his back and make sure he wasn't dead, but I thought if he was still alive and I touched him, he might die from it. I stood there with my arms wrapped around my stomach as the sirens slowed, and a fire truck and ambulance came bouncing down our narrow driveway. The lights flashed over the house, the apple trees, his unmoving body.

An EMT approached, someone I remembered being a seinior when I was a freshman. "He was like this when I found him."

Keeping it simple.

The sheriff interviewed me first. I told him to talk to Alex Fournier, who'd been in town that day to walk in commencement. Two days later, the priest came from the local church and tried to talk to us. Mom wouldn't let him in the door. Coach Gilroy came over and yelled like a crazy person. "Blunt force trauma! Who the hell hit him on the back of the head?"

"He was like that when I found him."

Then the uncle priest showed up. He wanted clothes for Gentry. They'd had to cut off everything Gentry was wearing that night. Mel was polite at first, asking for a bag, giving my mother the prognosis, talking about Gentry's broken jaw and bruised larynx, his cracked ribs, his concussion, his memory loss. He was so calm about it. But eventually he broke down and stood in our driveway, calling on God and demanding the truth. My mother just cried.

The sheriff came back and asked me more questions. He played a copy of the 911 tape while my mother listened. I sounded as young as Gretchen on that tape.

When the sheriff left, I sat at the table for a minute, just trying to breathe, remembering Gentry on that bed of glass.

Mom leaned on the sink, her clavicles standing out like cello bows.

"Marcialin? What really happened?"

"He was like that when I found him."

I stood up, went to the phone, and called my dad.

~

Dad was there in less than two hours to get me. He shoved open the door without knocking and walked past me where I sat in the kitchen with my suitcase, and charged into the living room to confront Mom about letting the sheriff talk to me. "Twice? You let them talk to her twice without a goddamned attorney present?"

Mom sat there, so small and blonde on her impeccable red sofa with her arms crossed, her eyes clear as ice. "She has nothing to hide, Michael. Nothing at all." My father scooped me up in his arms and carried me to the car like a child. He never asked what happened. The truth was less important than his daughter.

I always have my dad. He will always love me, always take care of me.

I think about that as I pass out.

Fiona

I heard Marci pull in here very late last night, music loud in her car, slamming around, mumbling. She sounded drunk. She woke me up, maybe she woke him up.

Maybe alcohol gave her courage.

He comes out early, which is fine, since I was up at dawn. "Feeling rested? You look rested. You look like you really got some power sleep. Where's Marci?" I wish I'd shut up.

"I think she's asleep. Her door was closed when I got up."

Her door. Meaning, she slept in a different room. "Well. Good. I mean, she got in late, right? I heard her. So good, she's getting some sleep." He seems confused. He frowns at me like I'm strange. Which I am, but he could at least pretend not to notice. I hand him a stack of pages. "Some of the 'so far.' I want you to read it and make sure it's okay." He sits down on the bed hard, blowing air out of his mouth like he's been punched in the gut.

He reads, pets Sam. Sighs. Reading and petting and sighing for about an hour. He slides the stack of pages under the side of the bed as if to get them out of his sight because they're so offensive that he can't even *look* at them, but he's too polite to say so, to say, Fiona, how can you waste your life writing shit like this, which is what Hugh says all the time. Then he pushes his hair off his face and sits there, silent.

"Gentry? Is it that bad?"

He gives me a bland smile. "It's fine. Just fine."

"What is it? Are you tired?"

"No. I think I was awake maybe four hours yesterday."

"But you're still tired."

"I can't seem to wake up."

"Is it Gretchen?" He's been taking care of Gretchen all summer. He's probably just tired because he can relax. "She's almost through this. She'll be all right, Gentry. She told me she always wanted to keep the baby."

He nods. "She did. She hid it. And when she finally told us, all the other parents kept saying how hard it would be on a girl her age to do this. Everyone but me. I was all for it." He stares into space, bereft and guilty and tragic.

I'd really like to hug him. But I touch him too much.

"You know, I was thinking. Let me make dinner for you tonight, all right?"

"Dinner?" Oh, that smile. "I didn't know you could cook."

"Me? I love to cook."

"Great. That would be great." And he lies back on the bed, closes his eyes and strokes that soft dog. "This bed is so comfortable."

"It really is, isn't it? It takes up most of the house, but it's comfortable." I type an email to my dad and one to Hugh. I have to beg Hugh to send me a recipe for something easy, because I'm supposed to make dinner. Oh, and he'd better send the grocery list for whatever it is, too.

When I look back over at the bed, Gentry and Sam are both asleep on their backs. Gentry's arms are flung out to each side. His shirt is pulled up. I can see his stomach, how it lifts with each breath he takes. I'm filled with longing.

I left because Gretchen told me I was destroying him, making him talk. She said to stay the hell away. I did, I stayed in Portland and worked on research and left him alone.

But it was killing me.

I was outside, moping and poking around the yard, when I saw Gretchen drive past in her mother's car. I walked out to the street and watched her slam out of the car into the house, stomping and sobbing and so impossibly, hugely pregnant. Tristan followed, guilt pulling down his shoulders. Kathryn looked seventy years old when she got out of the car.

I came inside and wandered around my kitchen, staring at the phone and thinking of his gentle face, his gentler hands, the soft feel of sweet Sam's fur, the salt smell of the water. I willed the phone to ring, and when it did my bag was already packed.

No, Gentry hadn't come to my door. But Jane returned to Rochester.

And so, I have I returned to Gentry. I watch him sleep. I want to curl up under one of those outstretched arms, to fit myself to him like a piece of a puzzle, the lost piece that will make everything complete. I want to gently lay my hand on the bare skin of his stomach.

But this is life, not a romance novel.

Gentry

I'm happy.

We're sitting at the table enjoying the fine meal that Fiona spent the afternoon planning and shopping for and preparing. She made a lot of noise in there, and she also had to call Hugh a few times. I heard her swearing.

I stayed out of the way.

I was a little nervous, but the food is excellent. "This is delicious, Fiona."

She shrugs and blushes. "I'm glad you're enjoying it."

"It's fantastic." This pasta has bacon in it. I usually only get bacon in the morning, but thanks to BLTs and bacon burgers, I can usually squeeze some in at lunch a few times a week. If I learned this recipe, I could eat bacon three times a day.

"What are you thinking about?" Marci asks this, studying me.

"Bacon."

"Bacon?"

"Yes. I'm thinking about bacon."

"You might be the strangest man I've ever met."

"Thank you."

Both of them laugh. I am happy to have amused the women at this table, as that seems to be my destiny. Marci seems rested for the first time since she got here.

Fiona says, "I actually don't think Gentry is strange."

"Oh PLEASE. He's a total weirdo."

"Again, thank you."

"You're welcome. But it's true. You're as strange as Gretchen. I don't know how you survived. My freshman year at college, I kept thinking about you trying to do it as a sixteen year-old. I couldn't *imagine* it. How did you do it?"

"I threw myself on the mercy of girls like you."

"Girls like me? What does that mean?"

"I mean, if I could get girls like you to tolerate me, I knew I'd be all right."

"You have no idea what I was like in college."

"I know exactly what you were like in college."

Her eyes are as green as money. "What was I like?"

"Hm. You started with Communications. That was too easy and you hated the group projects. Then, you got involved with Art or Art History, right? Art with a capital A. But your dad probably said no to that. You tried out Linguistics, but that was too hard. So then you made a stab at a useful degree like Econ or Marketing but you hated every single class. And then you took some creative writing classes, and you wrote bitter stories."

Her eyes broadcast equal parts amusement and hatred. "How do you *know* this?"

"You smoked briefly, and bought your clothing at thrift stores. There was probably a hat. Or a certain scarf. Tied . . . oddly."

"Shut. Up." But she's laughing.

"Did you listen to Tori Amos or Ani DiFranco? No, wait. PJ Harvey."

She throws up her hands. "No, excuse me, but those women are over. I listened to Sleater-Kinney, which is just as bad. How do you *know* all this?"

"I know that you broke a few hearts of artistic boys who never saw you coming. You found them boring, because they lacked a necessary robust quality." Her eyebrows shoot up at this particular insight. Hey, why else would I have enjoyed such success? I drove tractors in the summer. "You took some theater classes. Because you wanted to direct."

"I really hate you, Gentry."

"And you ended up back in Journalism, maybe because you had a crush on some professor."

"I actually slept with that professor. He was robust."

"Fine, but you found out you were good at it, Journalism, I mean, and there you stuck."

"Are you telling me that I'm just some type, some stereotypical girl who never did or thought or felt anything original in her life?"

Fiona pipes up. "I don't think anyone or anything is original. Art always expresses a common experience."

What is Fiona talking about? "What common experience?"

"The public experience of art makes the individual experience into a common one."

"Just because you're in the same space looking at the same thing? It's only common in the sense that it takes place in a shared space. But you overlook the individual response, Fiona. You're assuming each individual response within that common experience is the same."

"But the artist intends a response, correct?"

"But to assume a work will elicit that response is a fallacy."

"I know about the fallacy of authorial intent, Gentry." Fiona rolls her eyes. "I write. And it's absurd to think you can't figure out the author's intentions."

"Fine. Do you think whoever wrote 'The Sound of Music' intended my response?"

Fiona breaks into a cascade of laughter, and Marci taps her wine glass with a fork. "Excuse me? I think you both sound as ridiculous as I ever did, talking about Art with a capital A." She appraises Fiona. "Where did you go to college?"

Fiona shrugs. "I didn't."

I'm surprised. "Really?"

"Really. I always knew what I wanted to do, so I thought, well, I might as well just start doing it."

I stare at Fiona, trying to understand why I haven't asked her about this before. I've never asked Fiona about anything. I study her eyes, the feathers of her brows that I always want to smooth with my thumb, the tilt of her eyes, the length of her black lashes, the thin, inky ring around the silvery grey of each iris.

I know nothing about Fiona.

"It's my turn to talk about what you were like in college, Gentry." Marci is smirking. "You were that boy who never once spoke in class, but wrote brilliant papers."

I put my hand on my chest to acknowledge a direct hit. "You got me. I couldn't talk because there were girls in those classes. I hadn't been in school with girls since I was ten years old."

Marci tilts her head. "You were *never* around girls? Weird."

Fiona breaks in. "I went to St. Mary's, but we had co-ed dances. Didn't you even get to take girls to dances?"

"I don't dance."

Marci snorts. "You dance, Gentry. You danced with me at prom and people saw you dance up at the bar."

"You got a report every time I went to the bar, didn't you?"

"Well, I asked around, because the idea was, so, you know, bizarre. You up at the bar. Dancing. God." She snorts.

"I want to change the subject now."

"Of course you do."

We eat for a few more moments.

Fiona speaks up. "Were you shy, Gentry? In college? I bet you were shy and sweet and sensitive, and you courted girls with poetry."

Marci smiles. "He wrote a lot of poems, but he was anything but shy." She drops her eyes to her plate.

I'm confused. How would Marci know I ever wrote poetry?

I wrote poems for exactly eight months of my life, and they were all for Becca. And after we were done, she returned them all, every single poem, every single letter. I packed them away. In that envelope.

Which is upstairs in her closet.

She won't look at me.

"Hey Marci?"

"I'm sorry."

"Tell me you didn't open it."

"I'm *sorry*."

"That envelope's been sealed for ten years, Marci, *ten years*."

"I didn't think . . ."

"It said right on there, 'Do Not Open.' Mel never opened it, and Gretchen never opened it, and you did."

"I'm sorry." She moves her food around on her plate. I remember her moving her food around on her plate in high school.

My heart folds in on itself.

Marci sounds plaintive. "I found that box in my closet, just sitting there next to the other box, and I got curious. And that envelope was in there, and I opened it. Okay?" She glances over at Fiona, an uncomfortable, guilty glance, but she goes on. "I was shocked. You always seem so kind of, I don't know, innocent and pure. Especially back when you were my teacher. I mean, if I hadn't known about you and my mother, I'd have sworn you were a virgin."

My mouth falls open.

Fiona stares at me, her feathery eyebrows rise and those beautiful grey eyes look like they might explode right out of her skull in surprise.

Because I can't figure out what else to do or say, I eat. There's a long silence in which all I can hear is the sound of chewing, silver on plates, Fiona drinking water.

Marci clears her throat. "I was jealous."

Fiona blurts out, "Of your mother? Because I am. I mean, at *her age*? Wow!"

Marci lets out a hoot of happy laughter. "It's not still going *on*!"

"But I was so *impressed*." Fiona joins the laughter, they both sit there laughing and snorting and dabbing at their eyes with napkins.

"Hey, now. Stop. Both of you, knock it off."

"I'm sorry." Marci wipes her eyes. "I *meant* I was jealous when I read your college poems."

"Those poems were terrible."

"They were not. And I was jealous. All I ever got from Garret was dead fish."

"Dead fish?" Fiona is alert. "I'd like to hear about the dead fish?"

"I had a local boyfriend who was a fisherman, and he'd bring me the catch of the day. You know, to show me he cared. Because nothing says I love you like a dead fish."

Again, the two of them dissolve like girls at a lunch table, snickering and moaning and crying with laughter.

"He caught *good fish.*" Why am I defending Garret Blount's fish? But he brought over some fantastic fish. "I was always envious of those fish."

"They were *fish*. And I'd much rather have had some poem about my breasts being like peaches than . . ."

"Will you *be quiet.*"

"Peaches?" Fiona is, again, hyper alert. "I'd like to hear about the *peaches*?"

"Yes, it's a good one, just a second." Marci shoves away from the table and runs up the front stairs.

"Hey Marci?" My voice is loud with an edge of panic. "*Marci?*"

She comes down holding it like a baby in her arms. It's enormous, crammed full. "Don't," I say, and "Stop this," and "I mean it," and more useless words that she ignores as she dumps it all out, photos and letters and notes sliding all over the table.

God, look at all of that, spilled out all over everything.

Part of me wants to throw myself over this mess, to shield it from view. Another part wants to be alone with it.

Marci plucks up a picture. "See? Peaches."

"Could you please not look at that? Give that to me." Marci hands it over and I put it in my shirt pocket.

Fiona sits and stares at all of it. "Well. This is quite a. Quite a, well. Collection."

Marci smirks. "Obviously he wasn't a prude in college."

"I hate that word. Prude."

"I should make a note," Fiona mutters.

"Hey Marci? What exactly do you intend to do with all this?"

She smiles. "Oh, I don't know. I thought I'd scan it all and put it up on a website for your students to read. Or maybe just let Fiona read the poems."

Fiona brightens. "I like that second idea."

Marci starts sorting them out, handing them to Fiona.

"Do I have a say in this?"

"No."

Fiona frowns. "This is Neruda. So is this. I thought this was your poetry?"

"Just what's signed with my name."

"Like this?" She holds one up.

"Yes."

Fiona finds another of mine. She ignores everything but my bad poetry.

Fine, I will let her read my poems.

I start picking up the other part. Why did I save all this? I never save anything. These random notes from girls I barely remember. Why did I save this? This note. "*I hate you. You're a fagbanquet pussyface.*" Who wrote this? And why did I save it? And what does that mean?

All my letters from Becca, all mine to her. All these pictures. Why did they all give me pictures? Did they know how many of them I would forget? There are so many, here, from those years. Pictures of girls, and of me with one girl after another. I am so young in these. I look like Tristan. Ah. I remember her. Not her name, though. Maybe I never even knew her name.

Marci is smirking. "You should see your face."

"Be quiet. And don't read anything signed 'Becca.' I mean it."

Marci ducks her head and starts stacking. Making piles. Surreptitiously reading as she does. "What's a fagbanquet pussyface?"

"Um . . ."

Marci reads out again in a theatrical, emotional voice. "Oh, this one is perfect. '*Dear Gentry, I wish you'd stop hiding from me. I just want to talk. We need to get some of this stuff out in the open. I had no idea you were this much of a coward. Emily.*'"

Fiona seems amused. "Emily had issues."

Marci keeps reading out loud. "'*Dear Gentry. Had I known you'd fuck me like a beast all night and then disappear without saying a word to me, I'd have told you to go fuck yourself instead. Please feel free to eat shit and die. Morgan.*' I like Morgan better than Emily."

"Hey Marci? That's enough."

She stops reading out loud, but she doesn't stop reading.

Fiona sorts and stacks and gathers up my poems, there were more than I remembered. "I don't want you staring at me while I read these." And she carries away my poems. Marci stares at me for a moment, then stands up and goes into the kitchen.

I am alone with all those rectangles.

I wish I could leave out one of these other photos of Becca to show Gretchen. I want her to see her baby's grandmother. I wish my son could read these letters so he'd know how much we loved each other. I wish I could tell him that his family never gave him away, they found a different place for him within the family because he mattered, he was too important to just give away.

And I remember, now, why I have all this.

I moved in with Kevin when Daniel told me Becca was done with me. I moved out, and waited for her to come back and tell me herself.

One day there was a knock, and I opened it and she stood there with a bag full of all the letters I'd written to her, all the poems I'd copied out and slipped under her door, trusting the words of others more than my own to convey the contents of my heart. She held it out. "You can have all this back, Gentry." And I took the bag into my arms like a dead body and emptied it into the drawer where I kept everything she'd ever given me.

And then I tried to move on.

I set all the other notes and photos and threats and tears and accusations and self-abasements on top of our correspondence, burying it. When I moved from one room to another, from an underclassmen dorm to the grad student dorm, I took it all with me. It had become mixed, jumbled. I didn't want to sort through it, I didn't want to read through her words to me, my words to her. But I wanted to save them. And I sent all of it off to Mel for the same reason.

I take the picture of Becca out of my pocket. I gasped when she gave it to me, thanked her and put it away and never looked at it again. I was furious that anyone else had seen her like that. Who took it? Who saw her?

Dear God, see how beautiful she was.

Marci told me when she was in high school, she played a game where she could only use one word to describe a person. One word. I should have tried that with Becca, finding one word, because all my words were failures. I see Becca's twenty-year-old face, and I remember every poem.

One was a map of all the mysterious scents she carried. The invisible strawberries that grew in her hair, the secret musk of her ears and neck, the cedar smell between her legs, the vanilla of her arms and legs and feet. And I made love to her so one of her scents would be me.

I wrote a poem about eating potato chips in bed with her. She put those chips in my mouth, and I let them melt on my tongue like communion wafers. And then I sucked the salt from her fingertips.

There was one for her eyes, her green-eyed gaze was the signal, the light, the beacon. I lifted that right from Gatsby. And one for her mouth, it could be nothing but an opening rose, petals of velvet, giving of nectar, and I was the blind, bumping bee, drawn to her sacrifice to honey.

I wrote a poem about her breathing, the miracle of her respiration, how she was such a miracle that her exhalations blessed the air. I wrote a poem to her hair, the gold-shot river of red, parting over the delta of her smooth white neck. Even her bones, I wrote poems to her wrists, her collarbones. I wrote a poem to the fine, square line of her jaw, the geometry it held, the angles she created when she spoke. Her ribs, the delicate branchwork of hidden ivory fingers, holding and guarding her heart. How I envied her ribs.

I probably wrote ten poems to her breasts, the sweet, sweet peaches never touched by the sun. I suppose they were every southern fruit I ever tasted. I exhausted myself at those breasts, literally and metaphorically, and never did them justice.

I had no vocabulary at all for the sight of her from behind. I could only describe the catch in my throat, the ache in my gut the first time I watched her rise up from the bed and walk away from me. Because as beautiful as it was to watch her leave, what if she never came back?

I tried so hard to write one to her hips, the splendid, curving vessel that held what I could not name, no matter how I searched, no matter how I reached, I never found the words for her perfect, merciful bounty. I never found words for that particular miracle of red and gold, the softest miracle she let me enter. From that same soft miracle, she delivered our son.

Enough. I am no poet and never was. I used words to break a beautiful woman into parts.

I try to stuff it all back into the envelope, but it doesn't even begin to fit, which makes no sense. All the poems are out with Fiona, my adolescent longing and fumbling and failure is out in the little house being read over by her cool grey eyes. So why is this taking up so much room?

It's all been unfolded.

"Excuse me? Your friend messed up the whole kitchen. It's ridiculous how many bowls and pans she used. Do I have to clean it all by myself?"

I leave that chaos on the table.

I wash, she dries. Mel always says there is comfort in the tasks of the hands. But not tonight, not for this. I keep thinking about who took that photo, and I'm as angry and jealous as I was half my life ago. It was probably Daniel.

"What is it? You're still mad, right? Gentry, I'm sorry I opened that envelope. Okay? I'm really, really sorry. And I won't tell anyone what your name is."

Of course. My name is in that box.

"And I won't tell who Tristan's mother is. I figured it out by the dates on the letters. His birthday is in September. I just counted back sixteen years and nine months. It had to be the beautiful redhead, right? The girl you wrote all the poetry for."

Of course. She did the math. Marci knows everything.

"Gentry, will you please say something, or look at me, or break a plate or pop me with the dishcloth or something? Please?"

I turn to meet her green eyes. She cocks her head and studies my face. There are moments when Gretchen reminds me of her, but in this moment, that tilted head, that studying, she reminds me of Gretchen.

Ah, my heart. Unfolding. I'm not angry. I'm relieved.

"I need your help."

She smiles. "You want me to tell him who his mother is?"

"No. There's a reason he can't know, Marci. A reason you didn't find in that envelope." I turn my eyes to my hands, scrubbing what seems to be burnt cream out of the bottom of a saucepan. I study the scorching so she can't see my face. "She'll talk to him soon, I think. But not yet."

"He knows her?"

"Yes."

"Wow." Her voice is quiet. "Okay. I won't tell."

"That isn't what I need help with, though."

"What, do you want me to teach Fiona how to clean up a kitchen?"

"No. I want you to clean up what you did in the dining room. I can't stand to handle it." She needs a system. "Please sort out anything that's to do with her."

"The redhead?"

"Yes. All the letters to her and from her. The poems I wrote out for her. And the pictures? Any pictures of her or us. She took some of me at a farm, I'm up on a tractor or swimming and there are some at a cemetery. Sort that stuff out and put it back in the envelope and put it somewhere Gretchen won't find it. Could you please do that for me?"

She puts a hand on the small of my back. "Sure. I'm good at finding places to hide things." I remember that day in the attic of her old house, the box and the doll and her tears. It was safe that day to hug her. I want, so badly, to turn to her, to take her into my arms and make it all right.

I reach behind and move her hand away. "Thank you."

We go back to the dishes.

"What should I do with the rest of it?"

"Burn it."

"You don't want to save *any* of it?"

"No."

"Why not?" She sounds personally betrayed.

"Because it doesn't matter. It never mattered."

She concentrates on the pot she's drying. "So only Becca mattered? Because she's the one you really loved?"

"Yes."

Her shoulders curve in, her hair hides her face. "Those poor girls. It's not fair to do that to people, Gentry. It's wrong."

I don't know what to say. Except the one thing I never have.

"I'm sorry, Marci."

It's quiet in the kitchen, except for the sound of water. The ocean, the faucet. Occasionally I hear her sniff. It makes me want to die. But we stand there side-by-side, doing the dishes.

There is comfort in the tasks of the hands.

We work our way through all the big bowls, the sharp knives, the wooden spoons, and all the pots. I think this pan is ruined but I'll wait and ask Kathryn about it because there might be a remedy. Marci doesn't say a word about the scorch mark, she dries it off and hangs it on the rack above the island. And she wipes down the counters and scrubs the stovetop while I sweep. All through it, she sniffs.

I finally put my hand on her shoulder. She shrugs it away, gathers up the towels and dishcloth and takes them to the laundry room. I take that pan down from the rack and look at the scorched place. It doesn't seem right to hang it back there.

She comes out and stands facing me with her hands on her hips. She looks like she's about to start yelling. But she doesn't, she rolls her eyes and gives me a look of exasperation. "This is so typical. What is it? What the hell has *you* upset?"

I hold it out. "I'm worried about this pan."

"You're worried about the pan?"

"Yes. I'm worried that it's ruined."

She takes it, inspects it and hands it back. "She's a real pro in the kitchen, isn't she. It's a tiny scorch. Don't worry about it. You have to be careful for a while, because it will keep burning there if you're not careful. But it usually just wears away over time."

"Should I replace it?"

She gives me a look I hate, a look that verges on pity. "That pan cost over two hundred dollars, Gentry."

"Two hundred *dollars*? For a *pan*?" I hang it back up quickly, in case I somehow make the damage worse by handling it. I point to my blackened cast iron fry pan. "I've cooked with every pan in this kitchen and that's the best one in here. I paid sixteen dollars for it at Ace Hardware." I sit down on one of the stools, wishing for some coffee. She sits down beside me. And I sound every bit as pathetic as I feel when I say this out loud. "I liked the way your mother had this kitchen before."

"When the house was a dump."

"It wasn't a dump."

"It was. And you were comfortable here. You never understood that we had money, did you. Because Mom's car was so old, and this house was so old, and all the stuff in it was from her parents and her grandmother. You never had a clue until I took you to Portland. Do you have any idea what this property is worth, Gentry?"

I harden up my face, because I can't stand that she will see her direct hit.

"You're so clueless. You've always been so clueless." She stares at me, grim and green-eyed. "Rebecca St. Pierre is someone in his family, right?" I nod. I won't insult her by trying to deny the truth. "And from what Dad says about Tristan's adoptive mother, that family has money. A lot of money." I nod again. "I'd already figured that out from her letters. The things she talked about. The farm, her horse. A summer in Europe. Typical rich girl pastimes. And that one where she was going on and on about the night of her cotillion, how much she hated it. *It seemed so archaic and vapid, some outdated tribute to the idea of helpless Southern womanhood, which we know was just an excuse to develop a slave class.*" She approximates a Georgia accent for that perfectly rendered quotation.

For a rich girl, Marci sounds pretty contemptuous.

She shakes her head. "Okay. So is that why? Is that why you didn't marry Scarlett O'Hara? It's pretty clear it was you, Gentry, she was practically begging you in those last notes. Did you refuse to marry her because you didn't want to be with someone with that kind of background, because it made you too uncomfortable with yourself?"

My mouth falls open, but no words come out.

She waits, staring at me. "That's no excuse. You loved her, right? I mean, those poems, Gentry. Your letters. And her letters, too. You were both so overblown and melodramatic about it, but you loved each other. So when she got pregnant, why didn't you marry her?"

I shake my head. I could explain that I never knew about Tristan. But that isn't why. She loved me, and I loved her, but it was not enough.

It was never enough.

∽

I take Sam down to the water.

I wish there were no other face but hers, God. I wish there were no others. Four years like that, four years of barely knowing, never caring. An affront to You.

I almost died for it. I always almost die for it.

I apologize for what an idiot I was. But God? She was as euphemistic as Mel. "*Gentry, we need to get married.*" That's what she told me, staring at me, her clear eyes welling with tears. That's what she thought I would understand.

I thought she meant we should get married because we'd been together, and we needed to make things right in Your eyes, God. I didn't understand that she was pregnant. But I should have wanted to marry her anyway. I didn't want to.

It wasn't who she was. I was too stupid to know how much money mattered, never having been around any of it. It was who I was. I couldn't stand her knowing who I was.

I wish I'd told her, God. I wish I'd told her the truth about where I came from and what had happened to me, I could have let memory flow and told her the whole terrible truth and taken the risk that she would turn me away.

Instead, I turned her away.

But God? I swear this to You. It would have been different if I'd understood. If she'd have understood that her decorous Southern expression was lost on me. If she'd made it clear, or if I'd known. It would have been different if I had understood that she was pregnant. I believe that we would have figured out something. It would have been a mess, maybe even more of a mess than this is. I don't know what her gracious, horrified family would have done with me, a child who'd fathered a child on their elegant, educated daughter. I was penniless and parentless and barely able to speak out loud. What would they have done with me?

Maybe they would have adopted me.

I ask Your forgiveness, God, for my youth. I ask Your forgiveness for my disregard. Forgive me my stupidity, my carelessness, my weakness. It was all new, God, and I had no idea how to handle it. I shut it down, but I never truly despised the sin of my joyful blundering from bed to bed, never caring about any of them. Not until tonight.

I will try, now, as a man, to walk the path I couldn't walk as a boy. Forgive me, God, and I swear I will forgive myself.

Amen.

I can see the little house from down here. The window over the table is lit. She's up there translating pain into money, and I am on the beach, walking until I'm cold to the core. In the city, it's over a hundred degrees. Sam walks with me, but he hates to be cold. He stands at the foot of the stairs to urge me up to the house. He shakes and shakes his coat to try to rid it of water, but it's hopeless. I knock on her door, my door, Kathryn's door, who does this door belong to?

"Your poetry is beautiful, Gentry. So beautiful I cried. And you were only sixteen when you wrote it? Oh, look at you, you're shaking to death."

"I'm just cold. Hey Fiona? Can you keep Sam? I want a hot bath and he always gets in the tub with me. He'll scratch up Kathryn's doors if I leave him on the other side. Could he keep you company?"

"Of course. Come on, Sam. Sweet boy, come here." She coaxes him to her side, rubs his soaked head. "Wet boy, sweet wet boy," she says. "Let's find you a towel." She reaches for my hand. "Are you all right?"

She hugs me, I don't hug her back, I never hug her back but Dear God, I love it when she's close. She fits up so gently, breath on my neck, the sweet, sweet smell of her, God, forgive me. Because I know what will make me warm, and I know what I'll think about, and I have no right to it.

No right at all.

⌒

I'm building a rock wall. One of the many tasks I learned in North Dakota. Brother Harland taught me how, he showed me that a rock wall was like a puzzle, each stone fit to the next, how you hear the message of a rock when you hold it, you hold the rock in two hands and hear the shape and size and possibility of each one in your mind and your heart and your hand.

I am learning the vocabulary of rocks.

Each slides in with the next, perfect and tight. I don't find them in the dirt or on the ground of the baked Dakota prairie. I find the rocks in the pockets of Mel's overalls. That's what I wear, Mel's gigantic overalls, weighted with rocks. I had better stay out of the river, out of the lake. I can't ever go back in the ocean.

This wall will take years to build. Once I get it up, it will last forever. Except someone is on the other side of the wall, working from the bottom up, strategically pulling the rocks away, unsettling the fit. She makes it so the rocks can't talk to each other.

I keep on with my building. The weight of the rocks is pulling my overalls down. But I keep building.

There is comfort in the tasks of the hands.

Now and then a small stone comes over the wall at me, sharp and rattling, and I duck and wince when they hit but usually these stones miss on purpose.

Occasionally she throws higher, and a large rock fires off into the distance. I stop to admire those rocks. They fly so high and far that they turn into shore birds, curlews and sand pipers, gulls and terns. The flying rocks speak the shrieking language of beaks, the beating language of wings as they catch the current and fly off to the ocean and up to God in Heaven.

Who can throw like that? I know when she laughs.

When I speak, my voice is full of wonder.

Marci, *I say,* you don't throw like a girl.

"I don't *what?*"

"You don't throw like a girl."

She's over me, her teeth chattering.

I make a terrible noise and hit the bathwater in frustration and she shrieks, jumps back. "You have to STAY AWAY from me when I'm ASLEEP, Marci. You HAVE TO STAY AWAY."

"I didn't know you were in here! You *always* lock the bedroom door and it was open and the light was off! Plus you can *drown* falling asleep in the bathtub, did you *know* that?!"

"I'm ALIVE, could you GET OUT?" I make myself calm down, remember to breathe, cross my arms over what I don't want her to see. "I'm not dead. Okay? Get out of here."

"You get out." Her teeth are clacking, her lips are blue and she's shaking all over. She turns on the hot water, so hot it scalds my feet. "I'm cold, and I'm getting in this tub."

All right. I'm awake. I'm awake and I feel oddly calm. "Use the other tub."

"It's too small and it takes too long to fill. The old bathroom has bad water pressure." She stares at me, defiant, and pushes the water around with her hands to distribute the heat. "Get out if you're getting out, because I'm getting in."

"Marci, you can't get in this bathtub." I watch her peel off a jacket, the first layer of what I hope are many of her running clothes. She drops it on the floor. I can smell the rain and sweat and danger in that jacket. "Listen." My grasp on these things is rudimentary. "Don't get in this water. I'm afraid you could get pregnant."

She is laughing. "I won't get pregnant from the bath water!"

"Oh." Is that possible, anyway? I don't know. I should have asked in one of those classes. I imagine the reaction this question would get from the birth class teacher. *No wonder these children are pregnant.*

I hear the phone.

The phone.

The phone!

Oh Kathryn why did you put wood on these stairs instead of that black rubber mat because I'll fall to my death on my way to get the phone, the phone, and my wet feet I slip and ouch my hip but I'm up, there, I will not die before this baby comes and don't let the stupid answering machine get it, what was wrong with that old phone, anyway, I liked the old phone better "Hey!"

Kathryn. "It's time."

I shout, "MARCI! IT'S TIME!" and she jumps because she followed me down and she's standing right beside me so I shouted in her face, and then she shrieks "IT'S TIME!" and I jump because she's right there yelling in my ear and Kathryn says "Fly, Gentry," and I say "I WILL!" and Fiona walks in the kitchen with Sam and I yell "IT'S TIME!" and she just stares at me, is she deaf, did she not hear what I just said? "IT'S TIME!" and she stares at us and Marci yells "HURRY!" and runs up the stairs and Sam barks and I say "PLEASE KEEP SAM!" and Fiona stares at me and what is wrong with her? I start to run upstairs and then come back down and hang up the phone and go upstairs to get ready because it's time, it's time, it's finally time.

∾

I was so afraid to miss it, and I'm here Gretchen, I'm here and . . .

"I'M ALL RIGHT!!"

Gretchen's face is white with pain and she shakes, teeth gritted.

"You don't look all right, maybe you need to . . ."

"I SAID I'M ALL RIGHT!"

I see.

Tristan is afraid. "She's been here for three hours and they say it'll be five more."

"Five? Did you say five more? Five more hours?"

He's pale. "At least five. Maybe more."

"SHUT UP!"

More? Five more hours? Of this? I wait for a lull in her pain, when she collapses into panting. "Gretchen? You should let them give you something."

"I DON'T WANT ANYTHING!"

I look at Tristan. He looks at me.

"Okay. But if you change your mind . . ."

"I WILL NOT CHANGE MY MIND!"

"Okay. No problem."

She shakes through another one. I told them, I told them I couldn't do this, watching her suffer will kill me. Tristan takes her hands, and he does one of those breathing things they talked about in the classes. Is that helping? Does it help? Does that help in any way? Or is it just some inane thing for a man to do, to feel helpful, to dispel the truth of his uselessness?

"Gretchen, does that panting help?"

"YOU HAVE BAD BREATH! YOU NEVER HAVE BAD BREATH! DON'T BREATHE IN MY FACE!"

"I'm sorry. I ran out of the house and forgot to brush my teeth."

"DON'T CRY ABOUT IT, JUST BRUSH YOUR STUPID TEETH!"
Who is this girl? Where did they put my Gretchen?

I always have a toothbrush on me, but I guess tonight I forgot. I go down to the nurse's desk and explain the situation. A very kind nurse locates a brush and some toothpaste. I thank her sincerely.

She pats my back. "Is this your first time?"

"Yes. Not mine. I mean, um, this is not my baby. It's my first time, though. To be at a birth." Babble. And I fully intend not to be at this birth. I'll duck out as soon as I can get Gretchen to take something, and wait with Marci and Kathryn.

"*Oh*. You're with the kids. You look just like him." I nod. "His brother?" I shake my head. "You don't look old enough to be his father."

"I am."

She pats me again. "Well, I'm glad you're here. His mother was in here dropping him off and she had some words with the girl's mother. Yelling. It shook him up. That boy could use some kind words. This is hard on kids."

Not just on kids, Nurse.

I brush my teeth in the bathroom of Gretchen's room. When I look in the mirror, Tristan's haunted eyes look back at me.

Gretchen must be in between contractions. She smiles at me and I blow a little air at her. "Better?"

"Better. Sorry."

"I don't care." She pats the bed, and I sit by her shoulder. Tristan sort of sits in a chair by her side, but I say sort of because what he really does is sit down, and then leap up at her slightest movement, sit, leap, sit, leap. I imagine this might annoy Gretchen in her present state. I want to pat him. But a contraction starts, and she has hold of my hand, and my God, this girl has a grip, do You know that, God? "Tristan, do that breathing thing." He does, but this time he gets sent to the bathroom for his breath. "Use my brush." That poor kid.

The contraction passes. He's in there brushing his teeth for an awfully long time. He comes out. "Tristan, I want to go out and see Kathryn." He nods. Oh, my son, you're so pale. You're more afraid I am, I think. "I can send in Marci."

He seems relieved. "Okay."

God, who was there for Becca when she had my son? Who, God?

They rise up with hope when I enter the waiting room, but I shake my head. I tell Marci to go take my place. She's reluctant. "I don't want to go in there. Why do I have to go in there? What if the baby comes out while I'm in there?"

"It will be a long time."

"Are you positive?"

"Getting the baby out will be a process, Marci. You'll have time to leave the room." And hopefully, so will I. She reluctantly goes in to sit with her sister, and I sit by Kathryn. "Hey." I take a small, ice-cold hand in mine. She smiles through the tears in her eyes.

"Hi."

"Are you okay?"

"I am. Now that you're here to help."

"Oh, I'm a lot of help." I tell her about the teeth brushing. She laughs just the way I hoped she would. And then she weeps.

"I know it sounds trite, Gentry, but I remember it all so clearly. It wasn't that long ago. Not to me." I nod, what can I say, I know nothing of any of this. I only know how to nod. "I had a cesarean, so she was perfect, pretty, not all beat up from birth. I remember how beautiful she was. She was long and skinny and pale, I suppose she looked like a rubber chicken, but to me she looked just like she does now. Beautiful."

"Like a dryad."

"Yes. Except bald." She sobs. "And she never cried. The nurse said it was from the drugs, but that wasn't it. She was too calm to cry. She looked around, even then. She watched things. She watched."

I hold her now, sweet Kathryn, so cold and small.

"I was alone when she was born, Gentry. I was alone. Michael didn't even come up to the hospital. He said he had to take care of Marci, but he didn't even bother to come up to see her the day she was born.

"I just called him a few minutes ago. I called him to tell him it was time, I said I thought he should be here, and he hung up on me."

God, You should do something about him. You really should.

Marci rushes out, her face white, her eyes round with horror. "She just had something come out? Something called a bloody show? And I'm not going to stay in there anymore." She stares at me. "You go in there."

I go in there.

◡

The nurse says Gretchen should walk. So we walk.

We walk in the corridor, back and forth. I hold one side and Tristan holds the other and when the contractions hit, I feel them shake her body, lift it in pain.

"You should take something, G."

"Yes, Gretchen. You need to take something."

She stops, waits, gasping for air, for relief, until the contraction stops. We face her, watching. And then she says in her mother's voice, "If either one of you says that again, I swear, I'll kill you both."

We walk.

⤳

This has gone on for too long, now.

The doctor has come by to check on her. "Doctor, you have to do something for her. Now." She looks at me calmly. She's on call, she's not Gretchen's doctor, I have no idea who this woman is and she's not helping. "Did you hear me? I want you to help her. She's in too much pain."

"She's fine."

"She's in agony."

"Gretchen's doing the work of birth. That's why they call it labor."

"Don't patronize me."

"I'm not patronizing you." Her eyes flash under her frowning brows. "I'm just trying to tell you that she'll be fine."

"She's not FINE." Tristan moves to my side, I shrug away from his arm. "She's not FINE, she's in PAIN."

"She wants to do this naturally. I'm just respecting that."

"I don't think you CARE."

"Okay, whoever you are, I delivered Gretchen. I care."

She leaves. Gretchen wails.

I want to break something.

⤳

The nurses check her, there's no dignity in it, they shove their hands into her like she's so much meat, and it hurts her, I can see that, she blanches and cries.

"Could you be careful? Could you be a little more careful of her, would it KILL you not to HANDLE her like that?"

"Gentry, you'd better . . ."

"I'M SICK OF HER BEING HURT."

The nurse, threatening, "If he doesn't calm down, we'll have to get him out of here."

Gretchen, wailing, "No, please, I need him!"

My son, trying to calm me.

⁓

That doctor comes in again and shoves her hand up inside Gretchen.

"Hey Doctor? Why can't you do a cesarean?"

"That's not necessary."

"Her mother had cesareans."

"Gretchen is not her mother."

"She's suffering. Why don't you DO something?"

"Who are you? Why are you in here?"

"Could you answer my QUESTION, please?"

"I will not do a cesarean on Gretchen."

"Her mother had them."

"I know her mother had sections, I performed those sections. Listen to me. Her mother is smaller than Gretchen. Everything is going just the way it's supposed to. This baby is fine, and Gretchen is fine, and we will not do a section."

"She is NOT FINE."

"Get him out of here."

"I will NOT LEAVE."

"Get him out."

Tristan at my side. "Take a walk with me."

"No."

"Just for a second. Please." We walk into the hall.

He keeps trying to take my arm, pull at me.

"Let GO."

"You have to calm down. You have to, Gentry."

"You LET GO!" I take him against the wall, and HE did this to her, he did this to my Gretchen . . .

He holds his gut.

Dear God what have I done? God, what have I done to my son?

"Shit." He straightens up and his face is full of pain, and the shaking, I'm shaking, Oh Dear God. "Hey, chill. I'm just glad you hit me instead of that doctor. Look at me. You'd better pull it together or you'll miss it. I think it's time. It's time and they won't let you back in unless you straighten up. It's the end, now."

The shaking stops. I nod. We go back in.

"Hurry up." The doctor tells us what to do, Gretchen can't speak, her face is twisted, unrecognizable, the sound of her, I take one hand and he takes the other, and the nurse tells us that we need to pull her knees up and back, and her face is so red, her lips are blue, Oh God will this kill her? How can a baby come out of her, how will it happen, there's no way, no way that a baby can come out of what I see in front of me, it won't work, it will never work, they should just cut it out of her because this will never work, how does anyone, anywhere, ever get born, "Look away, look away you two," I look at him, I look in his eyes, our fear, there were scissors, oh God, scissors, "It's okay now, you two . . ." The noise she makes sounds like she'll scream, blood, and the head, all full of blood, and then I see, Oh God, the head of this child, this is a baby, not just pain, those sweet, bloody curls are red, red curls on a head with a face on shoulders, arms, oh, and the baby slides free, connected by a skin-covered telephone cord, a baby girl, my grandchild . . .

〜

"Gentry? Are you okay now?"

"I love you, Tristan."

"I love you too. Are you okay?"

"Don't let them give me a shot."

"I won't, but how about a cup of coffee?"

"Yes. Let me . . ."

"Stay down, slow down, don't . . ."

〜

"Gentry?"

Marci, oh, no, not again . . .

〜

"Gentry? Just hold on, okay? Sit up slow."

And I hold on to my son who loves me, and I sit. A ring of concerned faces peers down on me. "I'm fine, just fine. Go look at the baby."

The doctor's shaking her head. Mine hurts from hitting the linoleum floor. I can see why they don't have carpet, here, because of all the things that seem to pour out when, oh . . . no, I'm all right, I'm here. I'm right here. My son, who loves me, helps me to stand.

Everyone seems as relieved as I am.

The first thing I do is hug my son, who loves me. Then I hug the doctor. She lets me, she laughs a little. I hug Kathryn.

And then.

I sit down on the bed. Gretchen hands her to me.

Hey, little one. Hey, there. How did Gretchen know how to do this? How? To make you? You make my arms sing, do you know that, they sing from holding you. Oh, you are too fine for this world. Too fine for my words. Let me smell you. This is the best thing I've ever smelled, the back of your neck. You have these red curls. You have these little squashed eyes. Look at these beautiful ears. Perfect.

Hey, Granddaughter.

I whisper three things. I tell you that you're a Georgia peach. I tell you I love you. And I tell you my name.

God. This is to give thanks. Amen.

Gretchen lets out a gasping, snotty sob, wipes her nose on the back of her hand. She puts her wet hand on my arm. "Gentry? I think I know something, now." This little girl has always known everything. What more could she know? "I think I know what your face will look like when you get to Heaven."

Gretchen is the smartest person I've ever known.

Kathryn sees me with the baby in my arms, and there's grief in her face. What? What could make you sad on this fine day, Kathryn? Today is only joy. Today is the day we all know why we were born. For this.

Amen.

The doctor comes over and puts her arm around Kathryn's shoulders. They have a history, Kathryn and the doctor I almost hit. These women brought Marci and Gretchen into the world. And the doctor looks at me, and her eyebrows fly up, and she looks at Kathryn, and Kathryn nods, what? What is this womanly smoke signal?

Ah, forget them. This is a moment.

"Has anyone called Dad?" Marci injects this. Some moments are too fine to last. A cloud passes over the room and Gretchen's face. She holds out her arms for her daughter, soothed when she has her baby again.

Kathryn sounds like she's going to cry. "Can I please hold the baby now?" She holds out her arms, and Gretchen lets her mother have the baby. "Finally. I thought I'd never get my turn."

"Um, could I call Mike?"

"You?"

"Yes. I'd like to call him, if that would be all right."

"Well. Sure. The number is in the pocket of my purse. And you need to call your mom, Tristan." I never touch women's purses if I can help it, but I want to make this call. I take the card out of the side of her purse.

Everyone is puzzled because I won't call from the room. My son, who loves me, walks me to the waiting room. He keeps a hand on me. "Do you realize we both kind of became fathers in the same year, sort of, when you think about it?" He asks this in absolute amazement. My son is brilliant, making this kind of an observation. Just think how brilliant this child will be with these brilliant parents she has. Think of it.

First he calls his mother. "Mom? It's a girl . . . no, she's fine . . . both of them are just fine . . . it's okay, Mom . . . Eight pounds and four ounces . . . I know! . . . Twenty-one and three quarters . . . Gretchen is fine . . . I'm not mad. Just . . . come over, okay? . . . I love you, too . . . okay . . . okay. I love you too. But please come see her . . . I know. I know. I love you, Mom. Bye." He looks at me and rolls his eyes. "She lost it. Worse than you." I can taste his relief. No boy should have to forgive so much in a day, God.

I dial.

"Hello?"

"Hey, Eve."

"Oh, Gentry!" Her voice, her excitement. "Tell me it's a girl!"

"Yes, a girl."

Her glee. "Are they both all right?"

"Perfect. Both perfect. The baby is, um, apparently kind of enormous?"

"Well, that's good."

"It is?"

"Yes, because big babies sleep. Michael's at the office. Do you have the number?"

He's at the *office*? "Um, yes, I have that number. I'll call him."

"Would you?"

"Yes. I, um, have to go. Bye." I can't believe this.

Tristan keeps an eye on me. "Are you all right, Gentry?"

"I'm fine." I dial.

"Michael Mumford here."

"Hey Mike."

"Well, Gentry. What can I do for you?"

"What can you do for me? For *me*, Mike? Nothing. But maybe there's something you can do for your daughter."

"Don't you dare talk to me like that, don't you dare. You expect me to drop the important things I have to do, and unlike you I do have important things to do, just to come down there and wait for the arrival of the bastard of a bastard of a bastard, you little . . ."

"Shut up. You're a jerk, Mike, a godless, pompous jerk. But you're also Gretchen's father and you're a grandfather. The baby's here, do you understand? Your daughter just had a baby. I've never in my life seen anyone work harder to do something and you didn't even bother to show up for it. Just like when she was born. So shut up and come here."

I hang up.

"What did he say?"

"He said he'll be over here real soon."

"He did not. He did not say that."

"Yes. He said that."

"You really suck at lying."

"Sit with me a minute, Tristan."

"I was going to find you some coffee."

"No. Just sit here."

We sit, stretch our legs, study our shoes. Our feet are the same size. He has on trainers and I have on work boots, but I bet we have the same toes, same arch, same heel. I consider asking him to take off his shoes, to let me look, let me hold his hands, count his digits. He probably would, he's that sweet of a boy.

He loves me.

It takes a few minutes, but I stop shaking.

"Are you okay?"

"Yes."

"You were out for a little while in there, you know. That doctor said to just leave you on the floor until she was done, uh, well, sewing up."

Sewing up? Oh, Thank You God, for oblivion. "I was a wreck."

"No! You were great, really." I howl, I roar, really, this boy is a kind one. He's laughing too, we set up a racket, this is terrible. "No, I mean it. I couldn't have done it without you there."

"Yes, to serve as a cautionary example of how not to act in a delivery room."

"No, you really helped."

"What was most helpful, my yelling or my passing out?"

"Probably passing out."

And we have to laugh more. But we settle down.

"I never liked him."

"Mike?"

"Yeah. I even remember not liking him in preschool. He was so big, and he seemed too, I don't know, hearty, or something."

"I can't stand him. As a matter of fact, I want to hit him in the mouth."

He laughs again. "Have you ever?"

"Have I ever what?"

"Hit him?"

"Yes."

"Good. Why?"

"He said something a man shouldn't."

"Oh. Well, you really hit hard." I know I hit hard. I hit my son. "Hey, no, I understand, don't, please. Listen, you lost it, but it's okay . . ." He holds on to me while I whisper apologies into his hair. "It's okay," he says over and over while my tears soak his head.

Oh, Sweet God, Dear God, Please. Forgive me, because my son, who loves me, already has.

⁓

I'm not doing very well. Everyone else is sitting around, happy. Everyone else is fine. But I'm not fine. The Gilroys aren't back from Canada, so I can't call Lorrie. I called Fiona, who is on her way over here. I called Phyllis, which involved having

Fanny recognize my voice. Jesus still loves me. Phyllis was as happy about this news as if she knew who these people were. And I called Mel. I was fine until I talked to Mel. All I want to do is cry.

I stare out the window.

"So," says Marci, "what are you going to name your stupid baby?"

"Shut up! She's my perfect baby. My brilliant baby." Gretchen leans down and sniffs the red curls on the top of her daughter's head. Her eyes are dazed with love. "We do need to name her."

"We could name her 'Stupid Baby.' We can call her Tiffany for short."

"Do you want to give this another try? Here you go. That's it." Gretchen carefully puts her daughter to her breast. I carefully don't watch this. "I want to name her something happy."

"Something *happy*?" Kathryn sounds as tired as I feel.

"Yes. Tristan's name means sad. And we want something happy."

Time for synonym wars, I guess, because I don't want a grandchild named "Happy." What means happy? Felicity. Joy. Allegra. Gladys. I have to save this kid from some weird happy name. "How about Sarah?" No one says anything. "Or maybe Emily?"

Gretchen says, "That's my middle name. I never liked it."

Marci snorts. "It's better than Lavinia."

Just about anything is better than Lavinia.

"Those are the Dickinson sisters." Kathryn sounds defensive. "I named you after the Dickinson sisters."

"Yes, I'm the recluse poet and Marci is the church girl. So accurate!" And the girls snort and giggle.

"Mom, why couldn't you have gone with the Brontës and given me the middle name Anne?"

Because, Marci, your mother would have gone with Charlotte, and you would have hated that just as much. Besides, Marcialin Anne is almost as objectionable as Marcialin Lavinia.

I try again. "How about Hannah?"

"That sounds like a housekeeper." Marci snorts. "Scrub the hearth, Hannah!"

"Hey Marci? Was that nice?"

She ignores me. She takes her niece from her sister's arms. "What's this revolting yellow stuff on her lips?"

"Colostrum." I remember that from the birth class.

Marci coos to the baby. "Do you want us to name you Colostrum? Or we could name you Episiotomy."

Gretchen says, "We could name her Bloody Show."

Tristan dissolves in exhausted snickering. Marci laughs so hard that the baby stirs, complains. Kathryn says in a frosty voice, "Would you kids *please* straighten up?"

They're tired, Kathryn, these kids are tired. And they're kids.

"Sorry, Mother." Marci puts her face to the soft corona, inhaling that baby bouquet. She lifts her eyes and looks right at me. Her voice is loud. "Where did she get all this *curly red hair*?"

Marci, I'll get you.

Kathryn takes the baby from her daughter. She also leans down and smells the baby's head. Everyone in the world is now a hair sniffer. "Tristan? Do you have any ideas?" She uses her crisp interview voice.

My son sounds confused. "Well, no, Mrs. Fankhauser, I have no idea where she got that red hair."

"No, Tristan. I meant for names."

He thinks. "I like Sarah. And Emily." Ha! Votes for my names.

"Every grandparent should get a name veto, and I veto Sarah. Too old-fashioned." This is announced by the deep and manly vocal tones of a new arrival to the hospital room. Well, thank you, Mike. I notice you decided to show up here after all, you big jerk. In your suit, standing there with your hand on Kathryn's shoulder like you have a right to touch her. "And she got that red hair from my side. My brother Brian has red hair."

Brother? Mike has a brother? Why don't I ever know anything about anyone?

"Your mother has redheads in her people, too. So we always thought we'd get a redhead. And look at these blondies we got instead." Mike moves to the hospital bed to sit down by his daughter and put his arm around her as if he has a right to.

I stare out the window.

When she speaks, Gretchen addresses Mike as if she's picking up the thread of a very recent conversation. "It's recessive, Dad. That means Tristan has red hair on his side, too. Somewhere." Tristan turns to me and his eyes get round, and I turn away, because I can't bear to think of where that hair comes from right now and I can't bear not to tell him.

How did she do this without me?

Marci breaks the silence. "Let's give her a stripper name, like Amber or Tawny."

"Marci." Kathryn is ready to scold. "Be serious."

"I don't want my daughter to have a serious name."

A name, a name. At least I'm trying, here. I don't seem to be having any success, but I try. "Lauren?" The eyes roll, the heads shake. "How about Rachel?" Frowns. "Naomi?"

"I can't figure out why you want to name the baby after a supermodel," says Marci. "What's next, Tyra? Giselle?"

"Excuse me? What are you saying? I don't know anything about supermodels." I glance around the room and everyone is staring at me again. "I've offered several names, and everyone seems to hate them. But no one else has offered even one name in seriousness. Are there any other suggestions? Or am I the only person who cares?"

"Hey now, Dad." I feel my son's arm around me. "I like all the names you said." Ah. This my new name. Dad. I'm Dad, now.

"We need a baby name book." Kathryn's right. We need reference materials.

"What kind of name do you want, honey?" Oh, Mike, you'll give her anything she wants now that the hard part's over. You can BUY her a name. But where were you last night when your daughter was crying and screaming? Where were you all night? Who was here, making an idiot of himself, true, but who was here, threatening doctors and passing out cold, but who was here? I ask you that? Who bought her all that lotion and got her calcium for her leg cramps and loaned her his clothes and gave her all his underwear and took her to the doctor and those stupid useless birth classes and read her Harry Potter and Eisley essays when she was too upset to sleep because you wouldn't talk to her? Who took walks with her, and who cooked her soup? Who sat her on his lap when she cried and held her all night when she had bad dreams? Who took care of her, Mike?

I offer my care of her, God. As my proof.

"Sh. Hey Dad. Chill. It's okay." I didn't say anything, but my son hears me. He tightens his arm. We stare out the window together.

Gretchen's voice sounds like a little girl's. "All I want is a name that isn't sad."

"Well, I think I know one." Marci is ready with another ridiculous suggestion. "Doesn't Hilary mean mirth? The Latin root?" Everyone turns to me for confirmation, because I'm the resident Catholic altar boy Latin expert.

I can't speak.

Tristan's arm is strong. "Dad? What do you think of calling her Hilary? Is that okay?"

Gretchen's eyes are full of hope. "It's a beautiful name."

"Hilary? I don't like that name." The Voice of the Nation. Mike. Silent for months, and here he is now, refusing to shut up.

I wish Fiona were here to swear for me.

Marci sounds irritated. "You've already used your veto, Dad."

"What?" He sounds outraged. "Doesn't anyone care what I think?"

"Basically no, Michael. No one really cares what you think at this point." Kathryn smiles at Gretchen. "Hilary is a pretty name. One L or two?"

Tristan says it. "One."

"I think it's lovely. But what would we put in the middle?" Kathryn smiles at her granddaughter in Marci's arms. "My mother's name was Lynne." Her voice is soft with hope. "Does anyone know what Lynne means?"

"Lynne means 'of the waterfall.'" Oh, her voice. Fiona is here, finally, she's here. I want her to come over and insist on hugging me, but Fiona stands before Marci and holds out her arms. Marci surrenders the baby. Fiona leans down and inhales the smell of my granddaughter. She looks up, her grey eyes full of bliss and longing.

"Hilary Lynne." Gretchen nods. "Laughter and water. That works for me." Happy Waterfall. It sounds like a Chinese restaurant.

Kathryn smiles. "You know, Lynne was a controversial choice for my mother back in the day. It was a man's name. Nana Marit scandalized everyone in the Iron Range when she chose it."

Gretchen nods. "Hilary used to be a man's name, too."

I stare out the window.

I turn when I hear Fiona speaking. "Are you Mike Mumford?" She stands there staring at Mike.

He's puzzled but pleased, as if he knows his reputation has preceded him. "Yes. I'm Michael Mumford."

A shudder passes through her, like she's swallowed something so bitter that it makes her entire body recoil. And then she recovers. "Well, then. I guess this is your granddaughter. And every single person in this room besides you thinks her name should be Hilary."

I watch her carry my granddaughter over to the hospital bed, but she doesn't give the baby to her mother. He holds out his arms, no Fiona, Fiona don't do it. Don't you do that. She gives him the baby.

He leans down and smells the back of her neck, and I watch it sink in, imprint. I watch emotion suffuse his face. He will kill for this child if he has to. "There's no other smell like this in the world," he sighs. He touches her cheek. "Hello, Hilary."

My heart will crack.

I know, God. I know. I know this road, where it leads. I submit. Mike and I have to share this child, just as we've had to share her mother. And Mike is here. He's late, he's angry at my son, he's angry at me, but he's here. And he loves her.

But I held her first, God.

Tristan tries it out in his low, fine, voice. "Hilary Lynne Buchanan." Mike's eyebrows go up, way up. What did he think? Did he think this child was going to be a Mumford?

"Well?" Gretchen is watching me. I look around the room and everyone looks back at me.

Everyone waits. I swallow. I clear my throat. "I guess that's an acceptable name." Gretchen laughs out loud. I give her a look.

Hilary is fine for a girl, Gretchen.

But not for a man.

⌀

I called Mel and told him the name, and he cried over it. He asked me about the christening. And then he told me someone is hacking the email server. I told him I would call him later and try to help him figure it out but I can't think about the email server right now.

Eve arrived with her sons. Tristan brought his daughter over, but wouldn't let either of her uncles hold her. "No way. Forget it. Hands off the baby." He was all elbows and forearms, fending off their young unwashed hands. He did let Eve hold her.

Jack arrived, and oh, how he smiled. And Toni came to meet her little granddaughter. Toni was not surprised by the red hair. She held her granddaughter and hugged her son. And then she took a hard look at me and offered to drive me to Kathryn's house. I accepted.

Dear God, Thank You.

I gave Tristan my keys so he could get home on his own. He looked at the keys. He looked at me. It was trite, hackneyed. It was nothing but sentimental pap. It was more than my heart could bear. Giving the car keys to my son.

Get me out of here, Toni.

⟡

At Kathryn's house, Toni cuts the engine and stares out the window of her BMW. "She's such a beautiful baby. And all that red hair."

"Have you called her?"

"I have." Please, Toni. Please say something more. "She said to say 'Hey, Grandpa.'" I don't think she said that. Except, that's what she would have said, exactly.

"Hey Toni? I keep wondering. About Becca. About when Tristan was born. And where. Because, I know . . ." And I choke off.

"She was here. At the same hospital."

"Who helped her?"

"Doug and I were there. She was never alone."

"She had something for the pain?"

"No, she didn't want anything."

I hate the thought of Becca hurting. God, I've taken pain. I've never, ever, taken any pain like that. I know what pain is, now.

"She was fine. She did it beautifully, the way she does everything." There are tears in her eyes. "And he was a few weeks late, so he was a big baby. He was due in August. She thought she'd have him and have time to get back to school on time. Like nothing had happened. But he waited to make his entrance."

"What day?"

"The eleventh." I was already back at school, waiting for her. And she was in Portland having my son, and Daniel knew where she was and what she was doing. If he'd told me, I could have been there for the birth of my son. "She left two days later. Rose up out of that bed like a swan, held him one last time, and left without a tear. Her shirt was soaked but her eyes were dry, Gentry. So brave. And determined. And devastated."

God. How could You? And how could Daniel? How can I ever forgive him?

"Hey Toni? What's his full name?"

"Tristan Holt."

"Who chose it?"

"She did."

She named my son Sadness.

"What about Holt? Is that a family name?"

"No. She said it was from something you always said to her. A poem you wrote to her, and you signed your letters that way. She wanted something in his name to be yours."

Holt. The one poem that wasn't in that envelope. The one poem she saved.

I will always hold you.

I press my hands to my eyes, I hold it in.

"Do you remember Becca's wedding? She insisted that you be invited. We were all against it, but she said you were sweet and gentle and wouldn't cause any trouble. I was terrified. I thought, we all thought, that you were finally coming to see your son."

"I didn't know I had a son."

"No one knew that but Daniel. We all thought you knew. And I was so curious. I mean, it was clear that Tristan had taken after you. I wanted to see you for myself. I watched at all the men, wondering which one was you. At first, your blonde friend, the tall one who looks so much like you?"

"Sandy."

"I thought he might be the one, because my sister had said you were a beautiful young man. But Tristan had to have a brown-eyed father. I saw you. I thought, no. That boy? You were too young. But I had no doubt it was you because my son was the image of you. You and your friend there, all that hair, and your clothes. At the evening wedding of a Southern girl. The full Mass, Becca wanted the full Mass. And you two were dressed like that. Talk about disrespectful."

That was the year I set the monastery up as an Internet provider, because they needed a way to make money. I did it, all of it, my time and my money. I had no money for something like a suit that year, and I forgot to call Kevin to ask him to bring one. When he saw that I didn't have anything else, Sandy wore jeans. That was Sandy.

And the truth is, I had no idea how important it was. What I wore.

"I wore what I had."

"It wasn't just what you wore, Gentry. I watched you to see what you would do. And you only ever looked at Becca. You never once looked at Tristan. He was nothing to you. I was so angry on his behalf."

Did I see my son?

I remember her wedding. I remember Sandy holding me up when I saw her coming down the aisle all in white to marry someone else.

She came in behind those beautiful children.

God, I have never prayed for this before.

But please let me remember.

⌒

He walked down alone in front of four little girls. He carried a pillow. He was walking in time to the music. He was counting. One two. Three four. Whispering, counting to himself, ignoring the redheaded chaos behind him. He looked very proud when he got to the end of the aisle. He turned and smiled. He had a window in his smile.

He was so small. He waited there, because it was time for her to walk down the aisle. His eyes were for her. The music changed, and I stood with Sandy's arm around me. He looked toward her, never seeing who she was. And I looked away from him, never seeing who he was to me. But Daniel saw. He knew. And he knew what everyone in the church would think of me when my son passed by me and I didn't look at him twice.

"He wore a little grey suit. One of his lower front teeth was out. His hair was cut straight across. He had Band-aids on his thumbs. And I looked at those and I thought, those remind him not to suck his thumb. I saw him. I just never knew he was mine."

She stares ahead. "He was six. He turned seven that fall. He hated that suit. He wore it for Becca, though. And then he had to wear it again when they buried his father."

"Hey Toni? I'm his father."

I get out of the car. Sam waits for me in the yard.

Hey, my Sam. Did you miss me? Come here. Good boy.

We use the key, enter the house, go up to Gretchen's room.

Let's sleep here, Sam. Let's sleep in this bed where she sleeps, this bed that smells like our Gretchen.

Let's sleep.

Kathryn

I come in and see him lying there, his dog beside him. I lie down on the other side, fitting closely, my head on his shoulder. I wake to his arm tight around me, his face in my hair. "Hey, Grandma."

"Oh, my god, please. Not that."

"You don't want to be called Grandma?"

"No!" The thought of that. "We can't be grandparents, Gentry. I'm too vain and you're too young."

"If I were too young, I wouldn't be one."

"Do you mean that you have an old soul? Are you getting New Age on me, Gentry?"

The sweetness of his laughter echoing through his chest, through mine. "No. I'm getting scientific on you. I keep going to the library." He thinks for a moment. "I guess if you don't like Grandma and Grandpa, we could be Nana and Ong Noi."

"Nana. You're going to kill me."

He puts his face to my hair, inhales. "Did everyone finally leave?"

"Yes. Gretchen said she wasn't tired, but I made them all go. Well, Jack stayed up there. He loves hanging around the hospital. But everyone else went home."

"Tristan?"

"I sent him home to get some rest."

"Thank you. They're going to need their sleep."

"So are we. How can they be parents? They're *babies*. How can Gretchen be a mother?"

"You need to go to the library, Kathryn." Which makes me laugh, which is good, because I was ready to cry. His arm tightens around my shoulders. "We'll get them through this. We can do this."

I study his profile. "To think you might have missed it."

"Missed it? I would never have missed it."

"No. I mean, if you were still in Oklahoma."

"I wouldn't have been in Oklahoma."

I put my hand on his heart, and he sighs. "Where would you have been?"

He stares up at the ceiling. "Colorado. North Dakota. Here. If anyone had told me she was pregnant, I would have come back to help."

"And found your son."

He blinks. Tears run from the corner of his eyes along those sharp cheekbones, into his ears.

Oh it's wrong and it's reckless, but I can't help myself. I put my mouth to his face and kiss those tears and he moans and his eyes sink shut as if this were a dream. He tastes of youth. "Kathryn. Be careful."

"Of what?"

"Of me."

It is such a simple request. And so impossible. I have never been careful of him, have I? But I settle back against the pillow and watch the play of light on the wall. He settles his head on my stomach, wraps his arms around my hips. His heartbeat calms, his body relaxes. I feel him settle down.

"Are we ever really going to be friends, Gentry?"

His voice is so quiet and low. "I thought we were friends."

"Friends talk to each other. They tell each other the important happenings in their lives. They share their histories."

He's quiet for a moment. "Hey Kathryn? Ask me."

"Ask you?"

"Yes. Just ask me, directly, what you want to know. That's all you ever had to do."

It's my turn to think. I believe the question that's plagued me since 1996 was answered at the hospital, so I have to think of another. "How did your wife die?"

"She took an overdose of pain pills."

"I'm so very sorry, Gentry."

"So was I. It was my fault. I never made her happy." His jaw clenches as if it were wired shut. "Whatever I did, it was wrong. I was never enough. Not for her, not for anyone."

"You were always enough."

He shakes his head. "I failed her."

"Listen to me. She was wrong. And she knew it. She regretted everything, always, every day. She was a proud, vain, bitter fool. She was the biggest fool who ever lived, Gentry. And she knows that."

I stroke his head. He falls asleep. Safe.

∽

I give myself one hour to indulge my regrets. One hour.

The West Hills scandal, living at the coast with my beautiful young lover. The boy who worked on farms and went to prep school. Who quoted Whitman and the Romantics when he drank. Who interrogated the semiotics of one of Gretchen's cartoons one morning over coffee and made me laugh so hard that a sleepy Marci stumbled down to see what the hell was going on. Who came home from the library after checking out a book on the Bible and paced around the kitchen in a state of agitation asking, couldn't something be done about Harold Bloom?

He would have been mine.

And the girls? What would it have meant to them?

Marci would have been furious, but she would have gone off to college and found a young man. And Gretchen? I would have done the unthinkable and sent Gretchen to her father. Because even then I knew she needed a better education than she was getting. Gentry would have insisted. So no matter what path I chose, Gretchen would have attended that school and met Tristan and very possibly made the exact same mistake.

Could any of us have stopped her from happening?

Hilary Lynne. I close my eyes and summon up her smell. The downy red curls and navy blue eyes that will no doubt turn brown. That sweet little miracle who should never have been born, that innocent child of fallen children.

We are who we are. It is what it is. My life is my life. God grant me the serenity, and so forth. I hate all that. But there you have it.

It works.

∽

It's getting dark when Jack opens the door to Gretchen's bedroom and peers in. His face is almost fearful. But I'm just sitting here on my daughter's bed. Gentry's arms are still wrapped around my hips, his head still rests on my stomach. And he's still sound asleep.

Suspicion and hope play across Jack's wary, weathered face. "There you are. He's tuckered out, I see."

I give Gentry's hair a maternal little pat. "Yes. He's exhausted. But he needs to eat so I'm going to wake him up. I'll be down to cook in a minute."

"It's late, Kathy. I could go get us something. Is Elephants still open?"

"No, I'd rather cook. You know I love to cook for the kids."

"All right, Kathy. If you want to."

"Would you take Sam out?"

"Come here, boy." Sam jumps down, tail wagging. They go down the stairs, out to the yard. I sit in the pool of yellow light from the hallway, looking down at Gentry.

I stroke that fine, heartbreaking hair.

ANOTHER SEPTEMBER

Fiona

I've never seen anything as happy as his face. He looks down, trying to hide his beaming face. And then he gives up and just lets it beam. I know it's his grand-daughter making him smile like that. Or who knows. Maybe it's something else. Like, whatever it is that's going on with him and Marci Mumford, which really isn't any of my business.

Whatever it is, he's smiling.

He's finishing the last page. If he can smile while reading this, he can smile at anything. He sets down the manuscript. "Hey Fiona? You're sure my name won't be on this?" He's very, very concerned about that.

"The publisher's excited about the anonymity angle. The possibilities for hype are endless." He nods. "I think we've talked about everything. Well, almost everything. We still haven't talked about the sex."

"Hm. Well, there wasn't very much of that, so can you just make it up?"

Oh, the silly guy. Doesn't he know that the sex is the best part, the part I always save till last? Hugh often helps me with the sex, and we make each other sick with laughter.

"You don't have the right attitude about this. This is the fun part, Gentry. The sex."

"Well, maybe if it were good sex, Fiona, but we're supposed to talk about impotence, yes? Impotence is not fun."

"Trust me. Gentry, just trust me. Tell me what really happened."

"With Miriam?"

"No, no. I've already made all that up. I want to know what happened with Brooke."

He stops. "With *Brooke*?"

"Yes. I need to know what happened with Brooke."

He's blushing. "Hey Fiona? How did you, um, know something happened with Brooke?"

I cross my arms and try to seem omniscient. "Women know."

We know how to bluff, at least.

It starts with a sigh, of course. An expression of great shame settles across his beautiful face. And then he hangs his head and talks to his lap, his voice getting lower and lower until it is hardly perceptible to human ears. He explains that he spilled his guts to her within five minutes of meeting her. All the things I have just about killed myself dragging out of him, he told her before they ordered lunch.

Oh, I'm not mad. I'm furious. "Why did you tell her all this?"

He blushes a deep, scarlet, romance novel heroine red. "I could, um, tell that it, um, was, um, arousing to her?"

I can't believe this. But really, I shouldn't be surprised. I mean, he is a man.

He tells me that they went in the bar, and they danced, and he got a little drunk, and then he "Um, I, um, put her, um, hand on my, um." On his "um"? He put her hand on his "um"? If I went anywhere near his "um," I bet he'd jump out a window, but he put her hand right on it?

Oh, I won't hit him or anything. I'd like to, but I won't.

And then, apparently, they talked about this "um, wager" wherein, if Brooke were able to make him "um, hard," and from the look on his face, I see that this was not anything that was happening for him at that time, then he would publish the book. "And she, um, was willing to, um, well, um," and he says this part very quickly, "putmeinhermouthunderthetable."

"Wait, let me get this straight. She offered to blow you? In the bar?"

"Yes."

I can't believe this. "Did it *work*?"

He's shocked. "I didn't let her. I called her a whore."

This is the first time I've EVER heard a word like that come out of his mouth. "I see. I understand why Brooke hates you." My voice sounds artificially calm.

He says, "I wish for death."

I start to laugh and so does he. "Can I just ask you one more thing about this, Gentry? Did you get even just, you know, vaguely tumescent for her?"

He clears his throat. "No?"

Please. He really can't lie. I pretend to believe him. "Good. I mean, oh." He seems so relieved. He really thinks he pulled one over on me. "Well, I think this encounter with Brooke is going to be what I refer to as a 'galvanizing moment.'"

"Galvanizing? Nothing about me was, um, steely."

"No, but you got resolve, you received strength, you had an epiphany." I turn to my keyboard. I type. He pets Sam and waits for the transformation of his partial truth and Miriam's complete lies into whatever passable fiction I can manufacture. Finally, I read to him. "'Brooke Gilbert was one of the most attractive women I had ever met,' blah, blah, blah. I get sort of romance novel about how sexy and elegant she was, her nails and all, and what she was wearing…"

He stops me. "What she was wearing?"

"Yes. She had on a hot little suit, Jimmy Choos, you know."

"What?"

"Jimmy Choos? Those are shoes?"

"I would never talk about that, how would I even *know* that?"

"People like Brooke spend time and money to look expensive, and the only way it can be worth it is if people notice, so we're going to. To make her happy. I talk about some more crap, blah, blah, blah, 'After Mavis's death, I was too devastated to even think about the idea of sex with another woman. But looking at Brooke made me think about it, long and hard.'"

"Oh, I like that long and hard part. That's subtle."

"Thank you, Mister Literary Snob. Then I put some more blah, blah, blah in here about what you ate."

"I had a steak and she had a salad."

"No, you have oyster shooters, and some clam broth, and then you both have the broiled swordfish."

"In Oklahoma?"

"So then you go into the bar. You drink, you dance, you flirt a little."

"Read the dancing part."

"Let's see, here we go. 'She moved with catlike grace, and her narrow hips rocked mine with the promise of erotic, feline delight.'"

He laughs a little more. Three months of dragging this out of him, and he's finally enjoying this on our last day. "I was probably counting in her ear." He laughs again. "Okay. What do we drink?"

"You have single malt, she has some expensive red wine."

"Actually, I think we did. I think you got that right."

"I'll change it, then."

"No, that's okay. Just go on."

"'We danced close to the hot rhythms of the cool jazz, and we talked about what had happened with Mavis. I poured the story into her willing ear. In Brooke, I realized that I had found that rarest of rarities, a compassionate soul. I realized, as

I watched her smoky eyes fill with tears, that she understood. I realized she cared about me, not as an agent, not as a business woman, but as a fellow human being.'"

"I'm doing quite a bit of realizing."

"'Brooke was moved, deeply, by the tragic circumstances of my life. She comforted me in a way that touched me, deeply, to the roots of my soul.'"

"You use deeply twice, there."

"I know. Long, hard, and deeply work well for me. Also, deep-rooted soul touching. That works, too."

"Will my name be on this?"

"Anyway, after you two stare at each other longingly for a while, she makes her move. 'Her hand, burning hot, touched my manhood . . .'"

"My name had BETTER NOT be on this."

"It won't. I have some blah, blah, blah here, sex stuff. Anyway, after she fondles you, quite thoroughly, in great detail, out of pure compassion, with deep sympathy, you have your epiphany."

"Right there in the bar?"

"You realize, blah, blah, blah, 'if I could not respond to a woman like this, a woman this beautiful, this desirable, this compassionate, then I was completely impotent. Even though she was understanding and kind, I was devastated by my inability to respond to her. I burned to have her, to take her, to make her mine, but I could not. Despite her kindness, I was cruel to her, cruel because of my own savage disappointment.'"

"Ah, my savage disappointment." He is really laughing.

"'I resolved, as she walked away from me, to give up drinking entirely. I knew that drinking was the cause of my impotence, and thanks to Brooke Gilbert, I stopped drinking that afternoon. Had I continued drinking, I would be dead.

"I owe my life to Brooke Gilbert.'"

He flops back hard on the bed. Sam hits the floor, startled. "Will it make her happy?"

"It will make her feel like dog shit."

"Great. Send it."

"I can't wait until she calls." I type away, send off the garbage delivery to Brooke. This might be the end of it. "I bet you're happy this is almost done."

"Done?" I thought he would be happy. I thought I would be, too. I thought I would be happy to stop hurting this man, but I feel terrible.

"Gentry? Will you come see me a lot, I mean all the time, like, every day?"

He smiles, pleased and shy. "Of course."

"Good. Then we don't have to be sad."

"I'll be so lonely." And he looks like he would like to suck the words right back into his mouth.

"What about Marci?"

"Marci? She's going back up to Seattle."

"Really. I thought she might be staying."

"She thought about it, but she's realized that she hates it here."

"Even though you're here?"

He looks confused, then patient. "I told you, there's nothing going on with Marci. I told you that."

"Oh, clearly not. Clearly it's all innocent. Because you're a nudist or something."

He stares at me for a minute like I'm unhinged. "What are you talking about?"

"I'm talking about the night you got the phone call telling you Gretchen was in labor."

"The phone call?" Something dawns in his face, a horrified understanding and remembrance. He slumps back. "I can't stand this."

"So, what did I see?"

"Me. In the bath when the phone rang. Being an idiot. Being excited."

"You did look excited." His face is completely aghast. "No, no, Gentry, not that kind of excited. I mean, it looked like you were excited in a completely, you know, appropriate and nonsexual way about getting that phone call."

"Are you sure?"

"I'm sure."

"Okay." He swallows, steadies himself. "But she was *there*."

"I bet she was so excited by the phone ringing that she didn't even see you."

He sounds hopeful. "Do you really think so?"

I believe it would be a good thing to lie. "Yes. I'm sure of it. So don't be embarrassed. Just forget about it."

"I can't." His voice is so soft. "I can't forget about anything. Not anymore."

"Well, I'm going to forget it. I promise."

Yes, sometimes it's good to lie.

I start my daily email to Hugh, because he's so good about sending mail to me every minute of every day and being bitchy and impatient if I don't write back immediately. "Listen, I'm driving home in the morning to check on Hugh. I'll be back Monday, unless Brooke says this will do it."

"Oh." He sits up, gets up, and goes to the door. He turns back to me. "Could you come back for Sunday?"

Sunday. He wants me here for Sunday. "I'd love to, Gentry, I would absolutely love to!"

"And bring Hugh, of course."

"Hugh is one of those recovering Catholics. He avoids church. Sorry."

"Oh. Okay." He stands by the door and stares at the floor. "Well, I'll see you on Sunday, early?" His hand is on the knob.

"Very early. I wouldn't miss it for anything." I'm thinking about what to wear on Sunday. I usually just wear jeans to church, but this calls for a dress. And shoes, real shoes.

"Hey Fiona? I didn't stay like that."

Maybe I'll buy a new dress. I never buy anything new. "What, Gentry?" Something pretty, summery, because it's only September.

"I didn't stay like that."

Summer dresses should be on sale. The fall stock is in, now. I can go through every sale rack on Northwest 23rd. "Like what? I'm sorry, what are you talking about?"

He speaks very slowly. "I didn't stay that way."

I stop my typing. His face is so naked, so bare. He wants me to ask him. "You're okay now?"

"Yes. It was the drinking, and what happened at the fertility place."

Oh, he's just the kind to get all worked up over that. "So you had a little date with a Dixie cup, Gentry. So big deal. They didn't do anything with your sperm. They just tested it and threw it away."

"I know that. That's not . . ." He shakes his head.

I go over to where he waits by the door. He allows me to hug him without returning it. As he always does. And then he steps back, puts a hand on each of my shoulders, looks in my eyes. He wants me to see his face, to understand it. To understand him. His voice, when he speaks, is deep and rough and not his voice, except it is.

"Come here."

He puts his hands against my back and pulls me close. His heart beats a pulse so strong that I can feel it. He buries his face in my hair and I can feel his need and pain and hardness and how he controls it, all of it, no matter how much he wants to let go.

He lets me go and leaves.

I go home to Hugh.

Gentry

Hey, little Hilary. You have beautiful red curls. As you should. And you have brown eyes, Hilary. As you should. Perfect hair, perfect eyes. You're perfect. "Don't you think she's perfect?"

"Well, I guess. She's kind of puny compared to Geneva, but she's a little cutie, just like her mom. Only Mumford woman worth a shit, as far as I'm concerned."

"Hey, now."

"Ah, I'm sorry." His eyes smile, I know he's only kidding. We sit outside, it's warm today, so we sit on lawn chairs in the driveway in the sun. I worry about Hilary in the sun, she has such fair skin, she might get burned, she might get skin cancer, she . . . she's fine. Hilary is fine.

We christened her today. I brought everyone to my church. I made them walk in and sit down and watch the scary, dark, mysterious Catholic rites. They were suspicious, but they came. Kathryn and Jack and Eve and Spencer and Marci. Fiona came, and the Gilroys, but of course Vicki goes to my church, so she wasn't afraid like the others. We filled two pews. We sat near some graven images, and everyone tried not to look at them, but I caught Kathryn staring at the stations of the cross.

We sang a nice hymn that always makes me smile, one where all the white folks have to clap a little, and sort of sway. I didn't do either, of course. I did sing. I always miss my church in Detroit when this group attempts gospel. Marci snickered, and I frowned at her.

The homily addressed nuclear disarmament. The priest rings the church bell whenever there's a bomb test, and he's received some complaints from the neighboring vacation homes, and he spoke sternly. Marci snickered again. I frowned at her again.

Vicki, Fiona and I filed up to indulge in some ritualized cannibalism. As usual, I refrained from the blood drinking, but I chowed down on the sacred body of the Lord. I hope it all wasn't too grisly for my guests, all of us with our post-Christ-eating kneeling and praying.

A baby boy, Tyler Andrew, was christened along with Hilary. Tristan and Gretchen and Vicki and I stood up for her. Hilary was very brave as the forces of archaic superstition and patriarchal oppression claimed her soul.

The priest put the holy water on her, and the oil and ashes, and the white stole. She blinked, but she didn't cry. We held her up, and everyone clapped as my granddaughter received the first of what I hope will be all her sacraments. She has her name. Hilary Lynne Buchanan.

Afterwards, we went to the Catholic coffee room for some Catholic coffee and Catholic cake. I think it tasted much the same as the Protestant variety, though Jack sniffed his suspiciously. There were two cakes, one with a pink cross for Hilary, and one with a blue cross for Tyler. Mrs. Nguyen, Vu's mother, made Hilary's cake because I still can't bake. Marci cut and served it because I made her. I told her it was a snickering penance.

I ate one bite of cake and saw Fiona in her summer dress with ten buttons down the front. I saw my son, my Gretchen. I saw my beautiful, miraculous grand-daughter. I gave thanks. Amen.

I went back into the church by myself, and lit a candle. I will always light the candle. And then we came home.

Your three living paternal grandparents are Catholic, Hilary. The other four are nothing. Why should the nothing take precedence over the something, I ask you?

"Do you want to hold her?"

"Well, not really. I might drop her. And she looks less bouncy than my kids."

"You won't drop her." I put her in his arms. I like the look of Lorrie with a baby. He holds her up to his huge heart and she falls immediately to sleep. I want her back. But I restrain myself.

"This is one fucking tender moment."

"It is." I'm happy. Gretchen and Tristan will only be here for a few more hours, but I have them for that. The book is almost finished. I'm happy to get that over with. I try not to think about how much I'll miss Fiona, but she needs to go back to Hugh, to her life.

The school year has started and the kids will keep me busy, and I have Sam, and my own kids will visit for as long as the weather holds. I don't want them driving over the pass with Hilary when the weather is bad. And I'll visit them.

God, I'm happy. "On Tuesday, my son turns sixteen."

"Hot damn! He can get his license! This Tuesday?"

I nod. "I'm taking the day off work and he's taking the morning off school and I'm taking him to the DMV and then to breakfast."

"That's a nice deal. I'm sure you'll both always remember it."

I touch my granddaughter's head and pray to God that, yes, this will be a day he will always remember.

"So I don't suppose I could take advantage of the mood and get you to answer one question for me."

"Ask me anything, Lorrie."

"It's been five sonofabitching years. Who the hell did it? Tell me. Tell me, because I won't do anything stupid, I swear."

I wait for the way I feel to go away, and my memories and my fear to well up and hurt me. He had to make me remember, he had to ruin this day. Why did he have to ruin this day?

September, at the coast. Perfect. I'm still happy. And it doesn't matter. And I'm all right.

"Anything but that. Anything else, Lorrie. Anything." He turns away, disappointed. "When I say anything, Lorrie, I mean anything. Think about it. This is your opportunity to ask me absolutely anything else. Anything."

"You mean it?" His face lights up. He can't believe his good fortune.

"Yes. So make it good."

"I plan to. Sonofabitch. This is great." His mouth twists with amusement. He has a game plan. "I think what I'll do, you little asshole, is just describe questions that I MIGHT ask you, and watch you squirm. And when I get to the one that makes you squirm the most, I'll ask that one."

Oh, God, my mask, I've forgotten how to harden my face.

"Let's see. I could ask you your name. I could ask you if Kathy Mumford is as good at fucking as she is at being a bitch because if she's not I don't know how the hell you tolerate her. I could ask you if you'd sleep with my wife if you had a chance. I always did wonder what the hell happened in the back seat of Darlene's car, exactly. And I could ask you what the hell happened between you and Marci. I have an idea, but I would like to fucking know, instead of fucking guessing."

Please, please, there has to be some other embarrassing thing you want to ask me about. "But the thing I always wondered about . . ." Why did I say that I would do this? ". . . what I always wanted to know is . . ." Just ask me so I can stop being afraid ". . . the thing I can't figure out . . ." just say it, ask it ". . . is what the hell happened to that yellow Berkeley ugly stick with the Zebco reel? Because you caught more fish with that embarrassing piece of shit than you ever do with the Loomis."

Mel gave me that the first year I lived with him. *Now, this is strictly for learning, my boy. We'll get you something better, I promise, but this will teach you what you need to know.* And I did learn everything I needed to know. But I never let him get me another. I kept it, used it. I had it in Georgia, I had it in Detroit, I had it in Oregon. I almost drove out of town without it, but Lorrie remembered. I managed to hold on to it.

It was time to tell Lorrie the truth. "My wife gave it to Goodwill."

The shock on his face. The righteous anger.

"You should have told me, Jesus, Gentry, if I'd have known that's how it was for you, I would've been down there. There is a limit, a line, and for a woman to mess with your tackle, for Christ's sake, I have never hit a woman in my goddamn life, but I would have come to Oklahoma just to personally kick her ass. Goddamn." He shakes his head. The baby starts to stir.

I should have called him. I should have forgotten my shame and called him and asked for help. He would have helped me. "It was Garret."

"Hell, I knew that. I always knew that. Didn't you notice that the sonofabitch joined the Navy before you were out of the goddamn hospital?" His big hands rub Hilary's tiny back. His hands are careful, tender, and he puts his cheek against her red curls. "There was glass all over that driveway. Something happened. So Emmett came around here and asked Marci who did it. She said she didn't know, everyone liked you, no one would hurt you. Except maybe Alex. And he told her Alex was at that party with an airtight alibi. That's when Emmett knew she was covering for someone. Throwing that poor fucked-up kid under the bus when everyone knew that kid couldn't hurt a fly.

"So Emmett went to talk to that Blount kid she ran around with. And when he did, that truck was gone. Garret said it must have been stolen. And no one ever saw that truck again. I figure, you know, someone grows up here, he knows a few places to put a truck. Like maybe at the bottom of the ocean, if you have a friend with a big enough boat. Gar Blount has lots of friends with big boats."

He stares out at the water.

"So he lost his truck, but that wasn't enough. That wasn't nearly enough for what he did to you. I never touched him. I wanted to, see. But I knew you wouldn't want me to. So." He turns to me. "That kid wanted one thing in life, to be out on that boat with his dad. I tried to get him to go out for football, for wrestling, because he was one mean, hard fisherman's son, but he wanted to be out with his dad."

I wonder what that would feel like.

"I figured you found your place here, and you had to give it up, see, and the only fair thing in the world would be for that kid to give up his place. I told him to get his ass in the military."

"Lorrie, I have it back. I have my place back, now."

"Well, Garret has a boat now, a nicer one than his dad ever had. He runs drugs, mostly. His dad lost his old piece of shit boat when they closed up the run one year, but Garret and his dad go out together, now, they fish. And he's got another truck. I just never let him come back until you came back, Gentry, because it wouldn't have been fair."

Fairness. Justice. Rules of engagement.

"He was so goddamn scared of me. I never did anything about it. I never had to. I had plenty of chances when he was home on leave, and I'm not so dumb that I couldn't have made it look like an accident. I always knew it was him, Gentry. I just wanted you to tell me, that's all."

We're silent, then.

"I love you, Lorrie."

"I love you, Gentry, but if you ever tell anybody I said that, I will personally kick your ass." Hilary starts to wake up and she rubs her cheeks across his shirt, searching for something he doesn't have. Hilary is hungry.

"I need to go find Gretchen."

"Ah, little buddy, you're so goddamn sensitive, I bet you wish you could just grow some tits and feed this baby yourself, don't you?" And he laughs, Lorrie laughs, he laughs with his joke and I do too.

This is to give thanks. Amen.

And they all leave, they go home. Everyone but Fiona.

Sam and I, we sit on the couch rereading this Denis Johnson book. We finished the boy wizard to date, and after all that magic, I need some poetry. I read poetry when my heart is breaking and poetry breaks it even more. I've always done that.

Old habits die hard, don't they, Sam.

But we've made it this far, and we'll be fine, just fine. Hey Sam, this was a busy summer, but the fall is here, and we have work to do. We have papers to go over. We have lesson plans to finish. We have to do Lorrie's, too.

Fiona is putting the last of her things in her car. I know that she needs to leave. She comes in the door. It hurts to look at her.

I've been alone for too long. God, forgive me.

"Hey. There's coffee." She never drinks coffee. She pours some. She's upset, oh what is it.

We seat ourselves at the kitchen island. "I heard from Brooke. She's not satisfied."

"Oh." Why did I think she would be? Brooke is a vampire.

"She says she needs more. Only a little more from you, now. Just a little. She wants you to put in what happened when you were a kid, Gentry."

"You were supposed to make up something."

She sounds sad. "I don't think that's a good idea. I don't want to be like Miriam, making guesses and getting everything wrong. I need the truth. If you just give me a little, I can work it in the way she wants." She sips her coffee. "Marci says you can't remember your childhood."

"You asked the wrong sister."

"So you remember?"

I nod.

"Please, Gentry. We've talked about everything else. Every hard thing." She stares out the window at the water. "Could you write it down? Like a story? I'll stay here with Sam and we'll read or something. When you're done, I'll go out there and read it, maybe with you there, or maybe not, whichever you want. But then I'll have what I need."

What she needs. She stares out the window at the ocean and she won't even look at me. Because it isn't Brooke who needs this.

I go to give her what she needs.

∽

It takes all afternoon. God, I think this is right. There's no one to ask whether or not I got something wrong. So, this is it, this will have to stand, this will have to do.

Amen.

I go to find her.

Hey, Fiona. This isn't even my couch you sleep on, with my dog. He's always felt like our dog. I like sharing him with you. I would share it all with you, Fiona, everything I have, as little as it is. But you belong to someone else.

The grief of it, God.

I think about that poem. My favorite poem in the entire collection, and it's about memory. He's going through Kansas on the Greyhound and sees the farm burning, the figures of the family around the flames as if they'd chosen that moment to cry out to God for witness. It's awful, a house burning down. But that's not the part of the poem that hurts. It's the crack of the bones in the farmer's hands as his horses pull against the reins to return to the fire.

My thoughts are like that.

Sweet Fiona, stretched out on the couch, her brown hair around her shoulders. I kneel down beside her and breathe her in. She's close, I know that, too close to loving me. I won't do that to Fiona. I made sure of it by telling the truth. She'll read what I wrote and turn away because she's sane, and no sane woman would want a man who came from that. I'll be safe from my own stupidity, and she will be safe with Hugh. This will send her away.

But God?

I love her.

I sit on the floor and watch her until her eyelids flutter. She opens her grey eyes. "Hi."

"Hey."

"What time is it?"

"About seven-thirty."

"It's out there?"

"It's out."

She slides to the floor beside me. She takes my hand and leans her head on my shoulder. "I'll read it, then delete it."

"Don't delete it. I need to send it to Mel."

"Okay." She leans over and kisses my cheek. And then she rises up, graceful and easy and smooth, and she leaves.

When she leaves for good, God, please make it just like that. Graceful and easy and smooth.

Amen.

I lie down where it's warm from her, and Sam stretches out beside me.

We sleep.

THE BEGINNING

Once upon a time, he had a mother.

She came from the mountains. She knew the complete history of fourteen generations of barn cats. She remembered horses and hired hands, storms that killed neighbors, winters so cold it froze the ears off cattle. She told him these stories and whispered, do you remember? Don't you remember?

Someday, you'll remember all of it.

He watched her, her ways of doing things. How she made meals from cans, how her small hands turned red in the dishwater, the flash of her brown eyes when she laughed. He watched everything she did. She taught him to read fairytales. She believed in angels. She said angels and fairytales were not the same thing, and God was more than just another good story, and the best place to hear about God was church. The man, who was like the sleeping giant at the top of the beanstalk, went to church with them every Sunday. The boy loved the quiet, the safety, the candles, the Madonna's arms curving around the child.

But his mother flew away and she never came back. So the first prayer was simple.

Bring her back. Amen.

⌒

You're hungry? Is that right. Starve, for all I care. Fucking parasite.

He climbed up on the counter, he looked through the cabinets. Once the cans were empty, he ate oatmeal. When that was gone, he found some old peanut butter under the sink she used for mouse traps. He got it open and ate it with his hands. And then his stomach hurt so bad, because he had been alone and hungry for too long and he threw up, sick all over, everywhere, and the man came in and he put the boy's face in it.

Clean it up. If you sick it up you'll eat it again. You're so sad that she's gone but it's your fault. Every fucking bit of it. You're going to have to take care of yourself, now. Get used to it. I don't want you to look at me, do you understand me? Do you? Because it's more than I can stand, seeing that face on you.

He took off his belt.

I told you things were going to be different. No crying. No CRYING. Take your medicine. No, no crying. Take it like a man.

The second prayer was just as simple.

Make him go away. Amen.

⌒

He tried to be invisible. To be noticed meant the belt, so he tried to stay out of the man's way when he came home from the bar.

He liked to sleep with a light on. It wasn't just that he hated the dark, it was being able to see what was coming at him when he woke up. A face, a hand, a belt. With the light on, he had a warning.

He always slept in his clothes. It hurt less through his clothes.

He would lie there after and listen to the man slam around the rest of the house until he passed out. He would have to get up and clean it up before the man woke up. He would get it if the house wasn't clean.

I ask for just one thing from you, you little leech, and that's to keep this dump clean.

⌒

Sometimes when the boy woke up, the man would be passed out at the table, his head in his arms, the gun on the table. Sometimes the man's teeth were sitting by the gun. And the boy wanted to pick it up and hide it, or take it to the curb so it would disappear, but he was afraid to touch it. He was afraid of the gun. And he was afraid of the teeth.

The teeth guarded the gun.

⌒

Get up. Wear your Sunday stuff. Yes, I know what day of the week it is. Hurry up.

When they got to the school, he was the only kid there with a man. All the rest were mothers, except for two who were too old. They were grandmothers. In fairytales, grandmothers could either be good or bad.

The man leaned his face down by the boy's ear.

Don't talk.

One lady was smiling and asking his name. She asked again. He stayed quiet.

She looked at the man, tilted her head. He felt the pressure of the man's giant hand on the back of his head. That big face by his ear.

When this lady asks you questions, you can answer her. She's your teacher. So tell her your name.

He did.

She frowned. And you're really five years old?

I can bring in his birth certificate.

No, that's fine. We let out at 11:50. Will his mother be picking him up?

Look, Miss, it's just him and me. He can walk home. He knows where the key is.

He's so small to be walking home. He shouldn't be walking alone.

I could run.

The teacher laughed and touched his shoulder.

Don't baby him.

Of course, Mr. Gentry. Her skin was so dark and her smile was beautiful but her eyes were hard. The man stood there, tall, swallowing, his eyes narrowed. That was the look he wore before the belt. But he kept his belt in the loops and left.

He couldn't hit teachers.

༄

He sat up front because he was short. The teacher asked them questions. Did they know their full names? Their addresses? Their colors? Their days of the week? Did any of them know any letters of the alphabet?

School was where you went to learn things. Who didn't know these things? He felt angry.

When everyone else was having milk and crackers, she asked him to come to her desk. You can bring your snack, it's all right. Just come up here and talk to me. Do you want another carton of milk? You're welcome. You have lovely manners, young man. Now, look at this with me. What does this say? Can you read this?

She kept him up there while the other kids rested on big rubber mats that smelled awful. He could read every book in the classroom, tell time, add and subtract. He quietly recited his times tables through twelve, and then named all the states. And their capitals. And then the continents. And then the planets in the solar system.

She took him to a huge room where older kids ate from plastic trays. She sat him down and he stared at the table until she returned with a tray for him. I want you to have lunch while I go to the office. I'll be right back. He ate it all and then stared at the tray, wishing. But if he'd been given more, he'd have gotten sick. So he sat and stared at the tray while kids laughed and ate around him.

She came back. All done? Good. You can spend some time with me until recess is over. She worked at her desk and he played with a globe, closing his eyes and running his fingers over the mountain ranges.

Okay. Come with me. Here's the classroom. This is where you'll be this year. I'm disappointed to let you go, but you'd be bored in kindergarten.

The other teacher introduced him. When she said his name, girls giggled.

Enough. How would you like it if someone mocked your name. HE is going to be in with us this year, because kindergarten is a little too easy for HIM. More kids giggled.

Enough, I said.

The kids were giants. But he didn't care, because the books in that room looked like books he wanted to read. And besides, in second grade, you got to have lunch.

A note came in the mail. What's this? Do you hear me, what the fuck is this? That belt whipped out of the loops like a snake.

He read the note. Second grade? He shook his head. What the hell? You're five years old and they sent you up to second grade?

It fell across his face like a shadow.

You didn't get that from me.

It was worst of all when the man cried. It didn't sound like a person. It sounded like an animal.

The house had always been clean, but it was stripped bare. The library books went back, leaving one shelf of books the man used for work. The kitchen was emptied of food, no milk bottles in the window over the sink, no magnets on the fridge. Everything of hers was gone, packed in the night while the radio played and the boy hid under a blanket. He knew to keep his room as close to empty as possible, bed made up tight, his marbles and that book of fairytales under his bed, whatever he wore in the closet. He knew it was important to keep everything as bare and empty as possible.

But he wanted a dog.

He played in the street, and there were dogs there. Sometimes they belonged to people. Sometimes they didn't. Skinny and hopeful and ready to belong to someone. They went where they wanted to, like him. All sizes, all colors, all hungry but happy, anyway. They were dirty and skinny and no one wanted them, but he did. He wanted all those dogs.

Twice, he let dogs follow him home. Once it was a skinny yellow dog with blue eyes and a tail that whipped around in crazy circles. That tail was so wild, it made him laugh and he couldn't throw anything at that dog. Another time, it was a big one, dirty and matted. It ran with a limp.

He thought about it a lot when he was trying to sleep.

A dog could live in the alley where everyone kept their garbage cans. He could maybe make a little house for it back there out of things that wouldn't be missed, a cardboard box, a blanket from the hall closet. The dog could be a secret. But it was too cold in the winter for a dog to live outside. And he had nothing to feed a dog. He was always hungry himself.

And the man had a gun.

People threw things at dogs in the street, and that made him angry. These dogs had nowhere to go. But if the dog followed him, he had to be the one throwing the rock. He had excellent aim and only hit the ground near them.

Go on. Go away.

The neighbor knocked on their door. She lived on the right side, and he was not allowed to say anything to this woman or her daughter. He was not supposed to even look at their house. But she was yelling through the door that it was an emergency and he'd better open up, so the man opened the door. She had a piece of paper in her hand and she was yelling that there were gooks and commies moving into the neighborhood who would eat all the dogs.

The man said, cool. There are too many bitches around here, anyway.

You watch your mouth or I'll call child welfare, she said, and the man closed the door in her face while she was yelling. He sagged against the door like he was going to cry, but he didn't cry. He got angry.

Hands on his shoulders, those giant hands crushing him, lifting him up in the air.

There's going to be people from the state coming by. And you need to keep your mouth shut. Do you know what happens to us if they take you? Do you know? I'll go to prison and they'll give you to the nuns. Those nuns keep the kids in the basement.

Shaking him until his teeth rattled.

Are you excited about that? Going to live with the nuns?

⤫

There were neighbors to the left, then. An old man and an old woman.

He was concerned about the neighborhood dogs, so he went right over and looked in the window as they were moving in. They pretended not to see him, though the old lady smiled. They didn't have a lot, and a lady with a clipboard was with them, but no one could say any of the same words.

The lady left and the old people stayed inside. He stayed in his yard watching. His plan was to keep any neighborhood dogs away from their house, and maybe the cats, too, to be on the safe side. If they wanted to eat anything smaller, well, he wouldn't worry about that. He heard the old people yelling. Their kitchen door flew open and smoke billowed out. He ran to the door and saw them standing there, yelling and pointing at each other while a fire licked up out of the oven.

He ran home and got the baking soda.

Once the flames were gone, he looked in the oven, feeling a little afraid of what might be in there. There was a little pile of wood with an unopened can of soup sitting in the middle of it. The label had burned away.

That's not how you make soup, he told them.

They stood next to each other in the smoky kitchen, shivering. He walked out into their empty living room and found the thermostat and turned on their heat.

Then, he cleaned out that oven and made them some soup.

⤫

They were afraid of the police and loud noises. They didn't know about stoves, light switches, or toilets. He taught them all that, and they taught him their words and fed him. They ate all kinds of things, but never any dogs.

He had to help them understand their house, first. How the toilets worked, what to do with their trash, what a lock was. He had to remind them that the rule of electricity was that whatever you turned on, you had to turn off. Once they got the house figured out, they worked on the rest of it.

He'd taken the bus all the time before she left, so he knew about the bus, where to wait, which lines went where, how much it cost. He was only five years old and had never been to a bank, but he went along and asked the right questions and they figured out the bank with some help from a woman who was called a teller. He thought she was called that because she told them what to do with checks and deposit slips. He helped them understand the grocery store, the mail, the light bill.

If anyone was rude to the neighbors, he'd get mad, but he didn't show it. They fed him dinner every night. They called him Grandson. They took him back to church.

The new priest looked out over them. He was huge, but his hands flew up like little white birds when he spoke. Such a strong, strange voice, a different way to say the words.

We have new members. Some call them refugees, but they are our brothers and sisters in Christ. He smiled at the neighbors. Welcome to our family.

They didn't speak any English and they didn't know what the priest was saying about them. But they smiled politely and stayed quiet.

The priest kept talking about them. Some of you have been in camps and prisons for years. Families are scattered, children are missing. But we are your family.

He held out his hand, which was so small.

We are here to lend a hand.

❧

The neighbors were always working on their garden or on the laundry.

You should teach him some of the true ways. It's bad to use machines for everything. It makes you lazy.

So why should I wear out my hands scrubbing your dirty drawers, there is a machine to do this for me. Ask him. Is there a machine for it?

There's a machine for everything.

This boy is so smart. You know everything, Grandson, everything.

The old man was not convinced. *What happens if a machine breaks? What happens then?* They both looked at him, waiting.

Machines are made of parts. You just put in a new part.

Did you hear that? The little woman started to laugh. *I can think of a few new parts you could use, old man.*

The old man laughed so hard that he dropped his pipe.

The neighbors were always, always laughing. They could find a way to laugh about anything. They never quite got the idea of locks, so their door was always open for him. When his teeth hurt, which they often did, the old man packed them with chewing tobacco. When he fell too hard on his knees and the blood went all over, the old woman put something on there that made it stop. And he felt this warm bath of relief, that finally, if something hurt there was someone who cared, somewhere to go for help.

When he got lice, the women in the office let him go home on his own. He didn't know what to do, how to fix it, what the man would do if he told him about these lice. So he ran next door and told her he had bugs in his hair. The old woman put kerosene in his hair, combed it through, clucking and cursing and smashing every bug. *Fucking bugs.* It took hours. *Go wash your bedding,* she told him. *I won't tell.*

ᗡ

Notes came home from school. There has been a lice epidemic. Immunizations are required. Financial assistance is available. Lunch ticket assistance is available. Please fill out and return the attached forms. Please see to these immunizations or your child will have to be removed from school. Snow gear is a legal requirement in our district. Snow gear can be provided at no cost for families in need. The district is offering a free breakfast program. Financial assistance is available.

He ripped up the notes.

And then a teacher would hand him a pair of shoes. These look to be just your size. Or snow pants. Here, these should fit. This will keep you warm. Now you wear these, do you understand? I don't want to see you walking to school without snow pants. The school nurse handing him a rubber ball to squeeze. It will just be a pinch. There. You're a brave little man. Would you like to keep the ball? The school secretary copying a signature, squinting at an old form. Looks just like it, doesn't it? I should have taken up forgery.

The way women hugged him, pulling him to their soft fronts, the way they smelled, like shampoo and perfume, the soap in their clothing and the sweet secret scent of their necks. Their laughter, their hands, their gentle touch. Thank you.

What a help you are. Such manners. Where did you get all this dark hair? You are such a beautiful little boy. I wish I could take you home and keep you for my own.

He felt himself bloom like a flower at their words. He was confused and embarrassed, haunted by the kindness of women, which so often remained a secret.

～

So the things that felt good, those were secrets. Like how his neighbors were his real family. And how women hugged him. And stray dogs that followed him home, the dogs he played with, so afraid they'd be discovered that he couldn't even give them names.

The biggest secret was that he looked like her.

～

The man always warned him before he hit him. Like the instructions before a test. Don't ever fight me.

Better not to try to fight back, better to stay still and get it over with.

He got the belt for talking back, not making his bed right, slamming the door, leaving the back door unlocked, going into the garage for any reason, leaving the lid off the garbage can, sucking his thumb. There were a million reasons he got the belt.

And don't *look* at me. I can't stand you *looking* at me, you look just *like* her.

He knew the real reason he got the belt was that he looked like her.

～

One day, he looked in the mirror at his own face. She looked back. He took a pair of scissors and cut off his hair. All of it. It grew back, always, no matter how he hacked at it, it grew and grew and grew out of him, all this hair, like something from a story, a story he remembered from her, but he never thought about her, ever. Except in church. When he lit the candle. When he looked at the Madonna, holding the child. Imagine that. Imagine being as perfect as God, imagine being held like that.

He lit the candle and made himself forget.

～

Every few months, the man walked in the house with bags. Sober and seething. The bags went on the counter.

Take care of this, and then get your filthy ass in the tub.

The man would get his bottles out of the cabinet over the fridge and take them into the garage and lock them in the trunk of his car.

The first bag held the same things. One loaf of bread. One jar of peanut butter. A quart of milk. Six apples. Every single time, the same stuff. The peanut butter went in the cabinet next to all the other unopened jars of peanut butter from all the other times. The milk in the fridge, the bread and the apples on the counter.

He would take the other bag in his room. A pair of tennis shoes, two pair of jeans, a package of underwear, socks, and two shirts. Everything was different sizes, clothes for a kid whose parts didn't match. He would put it all away, thinking about the apples.

A hand on the back of his neck, tight. That face by his ear.

Someone from the state is coming. Keep your fucking mouth shut.

And someone would come. A man or a woman. That person would go through the house, open the fridge, check the cabinets. His room would be looked over. You make your bed nicely. Where are your toys? You don't like inside toys? You play outside? Are these your books? You can read this one? Will you read to me? Very good.

All he wanted was for the man to go to the bar so he could have the apples.

And then that person would leave. When the caseworkers left, they went to other houses, they checked on other kids. The city was full of kids like him.

Sometimes at school there was a boy or a girl who looked at him with eyes that held a password. Another child who had no idea what to do with the Mother's Day presents and cards they had to make every year. A girl whose hair snarled into a rat's nest over the dirty wool of her coat collar. A boy who had no socks to go under his boots. Another child who wore long-sleeved shirts and long pants, no matter how hot it was in the summer. Kids who swore, who stood up on the swings, who chewed tobacco and stole lunches. And they recognized and ignored each other until the other child moved or the boy moved up a class.

He didn't want to talk to anyone else who knew. But at least he was not alone.

These things were safe.

His neighbors. Their family was gathering, people scattered in the prisons and camps had come to America and they were finding each other. They sat at the table and told stories that made him see how much worse it could be, in a camp. They had all been in camps. They had a real grandson, then. That boy got to live there for a while. Then he had his own house in the neighborhood with his parents and two aunts.

He hated that boy, but he taught him English.

School was safe, if he tried not to fight, if he didn't get any notes sent home. And then there was church. Church was safe, except for the nuns. Nuns were only there once in a while, for reasons he didn't understand and didn't want to know. He thought that maybe nuns ran the places that the refugees came from. Once a nun came up to him and called him by name. He ran away. But other than the nuns, church was good.

And that was perfect, then, because he went with the whole family. They celebrated everything, a big family now, pushing into a pew and arguing and then settling and poking and complaining. Then worshipping. He listened to the voices in that Mass, the songs in Vietnamese and French, and sometimes it was so pretty that it hurt, hurt enough to make him cry, but he never cried, he just listened.

And he went to RE, and then he went to Reconciliation class, Communion class. He counted the time until Confirmation, he prayed for his Confirmation. More than anything, he wanted to be an acolyte. He counted the months until he could learn how to help the priest serve Mass. He prayed, he learned to pray in his own, quiet way, his own words and his own way, and it helped.

So this was enough. A place to sleep. Some food. School. People who cared, even if they weren't really his family. Church. Years can pass like that, years of playing in the street with other kids, meals with the neighbors and church on Sunday.

Years can pass while praying for someone to go away.

⌒

The priest was called Mel. He watched the boy, and the boy watched him. Mel was kind. Asked how things were going. We haven't seen your father in church.

He doesn't ever come to church.

Well aren't you lucky that the Nguyens can bring you.

Yes. I'm lucky.

Ah, but they're lucky, too. Lucky for your helping hand. Everyone needs a helping hand, yes?

I guess.

Do you need any help? The priest smiled.

No. I don't need anything.

He ran home.

⁓

He lay in bed that night, thinking about the priest. He wasn't sure priests were actually men. And they were always talking about the sacrifice of our Lord. He knew that God had died for his sins, but he didn't understand how God could die. And yet Jesus had died. Sure, He rose up, but He died first, and everyone seemed to think the resurrection was the miracle. That wasn't the miracle. The miracle was that He ever died in the first place because how could God die?

He turned it over and over in his mind, the difference between Jesus and God.

Jesus was God on Earth, but he was a man. He walked around on roads. He performed miracles, but he wore clothes and ate bread and drank wine. He let people kill him. That seemed human.

Nothing about God seemed human. God was invisible, infinite, mighty, all-seeing and all-powerful. The one thing God couldn't do was die. So he made a human son that could do it. The boy thought the church had it wrong, the idea that Christ died for the sins of all mankind. The son had to die for His father, not for mankind.

He didn't like to think about sons and fathers, so he thought about fighting, instead.

He could beat up anyone in the school. He wasn't even sure how he did it, but there was a way to go under when you couldn't go over, and that gave you an advantage, access to the lower parts of a person, which were not as fair to hurt as the head and face, but it worked. You didn't have to be the strongest to win.

He lay in his bed and thought about it, what worked on which boy at school, if it would work at home. Maybe when he got older, taller. Would he ever get taller? He tried to imagine himself as tall as the man but that seemed ridiculous, he'd never get that tall. He would, however, like to just break five feet at some point.

He got up and turned off the light. He didn't like the dark, but maybe that would help him fall asleep. He got back under the covers and put his thumb back in his mouth.

There was no denying how strong the man was. He'd turned over the fridge before he left for work that day. He'd been up all night drinking at the table, and when the boy came in the door after running home from church, the man was asleep with his head on the table. He woke up when the door slammed. He stood up swearing and pulled the fridge over.

The man was at work, but the fridge was still there, facedown in the kitchen.

Maybe that's why he couldn't sleep. He knew the man would have all those hours at work to sober up, and he was waiting for the moment when the garage door opened and the man walked in came in the bedroom and started yelling.

Which is exactly what happened. The door banged open and the light came on and he heard the man say, what the *fuck* did you do to the fridge? Get your goddamned thumb out of your goddamned mouth, you girl.

He sat up, rubbing his eyes. I didn't do it.

What, it just fell over?

You did it. On your way out. Don't you remember?

The man blinked. He almost looked afraid.

No more backtalk.

That's not backtalk. I'm just saying I didn't tip over the fridge. How could I even do that?

You mouthy little bastard. Grabbed up by the back of his shirt, the back of his pants and it hurt, so he twisted, trying to get away.

Are you fighting me? Are you actually *fighting* me? Don't you *ever* fight me.

Flying through the air out the back door into the snow.

The boy walked over to the neighbors and tapped on the door. Heard the slap of their feet on the floor. Their faces looked afraid until they saw it was him. *Oh, are you selling something, grandson? Collecting money for the orphans?* They chuckled. *Come in, sit down here.*

They sat at their table with the lights off, the streetlight shining on their grave and sleepy faces, and listened to it coming from next door. Crashing, swearing. Where the fuck did you go, you mouthy little girl. Come home. I'm not done with you.

He realized the man was tearing the fridge apart with his bare hands and throwing it into the backyard.

The old man said, *why should we buy a radio when we have this beautiful music to listen to?* The old woman laughed, her brown teeth flashing. *Let's make a game of it. Every time he says fuck, I win a point.*

He couldn't laugh.

Grandson. You can laugh or you can cry.

I never cry.

You'd do well in war, Grandson. Give him tea.

He got up to make tea. She patted his shoulder, put him in a chair between them and pulled his cold feet into her lap. She peeled off his wet socks and rubbed his feet warm. *Little ice feet. How about you hold the teacup with your feet.* He tried and it spilled and they laughed.

Hush, hush. He's still out there.

He fell asleep, his head on their table. He woke up with his hips on his chair, his head on the old man's lap, his feet on the little woman's. They slept with their heads falling back, their hands on him lightly. Keeping him safe.

He wanted to live there. But somehow he knew he couldn't, and if he let himself be taken away, he would never see his grandparents again.

∽

They fought, too. They fought about money, relatives, dinner. They called each other funny names. Old rooster. Worn out shoe. Bent grass. Broken bowl. The fights were words and threats, never the belt, never hitting, even though once, the little woman took off her slipper and shook it in the old man's face. *Do you hear me, old man?*

I will send you to live with your daughter.
Then who will cook for you, you lazy old man.
I'll get myself a new wife. One who doesn't waste five dollars at bingo.
A new wife doesn't want an old husband.
Well then, I'll get a pig. With five dollars I can buy a pig.
Maybe a pig would marry you.
A pig would be nicer than some wives.
Old man, I explained this ten times over, if you get a pig they will make us move. Do you want to move?
Chickens, then. Fresh eggs.

I can buy eggs here. Chickens stink.
Maybe I'll get a goose.
Are you crazy, old man? Do you want to have to move?

The boy would eat while this was going on, peeling the spicy shrimp, picking away the legs, spooning sauce over rice, waiting for what would follow.

You give me five dollars for bingo or I will pee in your soup.

The boy put his head down and laughed. And the old man threw back his head and laughed, and gave her the five dollars.

It always ended like that. With laughter.

❧

In the classroom, he liked puzzles. When the weather was too harsh to send them out at recess, he would sit and work a puzzle by himself.

This was a puzzle. If he'd never known any different, he wouldn't have tried to figure it out. But at one time he'd had a mother. And she'd loved him. And he knew it was supposed to be different.

The man had a job, so he made money. He was the supervisor, that's what the kids of the ironworkers said. They were all Indian, they stuck together and didn't talk to anyone else. But one of them had wanted to talk about it.

Your dad is my dad's boss. But my dad says your dad better stop drinking before he can't walk the iron anymore. Because of the shakes.

He had thrown a punch at that boy, who blocked it and shoved him back hard. He stared at the boy for a second, then shook his head with a small smile and walked away.

A puzzle.

The house was clean. He kept it that way inside, but outside, the man did that. In the winter, he shoveled the walks and the driveway. When it wasn't winter, the grass was cut, the bushes trimmed. The garage was clean, everything organized and interesting and perfect, even though he wasn't supposed to go in there to see that, sometimes he just had to go in there and look at how the tools were hung, the rags folded, the cans stacked on specially built shelves. The car was waxed. The man took care of all that stuff.

He could afford a new refrigerator.

So, some things where he lived got taken care of. But he didn't.

It had something to do with her, with looking like her. Which was dangerous. It was as dangerous to look like her as it was to do what the man did. He imagined the man walking easy on beams of iron, putting things together and welding them in place. Telling other people what to do, how to do it. He wasn't afraid. He just walked around up there, no belts, no nets, just those big work boots and a hardhat on his head, walking the beams in the snow, the wind and the rain, the summer heat.

That was a danger everyone understood. No one understood this other kind of danger, the danger of looking like your mother.

Danger, the boy decided, was part of life.

Danger was the part of life that could end it.

∾

Spring came. He liked spring because the days were longer and he could stay out later. Well, he could always stay out as late as he wanted, but when it was light out, other kids were allowed to stay out with him.

He was putting away his school books when he heard knocking on the back door. He wasn't supposed to answer the front door, but a knock on the back could be his grandmother saying come eat, or one of the neighborhood kids for kick the can. He opened the door and there was the priest. May I come in? He opened his mouth to say no but the priest moved lightly into the kitchen as if he belonged there.

He was looking around. Where is your father?

At work.

He works nights?

He works second shift. That's only part of the night.

Ah, so you are alone most of the time.

I like being alone.

All the time?

I'm not alone all the time. I go next door.

The priest nodded. He walked through the house, looking. He even opened the door into the man's room, which was absolutely forbidden.

He could breathe again when the priest shut that door.

Your father keeps an exceedingly tidy room. And this is your room?

Yes.

It's almost empty. Where are your things, your toys?

I'm too old for toys.

You're ten.

I like to play outside.

Ah yes, you like kick the can. I actually hear that you're the best.

He shrugged. He was quietly proud, but didn't want that pride to show.

Is everything all right for you?

Everything is fine. Just fine.

The priest shook his head. I want you to know that I am paying attention. The Church is always here for you. And so am I.

He didn't know what to say. So he nodded.

The priest went out the way he came, by the back door.

∽

Summer was hot and he liked it hot, but he missed eating breakfast and lunch at the school. Summers were like weekends, when he was hungry all day long.

He was ten years old and finished with sixth grade. This was a big thing because it was time for junior high, and no one thought he should go to junior high but they didn't know what else to do with him. He'd gone to kindergarten for half a day. He never went to first. He went to second grade for two years, and then third, and then a week of fourth and then up to fifth, and finally sixth. He was always younger, smaller, faster than anyone else in his class. He hadn't broken five feet, but he was growing up. He was confused by what he felt. What he looked at. What he wondered. He didn't know who to talk to about the things going on inside his head, or what he was doing to himself whenever he was alone.

Sometimes, at night, he would worry about changing schools. At the next school, the gym was different, and that meant he would have to dress down. If he had to take his clothes off, then his back, his backside, the backs of his legs, it would all show. He couldn't sleep thinking about what would happen if they saw the rest of it, what would the man do to him if he ever let anyone see all the rest of it.

If they took him away.

If he never got to see his grandparents again.

∽

This time it was a woman. A very pretty woman in a skirt that raised up high but not as high as he wished it would when she knelt down to look under his bed. None of them had ever looked there before, but it was clean because sometimes he hid under there so that was all right.

What's this? She held out a book he'd taken from the living room and hidden. Will you read to me from this? They went to the living room where he read to her about phase transition, his finger bothering the edge of a sticker that said USED on the spine.

You read aloud beautifully. When your voice changes, it's going to be so low. But I'm still not sure I understand what phase transition is. Can you explain it without the book?

It's when something changes from one state to another, like a solid to a liquid. But it retains all its properties. He scratched at his head, thinking. Water is always two atoms of hydrogen and one of oxygen, no matter if it's ice or water or condensation. It's still the same chemical composition, but it changes due to temperature. That's a phase change.

You explain things very well.

I'm going to be a teacher.

Her smile made his chest hurt. But she frowned when she looked at the man. Mr. Gentry, let's talk in the kitchen.

He went to his room and sat down on his bed. He could still hear them talking.

That's a very bright boy you have. He's delightful.

Is he, now.

Yes, he is. Get him a haircut and put a toothbrush on your shopping list.

I'll do that. We're just a couple of single men around here. It's a good thing the state sent such a pretty girl to tell us how to live.

She made a laugh. It was not a laugh he enjoyed hearing. He put his hands over his ears and closed his eyes but some of the noises came through. He thought about it, did the math. Caseworkers had been coming to the house for five years, and this had never happened before. He wanted to hurt them both. But he couldn't stop thinking about her looking under his bed. He rolled on his stomach, pulling down his pants to get to the old, soft sheets. He thought about her getting on her hands and knees, crawling under the bed. He followed and they were under there together.

It felt so good. And then he fell asleep.

◯

Get *in* here.

He jumped up fast and went to the kitchen, rubbing his eyes. Six red apples sat on the counter. The air smelled strange and it made his skin prickle.

The man sat at the table with a bottle and a glass. He had on his underwear, and his hair was hanging down all around his face like he just woke up too. But he didn't look angry. He looked tired, and he rubbed his eyes hard like he had a headache.

Don't stand there like a scared little girl. Tell me who you're talking to. They're only supposed to come twice a year, and this makes four, and it's only June. So someone said something. Who are you talking to?

He stared at the apples.

I asked you a fucking question. I want a fucking answer. Who have you been talking to?

His collar twisting in that huge hand, so tight he was choking.

You think you have it bad here? You just wait. I think I'll let them give you to the nuns. If they get a hold of you, you'll find out how bad it can be for you. You have no fucking idea.

This was insulting, this old lie that had scared him when he was five years old. He was angry.

They don't give *kids* to the *nuns*.

The man let him go.

I see. You're so fucking smart, now. You probably want me to go to prison, do you understand that they could send me to prison? And then what do you think will happen to you? Who'll take you? No one, that's who. You'll be out on the street like a fucking stray dog.

I don't care.

What?

I said I don't care. That's better than this. Anything is better than this.

The man went into his room. He turned around and leaned against the sink, waiting for the belt. But the man didn't have the belt when he came out of the bedroom.

He came out with the gun. He put it on the table and sat down.

Go to your room. Do you hear me? You stay the fuck away from me.

He sat in his room on the edge of his bed, holding his stomach. He could hear the creak of the kitchen chair, the sound of the man crying on the phone. He wasn't even drunk, but he was crying, what he was saying. That crying was terrible but what the man was saying was worse and he went under the bed to get away from it.

When the man left for the bar, he went into the kitchen. He ate the apples, seeds and all. That gun sat there on the table. Waiting. He touched it with one finger.

That's all it needed. One finger.

∽

He stayed in his room as late as he could the next morning, waiting for the man to leave. He was supposed to go to work. Maybe he had a headache but he would have been in bed if he had a headache, and he was up and moving around the kitchen, drinking coffee.

Clean yourself up. Put this shirt on.

That lady was just here.

Get changed.

But I didn't . . .

I told you, keep your fucking *mouth* shut. The man got out the bottle and drank right from it, then put it away fast.

He was putting on the new shirt when the doorbell rang. The doorbell belonged to the front door and was always ignored. But the man opened the door and some people came into the house, so he went to the door of his bedroom to see.

A man and a woman. They were both as brown as Indians, with dazzling white teeth. And so tall, they were both so tall.

Why didn't you tell us you lived in a slum, Payton.

Hello, Mother. It's good to see you.

You don't have to bother with that, I'm just here to see the boy. The lady had long hair that was many colors mixed with white. She showed her teeth in a smile.

Well, so here you are. You really take after your grandmother.

The man touched her arm, but gently. Veda.

Well, it's true. He looks like her. It's amazing. Remember when you first brought her home? He looks exactly like her, especially the hair. It's beautiful. *He's* beautiful. He doesn't look a thing like you, but he's enchanting. Like a beautiful little fairy.

Veda, you need to calm down.

I'm fine, I just want to . . .

She reached towards him and he ducked away.

Well, don't be like that. I won't *hurt* you. Don't you have anything to say to me? Can't you say hello?

Hello.

And she laughed. What a delicious little creature.

He thought of the witch in Hansel and Gretel and shivered.

Go easy, Veda. He doesn't remember us.

But when he looked at the old man, he did remember.

You brought me a baseball glove.

That's right, when you were three. You were too young for it back then. Do you like it now?

The man's hand on the back of his neck in warning.

Go get in the car.

∽

He had no idea what he was supposed to do, so he kept quiet and followed. Went to the car and didn't ask where they were going. Went in the restaurant, he had never in his life been to a restaurant. Sat where the man nodded for him to sit. Said nothing.

He stared at the tabletop.

What would you like?

The table was fake wood. Plastic wood.

Don't you want anything?

No thank you.

Darling, I tell you what, you can order anything on the menu. The woman clapped. You can order the ENTIRE menu.

What's ordering?

She laughed too loud. Oh he's a funny one, like his grandmother. You're just like your grandmother.

Veda, calm down.

Mother, I'll order for him.

It came, and it looked like a gigantic pile of everything that ever made his teeth hurt.

That big hand on the back of his neck. Eat it.

He shook his head.

He put his face right by his ear.

You eat it or I'll put your face in it.

He picked up the spoon and took a bite. The sweet hit his tongue and the cold hit his teeth and the pain was so bad he started to shiver. This was a terrible pain that radiated up from his teeth into his face, and he knew he could never cry, especially not in front of whoever these people were, these old people who laughed.

He dropped the spoon.

What the fuck is *wrong* with you.

Payton, your *language*.

He let himself slide under the table and curled into a ball, trying to stop the shaking, trying not to cry. The old lady's feet were long and bony in her shoes. The old man wore cowboy boots. His teeth sang with pain and he couldn't stop shaking.

That woman with her strange voice said it so loud. I guess he doesn't like ice cream.

He wanted to stay under that table forever, knowing what was coming when he got home.

⌢

Words could be so much worse than the belt, even the buckle end.

Hey bastard? You acted *retarded*. Did you forget how to talk English, is that it? Your friends next door trained the English out of you. You're *done* with those neighbors. Do you hear me? I don't want you over there at that fucking house anymore. *Ever*.

It was the first time he hit the man.

And the last.

He thought he was tough at school. But this was nothing like a school fight, and nothing like the belt. It was so easy for the man to knock him down until he couldn't get up, to kick him around the room. This is a game of kick the can, he thought. I am just the can. Cans don't feel anything. Cans don't hurt.

The phone started to ring. One last kick. The man looked down, his eyes hard. Maybe now you understand why I told you not to fight me.

He almost started laughing, but it hurt so much he couldn't breathe to laugh. The phone kept ringing.
The phone rang and rang and rang.

∾

He ran the water hot, because that helped. And then he did the other thing he did in the tub, because that helped more.

He never could believe how good this felt. He thought of that girl on the swing, her eyes, the way she smiled so shy after she kissed him, that and his hands were enough to make him feel so good, they were swinging together, her on his lap, her legs around him, the pumping.

Higher and higher and higher.

The door slammed open.

Stand up and turn around. Now.

He stood up in the tub shivering, his hands cupped over himself. Oh God, is it that bad, am I that bad, the way I am, what I do, and the way the man looked at him, he knew it was bad, so bad, it was that bad, it couldn't be that bad, but it was.

Turn around. Turn around so I can't see your face.

I don't want to.

Goddamnit, you turn AROUND.

He did, because of the look in the man's face. At least if he turned around, he wouldn't have to see his face looking like that. So he turned around and looked at the wall, the square white tiles, and he waited. Counting the tiles, basic, this many over, that many down, doing the math. Very easy math, the easiest. Waiting. He stood in the bathtub with the water going cold, his wet hair dripping cold water down his back. Waiting. He couldn't stand waiting.

You look just like her from behind.

He looked back over his shoulder.

The man had the gun.

∾

He jumped out of the tub, the man caught at him but he was wet and slipped free, he just had to make it to the back door, but the man was running on some diabolical fuel and he caught the boy by the arm and twisted it behind him, he twisted it so hard that he felt it pulling, ripping. He couldn't breathe with the gun jammed up under his chin. He felt the man behind him. That face at his ear, speaking so soft.

Look. Let's get this over with, right? Let's just get this over with. First you, then me. And then we're done. Finally.

He felt his arm tearing off his body. He felt the gun at his throat. The will to live leaked from him like blood from a cut, like the pure red of Christ's blood from the place where the spikes were driven in. That's what Christ was bleeding out, the will to keep trying, to keep fighting and surviving and going on. Because the son had to die. The Father was too strong to die, so the son had to die for Him.

Amen.

He stopped fighting and hung his head, waiting.

There was a rush of agony when the man let go of his arm to hang at his side like a dead thing. He would have screamed if he could make a sound. But screaming was part of being alive and he had already decided to be dead. He heard the sound of metal on wood. That was the gun, set down on the table.

The man turned him around and the man was crying.

Brushing the hair away from his face, tipping up his jaw, following every line of the boy's face with his fingertips. His eyes, his nose, tracing every bone and hollow like there was another face hidden under the boy's that he had to find with his hands, not his eyes. Those giant hands cupping his head, circling his throat, resting lightly on his shoulders. That body bending down without menace, that face, sad and beautiful, beside his ear.

One word.

Run.

⁓

He ran through the backyard, through the broken fence, to the house next door. The old man and the little woman exploded, *oh no, no, cover him,* they wrapped him in a blanket and they fought, they screamed at each other, the woman wanted to call the police, and the old man, he would not, *not the police, trouble, that's all the police would be.*

She pulled at the old man's clothes and she screamed at him, *look at this boy, look at his face, look at his arm, look at the bruises, look at the marks on his legs, he's running naked in the street.*

Woman, be quiet.

No I won't be quiet. I don't have to be quiet. This is America, there's no war here. Save this boy. When will you go get him some help? Will he be dead before you go get him some help?

The old man wiped tears from his eyes.

Fine, old man. Fine. She put on her funny hat and left.

The boy sat at the table and drank the bitter black tea that the old man brewed for him. The wool of that blanket burned his bare skin. The old man talked to him about fishing. He talked about fishing, and he talked about farming. That was what he always talked about. He missed both. He could not grow the familiar things in the backyard, but he tried new things, and he talked about what succeeded and what failed.

Gardening in America is God's way to teach us about failure. And do you know why things fail here? We flush our crap in America, instead of using it to grow things. What else do you use it for? Pee I understand, pee has no use. But crap is good stuff. Where does it go? I don't understand America.

He talked in his kindest voice, in the words like music.

And the boy listened, he didn't talk, his music was poor, he knew it, under the best of circumstances he was hard put to answer because his mouth didn't wrap around the words. He understood almost everything. When he tried to speak, they laughed, oh they laughed at him, but kindly. But not tonight. Tonight he couldn't try.

I'm telling you something, Grandson. I'm telling you that the best stuff grows from crap. You think before the war we were this strong? We were just a couple of farmers. And do you know what we knew? We knew crap. We worked and laughed and fought and went to church. And then the war came, and took everything. Our farm, our home, our town, our parents. But first, it took our sons. We had four sons. And then one of our daughters, but we still have three. Three daughters and two grandsons, one of them American. The war tried to take everything and it couldn't. And we're so strong, now. Because we grew from all that crap. Crap is a good place to grow from, if you want to be strong.

The old man wiped his eyes. *Drink some tea, Grandson.*

His arm hurt so much he couldn't move it. He used his other hand to lift up the bowl of tea. It was quiet.

They heard a sound like a car's backfire.

He looked at the old man, and the old man looked at him.

The boy stood up.

No, you stay here, you stay here, this is trouble, don't go over there, this is bad. The old man tried to stop him, but he was too old. The boy was young and fast.

He went across the yard, through the broken fence, through the back door into the kitchen and he slipped, fell down, slid across the floor. He sat on the floor and looked at the mess.

I'm not cleaning this up, I always have to clean everything up, this is not fair, what did he do this time, anyway, what is this stuff? It's everywhere, what is it? What did he *do*? Where is this *coming* from? It just keeps coming, what *is* this? I'm not going to clean this up, what *is* all this stuff, anyway? What *is* this?

What it was.

He screamed until his throat closed.

∽

When the little woman brought the priest, because she knew one place to go for help, Mel told her to wait outside. He came in the back door to the kitchen.

Oh Dear God in Heaven. Oh, Heavenly Father.

Mel did something to what was left of the face, closed the eyes.

May God have mercy on your soul.

He looked around the kitchen. He spoke softly. Well, there you are. I can see why that might be the place you want to be right now. It looks bad here, yes, it does. But you can come out from there.

Mel leaned down and took him by the arm, but it was the hurt arm and he made a sound. Mel tried again, and he was careful. Come on, now. It's okay if you step in it. It washes off.

He started to come out. But his foot hit something. It was the teeth. They slid across the floor, slid away through all if it.

He went back under the table.

Mel squatted next to him for a long time, his hand on the edge of the table. Come out, now. Come on, now. I know it's a mess. It's a terrible mess but we can leave it behind, my boy. We just have to walk through it one time. We'll walk through this together and leave it behind forever.

Come here.

He came out from under the table.

Well, there you are. Let's get this mess off you. He pulled the blanket away.

Sweet Mary, Mother of God.

Mel put the blanket over what was left of the man. He put a small hand on the shoulder that didn't hurt. Talking soft.

Come on, my boy. Let's get you cleaned up.

Mel let the cold water out, the cold, dirty water. He put the boy under the clean hot water. This will help, my boy. This is what you need. This is the ticket, a good, hot shower.

Let's get you dressed.

He took the boy into his bedroom. Mel put on his Sunday clothes, buttoned his buttons, folded down his socks, tied his shoes. It looks like you could use a pair of boots, my boy. And a haircut. Mel combed his hair.

There you go. All set.

He went to the phone. This is Father Melvin from Saint Dominic parish. I would like to report a death. Yes. No. Don't bother with an ambulance. Just send the police. They can call the coroner. I will be waiting next door with the neighbors.

Mel repeated the address and the phone number.

Mel took him by the hand and led him out of that house.

He sat next door at the wobbly little table with a police officer and the priest.

The old man and woman wailed, circled the kitchen, begging him to speak to the police for them, *don't leave us, Grandson. Don't let them take you away from us, we want you. Tell them that, Grandson, tell them we'll take you.*

Back up there, folks. Let him be. Back up. Do you understand me? The officer was shouting.

The old man threw his hands up in frustration. *I'm not deaf you fat idiot. I'm just old.*

The boy sat at the table and rocked, sucked his thumb, pulled at his hair because he wanted to go to sleep and that was his private way he did it, but he was so tired that he did it in front of everyone. He had never been that tired.

Are you finished? This boy needs to go to bed.

Father, there's a few more questions we need to ask.

Well ask them and be done with it.

Okay, can you hear me, son? Your father is dead. Can you tell us anything about what happened?

In God's name, Officer, do you honestly expect this boy to *talk*?

We have to ask, Father. The man is dead.

By his own *hand*, may God have mercy on his soul.

We didn't find a note.

That is *beside* the point.

Listen to me, kid. Can you hear me? Where were you when this happened?

Why are you questioning this boy?

Because Child Welfare has a file three inches thick on this address. The officer stared at the boy. Kid? Now look at me. How did you and your dad get along?

This is ridiculous. He can't answer your questions.

Well someone has to. And these people don't speak English.

His grandparents looked at each other and started speaking softly.

This is not good.

You don't have to tell me.

The old man put his hand on Mel's arm. He had no English, and Mel had none of the old man's music, but they understood each other.

Mel nodded and cleared his throat.

Can you tell me what happened?

The old man nodded.

You tell this fat, stupid policeman that he is a good boy, a very, very good boy. Without him we would have died of being idiots our first winter here.

He says that the boy came over this afternoon and they were drinking tea. Mrs. Nguyen went out to the market and stopped by the rectory to invite me for dinner.

He is a very good boy, Father, he is helpful and smart and taught our other grandson English so he can get ahead in this crazy country.

While they were waiting for us to arrive, they heard a gunshot. They were too frightened to investigate, so they sat at this table and prayed.

How a good boy ever came from a bastard like that man next door, I will never know. That bastard deserves to be dead. I wish I had the balls to kill him.

They waited here at the table until I got to the house. They told me they'd heard a shot, so I went over. I found the body. I covered it with a blanket and called the authorities.

He threw his son out in the cold, in the middle of the night. Night after night. He tried to break that boy. To break his own son. The old man smacked the table with the palms of his hands. *But this boy will never break. He just gets stronger.*

Mel smiled at the old man, and the old man smiled back, wiping a tear.

Mr. Nguyen says his neighbor has been extremely sad over his wife. But he says there's never been any trouble. No trouble at all.

The officer looked from the boy to the old man to the old woman to the priest. You swear to God that's that the old man says?

I do not swear to God, officer, as that is taking the Lord's name in vain. But I promise you that this man only speaks the truth.

And you just covered the body? You didn't move anything? Didn't touch the gun, nothing like that?

Mel nodded. That is correct.

Father, there are little bloody footprints all through that house.

He followed me into the kitchen. He was terrified, which is why he is as you see him. You walk into a scene like that as a child and see how you react, Officer.

Mel stared at the officer until the officer snapped his notebook shut and put away his pen. Well, you win. I guess that's that. The social worker should be here in a minute.

What did you say?

The social worker. She's on her way.

A social worker? How many have I sent over there in the last year? And you expect me to let a social worker take him now?

Well where's he going to go to? We can't find anyone to call. No letters, nothing. You think we didn't look? Not even an address book over there. Where else can he go?

He can stay here. With the Nguyens.

One of the cops started to shift, to clear his throat, to shake his head. Father. Come on. He can't stay with these people. They don't speak English, they don't have a phone. He has to go to foster care.

And Mel spoke, with his sweet, clear voice from God. Quiet, at first.

This boy is not going into foster care.

Father, come on.

He will not go into foster care.

Well, Father? Is he going to go live in the rectory with you?

Yes.

Father, be reasonable.

Oh, I am very reasonable, Officer. I am the soul of reason. Just don't cross me.

Father, look at him. A kid like this, just let him go. You can't help him.

What did you say, Officer?

Well I just meant, I mean, look at him. He's a lost cause.

DO NOT SAY A THING LIKE THAT! SWEET MARY, MOTHER OF JESUS, I WILL TAKE THIS BOY, AND GOD WILL SMITE ANY MAN WHO DARES TO STAND IN MY WAY!

The cop crossed himself.

Mel shook his head. He was calming himself. Getting control.

He put his hand on the table, reaching towards the boy. I'd like you to stay with me for a while. Do you hear me? Look at me, my boy. Please.

That hand on the table, reaching towards him.

He never looked into the eyes of the people around him. He kept too many secrets, told too many lies. But he looked in Mel's eyes.

And he lived.

ANOTHER BEGINNING

Fiona

The door opens. He has Sam. I look at the monitor so he can't see my face. "I'm staying tonight. It's gotten so late."

"Okay."

"I made the revisions. Brooke just sent me word. She's completely satisfied."

He turns to leave.

If he walks out that door, I may die.

"Gentry?" I want to cry, or scream, but I type, and I talk. "I mailed the photos to Evelyn. She called to let me know they got back to her. She asked after you. She said to tell you hello."

"Okay." His hand is on the doorknob. He doesn't want to talk about Evelyn.

Well, that's just too bad. "Evelyn's been helpful. She's told me some things about Miriam that you didn't know. She told me why Miriam stopped nursing. And she told me that Miriam was married before."

"She was never married before."

"Yes she was."

"She was?"

"She was. Her first husband was chronically unfaithful, and he left her." He moves to the bed like his feet weigh a ton apiece, and he comes down hard. His head hangs. "Did Miriam have good vision, Gentry?"

Gentry studies his lap. "Like a hawk."

"I thought so." And I turn, and I wait until his eyes finally meet mine, and I tell him the thing that eats at me night and day. "I hate her, Gentry. I hate Miriam. I think I turned her into more of a human being in this book than she ever was in real life. And I hate her. I need to go to reconciliation to beg forgiveness for how I feel about a woman who was so sick in the head that she accidentally killed herself and ruined your life."

"Don't hate her."

"I do hate her. She was . . ." She was everything that's wrong with him.

"She was my wife."

"Fine. She was your wife." I find that I'm angry. "You know, Gentry, you make yourself so alone. And you're not alone in everything."

"I'm not alone?" He stands, and oh, his face. The outrage. "You read that, Fiona. Was that your childhood? Was that your *father*?" The word breaks from him like something snapped off. "I didn't tell you this for your pity. I can't stand it if you pity me."

"I don't pity you."

"Because this isn't my whole life, do you understand that? This isn't *all* of me." He's shouting as quietly as he can.

"I know that. I know there's more to you than this."

He sits back down on the bed. The only sound is the tap of my fingers on keys.

He strokes Sam. I want to go over there and fix him. I want him to pet his dog and to fall asleep in that bed and to wake up whole. I want to reach out but I've hurt him enough by dragging it all out of him. I won't do this to him anymore, even if it kills me to watch him close up like he does.

When he speaks, he sounds on the verge of tears. "Hey Fiona? So this is done?"

"Yes. It's done. We'll have a CEM to go over, but that's it."

"What is a CEM?"

"Copy edited manuscript."

Sam jumps down and comes over to me. Oh Sam, you sweet, pretty pup. He puts his paws in my lap, stares into my eyes. Sam, sweet Sam. I kiss his nose.

Gentry leans forward so that he's sitting on the bed with his feet far apart, his elbows on his knees and his hands clasped. His sad brown eyes fix on some point on the floor. "Hey Fiona? I need to tell you something." His voice is deep, soft. The voice I know.

"I'm listening."

He shakes his head and swallows. "And before I tell you, I want you to understand that I know it won't change anything about your life. But I want to tell you."

"Okay."

He sits there, staring at the floor. "And also, before I tell you, I want you to know that I'm glad you have Hugh."

"Me too. He's completely without mercy, but he's the best brother in the world."

His head snaps up. "Hey Fiona? What did you just say?"

"Nothing. I wasn't talking. You were."

His eyes are strange. "No, what did you say about Hugh?"

"I said he's without mercy."

"After that."

"He's the best brother in the world."

"Hey Fiona? Are you talking about Hugh, at your house?"

"Yes." What's wrong with him? "You know, Hugh? The investment banker who likes roses, who makes fun of me all the time and writes me email every fifteen minutes? We live in our father's house?"

And suddenly, everything makes sense.

I speak very softly. "Gentry, Hugh is my *brother*."

"Your *brother*." He looks up at me with shining brown eyes. It's very quiet in here, even though everything is changing. The only sound is our breathing, the ocean, the orbit of the world and the wheeling of the stars as the universe is gently, perfectly rearranged.

He stands up and holds out his arms. "Come here."

I do.

He takes hold and pulls me in tight. We fit perfectly. I feel his heart beating all through me, sounding my body like his heart is mine, because it is. He breathes in my hair, and then, finally, he puts his hands behind my neck, holds my head just right for what's coming, the kiss I have been craving since I first saw him. But before he kisses me, he looks in my eyes.

I love you more than life, he says. And for all the rest of it.

Readers Discussion Guide

1. Who is the main character in Book Three? Why do you think that?
2. For early readers, Book Three opens the waterworks. Did you cry? When?
3. The events of Book One had strong effects on the Mumford women. Discuss how each seems to be affected as you first see them in Book Three.
4. Gentry is an expert at burying his memories. It has been his main survival tool for most of his life. What breaks loose the dam of his memories?
5. Discuss Gentry's decision to remember how he ended up in the hospital. Were you surprised? Who do you blame for that night?
6. When Tristan is introduced to the story, who do you think he is? Discuss how his existence changes Gentry.
7. Why are dogs so important to Gentry?
8. Fiona is the first person who has heard Gentry's entire story. Does he only open up for the purposes of their project, or is there more to it?
9. Do Fiona's reactions sync up with your reactions to the story of his time with Miriam?
10. Why is Gentry afraid of nuns?
11. Discuss Gentry's restaurant confrontation with Garret Blount. Did it surprise you?
12. Mike Mumford is both an unlikely ally and a serious adversary. What do you think of him? Is he a good guy, a bad guy, or just a guy?
13. It takes some time in this book, but we finally understand why Gretchen stopped writing to Gentry. Discuss her feelings of betrayal and guilt. Does growing up help her forgive him for what she saw in Book One?
14. What do you think of Lorrie's life? He seemed fairly happy in Book One. Is he happier now?
15. How about Kathryn? Is she happy in her current life? Why or why not?
16. Gentry is a key player in a serious decision that will change Gretchen's life forever. What do you think of this decision? Was this really the best for everyone involved?
17. What is Gentry's name?

18. Have you forgiven Miriam? Has Gentry?
19. Why does Fiona insist on knowing what happened in Gentry's childhood? Was it what you expected?
20. Where do these characters go next?

About Karen G. Berry

After a nomadic childhood that took her to South Dakota, California, Minnesota, Arkansas, Washington and Montana, Karen G. Berry settled in Portland, Oregon. She's stayed put for over thirty years, raising three daughters and walking many dogs. After graduating magna cum laude at age forty with a degree in English, Karen has worked in marketing. Aside from her novel endeavors, she is an extensively published poet, but tries not to let that sneak into her fiction.

Visit her at www.karengberry.mywriting.network/ to learn more.

Made in the USA
San Bernardino, CA
17 June 2018